MW01631932

The Irish Sisters Trilogy

MONTANA SKY SERIES

A Valentine's Choice

An Irish Blessing

A Rolling Stone

DEBRA HOLLAND

THE IRISH SISTERS TRILOGY
Compilation Copyright © 2017 by Debra Holland

A VALENTINE'S CHOICE
Copyright © 2015 by Debra Holland

AN IRISH BLESSING
Copyright © 2016 by Debra Holland

A ROLLING STONE
Copyright © 2017 by Debra Holland

ISBN: 978-1-939813-60-2
Print Edition

All other rights reserved by the author. The reproduction or other use of any part of this publication without the prior written consent of the rights holder is an infringement of the copyright law.

Published in the United States of America.

Acknowledgements

In gratitude to:
My editors:
Louella Nelson, Linda Carroll-Bradd and Adela Brito,
who always make my stories better.

To Delle Jacobs, friend and talented cover artist
and her brother, John Mitchell, who helps her.

To my beta readers:
My mother, Honey Holland
My aunt, Hedy Codner
Marlene Larsen,
I appreciate your sharp eyes.

To Ed Millner,
who rescues me from computer and formatting problems.

To Regina Reynante,
for teaching me the best way to tighten a corset

To Tom Hall, fellow USC friend and alumni,
for suggesting "Traveler" for Moss's horse.

To Katharine West,
for the information about childbirth

To all my Facebook friends,
who make suggestions when I ask for help
and are so eager for more Montana Sky Stories,
I'm truly blessed to "know" you!

Contents

A Valentine's Choice

Chapter One

SWEETWATER SPRINGS, MONTANA
January 1895

Bridget O'Donnell peered out the train window at the town of Sweetwater Springs, blanketed in white. She barely glanced at the wooden buildings, instead focusing her attention on the street. In spite of last night's storm, which had delayed their arrival until this morning, vehicle tracks and hoof- and footprints had churned the dirty snow to slush. Here and there a mud patch showed in the road.

Her sister Alana looked over Bridget's shoulder at their destination and sighed. "The streets aren't paved with gold."

"Well, we knew that," Bridget said in a brisk tone to hide her disappointment. "We haven't seen gold anywhere on our travels, and we've crossed half of America."

Alana sat back, her blue eyes sad. "Yes, but we still had hope."

On the long journey from their small village in Ireland, crossing the Atlantic to New York, their belief they'd have wonderful new lives had sustained them. But the reality of America had proven quite a shock to the twenty-two-year-old twins. The Irish were as much second-class citizens in the United States as they were back home. And in many places, the people seemed just as destitute as those they'd left behind. But they'd still hoped Sweetwater Springs would be different.

Now taking a closer look at their destination, the last of the dream of a better life that Bridget had held onto all the way to Montana trickled away like gold dust seeping through her fingers. But she didn't allow her sister to see her low spirits. "We'll just have to make the best of it."

Alana rose and stretched. She moved into the aisle.

Bridget frowned. Over the course of the voyage and overland train trip, Alana had lost weight. Her cheeks were hollowed, and her eyes shadowed. Her twin had left her appetite and, Bridget suspected, her wounded heart back in Ireland.

Bridget hoped once they reunited with family, Alana's spirits would lift and her appetite return. Grateful to move off that hard train bench, she stood and gathered their luggage.

The satchels they carried contained their scanty possessions. In addition to their clothing, Bridget's satchel held the family Bible and Alana's a volume of Shakespeare's plays as well as the dried medicinal herbs she'd gathered before leaving home. Each young woman also carried a heavy burlap bag filled with potatoes—the treasure of their family.

The enclosures of the common land in Ireland two generations before had restricted the poor to small rocky plots, with potatoes as their main crop. During and after *an Gorta Mór*, the O'Donnell family had dwindled, as relatives emigrated, and they'd lost touch with them. Only their Uncle Rory had sent a letter home once a year—first from Virginia, where he'd married and started a family, and then from Montana.

Once they alighted onto the platform, the cloudy gray sky made her mood bleaker. The wind blew, sharp and bitter, heavy with smoke from the train. Bridget was glad for the mittens and the knitted cap she wore, for she hated having her ears and fingers chilled. But even so, the bitter cold penetrated the wool. One cheery element nearby was the spritely yellow trim around the windows of the brown train station. She tilted her head in the direction of the building in a silent signal to her sister to head inside.

They moved around the corner of the building just as a man in a long fur coat jogged up the stairs to the platform. He saw them, halted, and touched fingers to the brim of his hat. "Mornin'." His voice was rich with a western drawl. He had kind brown eyes, a snub nose, and a wide mouth.

Instead of glancing back and forth between the two sisters as strangers did upon first seeing them—checking to make sure they were indeed two identical women—his gaze lingered on Bridget's face in respectful appreciation. His mouth crooked up, showing dimples and giving him an endearing boyish look.

Heat suffused her face, and tingles swirled in her stomach.

The man opened the door and gestured for them to enter the station ahead of him.

Alana hurried inside.

Bridget dawdled just a moment to give him a smile of gratitude.

He touched the small of her back, ushering her into the building—an intimate gesture from a stranger, even if she couldn't feel his hand through her coat.

They blew inside on a gust of wind, and the man quickly shut the door behind them. The main room, with two rows of long wooden benches, was cold and empty. The round stove wasn't burning. But at least they were out of the wind. A ticket counter was set into an interior wall on the left side of the room. The panels over the opening were closed, as was the door next to the counter.

The man lifted his chin toward the inner door. "The stationmaster will be in there, sitting next to his stove. The cold bothers his joints. Jack!" he called.

"Here!" From the other room came the sound of a muffled voice. "Head on back."

He extended a hand toward Bridget's baggage and one toward Alana's. "Allow me to help you carry those."

Bridget hesitated, unsure if she should accept the man's help, though he looked honest enough.

"I'm James Whitson. But you can call me James." He waved toward the counter. "And Jack will vouch for me."

Neither his words nor the humor lurking in his eyes reassured her. But an intuitive sense that she could trust him made Bridget hand over her precious bag of potatoes. Even if he had a mind to rob them, those potatoes had no value to anyone but them.

With a quirk of his eyebrow, James hefted the bag. "Rocks?"

Bridget laughed. "Potatoes."

"Potatoes?" he echoed in a tone of disbelief. "We do have potatoes in Sweetwater Springs, you know."

"Not these potatoes, you don't. *These* are the jewels of our family," she said with pride. "My grandparents' crops never succumbed to the blight of the Great Famine."

"Ah."

"Nor have they since, and thus enabled us to survive." *Survive, but not thrive.* "These were all we could carry with us. The sales from the rest of the crop helped pay our way here." *That and selling everything else we owned.*

Bridget couldn't help a pang of grief, remembering the loss of their family's possessions: the cow, a rocking chair and cradle her great-grandfather had made—the wood burnished to a patina by many years of use, a pair of silver candlesticks—a gift from the squire's wife when Ma had helped her deliver her babe safely, the pewter tankards and plates....

At least we have these. Bridget touched her grandmother's gold locket she wore under her dress. Alana had their mother's wedding ring on a chain under her shirtwaist. *The sacrifice will be worth it.* She repeated what she'd been telling her twin for weeks. Her sister hadn't wanted to leave everything they'd known. Neither had Bridget. But she was eager to make a new start.

"I plan to claim land and raise a crop to sustain us, as well as to sell or barter," she told the stranger, sensing his interest.

He raised his eyebrows in obvious admiration. "Well, I'll be the first in line to buy some. I'm mighty fond of baked potatoes. Easy eating when on the trail. Just stick them in a campfire to bake, or slice them with some onions to fry up."

"I'll be sure to save some of the best ones for ye, Mr. Whitson. For yer kindness."

He smiled and held out a hand to Alana.

Her sister handed her bag of potatoes to James and then slanted Bridget a questioning glance. She knew what that look meant. Babbling their business to strangers, especially a man, wasn't like Bridget. And the two had been careful to guard their meager possessions on the journey.

Bridget couldn't explain to Alana what impulse had gotten into her. *Was it really just a reaction to a lingering glance? James Whitson seeing me as an individual, not as part of a pair? A feeling about him?*

Carrying both bags, James headed toward the interior door. His boot heels clicked on the wooden floor, spurs jangling.

She wondered if his shoulders were as wide as they seemed, or if the fur coat cast an illusion.

After sharing sideways glances, the twins trailed after him.

James set down one bag to open the door and ushered them inside.

This room was obviously the post office for Sweetwater Springs. One wall held floor-to-ceiling shelves stacked with wooden boxes labeled with family names. In the middle of the space stood a small stove, emitting welcomed warmth.

Next to the stove, a man with bushy gray hair huddled in a low chair underneath some blankets. When he saw the twins, his eyes widened. He grasped the arms of his chair and struggled to stand. Once on his feet, he motioned them over. "Come in. Come in. Hurry up and git yerself warm." He was small, but his hunched-over posture made him seem tiny—a leprechaun in human form.

Bridget bit back a grin.

They obeyed, setting down their satchels and moving to the stove, spreading their hands over the heat.

James didn't follow. He shut the door and remained in the corner.

Perhaps he's giving us some privacy. Thoughtful of him.

"I didn't have passengers waiting to catch the train," the old man said in an apologetic tone. "So I didn't fire up the stove in the outer room."

"This is perfect." Bridget smiled at him. "Thank ye."

"I'm Jack Waite, postmaster and stationmaster all rolled up into one." He surveyed them with bright eyes. "Don't recall anyone telling me to expect two identical-looking ladies."

"We aren't expected." Bridget touched her chest. "I'm Bridget O'Donnell, and this is my sister Alana."

"Ah." The postmaster touched the side of his nose. "I thought I heard Ireland in your voice."

"We're here to find our uncle and his family. Do ye know Rory O'Donnell?"

"I do, indeed. Sends a letter to Ireland every year…to Siobhan O'Donnell." He pronounced the name *Soban* rather than *Shivawn*.

"Our mother," Alana offered in a quiet voice. "She passed away last year."

Mr. Waite's cheerful expression clouded. "I'm sorry to hear that. And even more to have to tell you…your aunt is very ill. Erik Muth has his dairy farm out in the direction of your kin. This morning, he drove into town to sell his milk at the mercantile and brought the news. He left word with Dr. Cameron to drive out to the O'Donnell homestead, then came here for his mail." He shook his head. "Most poor folks don't summon the doctor unless the illness is serious."

Oh, no! Equally concerned with the sad thought of their aunt being so ill and not wanting to impose on the family at such a time, Bridget glanced at Alana, seeing similar distress mirrored in her sister's eyes.

James strode across the floor of the small room and pulled off his black hat. "Ah, pardon me, ladies. I couldn't help overhearing, but I think I can offer a solution."

Mr. Waite's expression cleared. "Why, James Whitson. I believe I know what you're about to say. That's a right good idea."

Puzzled, Bridget glanced back and forth between the two men.

Mr. Waite tipped his chin toward the cowboy. "Ah, James, here, works at the Thompson ranch along with Harry O'Hanlon, who married your cousin Sally on New Year's Eve. A whirlwind courtship, that was. Heard tell, Harry came back from courting Sally on Christmas Day mighty determined to wed. With Wyatt Thompson's blessing, Harry and the rest of Thompson's hands built a cabin in just one week right there at the ranch."

"I know you'll be welcome there." James cut into the flow of Jack's words. He gave Bridget and then Alana a reassuring glance. "The Thompsons are kind people, welcoming people."

"But my cousin and her husband are newlyweds," Bridget protested, knowing the sisters would be in the way at the very time in a marriage when a couple most wanted privacy. *Here I'd thought once we reached Sweetwater Springs, all our problems would be solved.*

The stationmaster reached over and patted Bridget's hand. "Don't you fret none. You won't be staying there long. You two are as pretty as a picture. I have no doubt you'll be snapped up in no time." He shot James a speculative glance, an obvious matchmaking gleam in his eyes. "Why, you'll have a fine selection of cowboys at Thompson's place alone. What, ten?" He raised his brows at James for confirmation.

James grimaced, apparently uncomfortable with the topic of conversation. He shifted his weight from one leg to another. "Eleven. Moss never sends or receives mail, and he rode into town instead of taking the train, so you wouldn't know him."

Jack cackled. "Eleven's a right good number." He waggled his ears. "And I'm sure every available man in Sweetwater Springs will come a courtin' when he hears of twin beauties stayin' at the Thompsons. I'll bet we have Valentine weddings." He patted the arm of his chair and winked at Bridget, clearly pleased with his prognostications. "Valentine's Day is only three weeks away, ladies."

We couldn't possibly find husbands that quickly! But Bridget kept her own counsel. She liked the little man and did not want to contradict him.

James pulled out a letter and handed the envelope to Jack in a way that sliced off the postmaster's conversation. "Any mail to pick up?"

Mr. Waite shook his head. "Nothing today. But I haven't gotten up yet to fetch the mailbag from the train."

James set his hat back on his head. "I'll get it for you. Then I'll be off to the livery to rent the sleigh for the ladies. The recent storm has blocked the roads, so it's either ride on horseback or take the sleigh." He moved toward the door.

Bridget wanted to protest, to tell him that she could ride and save the cost of a conveyance. But Alana was scared of horses. The sleigh would be better. She reached for the thin pouch of money nestled in the pocket of her coat, knowing how few of their funds remained inside. "Let me pay ye."

James held up a hand in a stopping motion, flashed Bridget a grin, and continued walking out the door.

She stared after him. The idea of being beholden to a stranger, particularly *this* stranger, didn't sit well with her.

Yet, somehow, he doesn't feel like a stranger.

Feeling light-headed, James couldn't believe his luck. He pulled his thick raccoon-skin coat tighter against the wind. This morning his boss could have chosen one of the other hands to ride with the Thompson children to school. Usually, they traveled alone, but after last night's snowstorm, Wyatt wanted an escort for them.

James hurried across the platform and down the steps, as quickly as he could and still keep his footing on the icy wood. He moved through the familiar motions of mounting Dusty and riding the short block to the livery. But his thoughts remained with the woman he'd left behind.

Miss Bridget O'Donnell had skin as pale as milk, eyes the color of the sky at dusk, and kissable pink lips. A dimple on one side when she smiled made his heart race when it appeared. He liked the whisky-red curls that had escaped her hat to frame her face, and the way her words with their lilting accent shivered over his skin the first time he heard her speak. *I'm sounding like a poet,* James thought, half in amusement, half in dismay.

At the livery, he rented the small two-seater sleigh that Dusty could pull. Even with toting their bags of spuds and satchels, those young women wouldn't weigh much, but he worried about them on the long, cold drive out to the ranch. Their coats looked thin and shabby.

He only hoped Dusty would cooperate for a smooth drive. The gelding had pulled the Thompson's wagon a time or two, but only when hitched with his buddy, Two Bits. Pulling a sleigh alone would be different than driving in tandem.

At the livery, working in the dim light of two lanterns, Pepe Sanchez, the stableman, helped him hitch Dusty to the sleigh. Although not a talkative man, the good-natured groom usually had a shy smile for everyone. But ever since he'd learned James would be driving two young women to the ranch, he'd sported a broad grin. The man was as bad as Jack with his matchmaking ideas. Probably the fault of Pepe's recent betrothal to Lucia Perez.

"*Si, Amigo*, I have bricks warming on the stove and will send along a bear fur to cover them," Pepe said with a soft Spanish accent.

"I appreciate that," James said, relieved for the women to have the extra protection.

"Can't have your pretty ladies getting sick."

"I never said they were pretty," James muttered.

Pepe sent him a sly grin, his eyes alight with laughter. "You didn't have to. You have the look of a man interested in a *señorita*."

"'Spose you've been seeing that look in the mirror." James growled. But thinking of Bridget made him anxious to get back to her.

"That, I do," the stableman said, appearing undaunted by the reference to his feelings for Lucia. Pepe's expression sobered. "Don't make my mistake of waiting. Wasted time, and I almost lost her to another man." His broad grin reappeared. "Now we're soon to be wed. My Lucia refuses to wait."

Christmastime had brought a spate of engagements and marriages to Sweetwater Springs. The ranch hands had laughed and joked about the wave of matches, teasing Harry O'Hanlon unmercifully for being caught up in a holiday romance. But the cowboy had shrugged off their banter, like a slicker shed water, going about his work and the building of his cabin—a man lit with an inner glow.

James had secretly envied him. An odd restlessness overcame him whenever he saw the newlyweds together. The two had a sparkle about them—an obvious bond, not unlike the one that existed between Wyatt Thompson and his wife, Samantha, wed for only six months. A widow from Argentina, who'd inherited the neighboring ranch, she'd brought a passel of boys and midget Falabella horses with her when she married Wyatt. From that day on, the ranch had exploded with laughter and love and high jinx that seasoned the grueling work of ranch life.

But until Harry O'Hanlon had wed Sally O'Donnell, James hadn't believed he could even dream of a wife of his own. Before, such an idea seemed as far away as the moon. With living on an isolated ranch, near a town with few unmarried women, he hadn't seen anyone who took his fancy. Now he understood Harry—how the exchange of a few looks and words from a special woman could knock a man right off his course, sending him unexpected images and longings.

James climbed into the sleigh and gathered up the reins. He nodded good day to Pepe.

With a frown of concern, James realized he didn't have the

same clear field as Harry had possessed for his courtship. The other cowboy had met Sally O'Donnell in the mercantile, and then on Christmas rode out to the O'Donnell's claim on the prairie, taking with him a haunch of beef as a gift. Later that night, he'd returned to the Thompson ranch, an engaged man.

But Harry hadn't had any competition, no passel of cowhands to interfere with his courtship. James doubted Sally O'Donnell had set eyes on another suitor in the months before Harry showed up on her doorstep. She had mighty slim pickings out on the isolated prairie. Not that Harry wasn't a good guy. The two were obviously head over heels in love.

James thought of the eight other available cowboys who lived in the bunkhouse on the Thompson ranch. Deuce, thank goodness, was too young, and Sid was too old, but the rest of them were presentable enough—or at least they were after they bathed. Even though it was the dead of winter, he predicted there'd be a spate of bathing in the ranch hands' future as they slicked themselves up for courtin' the O'Donnell twins.

James sensed Patrick Gallagher would be his real competition. The man had brought a stud to the ranch for Wyatt to check out while he assessed the quality of the mare his stallion would breed to. He was staying up at the big house for a few days, maybe longer—plenty of time to court Bridget.

James had envied him the black Thoroughbred, but now.... Gallagher was a tall, well-formed man who knew his way around a horse and had dark good looks that would probably appeal to women. And the breeder knew it, too. He walked like a man who had land and plenty of stock—unlike James who was just a ranch hand, and up until right now, content to be so.

Defeat tried to edge in, dampening his hope. But he shrugged off the feeling.

First to the table, first to be fed, as his ma was fond of saying. He vowed to begin courting Miss Bridget O'Donnell as soon as she stepped out of the station.

Chapter Two

Bridget stood by the window at the post office, watching for James to return, weary but eager to see him again. Behind her, Alana sat in the only other chair in the room, engaged in a quiet conversation with Mr. Waite, asking him about his rheumatism and suggesting an herbal posset he might try.

Bridget had to tamp down her impatience to be moving, to finish this journey and see what awaited them at the Thompson ranch. She could barely keep herself from pacing the small space.

A faded brown sleigh pulled up in front of the station. She saw James, and her stomach fluttered. To distract herself, she focused her attention on his horse—some type of dappled gray. She wanted a closer look. "James is here, Alana. We must not keep the horse waiting in the cold."

"We mustn't keep *Mr. Whitson* waiting," her sister chided and rose to her feet, turning to hold out a hand to the stationmaster. "Thank ye, Mr. Waite, for allowing us to warm ourselves."

"Jack. Call me Jack." He pressed and released her hand. "No need to stand on formality with me, no siree." He struggled to get to his feet.

"No, no." Alana touched his arm. "Ye stay comfortable, and we'll see ourselves out."

"Uhh," he grunted, settling back.

Bridget donned the coat she'd removed earlier and pulled on

her mittens. She echoed her sister's thanks, gathered her satchel and potato bag, and bade the stationmaster good-bye.

Instead of going back into the main room, they left by the outside door, walking across the platform and down the steps.

James reached for Alana's bags and helped her into the back seat of the sleigh.

Bridget tilted her head toward the horse. "Yers?"

"My gelding, Dusty."

As soon as she handed her satchel and the potato bag to James, Bridget moved to the horse and ran her hand down his neck.

The gelding was tall, with a narrow-bodied, rangy build. But what interested Bridget was his coloring. He looked like someone had taken a gray horse and splattered paint across his coat, and then stood the mount in a vat of paint to his knees to create four white socks. Only the long mane and tail remained sooty gray.

"I've never seen anything like him."

The horse turned to snuffle her arm.

"Ye beauty." Bridget wished she had an apple slice or carrot to give him. "Next time I see ye, dear boy, I promise to bring ye a treat."

James walked to her side. "He's an Appaloosa. An American breed known by these spots."

"Unusual and striking." She felt more than saw Alana's long-suffering look. With a final pat to Dusty's nose, Bridget returned to the sleigh. *There'd be time later to become acquainted with the horse.* For the first time, excitement stirred in her about visiting a ranch. *I'll have my fill of horses.* She let out a happy sigh.

With a courtly bow, James extended a hand to help her into the sleigh, his gaze intent on her face.

Bridget smiled her thanks. She climbed inside, letting her hand linger in his longer than convention allowed.

The padded leather seat still felt warm from hot bricks wrapped in rags that James had moved from the seat to the floor.

Bridget snuggled next to Alana, who rested her head on the seatback, her eyes closed.

James covered them with a thick brown fur, solicitously tucking in the edges.

Bridget fingered the heavy fur, wondering what type of animal had a pelt so thick.

"Bearskin. Grizzly bear." After answering her unspoken question, James climbed into the front seat and gathered up the reins. With a jerk, the sleigh started forward, and he directed Dusty down the street.

The gelding tossed his head and took some mincing steps sideways, as if protesting the burden behind him. With the guidance of James's hands on the reins and his voice, Dusty settled down to the task of pulling the sleigh.

Bridget glanced at her sister. "This is cozy."

Alana raised her head and gazed at Bridget, her eyes troubled. "Mr. Whitson is a thoughtful man. But I don't like the idea of going to this ranch, instead of our uncle's home."

As she usually did, Bridget stepped into the role of giving assurance instead of voicing her own doubts. "Sally *is* our family, our cousin. Moreover, James and Mr. Waite told us the Thompsons would welcome us."

"I guess we'll find out," Alana said in a tired voice and rested her head on the seatback.

Bridget watched James with interest, assessing his skill. He had sure hands and a confident manner with both the horse and sled.

She'd driven carts and wagons plenty of times, but never a sleigh. When she was young, they'd had a stocky Irish draught horse. And as soon as she was old enough to drive, Bridget coaxed her father into allowing her to take the reins. Da, now gone to Heaven, bless him, had never resisted Bridget's persuasions. He'd allowed her to run wild in the outdoors she loved, as well as spend time at the squire's stables, helping out the grooms. The most heart-wrenching part of leaving Ireland was saying good-bye to her beloved horses.

Bridget sat back, tugged up the fur to cover most of her face, inhaling the smell of musty leather, and watched as they glided through the town, which on closer inspection proved bigger than she'd thought from her first glance through the train window. Two big buildings under construction rose three or four stories amid the false-fronted wooden ones. A few nice houses and one brick mansion seemed out of place next to the simple wood cabins.

Soon they left the town, gliding under brown-trunked trees, the branches laden with white crystals from yesterday's snowstorm. The beauty, like the cold, took her breath away, and she had to force the pine-scented air into her lungs.

James looked back over his shoulder and tossed her a grin. "You two lovely ladies all right back there?"

She lowered the bearskin. "As right as can be with such a skilled driver," Bridget said with a smile, grateful that Alana was snoozing and thus couldn't hear how flirtatious she sounded.

He winked and returned his attention to driving.

After about an hour, the novelty of riding in a sleigh had worn off. The bricks at their feet chilled, and they grew cold.

They passed from forest into open land. The earlier cloudiness of the day had given way to vivid blue skies and sunshine that sparkled off the snow, the brightness making her squint.

Even huddled next to her twin with the thick bear pelt over part of her face, Bridget felt the icy cold start to wear away at her energy and fatigue set in. Eventually, the strain of the their long journey caught up with her, and she dozed off, her head resting together with Alana's. Sometimes, the women bumped awake when the runners of the sleigh hit an unseen hole or rock, buried under the snow. Then they'd drift back to sleep.

Finally, James slowed the sled. He twisted in the seat to give them a sympathetic glance. "Last stretch, ladies. We've been on Thompson land for a while."

Bridget lowered the fur enough to expose her mouth. "It's thankin' the Good Lord I'll be when I'm warm again."

He laughed, although his face was ruddy with cold. "'Bout another ten minutes or so, and we'll reach the house."

He must be just as glad as we are to arrive at the destination.

Keeping the fur tight around the two of them, she wiggled to sit up so she could see. But the vista hadn't changed from snow-covered land and distant blue-gray mountains.

"Do you really think they'll welcome us?" Alana's voice quivered.

"Of course. We're kin to Sally and her husband." Bridget enthused more certainty into her tone than she felt. Alana, gentle soul that she was, had too many fears, and Bridget often needed to prop her up. *Or push or pull her.* She remembered the difficulties she'd had in convincing her twin to set out for America. Bridget hadn't wanted to leave "her" horses, but Alana clung to the people she cared about, especially her best friend, Timkin.

"There!" Bridget pointed with her chin. "I see buildings." A big two-story white ranch house blended into the snow around them. But the two huge red barns—one in front of the other—made a stark contrast against the arching blue sky. She couldn't wait to meet all the horses that must be inside.

In the corral on the left of the barn, Bridget saw a big man lunging a magnificent black stallion, his movements capable. She sat up, leaning over the side so she could study the horse. She glimpsed a well-chiseled head on a long neck, high withers, a lean body, and long legs. *A Thoroughbred.* The sleigh passed the barn, and she lost sight of the horse. *What are they doing with a Thoroughbred on a ranch?*

"Bridget," Alana chided. "Yer lettin' in the cold air."

"Away wi' ye, Alana. Aren't ye excited?"

"Nae, Bridget. I'm tuckered is what."

The sled pulled up between the house and the biggest barn. A picket fence enclosed an area around a side door. A brick walkway and steps leading to the house were cleared of snow.

The door opened, and Bridget spotted a woman in a navy blue coat step out. She wore a pale blue hat, scarf, and mittens, and apparently hadn't seen them arrive, for she stopped and shaded her eyes from the sun. Then she lowered her arm and moved down the walkway and through the gate to meet the sleigh, a warm smile on her face. She had bright blue eyes, even features, and auburn brows and lashes, which must surely match the hair hidden by her cap.

"Looks like you brought company for me." The woman addressed the words to James, but her glance at the twins was friendly.

"Well, not precisely for you, Miz Thompson," James corrected her. "Miz O'Hanlon's cousins. Bridget and Alana O'Donnell. All the way from Ireland."

The woman's eyes widened. "What a journey you two have made. I'm Samantha Thompson. Welcome." She gestured for them to step from the sleigh.

A lanky man ambled from the barn. Up close he proved to be young, perhaps seventeen, with orange hair and a freckled face. When he saw the twins, his eyes widened and he stumbled, pulling himself up abruptly. Color flooded his cheeks, and his Adam's apple bobbed up and down.

With an upward quirk of his mouth, James handed the reins to the young man. "This here's Deuce. He's really named Harry, but since we have another Harry, the one who married your cousin, we swapped out his name for Deuce." He introduced the twins to the young man.

Deuce ducked his head and stuttered out a greeting.

Mrs. Thompson patted him on the shoulder. "I was just on my way to check on Sally," she said to the twins. "The storm knocked down the north fence, and the cattle have scattered. My husband, Wyatt, and the hands rode out to round them up and string new wire. I intend to stay with Sally for a while because Harry is reluctant to leave her, for she's feeling poorly."

Is she ill like her mother?

Bridget's concern must have shown on her face for Mrs. Thompson waved her hand in a negating motion. "No, no.

Nothing serious. For the last three days, she's been queasy in the mornings…"

Alana gasped. "Sally's with child?"

Her sister had been the one to help their mother with healing and midwifery and so knew about such matters.

Mrs. Thompson's eyes twinkled. "It's early days, but I suspect so, since she perks up in the afternoon."

Bridget exchanged a concerned glance with Alana. Given her condition, their cousin couldn't possibly welcome visitors.

With a smile, Mrs. Thompson waved for them to accompany her. "After you greet Sally, I'll bring you back to the house. I know from experience what a long journey from another country feels like, and I'm sure you'd like a bath. We have indoor plumbing and a nice bathtub for soaking. Far easier than a small tin tub in Sally's cabin. And afterwards, Mrs. Toffels, my housekeeper, will make you something to eat."

"A bath sounds just heavenly." Bridget allowed Mrs. Thompson's charm to wrap around her like welcomed warmth, and her fears eased. Back home, an upper-class lady wouldn't dream of inviting the likes of them into her home for a bath and a meal. She wondered if everyone in this town would be as friendly.

The crunch of footsteps and hoofbeats in the snow heralded a horseman leading the black stallion. She recognized him as the one who'd been working the Thoroughbred, and her interest quickened.

With a gasp, Alana shrank behind Bridget.

Up close, Bridget could see the man was as magnificent as his horse. Big and broad-shouldered, he had patrician features with dark eyes and eyebrows.

He glanced at them, a glint of interest in his eyes.

Bridget met his gaze with a frankness of her own.

His eyebrows lifted, and he focused his attention on her.

"Mr. Gallagher owns a stud farm." Mrs. Thompson explained, touching Bridget's shoulder. "Patrick, I'd like you to meet Miss Bridget—" She brushed Alana's sleeve "—and Miss Alana O'Donnell, who've come a long ways…from Ireland. Ladies, Mr. Patrick Gallagher.

He removed his hat and swept them a bow. Straightening, he smiled with great charm and replaced his hat.

Something about the way his body shifted—shoulders back, chin firm, head slightly-angled, showed he was used to female attention. He made Bridget aware of her bedraggled state in a way that James had not. She stilled her hands to keep from smoothing the wrinkles of her skirt. She wouldn't betray any hint of self-consciousness to this man.

Like James, he, too, barely glanced at her sister. A novel reaction, not just because the sisters were twins but because at home Alana, with her gentle goodness, was beloved by all the villagers. Kindness shone on her face, and everyone, especially men, noticed her.

Confusion made Bridget glance away from the horse's owner and focus on his stallion. She wanted to move closer, but Alana grasped a fold of her coat. She couldn't pull away without exposing her sister's skittishness.

Is Patrick Gallagher looking at me because he can tell I'm interested in him? Does he see my longing to know his horse? Or is it just that Alana is hiding, and I'm the one in the forefront?

As if discerning that her thoughts were on him, he sent her a knowing smile.

Heat flushed her, bringing a sudden sense of optimism. *Perhaps there's some gold dust in Montana, after all.*

A few minutes later, as James carried the bags of potatoes, Bridget and Alana followed Mrs. Thompson down a narrow path through the snow to a small cabin made of squared-off logs. The door sat in the middle of the one-story house, with a small four-paned glass window on each side. The timbers still looked raw, with some kind of plaster sealing the spaces between the logs. There was no porch, unlike many of the houses she'd seen from the train, only a wooden step to the entrance. Cordwood was stacked to the eaves along one wall.

A privy stood to the left of the house, with a narrow path through the snow from the doorway. The wood of the small structure was as new as the home.

Mrs. Thompson tapped on the door, and then stepped to the side so the twins would be in view of whomever answered.

Her stomach tight, Bridget turned to give Alana a reassuring smile.

Her sister barely tipped her lips up in response.

The door opened, and a man looked out. He had a tan, rugged face and brown hair and eyes.

Mrs. Thompson waved toward Bridget and Alana. "Harry, I've brought visitors."

He looked at the twins with a bewildered expression but gave them a polite smile. "Come on in."

The group stepped inside. With just the light from the two windows, the interior was dim, although a small stove in a kitchen area emitted warmth that filled the room. A slight sour smell lingered in the air, remnants of Sally's nausea.

Harry gestured the twins forward.

Bridget moved to his left, and Alana flanked her other side.

On a bed tucked under a loft and taking up half the room, a young woman was propped against the pillows. She wore a navy wool dress. A shawl of the same color was draped around her shoulders.

Bridget studied her cousin, searching for a family resemblance.

Sally looked wan and tired, but when they entered, she slid her legs off the bed and stood. With her mouth in an *O*, she gazed at the twins.

When Bridget saw her cousin's dark blue eyes—the same eyes

she saw in her sister and in the looking glass—the O'Donnell eyes—she relaxed, feeling an immediate sense of kinship, although she envied Sally her thick dark hair and refined nose.

"I have a surprise for you, my dear," Mrs. Thompson said gaily. "These are your cousins Bridget and Alana, come all the way from Ireland."

Sally gasped. Her hand flew to cover her mouth. Then with a happy shriek, she lowered her arm and lunged forward to hug Bridget first, and then Alana before stepping back, laughing.

Bridget couldn't but join in her cousin's laugher

"Oh, you must think me daft!" Sally exclaimed. "But Da will be so happy. He's never stopped missing his family in Ireland." She glanced behind them as if looking for more people. "Your mother? Catriona?" She spoke with an American accent.

"It's just us," Bridget said with the bright smile she beamed to belie the pain of her stark statement. "We decided to come to our family in America."

"As well you should." Sally leaned forward to take the hand of each twin and squeezed.

James gave Bridget a questioning glance.

She figured he was asking about giving Sally the information about her mother, and she nodded for him to go ahead.

He cleared his throat. "I'm afraid I have bad news, Sally. Your mother is very ill, and your father sent word with Erik Muth to fetch the doctor to their place. That's why I brought your cousins here, instead of to your parents' home."

"My Ma!" Sally released their hands. "Oh, dear Lord. I must go to her." She whirled toward the bureau as if to start packing.

Harry caught her arm. "You cannot, love. You've been sick, too. You're in no condition to take care of your mother. You couldn't leave the bed this morning."

"No, Harry, I must! There's just Da and the children to nurse her."

He touched her cheek. "If what we think about your condition is true, Sally, you can't risk yourself or the babe."

Sally's eyes welled with tears, and she sank onto the bed, the back of a hand pressing against her mouth.

Harry took a seat next to her and placed an arm around her shoulders. "You know how competent Dr. Cameron is."

Sally nodded. "But he can't stay to care for her." Her voice quavered. "To see to the needs of my family…the children."

"I'll go." Alana leaned forward. "I'm quite skilled with herbs and nursing."

Bridget held her protest behind her teeth. She didn't want to be separated from her sister in this new land, but when she looked at her twin's stiff shoulders and the firm set of her chin, she held in a selfish complaint. Parting would be far more difficult on timid Alana. To leave the safety of her sister's side and go amongst strangers—no matter that they were kin—took courage. Unexpected pride surged in her. For this crisis, Alana was the best choice. "My sister is right," Bridget said, stepping close to Alana in solidarity.

Sally's shoulders slumped in defeat.

Bridget glanced from the couple to Mrs. Thompson. "Will…will it be all right for me to stay here? I could help Sally…"

Harry rose, his expression clearing. "I'd be obliged for you to do so, Cousin Bridget. You're welcome, indeed. I haven't felt right for Mrs. Thompson to remain here with Sally when I know how much else she has to do." He shot Mrs. Thompson a look as if to quell an objection. His gaze swung back to her. "It would ease my mind to have Sally's kin with her."

Sally touched Harry's elbow. "But how is Alana to get to my family's?"

James moved forward. His swift glance toward Mrs. Thompson obviously asked for permission. "I'll take her."

Harry made a negating motion with his hand. "Thank you for the offer, James. But I will do the honors for Cousin Alana. I know my way. And it's my duty to my new family."

"But not until tomorrow," Mrs. Thompson said firmly.

Sally made a weak sound of protest.

Mrs. Thompson leaned over and patted Sally's hand. "Alana has had a long journey and must rest. Even if they left this minute, she and Harry couldn't make it to your family's farm before dark. It's too dangerous driving on the prairie on a winter's night." She glanced at Harry. "And you're to stay there if they need you. We'll take care of your wife while you're gone."

Silence followed her words.

Sally exchanged an anguished look with her husband.

Bridget's heart went out to her. *Newly married, happy, a baby on the way, then this bad news to dash their wedded bliss.*

James cleared his throat. "I'll just leave these here and go see to Dusty." He hefted the two sacks of potatoes before setting them in the corner.

Harry nodded. "I'm sure you ladies would like some privacy. I've got to check on a horse or two, and there's plenty of work we can do in the barn. We've been putting off the leather repair until there was more time. One of my reins is wearing thin. 'Bout to snap any day now, probably when I'm after an ornery steer."

"I must go also." Mrs. Thompson glanced at Bridget and Alana. "Once the two of you and Sally have caught up, please come over to the big house and take advantage of our bathing room. Bring any clothes that need washing, and Mrs. Toffels will see they are cleaned. We'll hang them over the stove in the kitchen to dry. And of course, you'll have supper with us tonight. All of you."

Bridget stepped up to James and touched his arm—a daring gesture toward a man who was practically a stranger, even if he didn't feel like one. "I don't know how to thank ye for yer kindness, James. We would have been lost without yer assistance."

His gaze remained steady on her, although spots of color appeared on his cheeks. "I'm glad to help. I reckon you, uh, you and your sister are safe now."

Safe. She hadn't felt safe for a long time—not since Ma died and their funds dwindled. She'd known they had only a few months before they could no longer pay the rent on their cottage. They hadn't even had time to send a letter to Montana as a warning of their arrival.

Although Bridget didn't like to feel beholden to her kin, Sally and her family needed the twins' help, which made her feel purposeful and went a long way to soothe the pricking of her conscience at foisting the two of them on their family.

After James, Harry, and Mrs. Thompson left, the three girls looked at each other in curiosity.

Sally patted the bed beside her. "Come, be comfortable. Since we're family there's no need to be formal, is there?"

Bridget took off her coat and hung the garment on a peg by the door. Then she pulled off her cap and mittens and tucked them into the pockets.

Alana followed suit.

Sally scooted back so she was propped against the pillows, looking weary. "I'm a poor hostess, I'm afraid. Sick in the mornings, then a burst of energy midday, then tired and needing a nap."

Bridget sat on the end of the bed facing her.

Alana took her other side. "Not at all. Sometimes the early months of pregnancy can be trying. But then ye will feel better."

"I hope so," Sally said in a fervent tone. "My dear Harry is so worried." She pursed her lips. "Will you think poorly of me if I say I wish this baby had waited a few months? We've barely wed."

Bridget laughed and reached over to pat Sally's ankle. "Not at all. I think I'd want a whole year, not just months."

"Now—" Sally nodded. "Enough about me. Tell me about Aunt Siobhan and Catriona."

The twins exchanged pain-filled glances. Her throat tight, Bridget gave a slight dip of her head to encourage her sister to speak up.

"Our dear mother passed away six months ago." Alana said in a voice soft with grief.

Hearing the words, remembering their beloved mother, made moisture well up in Bridget's eyes. *I miss her so!*

Sally sat up straighter. "Oh, I'm so sorry. Da would often tell stories of your parents from when they were all young. I gather Aunt Siobhan had a forthright personality."

The twins laughed through their tears. "Aye," Alana agreed with a mischievous glance at her sister. "And our Bridget is much the same way."

Bridget wrinkled her nose. "And Alana takes after our da. She's as kind and gentle as ever a lass could be."

"And Catriona?"

Abruptly, the laughter left Bridget, replaced by an ache of guilt. They'd left their older sister behind…never even had a chance to say good-bye.

"Three months after mother died, Catriona eloped with a peddler," Alana said, her expression pinched.

Bridget laid a hand on Alana's knee in a silent gesture of support. "We never heard from her again." How Catri could have left them to such worry angered her. Instead of the three sisters supporting each other through their grief, Catri had selfishly left her younger sisters to fend for themselves.

"We hated to leave without her knowing…" Alana's voice died away.

But I made ye go. Bridget finished for sister. "We left a letter with our mother's dearest friend. We left word of our destination with several of our neighbors—" She nodded at Sally. "That of yer parents' farm. If Catri returns home, she'll know where we are."

"And if a letter from her arrives, Mrs. O'Bannon will forward it here."

Sally's eyebrows pulled together. "Do you think she's happy?"

Bridget shrugged. "The peddler was handsome…. In fact, that man with the Thoroughbred, Mr. Gallagher, reminded me of him. Dark Irish, with bold eyes, and a confident air."

"I never liked the man," Alana broke in with uncustomary

harshness in her tone. "I say a rosary every day for her."

Sally wrinkled her nose. "It must have been hard to depart, knowing you might never have word from your sister again." She shook her head. "I'll say prayers for her, too. And that soon you'll receive a letter."

"And we'll pray for a swift recovery for yer mother."

Alana's eyes filled with tears. "It will be hard not knowing what is happening to our sister."

"I know." *Oh, how I know. Sally will soon have the news about the outcome of her mother's illness—hopefully a good one. But Alana and I might never know about Catriona.* The thought made her heart ache.

Chapter Three

James hurried into the barn, glad to be out of the chill. The brief time in the O'Hanlon's cabin hadn't warmed him enough from the long sleigh ride. The barn was dim and cold, lit only by lantern light and weak sunlight filtering through cracks, but not nearly as bad as out in the open. He inhaled the familiar smell of horse and hay, feeling an odd sense of contentment and excitement. With the arrival of Miss Bridget O'Donnell, his life had just changed, and he was impatient to get on with the business of courting her.

In one stall, Deuce was busy rubbing Dusty down.

Patrick Gallagher worked on the same task with Thunder.

As usual, James stopped to eye the stallion, as fine a piece of horseflesh as he'd ever seen but with an unexpectedly gentle temperament. *You'd think a Thoroughbred as black as the night would have a devil temper to match. Gallagher had sure lucked out with this stud.* James checked his thoughts. *No, to give the man his due, the horse was well-trained.*

Gallagher caught him eyeing the stallion. His hand on the currycomb didn't stop, but he gave James a friendly nod. "So how did you end up bringing two unexpected lady visitors to the ranch?"

"Found them at the train station. They were planning to go to the O'Donnell's out on the prairie. But I'd stopped to speak to Erik Muth, a neighbor who was delivering milk to the mercantile, who told me of the illness of Mrs. O'Donnell. The ladies could hardly descend on a house of illness, so I suggested bringing them to their cousin, Sally."

"Quick thinking on your part."

James remained silent. He hadn't acted out of self-interest. The two women needed a place to stay, and he'd had a solution. But then he thought of his attraction to Bridget. *Well, at least mostly from unselfish motives.*

"I do like Miss Bridget, although it probably doesn't matter which one I'd chose…if I were to chose. They're alike as two peas in a pod." Patrick hesitated and appeared to think. "Well, the glimpse I had of Miss Alana, she was thinner, and I do like a woman with more meat on her bones."

James bristled. "You make Miss Bridget sound like a pig to fatten up for dinner."

"That's one way to put it. But I sure look forward to seeing her cleaned up and not wearing a coat and hat."

"She's pretty, just the way she is," James muttered, gripping the stall.

"Well, I'll wait and see. I have certain standards of what I require in a wife."

Wife. James's heart sank. He knew Gallagher traveled all over with his stud and had plenty of opportunities to meet women.

Why did he have to settle on the one I've chosen?

Clean from head to toe from their bath and wrapped in borrowed robes, Bridget and Alana sat with their backs to the stove in the Thompsons' kitchen, drying their long hair. Bridget had never seen such a big kitchen, replete with a table covered with a red-and-white checked cloth that matched the curtains, as well as an icebox, pie safe, china hutch, and great black cast-iron stove with its pipe angling up through the ceiling. *Why, the*

whole main room of our cottage at home could fit in here with space to spare.

Alana swayed in a rocking chair, petting the head of Matilda, the elderly black and tan dog.

Bridget had chosen a straight chair. The red seat cushion made it comfortable.

They chatted with Mrs. Toffels as she alternated between ironing their wrinkled Sunday dresses and cooking dinner. The short, plump housekeeper, with a cheerful round face and gray hair, had refused to let them help with the tasks, insisting they take their ease after such a long, arduous journey. Mrs. Toffels had washed their undergarments, which now hung over the stove, the water drips just missing the pot of beef stew and an iron heating up to be switched out with the one she currently wielded. The simmering stew filled the room with a rich scent.

"There." The housekeeper set down the second iron on the stovetop next to the other one and held up the blue dress. "You can go change, Miss Alana." She glanced out the window. "The children will be home from school any minute now. Of course, they'll have to see to their horses, but then they'll traipse into the kitchen to warm themselves up."

Alana accepted the dress, thanked her and left the room.

The housekeeper stared after her, a frown marring her good-natured countenance. "Your sister's too thin. I suspect it's more than the journey, else the two of you would look the same. Unless you didn't start out the same."

"We did. Alana's pining for home." *For Timkin.*

"Well, some of my good meals should do the trick, if I do say so myself." The housekeeper pursed her lips and picked up Bridget's dress—one almost identical to Alana's because they'd gotten the bolt of cloth at a discount. "Too bad she's not staying here. I'd fatten her right up. But don't you worry, Miss Bridget. I'll send plenty of food along with your sister."

"In that case, I won't be worryin' about *food.*" Bridget tried to inject a teasing tone into her words. "But with us parted, I'm sure I'll be fretting about her."

Mrs. Toffels spread the skirt over the end of the ironing board and picked up the heated iron from the stove. "Well, dear, I've lived a long enough life to know that one can spend time fretting over things that never happen. And there's enough that does. I ought to know. I've buried three husbands—all good men. Best leave the worry for when you know there's a real problem."

"Ye are right." Bridget fell silent, thinking about the woman's wise words. *Perhaps I worry too much about Alana.*

Lost in thought, she didn't notice Mrs. Toffels had finished the dress. "There you are, dear. I'll look forward to seeing you two in them. That color will be beautiful with your eyes." She gave the dress to Bridget. "Just leave the robes on the bed. Once you're dressed, head to the parlor—down the hall thataway—where everyone will gather before dinner to meet you." She waved in the direction. "I'll have someone light a fire in that room."

On impulse, Bridget leaned over and kissed the woman's wrinkled cheek. "I appreciate all ye are doing for us."

"It's a downright pleasure to have young ladies visiting." With a smile crinkling her face, Mrs. Toffels made a shooing motion. "Now off with you."

Bridget hurried upstairs to the guest bedroom, where they'd left their satchels on the big four-poster bed, spread with a pink and green quilt. The room smelled of roses from the dried petals in a crystal bowl on the nightstand.

Alana had already donned her dress but hadn't managed all the buttons down her back. She stood in front of a mirror hanging above a chest of drawers, braiding her hair. She smiled, her face reflecting back to Bridget. "Such a lovely big mirror." She deftly looped the braid over her head, tucking in hairpins. Reddish tendrils escaped to curl around her cheeks.

Out of long habit, Bridget walked over to her sister, buttoning the middle section and noting how loose the dress hung. But she said nothing. Over the past weeks, she'd nagged at Alana to eat more, to no avail.

They heard the distant sound of doors opening and closing, voices, and footsteps. The window reflected candlelight from the lamp on the dresser, with only darkness beyond.

"The children must be home. They would have had a long cold ride today with the snow so deep." Bridget slipped on her own gown and turned so her twin could button up the back. She used the hairbrush and then started to braid her hair. As the unruly mass dried, the curls tightened but were still slightly damp underneath. She coiled her braid into a bun at her nape and stabbed in the hairpins, fluffing her bangs. Like Alana's hair, some wisps sprang free to frame her face. The two of them would never present an elegant appearance.

Bridget tapped the wooden handle of the brush. "When ye leave ye should take this with ye, and I'll be keeping the comb. Unless ye'd prefer the comb?"

"We won't be sharing for a while. At least I don't need to worry about ye stealing a fresh shirtwaist and returning it to me crumpled and smelling of the stable." Alana adjusted Bridget's lace, pretending seriousness.

"Ye will have to wash and iron yer own clothes more often now."

This time, Bridget wrinkled her nose at her sister. Aside from the heated discussions over immigrating to America, in the past they'd only argued about Bridget's tendency to borrow Alana's clothing. Well, aside from Alana's frustration when the mess on Bridget's side of their small bedroom spilled into her own area.

With a playful smile, Alana tilted her head so both sisters could see themselves in the mirror.

With the contrast of their two faces before her, Bridget could see the hollows in her sister's cheeks and the shadows under her eyes. Guilt stabbed her for dragging her sister—despite her tears and protests—away from home. "Shall we wear our collars?" Their mother had crocheted them for the twins' eighteen birthday. They only wore them for church and other special occasions.

Her sister nodded. "I think we should look our best for our hosts as well as meeting the handsome cowboys." She walked over to the bed, reached into her satchel for the little roll of pink crocheted lace, and fastened the collar around her neck.

Her words, uttered in a placid tone, shocked Bridget, for the statement was so unlike her demure sister.

She secured her own collar, similar to Alana's except hers was white and had points to make it different from the rounded edges of her sister's. *If she's preening for the men, perhaps she's over Timkin Walsh,* Bridget thought with a surge of hope. "I thought both James Whitson and Patrick Gallagher seemed fine men." She made her tone as matter-of-fact as her twin's.

"Horsemen, both. Ye have a lot in common."

"Most men out here are sure to own a horse, Alana," Bridget pointed out, disappointed that her sister wasn't interested for herself.

"But they don't all make their living with horses."

Bridget opened her mouth to retort, then pressed her lips together. Trying to push Alana into the arms of any man, much less a cowboy, would only result in her usually docile sister digging in her heels.

But still…horsemen or not, perhaps one will captivate her enough to forget Timkin Walsh.

"Mrs. Toffels says we're to go to the parlor." Bridget leaned over and pinched her sister's cheeks. "There. Now ye have some color."

"Silly," Alana chided. "Ye know it won't last." She followed Bridget out the door, down the stairs, and around a corner to the hall.

Bridget walked into a parlor filled with several rose velvet chairs with high backs and a matching settee that held pillows embroidered with flowers. An enormous fireplace took up the far wall. A portrait of a blonde woman in a flowing pink gown hung above a mantle carved from dark wood. "A beautiful room," she murmured.

At first, she didn't see James crouching in front of the hearth, feeding a log to the fire.

He stood, and his eyes brightened. "Miss O'Donnell, you look…you look…" His ears reddened.

"Clean," Bridget teased, holding out her skirt.

"I was searching for the best form of the word *beautiful*," he said with mock stiffness, the crook of his mouth and his dimples betraying he was teasing her in return.

Alana entered and stepped to the side of the doorway.

James swept her a small bow. "Miss O'Donnell, how lovely you look." This time, there wasn't a hint of discomfort in his manner.

How come he's so courtly with her? Bridget suppressed a spark of jealousy.

Alana's cheeks, still slightly flushed from the pinches, pinked becomingly, and her shy smile at James was the widest Bridget had seen in a long while.

Alana and James would make a good match. He's a kind man, and that's what she needs in a husband. Bridget ignored how her stomach churned at the idea. To make her sister happy, she'd give up any interest in James Whitson.

She heard the clatter of feet and turned to see a group of children flood into the room. Upon closer inspection, she narrowed the count to five—four boys and a girl. But surely they couldn't be siblings? Except for two of the brown-haired, green-eyed boys, who looked even more identical than her and Alana, none of the children resembled each other.

The girl was the image of the woman in the portrait over the fireplace. She looked about nine or ten.

Bridget recognized Samantha's blue eyes in the youngest boy, who appeared to be about ten. But his dark hair, golden skin, and slanting eyebrows looked nothing like his mother's.

The oldest boy's skin was even browner than the youngest

one, and he had black hair pulled into a long tail. He caught her looking at him and gazed back with dark solemn eyes.

The rest of the children halted in front of the twins and stared at the two women, eyes wide.

The young boy hopped a step closer, and his eyebrows winged upward. "I'm Daniel. Are you twins like Jack and Tim?" Without waiting for an answer he rushed on. "Too bad you're so old, or you could marry Tim and Jack. They're twelve." His wide grin showed his delight with the idea.

Old? I supposed twenty-two seems old to him. Bridget's eyes met Alana's, and they both burst out laughing. *How good it feels to once again laugh with my sister!* Although giggles continued to bubble in her chest, she sobered her expression lest she hurt the boy's feelings.

But instead of looking abashed, Daniel watched them with an irrepressible grin.

Little imp, she thought, liking the boy right away. She'd never had a brother but had befriended the stable lads at the squire's. She suppressed a pang from missing them.

Daniel's comment caused one of his twin brothers to roll his eyes.

The other elbowed Daniel in his side. "Don't mind him. We try not to. When he goes on like that, usually we just sit on him." He jabbed Daniel again. "I'm Jack, that's Hunter—" he indicated the dark-skin oldest boy, who looked about fourteen "—and my quiet twin over there is Tim. He'll talk with you when he knows you better."

Tim gave the two of them a shy smile and a slight nod, before his gaze slid away.

"I know what ye mean," Bridget said to Jack in a mournful tone, all the better to get in a friendly dig at her twin. "Alana's the same way. Do you find ye have to talk for him?"

Alana nudged her, acting as if they, too, were children. "Sure and I can speak for meself, thank ye very much," she said, playfully thickening her Gaelic accent. She turned to address the girl. "I'm Alana. And my sister who talks too much is Bridget."

"I'm Christine." The girl tilted her head and studied Alana. "I like the way you talk. Sounds pretty."

"We're from Ireland, dear one. That's how everyone speaks there. In fact, we have our own language called Gaelic."

Samantha Thompson walked into the parlor on the arm of a man who must be her husband.

Mr. Thompson was tall and dark-haired, with high-cheekbones, a slightly aquiline nose, and a formidable expression. His gray shirt made his dark eyes gleam like pewter.

Mrs. Thompson wore a pale blue dress with a rose pattern, well cut, but not fancy.

Bridget doubted the woman was wearing her best. She probably hadn't wanted the twins to feel out of place in their simple gowns.

With a wide smile, Mrs. Thompson tugged her husband over to them. "Alana, Bridget, my dears. You must meet Wyatt."

"Mr. Thompson," Bridge bobbed a curtsey. "I must thank ye for allowing us to be guests at yer ranch."

He raised his eyebrows at his wife, and his eyes twinkled, softening his intimidating expression. "I doubt I had anything to do with it. So save your thanks. And please, call us Wyatt and Samantha. You'll find we don't stand on ceremony around here." He gestured to the children. "I see you've met our brood."

"They are darlings."

Daniel and Christine giggled.

He threw his head back and laughed. "When you know them better, you might not think so. Why, I could tell you stories—"

His wife elbowed him.

The gesture was so much like Jack's to Daniel that Bridget burst out laughing. "I see where yer son gets it." She mimicked the flying elbow.

Wyatt sent Samantha a smug look. "See. Miss Bridget agrees with me. All the mischievous qualities of our offspring are on your account."

Her face glowing, Samantha cast a loving look at her

children. A smile played about her lips. "I'm afraid I can't take all the credit." She shot Bridget an amused glance. "You've probably wondered at our assortment."

Not sure what to say, Bridget settled for a simple nod.

"This is Wyatt's and my second marriage. Christine is his from his first wife." She waved toward the portrait over the mantel. "Daniel is mine. His father was Argentine. The other boys are our adopted sons."

"Ah, that settles my curiosity." *Although it didn't, really.* Bridget wanted to learn more about them, hear stories of how the couple met and married and about their children. *There'll be time enough for that.* The thought gave her satisfaction—a feeling of putting down roots in this community.

Alana drifted a few feet away to talk to Tim.

The O'Hanlons entered. Sally, leaning on Harry's arm, came over to them. She looked refreshed after her nap.

In the light of the bigger room, Bridget could see her cousin's dress was the same navy blue as hers, although more stylishly made with fuller sleeves.

Sally looked from Bridget's dress to Alana's and held out a fold of her gown. "I'd say we all like the same color. This dress was a wedding gift from Harry." She stared at her husband with adoring eyes. "He thought I needed warmer garments than the dresses I had."

He reddened and shifted, then gestured from Alana to Bridget to Sally. "Not hard to discern why you're dressed alike. You all have the same eye color."

"You're right, Harry." Samantha agreed. "The family resemblance is strong. Navy is the perfect hue for the O'Donnell ladies, even if one is now an O'Hanlon."

In the pause, Bridget heard the slow tread of boots from the hallway.

Wyatt pointed his chin to a space by the settee. "Let's make way for the new arrivals. Harry, you can tell me how the leather repairs went." He guided his wife away, and Harry followed with Sally.

Bridget turned to see Patrick striding through the door as if he owned the place, followed by two men she hadn't met. One was about the stud owner's height, although not as broad. He had a shock of curly brown hair, hazel eyes, and a long nose over a wide mouth, which stretched into an appealing grin. The other was short, with blunt features, light blue eyes, and pale blond hair and eyelashes.

The two men jostled each other in a friendly way, trying to be the first to reach her side.

Patrick let them by, one eyebrow cocked indulgently.

The tall one arrived first. "I'm Moss. Have I the honor of addressing Miss Bridget or Miss Alana?"

"I'm Bridget, Mr. Moss."

"No, ma'am, not *Mr.* Moss," he corrected. "Moss Callahan.

The stocky man edged around him. "I'm Buck Skold."

Bridget smiled at their eagerness. "Is that a nickname, or do ye have another Christian name, then, Mr. Skold?"

"Yes, ma'am. Buchanan." He shrugged. "Could be worse. But I prefer Buck."

"Aye. And ye, Moss?"

"I do have a real name, Miss Bridget. But since my sainted mother isn't here to object to me using a nickname, I'll tell you only that I'm called Moss."

"Aye, for your eye color, then."

His smile widened.

James joined them in time to hear the last comments. He nudged Moss with his shoulder. "No, for rolling stone. As in no moss grows under his feet. Our Moss isn't one to stick around one place for too long."

She raised an eyebrow. "A gypsy are ye, then?"

Moss nodded, an expression of regret in his eyes as he looked at her, although his smile didn't dim. "I'm afraid I have itchy feet, Miss Bridget. But perhaps a lady such as yourself could tempt me to plant myself in Sweetwater Springs."

Bridget laughed, not believing him for a moment but amused

by his flirtation. She wondered what might have caused his wandering ways.

The shorter man, who was stout enough to at least hoist a bale without effort, turned to James. "Ah, you read last week's paper yet?" Buck asked. "President Cleveland made another darn fool statement." From that comment, the conversation drifted into politics.

Normally, Bridget would have paid attention to the discussion, but they were speaking of American politics, and she hadn't the least idea what was going on. She kept an expression of interest on her face and covertly surveyed the rest of the people crowded into the room.

Out of the corner of her eye, she saw Mrs. Toffels hasten to Samantha's side. Although she didn't move away from the men, Bridget was close enough to overhear.

"The rest of the hands are waiting in the kitchen. Shall I tell them to come in here first to meet the young ladies before they sit themselves at the table?"

Wyatt slanted a grin at his housekeeper. "I wonder how many of our shy cowboys would take you up on that offer?"

"A few, perhaps." Mrs. Toffels smiled, wrinkles fanning out over her face. "But I suspect, there's a couple like Sid who still haven't recovered from you bringing home a beautiful wife."

Wyatt laughed. "Sid will adjust…in about five years or so."

Samantha darted a speculative glance at Alana. "Our guests are very pretty. I'd like to keep them."

Wyatt grinned at Samantha. "My darling, at this rate, we're going to be sprouting cabins like mushrooms."

His wife laughed. "How wonderful that would be, Wyatt. In a few short weeks, Sally O'Hanlon has become a friend, and I'd love to have more women nearby. I'm sure Mrs. Toffels agrees." With a raised eyebrow, she glanced at the housekeeper.

The older woman nodded, and her two chins quivered. "I'd be delighted if Miss Bridget chose our James, and they settled down here."

Bridget found herself coloring, but she dared not look over to see if James overheard.

Wyatt shook his head. "I won't ask why you've settled on James for Bridget or who you have in mind for Alana. I'm staying far away from female matchmaking."

As much as she wanted to hear the reply, Bridget knew this conversation wasn't meant for her ears. With a smile she excused herself from the political discussion and moved toward Alana.

Her sister was teaching Tim some Gaelic words.

The young man gazed at her with an infatuated expression.

Bridget halted a few feet away. She couldn't help but smile at the sight of the two shy twins engrossed in conversation. Even better was the animation on Alana's face. In thankfulness, she placed a hand on her chest and exhaled a breath of relief.

Perhaps I can stop worrying after all.

But as she looked at Alana's thinness, doubt still niggled at her.

Chapter Four

The next morning in the O'Hanlon's cabin, the three women prepared for Alana's departure. The night before, they'd done their best with a damp sponge to clean the wool gowns they'd worn for traveling, then left the dresses and their coats hanging outside in hopes the wind would blow away any lingering sooty smell from the train. After breakfast at the big house, the twins retrieved their dried undergarments and rolled up all of Alana's things for tight packing.

Now, well-fed, clean in body and attire, Bridget should have felt a sense of well-being and gratitude. And she really did. But a tight band of unshed tears squeezed her chest.

We've never been parted for more than a single day.

Bridget and Alana donned their coats, hats, and mittens, as well as the new scarves their cousin had given them as welcome presents. Sally knitted scarves for the mercantile to earn extra money, and she'd allowed them to choose from several colors. They'd both selected dark-blue.

Sally had insisted on getting up and helping even though the pale cast to her skin indicated what the movement cost her. She still wore a robe over her nightgown and hadn't gone to breakfast with them. "If only I'd felt better, I'd have prepared meals to send along." She fussed with loading supplies onto the top of the table.

"Don't worry," Bridget assured her. "Alana is a fine cook, and Mrs. Toffels is sending food with her."

Sally frowned in obvious distress. "Harry and I were showered with foodstuffs as wedding gifts, and I want to share with them. Portions of rice, beans, coffee." She tapped each sack. "A jar of huckleberry jam, a hank of salt pork, and a canister of tea." As she spoke, she picked up each item and tucked it into a round basket with a curved handle.

Alana laid a hand on Sally's arm. "I'll manage the meals just fine, cousin. No need to fret yerself so."

Sally gave her a rueful smile. "I am fretting, aren't I? It's not as if my parents hadn't laid down provisions to last through the winter, even though at times, we eek out what we have with wild game. They expected me to be living with them still, so, in a way, you're just taking my place."

"Not that I can take their daughter's place," Alana said in a soothing voice. "But this experience will give yer family and me a chance to form the bonds of kinship that we've lacked all our lives."

"You're right." Sally relaxed and breathed out a sigh.

"I promise ye, I will give yer mother the same loving care that ye would."

Sally embraced Alana. "I can't tell you how thankful I am that you're doing this." Taking a step back, she glanced at both women. "You two are such a godsend—the answer to prayers I didn't know I needed to pray."

Alana touched Sally's shoulder. "Comforting, isn't it? That the good Lord knows our needs before we do."

Bridget didn't have Alana's unquestioning belief. After all, she was the one who often had to pinch and scrape for both of them. A sudden thought struck her. James had appeared at the train station at the very moment they arrived. *Perhaps my sister is right. Something to ponder later.*

"Now, back to bed with ye, Sally," Alana said firmly. "We'll see ourselves out."

Sally released her cousin's hand. "Thank you again."

Alana pointed at the bed in a silent command.

"All right, all right," Sally muttered in a mock grumble.

Alana picked up her satchel. She was also taking along the volume of Shakespeare, hoping to read to her aunt as she convalesced.

No sense sending the potatoes they'd stored in a corner of the loft. *Surely, we'll be reunited before spring planting.* Bridget threaded her arm through the handle of the basket, lifted it, and turned.

Alana smiled a good-bye to Sally before following Bridget out the door.

The cold wind caught them first, but the freshness was welcome after the close air of the cabin. Bridget and Alana trudged through the snow on a path made wider by the recent comings and goings to and from the houses.

They reached the area between the barn and the big house to find the rented sleigh, a brown horse hitched to the front. The plan was for Harry to drive the sleigh to the O'Donnels and on the way home, drop off the conveyance at the livery, and ride horseback the rest of the way to the ranch.

Samantha came out of the house, carrying a crate that she gave to Harry.

Without a word, he stowed it on the front seat. He took the basket and satchel from the sisters and placed them on the floor in the back. "Mrs. Toffels heated the bricks."

Samantha pulled a fur muff off her arm and handed it to Alana. "Borrow this for your journey, my dear."

"Thank ye for yer kindness." Alana stroked the fur then slipped the muff over one of her hands.

Samantha turned to Harry, ticking off her fingers as she talked. "Stop in town at the Camerons to warm up, heat the bricks again, and take along any medicine or instructions Dr. Cameron might want to give you."

Mrs. Toffels bustled out from the side door of the house, her arms around a giant basket. "There are quart jars of chicken soup and beef stew in the crate. In here, you'll find my Saskatoon preserves, a basket of eggs, several loaves of bread and butter, my elderberry cordial, and molasses cookies.

Harry inhaled a sharp breath, and then swallowed hard as if moved. "Much obliged, ma'am. On behalf of my wife and her family, I thank you." He glanced at Mrs. Thompson. "I thank you both." He shook his head. "I don't know how we can ever repay you."

"Nonsense, Harry." Samantha smiled at him. "Sally is one of us now, and we take care of our own. There will be plenty of opportunities for turn and turn about."

Alana moved to Bridget, extending her arms.

Bridget hugged her sister, holding her tight for an extra moment, her eyes stinging.

Alana clung to her, clearly just as reluctant to part. But she was the one to break away, kissing Bridget's cheek and murmuring, "*Go dtí le chéile againn arís.*" She climbed into the sleigh.

Bridget tucked the bearskin around Alana. Her throat clogged on repeating the words of farewell, so she thought them instead. *Until we meet again.* Then she, too, kissed her sister's cheek, and straightened.

From the corner of her eye, Bridget caught a movement and turned to see James heading their way, carrying a gunnysack. He had blood on his hands. "I thought Alana might want some extra meat to take with her, so I set snares for some rabbits. They're dressed out. Haven't had time to skin them. In this cold, they'll keep just fine."

"How kind, James!" Bridget exclaimed. "Ye must have been up before dawn to have caught these." His thoughtfulness helped ease the heaviness in her chest. She wouldn't have her sister by her side, but she was surrounded by good people—new friends. Her gaze lingered on James, and heat rose to her cheeks. *Perhaps, a special new friend.*

Although Alana appeared grateful and thanked James, Bridget noted no light in her eyes, as she'd seen before when her sister looked at Timkin.

Perhaps she truly isn't interested in James.

But Bridget wasn't so sure about James, who'd just given Alana a dimpled smile.

Harry climbed into the front seat, gathered the reins, and released the brake.

Her throat tight, Bridget waved good-bye. Shading her eyes with her hand, she watched the sleigh until the vehicle dwindled to a speck, and then passed out of sight. She inhaled a bracing breath, determined not to cry. Her new acquaintances didn't deserve a moping newcomer in their midst. She plastered on a smile and turned to Samantha. "Would ye mind if I spent some time in the barn becoming acquainted with yer horses?" Shrugging, she gave a self-depreciating laugh. "I'm horse mad, ye see."

Samantha's eyes twinkled. "So am I. I'm going to check on Sally and see if she wants the broth Mrs. Toffels made. You go meet the horses. I promise you, there will be some that surprise you."

Again, James's smile showed his dimples. "I'll join you after I've washed up, so I can show you around."

Her spirits lifted, and Bridget wondered if the rise was due to the idea of horses, especially surprise horses, or James's company. *Probably both.*

Bridget moved toward the barn, careful of her footing on the icy spots. She pushed open one of the great doors and stepped inside, pulling it shut behind her.

For a moment she closed her eyes, just taking in the scent of horses, hay, leather, and manure. Behind her lids, tears pricked her eyes, and she inhaled a deep breath, feeling a blissful sense of homecoming.

A horse nickered, and she heard the stomp of a shod hoof. Unable to bear the suspense any longer, she opened her eyes.

The squire's barn had been several centuries old, the walls made of stone, the ceiling lower and the light dimmer than in this soaring wooden structure. The immense space seemed empty, with only a few horses poking their heads over the stall doors. Most of the cowboys must be out on the range.

Deuce worked with his back to her, mucking out a stall at the end of the aisle.

Bridget decided not to disturb him, instead wanting to explore a bit on her own before James caught up with her. Scanning the aisle of stalls, she recognized the sleek black head of the Thoroughbred and walked toward him, her gestures slow.

The horse eyed her with curiosity.

"*Is buachaill álainn thú'*," she murmured, while rubbing his neck.

"Thunder doesn't know Gaelic." A man spoke from behind her.

Bridget turned to see Patrick Gallagher looming near. She'd been too engrossed in his stallion to notice his approach.

He wore a black shirt that enhanced his dark eyes and hair. His eyelashes were long. But the chiseled planes of his face and the square chin kept him from looking soft.

He's attractive, indeed. She couldn't help but respond to the sheer magnificence of the man and his horse.

"I don't speak the language, either," he admitted with a small shrug. "Too many generations away from the old country."

"I told Thunder he was a beautiful boy," Bridget explained.

"Aye, beautiful," he said, staring into her eyes and dropped a hand on the stall door next to her.

She blushed and dropped her gaze. Uncomfortable with his closeness, she sidled to Thunder's other side, putting the horse's head between them. "Why a Thoroughbred here?" She rubbed Thunder's nose.

"We have racing in Montana, you know. Even here in Sweetwater Springs. It might not be up to Irish standards, but we have our share of splendid winners."

"The squire of our village was heavily into racing. From an early age, he allowed me to spend time at his stables helping out."

"He must have trusted you, then."

"Aye. He's a dear man. 'Tis grateful, I am that he didn't let the disapproval of his wife and son prohibit me from the place." She patted Thunder's muscled neck. "This one must be fast."

"As the wind. Thompson has a mare who won the horse race here last August. He wants to breed her. I brought Thunder for Thompson to inspect and also so I could look over the mare. I plan to drop by the Carter and Sanders' ranches as well. But Thompson and his missus have made me welcome, invited me to stay a while." His gaze dropped to her mouth. "I've taken them up on their invitation."

Eager to find Bridget and spend some time together, James strode to the bunkhouse where, during the day, a kettle of warm water was kept on the back of the stove that heated the room. He stripped off his gloves and coat and unwound his scarf. He poured some water into the basin, washed, and shaved—something he hadn't managed in the early morning darkness. Once he dried his hands and face, he donned his outerwear again and strode to the barn.

The sadness in her eyes as she'd watched Alana leave had made his belly tight, and James wanted to do something, anything, to bring a genuine smile back to Bridget's face. And he knew just the trick—the Falabellas.

According to Samantha, the midget horses had worked miracles on her once-troubled adopted sons. Every man on the ranch loved the small creatures, even if a few grumbled about having nothing to do with such *toys*—although on several occasions, he'd caught one or the other of those same cowboys secretly slipping carrots or apple slices to a Falabella and even using *baby talk*. James snickered at the memories. He hadn't said anything yet to the culprits. He was saving the revelations for a time when they'd have the most impact.

Now, James was certain the little ones would have a similar magical effect on Bridget. Just thinking of her reaction, he couldn't help but grin.

Inside the barn, he saw Bridget talking to Patrick Gallagher while she stroked his horse, and James's cheerful feelings gave way to jealousy. He stalked toward them, nodding at Gallagher but giving Bridget a warm grin. "Are you ready for your tour of the barn?"

"I am, indeed."

Patrick frowned. "I'll go lunge Thunder."

Bridget cast the man a reluctant glance, as if wanting to see him work the horse. She gave a final pat to the stallion's nose. "I'll see ye again, sweet boy." With a smile at Gallagher, she moved to James's side.

"Come this way." He led her to the middle of the barn. "I'm assuming you'd rather see the horses than the tack room or the hay loft."

She nodded, a wide smile on her face.

"Wyatt had these doors shortened so the horses can see over them." He gestured for her to look into a stall.

Bridget peeked over, and her eyes widened. "Oh." She inhaled sharply in obvious delight at seeing the tiny black mare. "Why, I've never seen the like! Tell me, Jamie—" the nickname slipped out "—what is this dear wee creature? Surely not a pony. She's too small."

There's the smile I was hoping for. He liked how Bridget called him *Jamie*, the word taking on a different cadence when uttered in a musical Irish accent. Although he might have to beat up a man who called him Jamie, the name coming from her seemed intimate. With a sense of longing, he wondered if he'd ever hear her whisper his name while they were together in the dark of the night.

James realized Bridget was waiting for his answer. "A Falabella. Her name's Chita, and she belongs to Daniel. Mrs. Thompson brought them from Argentina."

"Them? There are more?"

"Yes. And you'll see more around town because we only kept one foal. Let me introduce you to each Falabella, then you can choose which to get acquainted with first. They're all good-natured and very playful." James took Bridget's hand and led her down the row, hoping she wouldn't pull away. He tried to act casual, but his heart thumped so loudly he heard the pulse beat in his ears. "The chestnut is Bonita, the brown mare is Pampita. Mariposa is the gray. The Falabella stallion is Chico."

"Such darlings." Her face glowed. "I'm in love already."

So am I. He cleared his throat. "They do have that effect on people." He stopped before the last shortened door. "This brown sweetie was born here. She belongs to Christine, who named her Tulip."

"'Tis adorable, she is. I'll start with her."

"Go right ahead." He opened the stall door and stood back.

Bridget took two steps inside and sank to her knees in the straw. Luckily, Deuce had already mucked out this stall.

At first, James thought to wander off and do some work, for there were always jobs around the barn. But he couldn't tear himself away for long. Instead, he grabbed his bridle, a can of linseed oil, and a rag, and rubbed the leather while he leaned against the opposite stall and watched Bridget.

She never even noticed his regard, so absorbed in the Falabellas was she. She moved from stall to stall, spending about five minutes with each Falabella.

Right now, James could see by the way she smiled and caressed the horses, even kissing their noses, that no worries about her sister or her aunt crossed her mind. He wished he could make this time last—always keep her free from care. *But at least she has a respite.*

After about half an hour, he stirred from his spot and quietly called out. "Bridget, if you want to see the rest of the animals, we'd best be going."

"Oh, goodness, yes." She ran a hand over Mariposa's gray back and stood. "Sally will be waking soon, and I should be back by then."

He took her toward some of the other horses, pulling a carrot from his pocket when they reached Dusty and offering it to Bridget.

"Oh, thank ye for helping me keep my promise to him."

Her grateful smile warmed James all the way to his toes. *Who needs hot bricks when Bridget O'Donnell is around?*

She held out the carrot, petting Dusty's nose as the gelding happily crunched away.

James envied the horse her touch.

She tilted her head, closely examining the gelding, then stepped sideways to view one of the extra mounts, before sliding back to his side. "They're different from our horses back home. I'm not talking about the Thoroughbreds, but our draught horses. Fine creatures, indeed. They're short-legged and powerful. Deep of girth and strong of back and quarters. Light and fast on their feet for such heavy horses and—" she held up a finger and flicked it upward "—good jumpers."

James liked the way Bridget's eyes lit as she waxed eloquent. "What about their temperament?"

"Intelligent and gentle natured, reliable," she said in a proud tone. "They're bred for multiple jobs—to plow, sow, mow and reap, hunt, ride, and drive the family to church."

He chuckled. "I guess that's more than chasing and cutting cattle or riding into town." He patted Dusty's neck. "Although, as you saw, this one proved quite good at pulling the sleigh."

She stroked the gelding's head. "Ye did a fine job, Dusty, me boyo," she said thickening her accent.

They moved on to meet Samantha's mare, Bianca, a wedding present from her husband. The black beauty had four white stockings and a blaze down her nose. The mare nickered and snuffled Bridget's arm.

"Oh, my." She rubbed Bianca's nose. "What a lovely lady ye are."

"She's a sweet goer, a perfect mount for the missus."

He gestured to a chestnut mare in the next stall. "And this is our speed demon, Miss Midnight, although we call her Missy unless we're trying to intimidate or impress people."

"I would love to see her race."

"She is something." James placed a hand on her arm to guide her toward the back door. "Let's go see the old barn." He took her out and through a covered breezeway built last fall. Amazing the changes the boss had made around the place for the pleasure and comfort of his bride.

This barn was constructed when the previous ranch owner lived in a log cabin. The structure was smaller than the first and housed the goats, pigs, and milk cows.

Half of the space was taken up by a fenced-in area spread with thick straw where the small herd of goats milled around. Some were black and others dun-colored.

Holding on to the top rail, she leaned over the enclosure. "Somehow, I never thought to find goats on a cattle ranch."

"They're relatively new. A lot of things changed around here when the boss got married."

She chuckled and nodded.

The musical tone of her laughter caused a flutter in his belly.

"I imagine so."

He wrenched his thoughts back to the topic. "Mrs. Toffels has the knack for making cheese, and we learned to like the taste."

"I love goat cheese."

"Jack and Tim had a goat when Samantha adopted them. Actually, the story is that they didn't have the goat anymore. They'd been staying with Widow Murphy, and she kept the goat—claimed it was in payment for the boys' care."

She turned and stared with a wide-eyed look. "How mean!"

His mouth turned up. "The twins stole back Nanny, and Samantha paid off the widow. After their marriage, Wyatt bought the boys another pair, one of which came with her two babies. He also acquired a billy goat. Now two of the dams have given birth. Twins each. We're practically overrun. We'll soon have more goats than cattle."

Again, she laughed. "I'm sure ye are a long way from that."

"Well, you know goats can breed twice a year and have two, and sometimes three babies..."

She shook her head at him, a smile pulling at her lips. "Can I go into the pen?" She waved toward the center.

He unlatched the gate of the enclosure and followed her inside. "Just be careful. Reggie will try to eat your skirt."

Several curious goats approached. But the two mothers glowered and kept their kids tucked away in the corner.

"What are the rest of them called?"

"The twins are particularly fond of names beginning with R. Reggie, Rufus, Rocky, Roland, Ruff." As James said each name, he pointed to the animal. "Then there's Scruff, Bessie, Dessie, and Chessie." He patted one on the head. "And here is Jack's original Nanny."

Nanny butted Bridget's leg, and at the same time, one of the other goats bumped her from behind, collapsing her knee. She took a faltering step sideways and caught her foot in the hem of her dress, further unbalancing her stance.

James grabbed her before she could fall.

Bridget ended up pressed against him, one hand on his shoulder. She glanced into his eyes, and their gazes locked, their mouths only inches apart.

James couldn't resist the temptation to kiss her. He lowered his lips to touch hers just as Nanny banged into him, making him jerk and straighten, and bringing an awareness of their circumstances. *Anyone could have come in and seen us.* He wouldn't for the world want to sully her reputation or make her feel forced into marriage.

Although he wanted to pull her close to him again, James held Bridget away from his body until he was sure she was steady on her feet.

Her color was high, making her eyes vivid, and she gave him a shy smile. "I think I'd best be getting back to Sally."

Reluctantly, James released her, but as they walked out of the enclosure, a new awareness shimmered between them. He escorted Bridget out of the barn and watched her walk to the cabin, wondering what the future would bring.

Chapter Five

The next day, when Bridget first awoke to silence, she lay disoriented in the dim light. The dark slant of the roof over her head gradually brought her the realization she was in the loft of her cousin's Montana cabin.

She listened for sounds of Sally stirring but didn't hear anything. *Well, Sally has no cow to feed and milk at first light.* She thought of Bo, the soft-eyed Guernsey she'd left behind, and felt a pang of homesickness.

Thinking of Bo reminded her of playing with the Falabellas and the goats...and of her very first kiss, the lightest brush of their lips before the goat's head butting interrupted them. She wondered what a real kiss would feel like. *I hope I find out soon.*

Bridget pulled the coverings closer around her shoulders, grateful for their warmth in the frigid air. She didn't look forward to crawling out from her warm cocoon to dress. Until her hostess arose, she'd not venture from her bed.

Last night she'd been so exhausted, she'd dropped right into a deep sleep, barely noting the lack of her sister's presence on the pallet beside her.

But now, Alana's absence hit her, tightening her throat. For the first time in her life, Bridget had slept alone. Even in the third-class cabin on the ship, they'd squeezed together on the same bunk. She slid her hand over to where Alana should be and ached for the presence of her twin.

Bridget tried not to think of the empty place on her other side that had always belonged to Catriona. She'd had months to get used to the fact their older sister had abandoned them, and she supposed eventually she'd get used to Alana's absence, as well. Then she chided herself for being so fatalistic. *Alana will be back. Soon we'll be reunited.*

But an awareness of future changes hit her in a way that she'd never thought of before. *Someday, maybe soon, we'll be married and no longer living together. Someone else will sleep next to me and to Alana.*

Bridget had always had a vague awareness of that fact. After all, marriage is what happened when one grew up and became an adult. But no man in their small village was suitable—for the sisters' ages and station in life anyway.

Unfortunately beautiful Catriona had set her sights on the squire's son and had for a long time had eyes for no other. Bridget suspected her yearning for the man combined with grief over their mother's passing made her susceptible to the peddler's blandishments.

And even if available bachelors or widowers lived nearby, she had always assumed Alana would be the first to wed. That is, if her twin ever got over her secret love for Timkin—another reason to leave their village, for Bridget had always doubted that young man, who seemed more fey than human, returned her sister's love.

And even if Bridget caught the eye of a man she wanted to wed, she couldn't leave her sister—for timid Alana couldn't live on her own. Any man who chose Bridget would end up with the pair of twins on his hands.

Nostalgic pain for her childhood, the closeness with her parents and two sisters—all five of them together—clogged her throat. *Now I'm alone.*

A different sadness, as wispy as a spider web, threaded through her pain—feelings she'd never allowed herself to feel before—the longing for someone to love and be loved by in return. As things stood back home, there'd been no one.

But, unlike in Ireland, here she had hope. Her thoughts lingered on James, then skittered to Patrick.

From the way the stationmaster had talked, the twins could have even more men interested in them. For the first time ever, they might have an abundance of suitors to choose from.

I have possibilities for a different future.

She imagined a husband lying in the empty place beside her. *But which man?* She felt attracted to both Patrick and James, and as the purple shadows lightened, she pictured first one then the other beside her, and both men felt good.

The heady thought excited and overwhelmed her.

A week later, Bridget curried a placid Falabella mare, taking advantage of Sally's nap time to escape to the barn to play with the little horses she'd fallen in love with.

Aside from handwork, she had only a limited amount of household tasks, for Samantha and Mrs. Toffels insisted the three of them take meals at the big house.

While she enjoyed sitting with her cousin—doing handwork, knitting, mending, or darning socks—and talking about everything under the sun—well, under an Irish or Montana sun—Bridget was used to being outdoors or in the stables.

So when Sally napped, Bridget felt free to do as she pleased. But she also felt an obligation to stay by Sally's side and try and keep up her cousin's spirits, not let her fret about her mother.

Two days after he'd left, Harry had returned with distressing news. Dr. Cameron had diagnosed Henrietta O'Donnell with influenza, a serious illness that caused far too many deaths. Sally not only worried for her mother, she feared the rest of her family would succumb.

Bridget couldn't help worrying about Alana. To be sure, her twin had often nursed the sick and remained as healthy as a horse. But now, she couldn't help but wonder if her sister's broken heart and weakened appearance would make her more susceptible.

Harry had also spoken of the warm welcome the family had afforded Alana, which reassured Bridget. Both hers and Sally's thoughts and prayers tended to often stray to the far-away house on the prairie.

Gradually, Bridget had also gotten to know several of the cowboys. A few, like Buck, were gregarious, obviously grateful to have a woman to talk with. But others acted shy and barely made eye contact with her. A few, she suspected, hadn't yet adjusted to the presence of beautiful Samantha Thompson, much less having Sally, and then Bridget, drop into their world in rapid succession.

Deuce trailed after her like a puppy dog. Moss had a sense of humor that made her laugh. The oldest cowboy, Sid, pretended she wasn't there at all.

Of all the men, she spent the most time with James and Patrick because those two singled her out. Each day, her liking for them increased.

She also spent time riding, although it was too cold to go far. James often lent her Dusty, and when he worked away from the house, she rode Samantha's black mare Bianca.

Today the cowboys were out and about, and she had the barn to herself. Bridget was so occupied with grooming Pampita she didn't hear James until he spoke. "Hello, Bridget."

Startled into gasping, she almost dropped the comb. Her heartbeat quickened and not just from surprise.

"I'm sorry. Didn't mean to sneak up on you." James extended a hand to her. "Come with me. I want to show you something."

"I haven't finished with Pampita yet."

"There's not much of her, so I'll bet you'll be through in a few minutes."

"Where are we going?" She continued pulling the comb through Pampita's shaggy winter coat.

"You'll see. It will be a bit of a walk."

Bridget finished the last spot on the brown mare's rump. "You're right. They're so small, it doesn't take long to groom them." She kissed Pampita's nose and reached up to place her hand in James's.

He helped her to her feet, his grip warm and sure, and released her.

Bridget grabbed her mittens from the edge of the manger and pulled them on. She stepped out of the stall, latching the door behind her, then followed James down the aisle and out the door.

Outside, the day was sunny, the warmest she'd experienced since her arrival, although still cold. Much of the snow, especially in the trodden areas, had melted to mud. Luckily, the area between the barn and the house had stone pavers, but their protection didn't last past the far edge of the barn.

They walked in companionable silence for about fifteen minutes, until they reached an area with unbroken snow. A trail led to a crescent of trees—most with their branches empty, but some firs stood in all their year-long green finery.

"I broke a path through here earlier."

James led her through the trees.

She breathed in the spicy scent from the firs. The rows of trees thinned to bare land.

They continued to the top of a small rise that seemed flat, gradually sloping to a snow-covered meadow.

James raised a hand in a signal to halt. He sent her a glance filled with mischief.

Try as she might, Bridget could see nothing special about her surroundings. Slowly, she turned in a circle, viewing only sky and trees and snow. "What is this? Why did ye bring me here, Jamie?"

A smile played around his mouth. "To see your dreams."

She shrugged and raised her eyebrows in puzzlement. "I give up. What am I supposed to see?"

A slow grin spread across his face. He waved an arm to encompass the whole space. "Your potato patch."

"My what?"

"No one's using this plot of land. Too many trees around the area to be able to run cattle through here. Too far from the big house to make it easy to cultivate for the kitchen garden. Potatoes don't need the tending that other vegetables do, or at least, I assume." He raised an eyebrow in inquiry.

Heart beating fast, she nodded in agreement.

"So it's a practical area for you."

"But this is still the Thompson's land."

"I think if you offered them a share of your crop in exchange for the space to plant, they'd be fine with your enterprise. Certainly wouldn't hurt to ask."

Excitement tingled through her. She imagined the rich dirt beneath the snow, the budding crop, harvesting potatoes in the fall, filling the larders of the Thompsons and the O'Hanlons, and still having enough left over for a cash crop. Breathing deep, she stretched out her hands, fingers spread, feeling her dream take hold.

James watched her as if he saw something wondrous. His gaze captured hers, and he stepped closer, clasped her hand, drawing her to him, and gently touched her cheek with his other hand. He smiled just enough for those dimples to show.

Obeying a strange compulsion, she boldly leaned forward and pressed a kiss into the nearest one. Then, realizing what she'd done, Bridget gasped and pulled away. *Holy mother of God, what came over me!*

"You missed."

"Missed?" Confused, Bridget only knew her face must be beet red.

He tapped his lips, laughter in his eyes.

"Oh, ye." She swatted at him, but the urge to kiss his dimples again remained, unnerving her. Her face hot, Bridget turned and hurried toward the copse of trees. When she reached their shelter, she looked behind her to see what James was doing.

He grinned and waved, but made no move to follow her.

Her hands flew to cover her burning cheeks, and Bridget fled back the way they'd come and didn't stop until she'd reached the safety of the big barn.

Once there, she thrust open the door, stepped inside, and shut it behind her—far harder than necessary—and tried to catch her breath.

In Thunder's stall, Patrick groomed the horse. His attention was fully absorbed in the stallion. His hands were gentle, and he murmured to Thunder in a quiet voice.

Bridget couldn't make out the words, just the warmth of his tone. She'd never seen a more perfect picture of masculine beauty—both man and beast—not that Thunder was a beast. No, far from it. The stallion was as sweet as clover—an unusual temperament for a Thoroughbred.

"I'm not sure who likes the grooming more—him or ye."

With a jerk, his head came up, and he slanted her a glance. "I was looking for you."

Calmer now, she came to the stall door, unlatched it, went in, and walked to his side.

"Thought you'd like to work with Thunder." Patrick shrugged. "But when I couldn't find you I did the job myself." His posture radiated displeasure.

"Oh," she said in disappointment. All week, she'd been angling to work with Thunder—had striven to build Patrick's trust in her skills with horses. *Have I ruined my only chance?*

"James took me to see some land where I could plant my potatoes."

His brows pulled together in a frown. "Potatoes?"

With a shock, Bridget realized she hadn't shared with Patrick her dream of a potato farm. *Strange how that hasn't happened, for I've told anyone else who's shown the slightest sign of interest.*

Perhaps he hasn't given me any. Their talk had been only of horses, with some sharing about their previous lives. "Alana and I brought potatoes from Ireland. I plan to raise a crop to sell." She went on to tell him the story about her family surviving the famine, including her pride in their achievements.

His frown didn't abate. "I've nothing against a good spud, mind you. At my house, we have a well-stocked garden, which, as my cook tells me, leads to a well-stocked pantry and root cellar." His jaw tightened, as if he'd planned to say more, but stopped himself.

Bridget had a feeling she wouldn't have wanted to hear the rest.

"Did I ever tell you about my house? My horse farm is outside of Crenshaw. A couple hours journey by train from Sweetwater Springs."

His abrupt change of topic confused her, but she managed a shake of her head.

"My place is about the size of the Thompson's here, in a snug green valley with lush grazing." He tilted his head in the direction of Samantha's home. "My house is perhaps a little narrower. Bigger porch. It's painted blue instead of white."

"Blue?" Bridget queried, intrigued, and wished she could see the place.

"I'm partial to blue. It's sort of…" He looked around as if seeking something with the color he wanted. "Dark blue. With white trim."

"Sounds attractive."

"Matching stables and a small barn for the other livestock—pigs, cows. No goats, though."

She laughed. "Ye might need to acquire some." Thunder seemed quite taken with the goats, but Patrick had shown silent, although clear, disapproval about the way the twins' goats visited the horses, often remaining in their stalls to keep them company.

Patrick scowled. "If Thunder becomes attached to one, he'll pine when we leave. Luckily, the boys have been changing up the goats, so no one single animal is left with him. But, it's only a matter of time. Of course, I can offer to buy the creature, but those twins obviously love their goats."

Pain in either choice. Bridget thought it best to return to their previous topic. "That's a lot of blue."

He looked deep into her eyes. "I'm partial to blue," he repeated.

"So am I," she whispered, drawn by the intensity in his gaze.

He leaned toward her.

He's going to kiss me. Uncomfortable, Bridget rattled out some more words and took a half-step backwards. "But a house isn't what's important to me. The potatoes are what matters." *Security matters.*

Patrick pulled back, an expression of annoyance crossing his face. "Those potatoes again. Do you realize the backbreaking amount of labor you'll do to dig raw land? It's not like working your garden at home that's been shoveled over and over again through what…hundreds of years?"

Well no, I haven't thought of that. Although daunted by the idea, Bridget raised her chin, determined not to let Patrick know he'd shaken her.

Chapter Six

Sunday morning saw the Thompson family as well as Bridget, Patrick, and Mrs. Toffels squeezed into their regular pew near the front of the Sweetwater Springs church.

Toward the back, James sat between Buck and Deuce, his attention centered on Bridget far more than on the sermon preached by Reverend Norton. She wore her best dress, the one that made her eyes so blue. But he figured she could be in rags and appear just as pretty. He planned to do some courting after the service.

The Thompson hands who'd chosen to attend the service sat among a group of cowboys from other ranches. Their boss wasn't a stickler about church attendance for his men. When the work permitted, he left the choice up to them, but other ranch owners weren't so lenient.

Winter light streamed through the side windows but provided no warmth. The heat from the stove in the front corner of the church didn't reach the entire room, so the cowboys kept their coats on. Reverend Norton, preaching in front of the altar, probably was the warmest person in the building.

With dismay, James noticed several other men casting surreptitious glances Bridget's way. A cowboy from the Carter ranch nudged the man next to him, pointing her out with a lift of his chin. An unmarried woman, newly come to town, always provoked male interest. And a *pretty* miss was a treat to behold.

Before the service, he'd kept his eye on Banker Livingston who, rumor had it, was in search of a wife. James had seen the man glance at Bridget and then dismiss her, probably because she wasn't wearing highfalutin' clothing. *More fool he.*

Livingston's focus on status and outward appearance could cause the man to end up married to a well-bred, beautiful shrew, who'd make him miserable for the rest of his days. But with the handsome, wealthy banker out of the way, James could keep a dogged watch on any other man sniffing around Bridget and prepare to cut him out.

After the service ended, the congregation milled around outside, but not for long, for the temperature was too cold, unlike in summer when the close of the service heralded the start of a lively social hour.

James tried to move to Bridget's side, but stopped when he saw Samantha introducing her to the Carters and the Sanders—two prominent ranching families.

After a few minutes, the crowd dispersed—some to head home and others to visit the mercantile, which only opened for an hour after the service.

The hands all traipsed behind the Thompson family to the mercantile—not that the cowboys tended to buy much. Most of them—at least, the ones who'd attended church today—were a thrifty, temperate bunch—rarely even visiting the saloon. But Deuce had a sweet tooth and wanted some candy, and Sid needed more tobacco. James went along because of Bridget, even if Gallagher—the lucky dog—was the one escorting her.

Crossing the street, Buck nudged him. "Better look sharp or Miss Bridget will be swept right out from under your nose, and maybe Gallagher's as well."

James shot his friend a sharp look. "We have the advantage. Except for times like this—" he swept his arm to indicate the whole town "—she's on *our* territory."

"You're right about that. Guess the race is between you and

Gallagher then. My money's on you, boy." He gave a wide grin. "So don't let me down!"

Let him down? "What?"

Buck's expression was smug. "We have a wager. Each man chipped in four bits."

James groaned. But what could he do? With cowboys, bettin' was inevitable.

The mercantile was crowded with churchgoers taking advantage of their trip into town. The customers knew they couldn't linger to gossip like they might on another day.

James roamed the periphery of the store, touching a finger to his hat to acknowledge the women and exchanging greetings with those he knew. Two ample-bodied ladies caused him to swerve wide to go around them, and he ended up near the front counter, where a row of Valentine's cards propped up in a cardboard holder caught his eye.

They seemed to be frivolous, probably expensive, bits of colorful paper. He doubted the practical, hard-working people of Sweetwater Springs would go for such nonsense. But he couldn't help another look at the hearts and the lace, and noticed the wistful glances women gave the cards, even one lady old enough to be his grandmother. *Maybe womenfolk put higher store in such things than I do.*

With a sudden flash of brilliance, an idea came to him. *I'll return and buy a card for Bridget!* There was no way he'd choose one now with what seemed like the whole town looking on. Besides, he wanted to take his time and make the perfect choice.

Anticipation filled him at the thought of purchasing a card, presenting it to Bridget, and asking her to marry him. *What a perfect way to propose!*

James carried the secret excitement with him during the trip home.

Samantha drove the wagon with her children in the back and Mrs. Toffels and Bridget on the seat beside her. Even seeing the way Patrick rode close to Bridget didn't dampen James's enthusiasm.

In spite of James's wish to return to town for the card, he and the other ranch hands had themselves two miserable days. A panther had spooked the herd, driving the cattle toward land made marshy by the melting snow and pocked with pits.

In the frigid cold from first light until dark, the men—even Wyatt, Gallagher, and the three older boys—wrestled filthy cows out of holes that held the animals as though they were caught in quagmires filled with glue instead of mud. They saved most of the cattle, but each one they lost hurt—even though they tried to tough out the pain.

They returned late to the ranch and saw to the needs of their horses. Then with stiff, aching muscles, they moved like elderly men into the big house and tracked dirt all over Mrs. Toffels's clean kitchen. After, hurriedly washing up, they gobbled down the enormous and filling meal she'd kept warm for them and returned to the bunkhouse to fall into bed, only to repeat the whole wretched process the next morning.

Wyatt sent off Buck, his best hunter, to track down and kill the panther, but the man lost the big cat's trail, only to pick up the spore near dusk on the second day and make his shot. With the cougar dispatched, the cowboys were able to drive the cattle to firmer ground, where, hopefully, they'd stay.

For two full days, James hadn't caught sight of Bridget, barely even thought of her except when they rode by the O'Hanlon cabin, and then he always said a prayer that all this would be over before Valentine's Day. At night in his bunk, he tried to picture her face, but he was too sore and exhausted to see more than a rosy smile before he dropped into deep sleep.

On Wednesday, Wyatt decreed a day of rest. With only the

most necessary chores to attend to—mucking out stalls and feeding and watering the livestock—James approached the boss for permission to ride into town.

Wyatt stared at him for a minute. The man's face was drawn, with lines of fatigue around his eyes. "Can't you wait until Sunday?"

James fought back a grimace. "Tomorrow's Valentine's Day."

Humor sparked in Wyatt's eyes, and he looked more like himself. "Ah…I'd forgotten."

"You're newly married." James pointed out the obvious.

Wyatt tapped his chest. "Yes, but I'm not fool enough to leave Valentine's trinkets until the last minute."

James made a mental note to learn from the man's example—if, that is, he was lucky enough to spend his life with a certain lady.

"Check with Mrs. Toffels before you leave to see if she needs anything. Our devouring horde may have cleaned out her cupboards."

"Will do." He gave the boss a two-fingered salute and loped to the kitchen. The sooner he started out, the sooner he'd be back.

During the two days the men had been working on the range long into the evening, both Bridget and Sally moped. Well, they moped on the inside. Bridget covered her feelings with cheerful conversations. And since Sally was equally pleasant, Bridget could only conclude her cousin felt the same pang over the men's absence—or rather, her husband's absence.

On Monday, Sally napped, giving Bridget time to play with the Falabellas and the goats and keep Thunder company. Patrick wouldn't risk the valuable Thoroughbred out on the range and had borrowed one of Wyatt's mounts, so he could ride out and help the men save the floundering cattle. She wished for the chance to exercise the stallion but didn't dare do so without permission.

The first night when Harry finally came home, he was so filthy, except for his face and hands, that he wouldn't let Sally near him until he'd stripped off his clothes and donned a nightshirt.

Bridget played least-in-sight, hiding in the loft until the couple was in bed. For the first time, she felt like she was imposing, for the newlyweds didn't have privacy and a chance to spend any time alone. Not that it mattered, for judging from the ragged snores, Harry was asleep as soon as his head hit the pillow.

Bridget spent Tuesday helping Samantha and Mrs. Toffels wash the men's mucky clothing, an arduous job given how dirty the water turned, and how often they had to empty the big wash bucket and fill it up again.

Bridget gave thanks for the indoor plumbing. Back home she'd had to haul water for twenty feet from an outdoor pump.

When they'd finished the washing and hung everything outside on the clotheslines, they tackled the ironing from the washing Mrs. Toffels and Samantha had done the previous day. Then as evening approached, they brought in the wash, frozen but no longer dripping, and hung the clothes on lines strung across the cellar. By the end of the day, Bridget's arms and back ached, but she'd enjoyed spending time with the two women. Their light-hearted conversation had made the hard work easier.

On Wednesday, Bridget couldn't wait to see James and Patrick and hear the stories of what they'd been through. The night before, Harry had told them about Wyatt decreeing a lenient workday, and, thus, all of them had slept in later than usual. In the morning, Bridget dressed and left the house, pointedly telling the couple, who were still in bed, that she'd be in the barn for most of the day and would see them at the big house when it was time for supper.

Once in the barn, Bridget looked for Dusty, expecting to see the Appaloosa in his stall and hoping she'd see James, as well. But neither was around.

Deuce and some of the other men were raking out stalls. Before she could ask about James, she saw the boy straighten, moving as if his body ached and leaning on the rake.

"If you're looking for James, he's gone to town."

"Oh." She tried to hide her disappointment.

Deuce shrugged and gave her a tired upward turn of his mouth before bending back to his task.

She glanced at the other men, who moved equally as slow and smelled of liniment. "Would ye like some help with the stalls?"

This time, Deuce's grin reached his eyes. "Mighty kind of you to offer." He jerked his head at the others. "But I have plenty of help today."

With a nod and a smile, Bridget walked away. She didn't want the men to know she was miffed with James for leaving without seeing her. *Surely, he could have delayed for a few minutes.*

Maybe he doesn't care about me the way I thought he did. She tried to suppress her hurt.

Patrick entered from the back and made his way over to her. He, too, had a stiffness to his walk.

"Thunder will be glad to see ye."

"He gets antsy when he's cooped up too long."

"So do I," Bridget murmured.

"Well, after the last two days, I can stand a little cooping up. I'm taking the boy for a ride. When I return I might sit by the fire. Maybe read. Unless someone wants to keep me company."

"Maybe I will." Especially since a certain cowboy didn't seem to want her company. "It was kind of ye to help out with the cattle, especially since ye are a guest here."

Patrick gave her a wry smile. "Sit on my hands while my host fights to save his herd? What kind of man would that make me?"

"I'm sure there are plenty who'd choose such."

"Well, all I can say is, I'm glad I don't run cattle. I'll stick to horses!"

She glanced over at Thunder. "I entirely agree with those sentiments."

Chapter Seven

James strode into the store and was about to head straight toward the Valentine cards when he glimpsed Widow Murphy standing in front of the counter, a basket in her arms, chatting with Mrs. Cobb, the shopkeeper. All the ranch hands, and probably every other man in Sweetwater Springs, knew to avoid the two cantankerous women.

He sidled behind one of the standing shelves and out of sight. He didn't want to choose a card with the widow close by to see and spread gossip.

After a while, James gave up waiting for the two women to stop their chat-fest. He eased around the other side of the shelves and headed toward the bags of flour stacked near the front of the store. Mrs. Toffels wanted him to return with two.

His plan was to take them to the counter and pretend to discover the cards, casually glance over them, and select the best. Then it wouldn't seem like he'd made the long trip into town just to buy a Valentine's Day card. With a bag of flour in each hand, James approached the counter.

Sharp-faced Mrs. Murphy gave him a disapproving shake of her head, which made the rooster wattle under her chin quiver. But, mercifully, she moved out of his way without saying anything.

No skin off his back, she was judgmental about everyone.

Doing his best to avoid eye contact with either woman, he set the bags on the counter. "Put these on the Thompson's account, please." He glanced toward the end of the counter but the cards weren't there. His body went rigid, and he scanned the entire area.

Has Mrs. Cobb moved them? They were nowhere in sight. Forgetting his subtle approach, James blurted out, "Where are the Valentine cards?"

"We sold out on Sunday," said Mrs. Cobb with a smug expression. "In fact, your visitor, Mr. Gallagher, bought my very last one—the most *expensive* one."

Hours later, James rode into the Thompson's yard, despondency weighing down his shoulders. He'd felt so sure the card would do the trick—express his sentiments, make Bridget feel special, and show her he was capable of the kind of romance women liked. Now, not only did James not have the card, but Gallagher had the fanciest one in his possession. The man had out-strategized him. Gallagher already had every advantage, and now he'd beaten James in the one area he'd thought would win Bridget's regard.

I have to come up with another plan.

The whole ride home he'd pondered and discarded ways and means, but the thought of Gallagher loomed so large, that each of James's ideas didn't pass muster. Finally, he shoved the whole mess out of his mind. Maybe if he stopped twisting his brain in knots, something would come to him. He dismounted by the side door of the big house.

Deuce walked out of the barn and over to him. "I'll take him for you."

"Thanks, Deuce. I need to drop off the flour for Mrs. Toffels." *And maybe a certain Irish lass will be there.* Then James remembered he had no card for her. "I'd appreciate you attending to Dusty 'til I'm back out." He unloaded the flour sacks from his saddlebags. His mood heavy, James walked through the gate of the picket fence and up the brick walkway to the side door, where he entered the house.

He followed the smell of fresh oatmeal cookies into the kitchen.

All five children sat around the table working on a project. The red-checked tablecloth had been replaced with one of brown oilcloth. The surface was strewn with pink, red, and white paper, two pairs of scissors, some saucers of flour paste, pencils, several damp rags, and an ink well and pen.

The children looked up when he entered and greeted him, then with unusual industriousness returned to their projects.

He found Mrs. Toffels ironing, a stack of neatly pressed and folded shirts and pants on the counter next to her, a towering mound of laundry in the basket at her feet.

Have I gotten the days wrong? He had to stop and count from Sunday's church service to today—not easy when the mess with the cattle had made the last few days a blur. "Isn't today Wednesday?" He hoped so, for Valentine's Day was supposed to be tomorrow. But the housekeeper always ironed on Tuesday, not Wednesday, and her routine was set in stone.

Mrs. Toffles looked up and smiled. "The days do get away from you sometimes, don't they? But yes, it's midweek."

"Then why are you ironing? I thought that chore was for Tuesdays."

"Until the lot of you decided to wrestle with muddy cattle. Aside from your best, you're probably standing in the last stitch of clean clothes you own, James Whitson."

He glanced down at himself to see what he wore. As usual, Mrs. Toffels was right on the mark. "Ah…well, uh, thank you." He eyed the massive pile of men's clothing. "Guess I don't have to tell you that we're much obliged for how well you take care of us all. We consider ourselves lucky, we do."

Her wrinkled cheeks pinked. "You're a good man, James

Whitson." Her gaze dropped to the flour bags. "And you've brought just what I need to make more cookies so the children can take some to school tomorrow."

His stomach rumbled. "Can I sneak one?"

"Of course." She beamed at him, always happy to feed hungry men. "The children were just about to have some milk and cookies. Would you like to join them?"

"Is there tea in China?" James dropped the bags next to the flour bin, stood for a moment near the stove to absorb the warmth before taking off his coat and scarf and hanging them on the wall pegs near the doorway. The gloves went into the pockets and his hat on top of the scarf. He moved to take a seat with the children at the long table. "What are you all doing?"

Christine, her blonde hair pulled back in braids, smiled, her blue eyes alight. "We're having a party at school tomorrow, and we're making Valentine's Day cards for our teacher and friends—"

"*You're* making cards for your friends," Daniel interrupted. He thumped his chest. "*We're* making cards for Mrs. Gordon. Boys don't give cards to their friends."

"Well, Hunter's making one for Ruthanne," Christine pointed out.

Hunching his shoulders, the Indian boy rolled his eyes. "It's supposed to be a secret."

"James won't tell," the girl said in a chirping tone. "Will you?"

He'd frozen, staring down at the table. *Here's my solution!* Relief swept through him. "I'll keep the secret if you'll keep one of mine. May I join you and make a card, too?"

Christine tilted her head in askance. "Who do you want to make a Valentine card for?"

"Who do you think?" Jack retorted with a snort. "It's as plain as the nose on your face. Miss Bridget, of course."

Her eyes widened.

Daniel bounced in his seat. "Oh, I like Miss Bridget."

Christine gave an imperious wave. "Do sit down, James. I'll help you with the card."

"He doesn't need help," Tim mumbled. "He's a grown up."

"Thank you for your confidence in me, Tim."

Christine handed James a piece of pink construction paper. He reached for the inkwell. *I'll get the hardest part over with.*

"You'd better use the pencil first," Daniel warned, eying James's movements. "If you make a mistake, you can erase it. Then you can go over the writing with ink."

"Good idea, Danny boy."

"What are you going to write, James?" Christine asked. "I think you should write a poem."

He shook his head and folded the paper in half to make a card. "I don't have time to think of a poem, even if I was inclined to make up poetry, which I'm not."

"You can use someone else's poem. Do you know any?"

"Of course, I do. My ma was a schoolteacher before she married my pa. But, somehow a poem seems too…flowery." He couldn't believe he was having this discussion with the children—that he was having the discussion at all, for that matter.

"I think you should write, 'I love you, truly,'" Jack teased.

"How about, 'Marry me, and I'll love you forever?'" Christine's brow furled, and leaning close, she gave James an anxious glance. "You *will* love Miss Bridget forever, won't you?"

He tapped her on the nose. "Forever, I promise."

"'Til death do us part," Christine quoted. "That's what Reverend Norton said when Pa and *Mamá* married." She and her adopted brothers had taken to using the same Spanish pronunciation as Daniel to distinguish Samantha from the mothers they'd loved and lost.

Daniel put both hands on his chest, elbows out. "I think you're the most beautiful lady in all the world," he said in a girlish voice, then pretended to faint against the back of his chair.

Grinning at the boy's performance, James made a stopping

motion. "Enough, you little bagpipes. I can think of what to say on my own."

With some mutters, the children returned to their work.

But, as James stared at the card, he realized those all-important words weren't coming to him. *What is usually written in Valentine's Day cards?* He tried to think of the time his sister had every young man around sending her cards, which she proudly displayed on a table in the parlor. He recalled making a paper airplane of one. *Be Mine.* That's what it said. *Perfect. Simple. Honest. Not flowery, but Valentiney anyway.*

Disregarding Daniel's suggestion of the pencil, he dipped the pen into the ink well and used his best copperplate, instead of his regular scrawl.

Be Mine

With all my love,

Your Jamie

He blew on the ink to dry it, and then rummaged up a vague memory of fourth grade, when they'd made Valentine cards in school. Miss Higgins had taught them how to construct doilies from cut-outs on a paper. But first, he folded a red paper and cut out a heart. The shape ended up lopsided, and, with the scissors, he shaved off one side. It still wasn't balanced, but when he glanced at the table, James saw he'd used up the last red sheet. *This will have to do.*

Taking a white piece of paper, he cut out a circle. Carefully, he folded the shape and snipped small squares, then folded in a different place and cut out triangles. He opened the circle and checked his work. Even though James was careful, the shapes weren't the same size and didn't properly line up when he compared one side to the other. Doggedly, he continued, folding and snipping, folding and snipping.

A few times, he cut one shape too close to another, making an extra gap. But he figured when he glued the doily to the card, it wouldn't show too badly. Or so he hoped. Finally, he made scalloped edges.

James opened the doily, which looked ragged, rather than elegant. He tried holding the paper at arm's length to see if that made an improvement. It didn't.

Perhaps when I place the heart in the middle, it will make it look better. He glued the doily onto the pink card, and then pressed the heart on top. Carefully, he dipped the pen into the inkwell and wrote Bridget's name in the center.

If he squinted, it sort of looked like lace surrounded the heart. But when he opened his eyes, his efforts looked worse than the children's.

Setting down the pen, he surveyed his handiwork. The card did *not* match the picture in his mind. *Maybe I should tell Bridget to squint before I hand it to her.*

The children leaned over for a closer look. For a moment, they stayed silent.

Tim shook his head. "I was wrong. You did need help."

James sat back with a frustrated sigh, trying to hide his disappointment. He'd have to think of another plan to win Bridget's regard. *Problem is I'm all tapped out of ideas.*

"You can make another." His eyebrows riding high—a sure sign of his distress—Daniel looked around the table, littered with leftover scraps. "I guess you can't."

Discouraged, James rose. "Well, it was worth a try." Leaving the card on the table, he managed a smile for the children, trying to ease their obvious distress. "Thanks for letting me join you."

Christine grabbed his shirtsleeve and held tight. "But aren't you going to give your card to Miss Bridget?"

His heart heavy enough to drop into his boots, he thought of the fancy Valentine card she'd be receiving from Gallagher. His homemade effort would only serve to illuminate the differences in what the suitors had to offer. *Perhaps it's best I just give up. Bridget would probably be happier with a handsome husband, a big house, plenty of horses….*

The girl looked up into his face, her eyes anxious. "Aren't you, James?" she repeated.

He touched her nose with one finger. "No, darlin', I'm not."

Chapter Eight

The next afternoon, Bridget sat in the parlor of the big house next to the fireplace, reading. She'd escaped the O'Hanlon cabin again because Harry had stopped by between his chores.

Bridget wanted the couple to have some privacy, but she also had a craving for some time alone. Too many men worked in the barn today, and the parlor, with the scent of dried rose petals from a bowl on the side table and the soft rose and pink colors, soothed her agitation over James's absence.

She immersed herself in *Pride and Prejudice*, loaned to her by Samantha, and savored the luxury of reading a book other than the Bible or Shakespeare. Bridget found herself drawn to the heroine Elizabeth Bennet's conflicted feelings for Mr. Wickham and Mr. Darcy. Although Patrick was much nicer than Mr. Darcy, she recognized both men possessed some of the same arrogance. James, of course, was a far more honorable man than Mr. Wickham. Even if she hadn't known him for long, she'd sensed his goodness from their very first meeting.

He reminds me of Da. The realization struck her, and she missed her father with a fierce ache that stole her breath. *How I wish he were here.*

She needed a hug and his wisdom, for she feared James wasn't as taken with her as she'd thought. *Why else would he have left the ranch for a second day in a row without seeking me out?* Nor had he made any attempt to find her last night, not even appearing at the big house for supper.

"Miss Bridget."

She looked up. "Yes?"

Hunter, the Indian boy, stood in the doorway, an uncomfortable look on his face. He had on an oversized blue and white shirt, which seemed to be the only kind the boy wore. In one hand, he held an envelope. "Mr. Gallagher asked me to give you this. I think it's a Valentine card." He crossed the room and handed it to her, then escaped as quickly as he could.

Bridget had to smile at Patrick's choice of a cupid. He'd probably selected Hunter as the child least likely to linger out of curiosity.

She looked down at the envelope and found her name written across the front in bold script. With a clutch of her stomach, she opened the flap and drew out the Valentine. She held the card for a moment, not opening it. The card was everything she would have wished for if asked—paper lace and hearts, violets, gilt, a chubby cupid—a beautiful creation. Yet, instead of feeling excited about opening it, Bridget realized she dreaded knowing what words were written inside.

Slowly she lifted the cover and read, *Be Mine.*

Underneath the two words, Patrick had written, *I've come to admire and love you and would be honored if you would spend the rest of your life at my side.*

Bridget gasped. Although she'd wondered, and at times hoped, she really hadn't expected a proposal from the man, especially one made in such an indirect way. Patrick Gallagher struck her as someone who'd seize what he wanted with both hands.

Why aren't I thrilled? Her lukewarm reaction surprised her.

Maybe I'm numb with shock.

"Miss Bridget." Christine's face peered around the doorway, her blue eyes full of mischief. "I have something for you."

"Come in, dearie."

The girl walked over to her. Today, instead of her usual braids, her blonde hair was in loose curls held back by a ribbon. Christine was clad in the pink dress with lace and satin ribbon on the collar and hem, the pretty creation she'd worn to school for the party. She held out a homemade card.

Bridget set Patrick's card in her lap and took Christine's offering. "Oh, how lovely of ye to make me a Valentine."

"I didn't, Miss Bridget. It's from James."

"James!" Just saying his name made Bridget's heart thump against her chest.

"We all made Valentines yesterday. Ours for school and James's for you." She scrunched her face and shook her head. "His doesn't look so pretty. But he tried. I just think he needs more practice."

A lump rose in her throat, and Bridget had to swallow before she could speak. "Thank ye, child."

Christine whirled, so her dress spun out. Then on tiptoe, she danced out of the room.

Bridget glanced down at the card and touched her name with a fingertip. The crude lace of the doily, if it could even be called that, looked like James had put a lot of effort into making the gift for her. *How very sweet of him.*

This card she opened with excited anticipation. Inside, she saw the same message as on Patrick's. *Be mine.* But this time, there wasn't a bold declaration. Like the man, his message was simple, loving.

Bridget balanced the cards, one on each knee, studying them in the same way she needed to balance her choice. Both good men, attractive men, men who sparked her interest. With Patrick, she'd be secure and never again fear poverty. She could take care of her sister. With such a big house, surely he wouldn't mind Alana living with them. And his horses… She could see Thunder every day. Coax Patrick into letting her ride the stallion. Probably have her very own mount. Help train Thunder's foals… *Such a life would be a dream come true.*

But… Bridget looked down at the card and reread the message. She'd be at Patrick's *side*, and, she suspected, not the center of his heart, or his life. His needs, his wants, would come first, and her own might not matter. She had no doubt he'd allow her potatoes to grow in the garden with the other vegetables, but not in a big field. The treasure of the O'Donnells' would be for his table only. *But*, she argued with herself, *there'd be no need to grow a potato crop to sell, for Alana and I wouldn't need the money to survive.*

In the distance, Bridget heard the sound of the side door, and then the firm clicks of male boot heels and the jingle of spurs on the wooden floor. Quickly, she tucked both Valentine cards into the book and closed it.

James burst into the room. "Bridget, I have good news for you!"

"What?" She dropped the book onto a side table and stood, moving to meet him.

He clasped her hands. "I rode to town to see Dr. Cameron. He visited your aunt just yesterday and told me her fever had broken, and he expects a full, although slow, recovery."

"Oh, Jamie!" She threw herself into his arms, tears of joy in her eyes.

He hugged her tight. "And there's more."

She pulled away enough to gaze into his dear face.

"Dr. Cameron says your sister has a good appetite, has put on weight, and has lost the shadows in her eyes." He grinned, showing his dimples. "I figured an update on your family would be the best Valentine's Day gift I could give you."

"Ye figured right!"

The weight Bridget had been carrying for weeks—no, if truth be told, for *months*—lifted from her shoulders, and she burst into tears of joy, sagging against him.

His arms tightened around her, and he kissed her head. "Go ahead and cry, dearest. I know how worried you've been."

She took full advantage of his offer, sobbing out the strain and fear of the last year.

He held her until she wept out the pain, then with one arm still around her shoulders, James fished a handkerchief from his pocket and handed her the cloth.

Bridget mopped her eyes and turned her face from him to blow her nose. She became conscious that her eyes and nose must be red, not the appearance she wanted to present on such an important occasion. "Oh, dear. I must be a sight."

"A beautiful sight, my love."

"Sally!" Bridget clutched his arm. "Have ye told her?"

"No. I came straight to you."

"We must go to her this instant. Oh, how happy she'll be!" She turned to rush out the door.

James grabbed her arm. "Wait! The news can keep for a few more minutes, for I need to ask you an important question."

"Oh, I know." She practically caroled the words.

He cocked an eyebrow and pressed his lips tight. "You do, do you?"

Bridget wiggled from his grasp, picked up the book, and pulled out his Valentine, trying to take care so he wouldn't see Patrick's. But the edges caught, and the fancy card dropped to the floor. She let it lay and held up James's. "I *will* be yers, my dearest Jamie."

"Where did you get that?"

Puzzled by the question, she cocked her head. "From Christine."

"That little rascal. She sure put one over on me!" Shaking his head, James laughed. "I'd planned to buy you a card like that." He pointed toward the floor. "But I didn't do so soon enough. Mrs. Cobb told me that Patrick had bought the last one. So when I saw how poorly mine turned out, I gave up on the idea."

"'Tis a *lovely* card, Jamie. I won't have you disparage your gift. I shall treasure yer Valentine all my days for ye made it with yer own hands." She set the card on the table and held out her hand for his.

James drew Bridget toward him, staring into her face, his eyes full of wonder.

His gaze penetrated all the way into her heart, which swelled with happiness.

"So you'll marry me, my darling?" he asked. "Soon? I know from experience that we, the men of the ranch, can build a house in a week—winter or not. Although we'll need an extra room for Alana, so the construction might take a few extra days."

He understands! Misty-eyed with joy, Bridget gazed at him. "Mr. Waite prophesied a Valentine wedding," she reminded him.

He kissed the tip of her nose. "Well, we came close. But I'm sure you'll want to wait until your aunt has recovered and your family can attend. I'd like to invite my sister as well. So I think mid-spring would be best."

Relieved, she cupped his cheek. "That would be lovely."

His thumb brushed along her jaw to the corner of her mouth, and lingered. "I love this dimple."

She reached up and touched his dimples with both her forefingers. "I think I fell in love with ye the first time I saw these. I just didn't know it yet."

"You poleaxed me from the moment you came around the corner of the train station." James captured her fingers and drew her hands down. Then he kissed her—softly, gently, as if she was a skittish foal, and he was afraid of startling her.

Bridget kissed him back and pressed her body against him, needing to show James that, in spite of her recent bout of tears, she wasn't fragile and would be his partner in all ways.

I will be yers for always, my darling. And ye will be mine. Then Bridget became lost in their kisses, and all rational thought fled.

Dear Readers,

I hope *A Valentine's Choice* brought you a feeling of love and romance regardless of the time of year in which you read the story. I'm sure you'll be pleased to know that the saga of the O'Donnell sisters isn't over. Read about Alana O'Donnell and Patrick Gallagher in *An Irish Blessing* and Catriona O'Donnell and Moss Callahan in *A Rolling Stone* (January 19, 2017) Sally and Harry o'Hanlon met and fell in love in *Irish Luck*, a short story in *Montana Sky Christmas*. Samantha and Wyatt Thompson's story is *Starry Montana Sky*.

While you are waiting for me to finish writing my stories, try reading Montana Sky Kindle World books. The Kindle World books are stories written by other authors set in Sweetwater Springs and Morgan's Crossing, using my characters as background characters. Currently there are 24 stories, with more to come. Look for a whole new batch on December 15, 2016, just in time for the holidays—although they won't all be holiday stories. The Kindle World tab on my website takes you to these books. Some of the authors are creating their own mini-series within mine, so scroll down and see which authors have two or more books.

I hope you enjoy the *Montana Sky Series*, and I look forward to bringing you many more stories in the years to come.

Debra Holland

An Irish Blessing

Chapter One

SWEETWATER SPRINGS, MONTANA
January 1895

(One day after the beginning of *A Valentine's Choice*)

As the sleigh carrying Alana O'Donnell left the Thompson's ranch to travel to her Uncle Rory's home on the prairie, she took a deep breath, experiencing an odd sense of relief. *Finally, I'm alone.* The pressure that had wrapped like a tight band around her chest for the last four weeks suddenly eased enough to inhale without physical pain.

Not that she was really *alone*, for her cousin Sally's husband sat in the driver's seat. Harry had his back to her, his attention focused on the gray Appaloosa pulling them down the snow-covered road. However, for the first time since leaving Ireland, Alana wasn't in close proximity to her twin Bridget, who'd remained at the Thompson ranch as a companion to Sally, who was newly with child and prone to morning sickness.

By nightfall, Alana would arrive at her uncle's homestead on the prairie in order to nurse her ailing aunt who had influenza. Although these isolated relatives were strangers, for Rory O'Donnell had immigrated to America before the twins were born, she knew they'd be welcoming. Still, only the urgent need for her healing skills would have parted Alana from the twin who'd been her companion since birth.

Inhaling the frigid air and the musty leather smell of the bearskin covering her, she took a shuddering breath. Alana welcomed the privacy she'd have during the journey, but she already missed her sister and constant companion and wondered how she'd fare during the weeks apart.

Now I can finally cry. The heavy weight of secret sorrow in her heart, frozen since saying good-bye to her true love, melted into tears.

Her beloved, Timkin Walsh, was a slight man with wiry strength. He moved like a dancer, graceful whether he was digging in the garden, walking down the road, or treading the measures with her at a *Cèilidh.* His deep green eyes, gilded hair, and slightly pointed ears gave him a *fae* look—lending credence that one of the *Sídhe* had fathered him.

He'd always made me feel safe…cared for…understood.

In fact, after weeks of arguments with Bridget, the reason she'd reluctantly agreed to her sister's plan for the two of them to immigrate to America and live with their uncle's family was because Alana believed she *wouldn't* be leaving Ireland; she'd be married to her Irish sweetheart. Therefore, her twin would not be going, either. The sisters would remain in their dear familiar village, living much the same life as always—except Alana would be wed, and they'd both reside with Timkin Walsh and his mother.

So when she'd told Timkin she was leaving for America, Alana had hoped, expected even, that the threat of her departure would *finally* stir her beloved to propose. Instead, he'd stared at her, his face going pale.

Shaken by his lack of response, she'd pressed her lips to his. His arms at his sides, Timkin had stepped away from her, a desolate look in his green eyes. He'd tried to smile but, instead, the stiff upturn of his lips looked more like a grimace.

Then as now, tears spilled over. Dampness chilled her cheeks.

I know he cared for me. So why didn't he speak of marriage?

She and Timkin would never again walk side-by-side in the gloaming after the day's tasks were finished, or work together to heal a small animal. The sound of him singing—his tenor so rich and beautiful that goose bumps shivered over her skin—would only be a memory. Never again would she gaze upon his dear countenance, for the whole ocean and most of the American continent lay between them.

From the moment he'd spurned her advances, hurt and shame and bewilderment had churned within Alana. But in the flurry of her and Bridget's leave-taking and weeks of travel, she had no privacy to release the emotions. Nor did she want to reveal to Bridget the depths of her foolishness, for her twin had long ago warned Alana that she needed to stop trailing after Timkin like a shadow. No, while Bridget would have listened with concern and been sorry for Alana's pain, she believed the break was for the best.

I couldn't bear to hear her say those words.

Her memories built to a terrible mourning, for her pain was more than a broken heart. Too many losses filled these three years past—the deaths of her parents…her sister Catriona running away…the twins leaving their beloved home.

She slid down in the seat, ducking beneath the fur so she could cry without freezing her eyes and face or worrying that Harry would glance back and see her distress. In the close darkness under the covering, Alana welcomed the sobs.

Pulling a handkerchief from the fur muff borrowed from Mrs. Thompson, she blotted her eyes, but the tears didn't stop. Under the protective covering of the bearskin, Alana wept for a long time. Remembrances—at once both dear and painful—flowed through her mind. From time to time, she blew her nose and then cried some more at a fresh recollection.

Now, far across the sea, in a frontier wasteland as different from home as could be, Alana was alone and bereft in wild Montana—never to have the life she'd dreamed of. The thought made her body tremble with grief.

Gradually, her tears slowed from a gush to a trickle, and then stopped. Weeping had done her good, drained some of the heaviness from her chest and numbed the jagged edges of her pain. For a final time, she blew her nose into her handkerchief, the cloth sodden and cold from her tears.

Once her face was dry, Alana lowered the bearskin and sat up, peering over the side of the sleigh at the evergreen forest around them. She took a deep breath of the crisp pine-scented air. The cold hurt her face, and she scooted back down under the fur, pulling the edge above her nose.

Harry slowed the horse, turned around, and grinned. His face was too rugged for handsomeness—not like Timkin's even-featured countenance. But she could see how his smile had charmed her cousin Sally into a whirlwind marriage. Yesterday, the cowboy had kindly welcomed the two unexpected visitors from Ireland who'd dropped in on the recently wedded couple.

"All right?" he asked Alana. "We'll be stopping to change the horse soon."

She lowered the bearskin a few inches so Harry could see her attempt at a smile, hoping he attributed her red eyes and nose to the brisk breeze. "I'm fine," she lied.

"Not much farther to Sweetwater Springs, and you'll have a chance to get out and warm up at Doctor Cameron's house."

"I'll be glad of it." *That at least isn't a lie.*

"We'll break our fast, too." He winked before turning back to his driving.

The small exchange brought her into the present—to the sound of hoofbeats and the grate of the sleigh runners on snow; the stark blue sky glimpsed through crystal-white treetops. *No*, Alana realized, she wasn't—as she'd sometimes thought on the wretched journey to America—going to die of grief.

Although, she also knew, to have any chance of happiness in this new land, she'd have to purge her old hopes and dreams, along with all the love in her heart for her *fae* lad and the mystical emerald-green country she'd left behind. The task seemed almost impossible.

Somehow, I'll have to find new dreams.

The slowing of the sleigh woke Alana from the doze she'd fallen into. She blinked several times to moisten and focus her eyes. From the position of the sun, she suspected the time must be near noon.

The sleigh pulled up in front of a two-story white house with a broad front porch. Green boxes hung under the windows. Bare-branched trees sheltered a yard enclosed by a white picket fence. Here and there along the fence, the snow level dipped enough to show the pruned stubs of rose bushes. In the summer, she imagined, the yard would look beautiful.

Harry turned. "I'll drop you off here to confer with the doctor about your aunt. I'll head to the livery to change horses." He pointed his chin in the direction of the house. "Use the front door."

Alana hesitated, not liking the idea of barging in on strangers.

Harry gave her a reassuring smile. "The doctor is accustomed to people dropping by. If you were in need of medical attention, you'd go around to his office in the back."

She shoved aside the bearskin and stepped from the sleigh. The snow was tamped down, as if many had trod this way today. The town spread on both sides of the house. Clapboard, log, and brick structures flanked a wide street. To her surprise, the buildings weren't crammed close together like so many of the towns she'd seen from the train windows on their journey across America.

She pushed open the gate and walked through. Eager to get out of the cold, Alana hurried up a cleared brick pathway. She knocked on the door and waited. When nothing happened, she wondered if anyone was home or if, perhaps, the doctor was out seeing a patient.

Alana knocked again, louder this time, hoping she wasn't sounding rude—or worse, as if she were injured and in need of medical attention.

The door flew open, and a man stuck out his head. His unruly red hair seemed at odds with his formal Prince Albert suit. Blue eyes intent, he quickly scanned her from head to toe, obviously seeking signs of illness or injury.

"I am well, sir. I don't need medical assistance." She rushed out the words. "Harry O'Hanlon dropped me off here so I could talk to ye. I'm Alana O'Donnell, and he's driving me out to nurse my aunt."

"Aye, lass. I'm Dr. Cameron," he said, in a Scottish brogue. Offering a kind smile, he waved her in.

In another room, Alana heard a child crying, the sound shrill.

With a harried look, the doctor ran a hand over his head, rumpling his hair. "Thinking it was quiet, my wife chose this time to go to the mercantile. Then two families with wee ones in distress descended upon me at the same time. I'm surprised I even heard your knock on the door. Luckily the screamer, *puir* laddie, paused for breath at the right moment."

Dr. Cameron ushered her into a parlor, done up in comfortable shades of green and brown. A cylindrical stove gave out heat. "Make yourself at home, lass." He pointed to a hallway on the right. "The washroom is there."

The screams grew more piercing.

He frowned, the lines around his eyes deepening. "If you will excuse me." The doctor headed toward a door in the opposite direction that must lead to his office.

Alana moved around a green velvet settee to reach the stove. She pulled off the muff and mittens and tucked them under one arm while she warmed her hands. After a few minutes, she became comfortable enough to pull off her knitted hat and set it and the muff on the settee. She slid the mittens into the pockets of her coat and unwrapped her new scarf, knitted by her cousin Sally, and walked over to a coat rack to hang it up.

She sloughed off her coat, set the garment over the scarf, and hurried down the hall to the washroom. There, she discovered that, like at the Thompson ranch house, the Camerons had the luxury of indoor plumbing—a toilet, sink, and claw-footed tub. Dark-blue trim edged the gleaming white tile on the walls.

After using the toilet, she washed her hands and face with the rose-scented soap, holding the small pink bar to her nose for an extra sniff of sweetness. The hand towel was thick and soft, and Alana allowed herself to enjoy the plush feel of the cloth. *Someday I want a washroom like this!* The wish felt like an impossible dream.

When she left the washroom and walked down the hall, Alana heard a second, high-pitched cry join the first, causing a pain-wracked cacophony. *An infant*, her experienced ears told her. *Perhaps colicky*. She glanced out the window at the sunlight. *A little earlier in the day than most babies experienced the discomfort. Perhaps something the little one had eaten.* Eager to help, Alana bypassed the parlor, moving toward the noise.

In a wide hallway, lined with chairs and leading to a back door, sat an elegantly dressed blonde woman, holding the screaming baby. A fur coat and hat hung from a row of pegs on the wall opposite the chairs. Various-sized coats, scarves, and hats lay on several chairs next to her. From the worn condition of the garments, Alana surmised they belonged to the family currently with the doctor in his office.

Normally, the woman's obvious upper-class status would be enough for Alana to keep her distance. But with the baby's cries spurring her on, without stopping to think, she acted on her healer's impulses, stooping to feel the infant's forehead under the blue knitted cap. "No fever, thank goodness." She smiled at the mother, seeing the fatigue on the woman's beautiful face. "How old is yer wee one, then?"

"Five weeks. She cries like this for hours. I don't know what to do for her." Distress shadowed the woman's blue eyes.

Alana took a seat on the empty chair on her other side. "In Ireland, we call such times the witching hours." She raised her voice to be heard over the baby's cries. "Some say it's because the wee ones are bewitched," she said in a matter-of-fact tone. "But I think such superstitions come from the frustration, aye, even anger, a mother experiences at such times. Makes her *feel* like a witch."

The woman leaned back against her chair, releasing a sigh of apparent relief. "That is so. I have felt wicked to have such frustrated thoughts when my poor Carol is in pain."

"Yer not the first mother to feel so," Alana assured her, wishing she could hold the baby. Her methods usually soothed fractious little ones.

"I love her so much." She dropped a kiss on her daughter's forehead before turning to look at Alana. Her eyes held the sheen of tears. "Her arrival made my life complete."

Envy squeezed her chest, but Alana thrust away the feeling to concentrate on the mother and child. "Luckily, yer Carol does have to sleep sometime and, I'm sure, looks like such an angel, ye wonder how she could work up such dreadful screechin' when she's awake."

The woman smiled and dropped another kiss on her wailing infant's head. "You've made me feel better, Miss…?"

"I'm Alana O'Donnell, just come from Ireland, I have. And I nursed plenty o' babes at home. My mother, God bless her soul, was the midwife of our village."

"I'm Elizabeth Sanders. Are you related to the O'Donnells who have a farm on the prairie?"

"Aye, and I'm about to descend upon them unannounced."

"I'm sure they'll be thrilled. Out here, visitors are always welcome, especially family." The child whimpered, and Mrs. Sanders drew a fine hand over little Carol's bright cheek. "I'm afraid a crying baby isn't a good welcome to Sweetwater Springs."

"*Nay*. 'Tis the best, for I feel needed." Alana held out her arms toward the baby. "Would ye mind, Mrs. Sanders? Let me try a few things for Carol while we wait for Dr. Cameron to see to her. Ye never know what will help."

"How kind of you." The woman handed over her daughter.

Alana held the baby tight for a moment, murmuring soothing words in soft Gaelic. The infant was a miniature of her mother with a wispy blonde curl peeking from under her cap and bright blue eyes. Although it was hard to tell with her little face red and scrunched in pain, Alana suspected the baby was beautiful. "Let me quickly show ye what to do. I'm going to unwrap her, but I don't want her to become chilled."

Mrs. Sanders gestured toward a closed door across from them. "Let's go sit by the stove in the kitchen."

Alana lifted an eyebrow in askance.

"Don't worry," Mrs. Sanders smiled, obviously amused. "I'm well enough acquainted with the Camerons to barge uninvited into their kitchen. I promise you, Alice Cameron will not mind a bit." She rose and led the way.

The room reminded Alana of the Thompson's kitchen—comfortable, with a big stove against one wall and a long table covered in oilcloth in the middle. A faint smell of bacon came from a can of congealed grease on the counter, obviously set out to cool. The wooden floor was painted brown, curtains of green chintz were pushed back from the window, and wallpaper patterned with green and yellow flowers gave the room a cheerful aspect.

Holding the squalling baby in one arm, Alana pulled a chair from the table with her free hand and set it next to the stove. Taking a seat, she laid Carol on her lap, unwrapped the blanket from around the infant, and eased her arms out of her tiny wool coat but left on the rest of her clothing.

Mrs. Sanders added some wood to the banked coals of the stove and stoked the fire before sitting down next to her.

Gently, Alana rubbed the infant's head, cheeks, arms, legs and feet, and then lightly made circular motions on the babe's stomach, at last moving the tiny legs back and forth as if pedaling.

The volume of the child's cries dulled to whimpers.

Alana smiled at Mrs. Sanders. "Just a short massage like ye just saw can relax her." She pulled the edges of the blanket snuggly up, over, and around the little body. "Swaddle her tightly, instead of loose like ye had her before. She'll probably start crying again soon, unless she's able to fall asleep. But even a few minutes of peace during the witching time is a godsend, aye?"

"Aye," Mrs. Sanders echoed, accent and all.

"A hot water bottle on her stomach might help, although not too hot, mind ye. Just warm enough to feel good to yer fingertips. I'm sure Dr. Cameron will agree that weak chamomile tea will be good for her—calming. Cooled, of course."

"Now why didn't I think of that?" Mrs. Sanders asked in a self-condemning tone. "Chamomile is always so soothing. I'll give your suggestions a try."

"Yer a new mother. Experience comes with time. What I will tell ye is that this won't last forever. Babes seem to grow out of colic by four months of age, if not sooner." Alana laid the swaddled baby on her lap and rocked her from side to side. "See how she likes this?"

Mrs. Sanders watched her every move. "Thank you for your kindness to my dear Carol, Miss O'Donnell. May I call you Alana? Such a pretty name. And please call me Elizabeth."

"I'd like that." Warmth surged through her. No matter Elizabeth's elegance and status, they were two women together forming the bonds of a potential friendship in their efforts to soothe a fractious child. As Carol remained calm, the strain eased from Elizabeth's face.

"Now tell me about yourself, my dear Alana. It's always so exciting to welcome another woman to Sweetwater Springs."

"Two women. My twin sister Bridget remains at the Thompson ranch with our cousin Sally and her husband Harry O'Hanlon."

Elizabeth shook her head. "I haven't met Sally, but I heard about her when Mrs. Thompson paid me a visit. Samantha has become a dear friend, and her husband brought her in the sleigh to see the new baby. We had a lovely, although too short, visit."

"Sally is newly with child and isn't feeling well."

"I hadn't heard, poor girl. I remember that time." Elizabeth gave her daughter a Madonna smile. "Fussy baby and all, a child is worth all the sickness, discomfort, and pain. Such unimagined joy."

I might never know. The thought tugged at Alana's heart.

The two women fell into easy conversation, and, in the presence of Elizabeth's genuine interest, Alana soon found herself sharing far more about her life in Ireland than she'd intended, especially about her disappointment with Timkin. She hadn't confided this much in anyone, even her twin. Like with her crying spell, the release of talking to a sympathetic listener eased her heart.

The screaming from the inner room diminished to whimpers.

"Ah. Blessed silence." Alana exchanged a grateful glance with Elizabeth. She tilted her head toward the hallway. "Best we go wait for the doctor." Standing, she handed Carol back to her mother.

They moved into the hall and took a seat.

"Now, ye try rocking her on yer lap."

Elizabeth kissed her daughter's cheek before laying the baby on her lap and rocking her until Carol fell asleep.

The door to the doctor's office opened, and a flock of children flew out, arms and mouths moving in excitement as they talked about the bug in Gordie's ear. They tugged on coats, scarves, hats, and mittens. A plump mother followed, a toddler in her arms. She made clucking sounds and looked harried as she tried to herd her brood. Her brown hair straggled from a haphazard bun, and she'd buttoned the front of her plaid shirtwaist crookedly.

Alana stood and smiled at the mother before directing her attention at the boy in her arms. "Are ye all better, dearie?"

"Aye," Dr. Cameron answered for the woman and child. "A bug had crawled into the laddie's ear. I dropped in some mustard oil, and the wee beastie floated right out."

The mother pulled an embarrassed face. "These children will be the death of me. I should have let them walk to school, even with the deep snow, for we ended up having to come here, anyway." She shook her head in obvious annoyance. "I let them take Gordie to play in the barn, and he fell asleep in the hay."

"Well, much better a bug than an ear infection," Alana said in a practical tone. "Yer little man would be in pain for much longer, if that t'was the case."

One of the older boys pulled on the woman's arm. "Come on, Ma!"

The woman handed Gordie to the oldest girl and donned her outerwear before being swept through the back door by her boisterous brood, calling good-byes. Cold wind rushed in through the door. The last child slammed it shut.

Carol startled and let out a cry.

"That's done it," Alana muttered.

The doctor gestured to the office. "Come in, Elizabeth, and let me see to wee Carol. She sounds colicky, but I'd best examine her." He glanced at Alana. "If you want to brew yourself some tea, you'll find the tin clearly labeled in the cupboard next to the sink."

"Thank you." She wandered into the room and took a seat by the stove. She suspected Harry would soon return, and she'd better soak up the warmth while she could. Although Alana would have welcomed a cup of tea, she wasn't about to go rummaging through another woman's kitchen to make herself one.

In the hall, the office door opened. Alana heard footsteps and the sound of Dr. Cameron and Elizabeth talking, as little Carol cried.

Elizabeth was already bundled in her fur bonnet and coat and carrying her fussy baby when she stepped into the kitchen.

"Thank you again, dear Alana. All my best to your aunt, and I hope to see you soon."

Alana waved, but before she could say more, Elizabeth vanished, the sound of her footsteps hurrying across the boards.

Dr. Cameron entered the kitchen and sank wearily into a chair. "Times like this make me realize how much I take my dear wife for granted. Somehow, Alice always manages the chaos." He leaned forward. "Now, lass. About your aunt…I saw her yesterday, and she is quite ill. Do you have much nursing experience?"

"Aye. My mother was a midwife and healer, and I learned from her which herbs and such to use, how to deliver babies, stitch up cuts, set broken bones, as well as how to keep an ailing body comfortable. After she passed six months ago, I continued her work with the villagers. I've brought along some herbs and tinctures, although not much compared to what I left behind."

He let out a slow breath. "That relieves my mind, and we can always use more women with nursing experience here. Our community is quite spread out."

"Dr. Cameron, would a *carragheen* tonic help my aunt? 'Tis good for what ails a body."

He jerked up his chin and gave Alana a sharp look. "Did you bring some of the moss with you then, lass?"

"Aye."

"Wonderful!" He rubbed his hands together. "Most American doctors would na know what to do with it." His accent thickened. "But since I hale from the shores of the old country…." He smiled, crinkling the care lines around his eyes.

She couldn't help but smile back.

"Feeding Mrs. O'Donnell such a tonic would be the best cure I could recommend." Dr. Cameron held up a hand in caution. "And, I'm sure I don't need to tell you how infectious influenza is. I have no wish for another outbreak of the illness. The last one did enough damage. By the grace of God, I only lost a few patients, although some had close calls." His eyes looked tired.

"Have the rest of the family take your tonic to stay healthy." He eyed her and frowned. "And you as well, lass. Something tells me you're not usually so thin. A long journey, eh?"

"Aye, Doctor." *Best he think that's the reason.*

"Now, your aunt had a good stock of chamomile, and I left instructions with your uncle to try to get three cups a day down her. 'Twill help with the aches and pains."

"Ah, good," Alana said in relief. "I left all my chamomile with Sally to ease her morning sickness, for she hadn't brought any with her when she married."

He gave a wry shake of his head. "Newlyweds don't usually consider illness when they're setting up a household."

Alana couldn't help but think of the well-stocked medicine cupboard she'd once planned to take with her when she wed Timkin and moved to his home. Her heart ached. She hadn't realized how much she'd woven her future around her beloved. *I still have too many threads wrapped around him. Many are invisible to me until I inadvertently tug on one.*

Alana wished she could cut herself free but figured each strand might have to break on its own. She forced her attention back to the conversation.

"I'd advise plenty of warm soup and bed rest. Your aunt is strongly-built, so…." Frowning, Dr. Cameron rubbed his chin. "The worst of the illness should run its course in the next week or…." The doctor didn't preface his statement with, *if your aunt survives*. He didn't have to.

Please, Lord, make me an instrument of Thy healing, she recited St. Francis of Assisi's prayer, changing *peace* to *healing* to fit her aunt's dire situation. *Please may I help Aunt Henrietta pull through.*

Chapter Two

As Harry drove the sleigh away from Sweetwater Springs, heading toward the open prairie, Alana remained lost in thought, pondering her all-too-brief stay at Dr. Cameron's. Elizabeth's friendship and the gratitude the woman expressed had warmed Alana's insides as much as sitting by the stove heated her outsides. Just remembering the encounter made her smile, and she hoped to see the woman and her child again.

Discussing medical matters with Dr. Cameron had been another treat, one unfortunately cut short by the arrival of Harry. *If only I could assist Dr. Cameron with his practice.* Imagining such a future made Alana's hopes rise. *I could learn much from him.*

Her smile fled when Alana remembered that she and Bridget had no settled home. Of the two possibilities, neither the Thompson ranch nor the O'Donnell house on the prairie would be close enough to town for her to help the doctor with his patients.

Her spirits, briefly lifted from her encounter with Elizabeth and conversation with Dr. Cameron, returned to melancholy. Alana stared out over the vast cold prairie, blanketed with a heavy covering of snow—the bright whiteness foreign to her eyes after a lifetime of green. Once again her future looked as bleak as the horizon. Ahead of her, the only sign of human civilization—the tracks of sleigh runners and hoofprints from other travelers—seemed to go on forever with no destination in sight.

Dried grasses and the withered stalks of vegetation poked through the snow. White crystals dusted the brown branches of a fringe of trees marking a stream.

Out here, with the mountains distant, all she could see was the wide plain and the harsh blue sky dotted with wheeling black specks. She wondered what kind of birds they were.

Along the way, they drove by a few homesteads, located far apart. The thought of living so isolated—without nearby neighbors—made a lonely shiver rush down her spine.

As the day passed, the bright heavens faded to gray-blue. The rays streaming from the ball of the setting sun, just beginning to dip behind the distant peaks, reflected white and gold on streamers of clouds. They passed a placid stream, the shimmering golden light and clouds reflecting on the glassy surface—a beauty as different from her home near the shores of the Emerald Isles as could be.

"Next place is your uncle's," Harry tossed the statement over his shoulder.

Thank goodness! She watched two small structures grow ever larger, until they appeared as a house, barn, as well as some small outbuildings—a henhouse and privy, perhaps. Now that they were almost at their destination, Alana couldn't help wondering what her relatives would think of her unexpected appearance. Her stomach roiled.

"Whoa, now." Harry told the bay horse he'd switched to at the livery. He pulled up in front of a single-story house, which looked built of boards and some kind of mud bricks. Two small windows showed faint light within. The mud-brick and wood barn looked large enough to shelter a few animals. All was blanketed in white.

A boy, bundled against the cold and carrying a pail, trudged from the barn toward the house. He stopped and turned toward them, his free hand shading his eyes.

A bulldog charged the sleigh barking before being shushed. Then the boy must have recognized Harry, for he grinned, waved, and rushed toward the sleigh. Her cousin Charlie, she supposed, for he looked much like Sally.

A bearded man stepped out of the house, buttoning his coat as he moved. He hadn't lingered inside to put on a hat or scarf, and his dark hair was the same shade as Alana's da.

Charlie—who looked about thirteen or fourteen—stopped to pet the horse.

Uncle Rory headed toward them, a smile on his face. He pulled up short, apparently realizing the woman in the sleigh with Harry wasn't his daughter Sally. His eyebrows rose. "And who have you brought me, then, Harry, me boy?" Without waiting for an answer, he stepped closer to Alana, studying her face.

Seeing her uncle caused her a pang of grief and a familiar tightening in her chest. He looked so like her da—his features more weathered and angular, perhaps, his hair threaded with gray but similar enough. And those blue O'Donnell eyes gave her an immediate feeling of familiarity…of kinship.

His mouth quirked into a crooked smile. "You have the look of an O'Donnell, *mavoureen*. Are you, perchance, one of my kin?" His years away from Ireland had smoothed off some of his accent.

"Aye, Uncle Rory," she said, delighted by his instant recognition. "I'm Alana."

"My brother's girl!" His eyes sparkled. "Welcome you are, niece, to your American family."

The affection in his expression and tone eased the tightness in her chest. Her stomach settled.

Her uncle extended a hand to help her out and then bundled her into a hug.

Enveloped in her uncle's embrace, Alana let out a sigh from her very depths. *I'm with family.* The thought brought tears to her eyes. Without their mother and older sister, the twins had felt so alone.

Stepping back, her uncle touched her cheek. "I see my mother in your face, bless her dear soul. Aye, and you've the look of my daughters as well." His sudden smile charmed her. "Beauties, all of you."

"Thank ye, Uncle Rory."

"Now remind me. Are you two years older than my Sally or three?"

"I'm twenty-two."

"Ah, three." He gestured to the boy who was stroking the mare and talking rapidly to Harry. "Your cousin Charlie is horse mad. He's over the moon that his sister married a cowboy. He'll be chewing Harry's ears off for a while."

"A mere female cousin come from Ireland couldn't possibly compare to a horse."

Uncle Rory barked a laugh. "Right you are. But manners are important, too." He guided her toward the boy. "Where are your mother and sisters?"

The pain of her losses stabbed through her, but she swallowed hard to give him the sad news. "Mama became ill and died six months ago."

He made an exclamation and brushed a hand over his face. "Yer mother was the most beautiful girl for miles around, and my brother the lucky man who won her." His accent was heavy, his tone thick with grief. "But had I been older, I'd have given him a challenge." The faraway look in his eyes remained sad. "I know—" Rory tapped his head "—in here my brother has been gone these three years past. But in here—" he placed a hand over his heart. "Your father lives still at home with the beautiful wife and the three young daughters who brought him such joy."

Alana's eyes grew misty.

A look of horror dawned on his face. He dropped his hands. "Don't tell me your sisters—"

"Nay, uncle," Alana hastened to assure him. "Bridget is staying with Sally. And Catriona…" Guilt mingled with her sadness. Their sister's elopement with a peddler had made the twins angry…*until we left her behind, her whereabouts unknown.* "She is married." *Or so we hope.*

"Thanks be to God that you three are well. Now, tell me, niece, what brings you to these parts?

"I've nursing experience, and I've come to help care for Aunt Henrietta."

His expression shifted into seriousness, and his eyes shadowed. "Then you're doubly welcomed, *mavoureen.* We dearly miss our Sally at such a time. I've been seeing to Henrietta's needs." He dropped his hand on the boy's shoulder. "Charlie has taken over my chores. My twins are managing the household as best they can, but they are only ten."

Harry walked over to greet Rory. The two men shook hands.

With obvious reluctance, Charlie tore his gaze away from the horse. "Where's your pinto, Harry?"

"Loper couldn't be persuaded to pull the sleigh. I started out with James Whitson's Appaloosa, and we switched horses at the livery in town. Bess, here, belongs to the livery. Can I count on you, Charlie, to do what needs to be done for her?" Harry patted the horse's neck.

"Oh, yes!" A grin stretched the boy's mouth.

Harry chuckled and glanced at Rory. "The Thompsons and Mrs. Toffels sent along enough food to feed an army."

"'Tis kind of them." Uncle Rory gestured toward the house. "Alana, go ahead inside and warm up. We'll unload the sleigh."

Glad to be out of the cold, she made a wide berth to avoid walking near the horse, pausing to give her hand to the bulldog to sniff.

"That ole boy is Sian," her uncle called. "You can pet him. He's friendly."

"Hello, Sian." She rubbed his head, then opened the door and stepped into the house. Inside, a main room combined a kitchen and living area. She inhaled the familiar smell of boiled cabbage and welcomed the warmth.

A girl, her hair in two braids, stood near a small stove, stirring a pot she could barely see over. A second girl peeled potatoes. Both looked at her with the eyes of her sisters and her father.

Her smile broke out. *Bridget and I must have appeared like this at the same age.* The familiar saying, told to her and Bridget all their lives, sprang to mind—*as identical as two peas in a pod.* For the first time, Alana experienced being the one staring at twins and trying to figure out how to tell them apart.

Their hair was dark like their father's, unlike Alana and Bridget, who'd inherited their mother's whiskey-colored frizzy curls. Their skin had a warmer hue than hers—from the sun, perhaps—and they had the same oval-shaped faces and refined noses as their older sister Sally.

Both girls came toward her. One, in a blue dress, covered by a faded gray pinafore, carried the wooden spoon. The other in a green dress and pinkish pinafore still clutched her potato and peeler.

"I'm yer cousin Alana."

Their eyes widened.

The girl in green edged closer. "Alana...like Bridget and Catriona and Alana?"

Her heart panged at the thought of Catri. But Alana didn't let her smile dim. "Yes. Cousins, we are. And ye must be Idelle and Isleen. Ye are just as pretty as yer sister Sally." *Surely a newly arrived cousin is allowed to compliment their looks without turning the girls' heads.*

"You talk like Da," said the one wearing green. "But you sound more Irish."

"That I do. The accent of our homeland." Alana glanced around for a safe place for the fur muff and placed it on a chair.

"Sally's peg is the empty one in the middle." The twin in the blue dress pointed to a row by the door holding an assortment of outerwear. "You can hang your things on hers."

Alana obeyed, shucking off her coat, tucking her mittens in the pocket, unwrapping her new scarf, and pulling off the woolen cap. After hanging up everything, she smoothed her hair.

A wooden plaque in the shape of a four-leaf clover hanging on the wall caught her eye, and she leaned closer to read the saying carved into the smooth wood and painted over in black letters.

May your blessings outnumber
The shamrocks you grow.
And may trouble avoid you
Wherever you go.

Reading the inscription made a lump leap into Alana's throat, for they were Timkin's final words to her. Even now, the memory made her bitter. *My family's had nothing but troubles.*

"Da made that for Ma for Christmas," said one of the girls.

"A fine gift." Hoping she appeared composed, Alana turned back to the twins. "Now—" she said in a brisk tone "—which one of ye is which?"

The one in the green gave a little bounce. "I'm Isleen. You can tell because I wear green."

Alana couldn't help but smile. "Then Miss Blue here must be Idelle."

Idelle beamed. "Yes, Cousin Alana."

"Clever of ye to wear different colors. Bridget and I always dressed alike. People could never tell us apart."

"Our Ma's idea." Idelle's smile fell away.

She could read the child's expression of worry. Remembering well the fear she'd experienced during her mother's final illness, Alana stretched an arm around the girl's shoulders and gave her a squeeze. "I'm here to help ye two care for yer ma. Let's see if a little Irish magic will bring her back to health."

Isleen clasped her hands to her chest. "Can you really do magic, Cousin Alana?"

The hopeful look in the girls' eyes made Alana's stomach squeeze. *Am I giving false hope?* "Mind, I'm not saying influenza isn't a very serious illness. But we will give yer ma all the healing that love can provide and with the blessing of the Good Lord, she will pull through."

Dear Lord and the Blessed Mother, make it so.

The door opened. With a gust of cold air, Uncle Rory and Harry entered, carrying Alana's satchel, the food sent from the Thompson ranch, and a small sack of potatoes taken from the load she and her twin had brought from home. The O'Donnell potatoes had never fallen to the blight, preserving their family through the famine that decimated so much of Ireland.

Uncle Rory handed her the satchel. "You traveled light," he commented.

"We sold almost everything to pay for our passage. I've some clothes, my herbs and tinctures, a volume of Shakespeare, and some small bits and pieces." She shrugged. "But that's it."

"Well, that's more than I left with." Rory hefted the sack. "But Harry tells me you brought the family's good luck with you."

"Aye, Bridget thought to grow a crop here. Hopefully, the potatoes will do well in the new world as they do at home. I brought some with me, but most are with Bridget, who guards them as if they were gold. I brought a few for ye and yer family."

"A wonderful gift! We grow a crop of potatoes, but they aren't the same as the treasure of the O'Donnells." Uncle Rory lowered the sack to the floor near the wall. "I want to hear all your news…how you and Bridget came to be here, but later, if you don't mind." He tilted his head toward an inner door. "Your aunt's in the bedroom." He eased out of his coat and hung the garment on a peg by the door. "Let me take you to her."

Alana followed her uncle into a stale-smelling room made of mud bricks and located in the front corner of the house. A bed took up most of the space. Two small windows—one in each outer wall—let in feeble light. A trunk sat at the end of the bed. A wooden washstand with polished curves showed of better times. Crumpled linen lay in a pile in the corner. Although no fireplace or stove warmed the room, the thick walls made the temperature almost cozy.

Rory took Alana's hand and led her to the side of the bed.

The woman lying there stirred and turned her head to them.

"Look here, *A ghrá geal,*" Uncle Rory said in a gentle voice. "Our own niece Alana has come to take care of you." He gently touched his wife's cheek.

Bright love, he'd called his wife in Gaelic, and Alana imagined when Henrietta O'Donnell was well, she must have appeared vibrant, indeed.

Now, however, Henrietta was pale and wan, her auburn hair dull and lifeless. She looked familiar, perhaps because of the resemblance to her daughters, for they'd inherited her features. But a hard life had mapped wrinkles around her eyes and mouth and lined her forehead.

Henrietta managed a weak turn of her lips. Her mouth moved, but the words didn't come.

Alana felt a sense of purpose twining her to these people, and to this place. *My kin, my new home.* She welcomed grafting herself to the American branch of her family. *I've been rootless for too long.*

She smiled down at her patient. "Now, dear Aunt Henrietta, let's see what we can do to make ye well."

Chapter Three

Three Weeks Later

Patrick Gallagher rode his Thoroughbred stallion, Thunder, away from the Thompson ranch toward town, intending to catch the next train out of Sweetwater Springs. He couldn't shake the mud of this place off his boots fast enough. The memories of his stay at the ranch and of the rejection of his marriage proposal by Bridget O'Donnell and her acceptance of another man—a poor cowboy—stung like angry bees, goading his escape.

Once rejected, Patrick barely stayed long enough to pack and bid a curt farewell to his hosts. At another time, he might be ashamed of his lack of manners, but he'd seen the sympathy in Mrs. Thompson's eyes and knew the word had already spread around the ranch of Bridget's acceptance of James Whitson's suit.

When Patrick reached the outskirts of Sweetwater Springs, something made him pause the stallion. He'd planned to travel home to his stud farm outside of Crenshaw in triumph, appearing with a pretty wife on his arm. He didn't like the idea of returning with his tail between his legs, even if no one at his horse farm knew of his proposal and rejection.

An idea struck him with the force of a horse's kick. *There might be a way to save my pride. Bridget has a twin sister, who's living with family on the prairie.* He struggled to remember her name. Something with an *A. Surely one is as good as the other.*

Patrick thought back to the glimpses he'd had of the other woman. He couldn't remember seeing more than an identical female, quieter, and definitely without Bridget's curves. He felt a pang at that loss, but then dismissed the emotion. He'd been most attracted to Bridget's pretty face—especially her indigo eyes.

"The *A* twin might not have Bridget's spunk, but perhaps that will be for the best," he said aloud. "Not so stubborn, more manageable."

Thunder's ears twitched.

"Probably she'll be grateful to receive an offer of marriage," he told the horse.

With a grim smile, Patrick stared out at the town, barely noting the false-fronted buildings, the banker's brick mansion, the white steeple of the church.

Maybe seeing me with her sister will make Bridget remorseful. His damaged pride liked the thought of rubbing the woman's nose in what she'd thrown away.

What excuse do I have to visit?

I can pretend to come bearing news of Sally and Bridget, and it's really not pretend. I do have news. He winced, once again remembering the humiliation of Bridget's engagement.

But he couldn't arrive at the O'Donnell's empty handed, especially if he came a courtin'. *I'll buy sweets, candy, and cookies. They will also need substantial supplies to feed a man of my size.* He didn't want to be a burden to the family.

Patrick remembered the story he'd heard…when cowboy Harry O'Hanlon had gone courting Sally O'Donnell on Christmas Day, he'd brought the family a haunch of beef. *I can do better. I'll take a ham.*

Sugar and white flour. Patrick ticked off a mental list. *Some grain and carrots for Thunder.*

Patrick hesitated, rationality returning for a moment, and squinted at the sun. The day was unusually temperate for mid-February. If he had to guess, he'd say about forty-five, maybe even fifty degrees—sunny and cold, the stark blue sky cloudless.

As fine a day as any to take a long ride on the open prairie.

Am I foolish to ride my prize stallion alone to some hovel in the middle of nowhere to court a woman I don't know? Risk harm to my horse because of my fool pride?

Thunder was the foundation of his stables. Taking the stud from his horse farm to the train, traveling for half a day to Sweetwater Springs riding in the stock car with Thunder, then journeying with an escort to the Thompson ranch was one thing. Not much could go wrong on such a trip. He hadn't thought twice about leaving on his own, for after attending church several times, the well-trodden road from the Thompson ranch to town had become familiar.

Patrick glanced at the sky, which looked clear in all directions as far as the eye could see. Not that a storm couldn't blow up, but all his senses told him otherwise. Squinting at the sun, he calculated the hours until darkness and what he'd heard from Harry about where the O'Donnell place was located.

If he were to make this trip, dropping Thunder off at the livery while he shopped at the mercantile would give both of them a chance to warm up. From his coat pocket, he pulled out the map rancher Wyatt Thompson had given him of Sweetwater Springs back when he'd first arrived. Thompson had informed him the map was up-to-date as of the previous year.

Patrick offered up a little prayer to the Almighty that all would be well—with his horse, with his courtship. With the decision made, he urged the stallion into town.

The main thoroughfare of Sweetwater Springs looked like many of the other small towns he'd ridden through—maybe nicer than a few, with the buildings spread apart instead of crammed together. A typical blend of structures found in a Western town—including a false-fronted green saloon and a white-steepled church, as well as some homes, both plain and fancy, shops and businesses.

As he rode up the dirt street, Patrick heard the banging of hammers and scritching of saws as workers on two new buildings took advantage of the fine day. One was a large hotel owned by the banker, and the other an office building for the newspaper owner. He'd met both men one Sunday.

No one was around the front of the livery, a weathered gray building, so he dismounted and led Thunder toward the big barn door, which he slid open a few feet and stepped inside, still holding the reins. The wooden floors were clean, he was glad to see, and only a couple of stalls were occupied. A surrey and a sleigh were parked at the end of the barn, with plenty of space for extra vehicles.

Today was his first time inside the livery. On Sundays, when almost everyone on the ranch came to town for the church service, some of Thompson's cowboys took charge of everyone's mounts, including the piebald gelding Patrick often borrowed from his host for general riding.

Two men studied a piece of paper tacked to a wall, so engrossed in their discussion that they didn't hear him enter. One was elderly, judging from his white hair, and the other a young dark-skinned man—Indian or Mexican, Patrick supposed.

The older one tapped the paper. "Good thinking about leaving a door here in the back," he told the younger man. "What with your Lucia hastening to wed, you can make do with the one room, and this design will make it easy to add a second room when your babes start coming. And come they will, I'll bet." He nudged his companion with his elbow. "One right after the other, and, if you're uncommonly blessed, they'll all thrive and live to adulthood."

Patrick had no desire to hear about another man's approaching nuptials, so he deliberately cleared his throat.

The two looked over and nodded a welcome.

He led Thunder inside, the hoofbeats loud on the rough plank floors.

Their gazes quickly left him to take in the horse.

"*Madre de Dios*," said the younger man with an awestruck breath.

That settles the Indian/Mexican question.

The young man's grin split his round face. "That's some horse you have there, *señor*," he said with a Spanish accent.

Despite his low mood, praise of his prized stallion made Patrick feel good. "I think so, too. Thunder's a Thoroughbred, bred to race, but as gentle as a winter's night is long."

"I've heard tell of this one." The older man approached and walked in an admiring circle around the stud. "You match him with Thompson's Miss Midnight, and their foals are going to be something special." He straightened, seeming to recollect his manners. "I'm Mack Taylor, owner of this place, and my man, here—" he said with a jerk of his thumb "—is Pepe."

"Patrick Gallagher." He tilted his head in the direction of the mercantile. "I need a few things, and I don't want to leave Thunder unattended."

"Rode in from the Thompson ranch, did you?"

"Yep."

"Then we'll see to this gentleman's needs." Mack ran an expert hand down Thunder's neck. "Don't you worry none. Will be a right treat for us to care for such a one."

Pepe pulled out a carrot stub from his pocket and held it up with a quirked eyebrow for Patrick's permission.

"Go ahead." Having a good feeling about both men, Patrick transferred the reins over to Mack. "I'll be back soon." He strode out the door, sliding it closed behind him.

He walked up the street, avoiding as best he could the worst of the manure piles and mud puddles from the melting snow. He tipped his hat and gave a charming grin to a pinch-faced elderly lady passing by with a basket on her arm, startling a smile from her.

The mercantile was a brick building with a big glass window, with wares displayed and *Cobb's Mercantile* on the front. He turned away from the sight of a fat pink pillow shaped like a heart, probably left over from Valentine's Day yesterday, but not before feeling a pang in his chest. He pushed the thought of Bridget from his mind. Or tried to, at least.

At the steps, he scraped off the worst of the mud from his

boots and then vigorously slid his feet across the woven straw mat in front of the door to clean the soles as much as possible. He opened the door and strode inside, enjoying the scent of cinnamon cookies, his favorite kind. The room looked big for a small town mercantile. Although space remained in front of the back counter, almost every other inch displayed goods—whether on tall shelves running down the middle of the room, in barrels near the door, on pegs drilled into the wall above display cases, and even hanging from beams overhead.

The clerk standing behind the counter—a heavy-set woman who looked to be in her forties—glanced up, scrutinizing him with sharp, close-set eyes.

Mrs. Cobb, he assumed. He vaguely recalled seeing her on the Sunday he'd been in to buy a Valentine's Day card for Bridget. The place had been busy with many people stopping in the store after church, and Mr. Cobb had waited on him.

She eyed him up and down before casting him a simpering smile at odds with her age.

Patrick suppressed an eye-roll. He'd received plenty of such glances from ladies, especially in Crenshaw, where he was known to be an eligible match. But usually they came from women who were younger and trying to hook him into bestowing the title of Mrs. Gallagher upon them. This one, he suspected, was out to hook the money from his pockets.

"Welcome to our store, Mr. Gallagher." At his surprised look from hearing her address him by name, Mrs. Cobb coyly shook a stubby finger at him. "I saw you on Sunday but didn't have a chance to be formally introduced." She leaned over the counter. "Now, tell me, how did Miss O'Donnell like the Valentine's card you bought her?"

His stomach clenched in a painful knot. *I have no idea.* He'd used one of the Thompson boys as his messenger, and soon after, the news of her acceptance of James had forked around the ranch like lightning. Bridget's stilted apology for her rejection hadn't included mention of the card.

Mrs. Cobb waited, an inquisitive expression on her face.

No doubt salivating for the latest gossip. If he could have politely turned and fled the store, he'd have done so. Once he told her the news, Patrick had no doubt the juicy tidbits of his rejection and Bridget's engagement to another man would be all over town in less than an hour.

"Miss O'Donnell must have preferred another card." He made himself sound unconcerned. "She accepted James Whitson's proposal."

Mrs. Cobb's eyebrows drew together. "I don't recall that Mr. Whitson bought a card. I kept careful track of who purchased each one." She shook her head and pressed her lips together. "I can't imagine why that girl would choose a mere ranch hand over *you*."

I can't either. Patrick shrugged as if he didn't care. "I'm on an errand of mercy, traveling to the O'Donnell family on the prairie to bring them word of their daughter and niece. I understand Mrs. O'Donnell has been seriously ill, and I'd like to take them some provisions."

"I've heard Henrietta has turned a corner and is no longer at death's door. Erik Muth, their neighbor, is here several times a week delivering milk. He regularly brings us news. Their niece, Miss Alana O'Donnell, has been quite a help." Avid speculation lurked in her eyes.

Patrick's gaze fell on the jars of candy on the counter. "As well as some treats." Not wanting to further the conversation, he tapped the nearest jar. "We can start with peppermint sticks. I believe they have several children besides their married daughter."

Mercifully, the shopkeeper went along with his change of subject. "Three." She pulled a sheet of waxed paper from a roll. "How many?"

"I'll take six. And two dozen of your cookies. Actually, throw in another half dozen." *I'll eat some on the way rather than using the food Mrs. Toffels packed for the journey.*

While she selected and wrapped the candy, Patrick reeled off the list he'd mentally compiled.

The woman nodded at each item but didn't stop to write down anything. She bustled about, gathering what he needed and wrapping the goods into parcels.

In the meantime, Patrick strolled around the store to see if anything else would catch his interest.

A narrow shaft of light from the front window penetrated between two rows of shelves to glitter on some jewelry inside a glass cabinet next to the counter. Patrick bent to peer closer. He avoided glancing at a row of rings—both plain gold or set with jewels. To show up uninvited and present Miss O'Donnell with an engagement ring would be too presumptuous, even for him.

He eyed a cameo with a delicate female profile, and then a mourning brooch made of jet with a space for the deceased's lock of hair. He passed his gaze over a pearl bracelet, then lingered on a necklace with a gold charm in the shape of a shamrock.

Patrick thought of Bridget's musical Irish accent and supposed her twin's was the same, although the woman hadn't uttered a word to him that he recalled. *An Irish trinket for an Irish young lady.*

Perfect.

If Miss O'Donnell accepts my courtship, I'll give her the necklace as a token of my esteem and intentions. The ring can come later.

Feeling quite pleased with his plan, Patrick tapped on the glass and pointed at the shamrock. "I'll take that one."

Mrs. Cobb's sharp gaze flew to his face, evidently probing for hints.

He ignored her. *This time I will keep my intentions to myself 'til I have the answer I want.*

Alana sat in the main room with her aunt and the twins, the four of them doing handwork. A cheerful fire burned in the fireplace and the bright afternoon sun gleamed through the small windows. The twins embroidered their samplers, her aunt knitted, and Alana darned Charlie's stockings.

In the midst of one patch of light, the girls sat close, their knees angled toward each other to make the best of the brightness. Alana and Henrietta worked in the sunny area of the other window.

Today was the first day Alana had allowed Henrietta out of bed. The dreadful illness had taken her aunt to heaven's pearly gates and back, and her recovery had been slow.

While Alana's fingers moved through the familiar task, she kept a sharp eye on her patient. As soon as Henrietta showed signs of tiring, back to bed she'd go.

Stew made from a rabbit Charlie had snared this morning, thick with carrots, potatoes, and onions, and spiced with some dried rosemary leaves brought from home, simmered on the stove, sending an enticing smell throughout the room. As in Ireland, fresh meat came seldom enough to be a treat, and Alana had cooked up a double batch to last through two meals. From time to time, she rose and went to the stove to stir the pot.

Earlier, the girls had recited their spelling words and the Bible verses they'd memorized under Alana's tutelage, but now the four lapsed into companionable silence.

Isleen wrinkled her nose at her sampler and stirred as if to complain. She glanced at her mother and settled back in her chair.

Alana suppressed a smile. Isleen reminded her of Bridget, who'd struggled with her hated sampler. Both Isleen and Bridget had more outgoing personalities. Her active sister preferred being outdoors with the horses and would rather dig in the garden than sit still and do handwork. Sometimes, Alana had worked on Bridget's sampler in secret so her twin could escape.

For the first time, thinking of home and of her herb garden, didn't send a stab of homesickness through her. These last three weeks had worked wonders for her low spirits. Although her heart still hurt, the warmth of her American family gave her a sense of being loved and needed. Her appetite had returned, and she took satisfaction in seeing her aunt's slow but steady recovery.

To her surprise, living away from the shadow of her mother's formidable reputation as a healer and midwife, with no one who'd known her as a babe judging her skills, had given Alana a newfound feeling of competence. Even their nearest neighbor, Erik Muth, had stopped by to have a cut in his arm sewn shut, and he'd admired the neat stitches.

If only I didn't miss Bridget so much. Being away from her sister had turned into a constant ache, as if a part of her was missing. Ironic how with the pain of losing Timkin easing somewhat that of being parted from her sister increased. *Hopefully, we'll soon be reunited.*

She checked on her aunt again.

Henrietta caught her look. "No need to worry, dear Alana. I've already promised I'll nap when I become tired."

"I know. But it's common to think yer doing well, push too hard, and cause a setback. I won't allow that to happen." Alana made herself sound stern, although she couldn't help but smile. "Soon ye'll be completely well, Sally will be past the time of her morning sickness, and Bridget will arrive here.... Why, everything will be perfect." Or as perfect as possible in this new life of hers.

Her aunt arched an auburn eyebrow. "I've heard you talking with Rory about planting your potatoes and herbs."

Alana cast a glance out the window at the cloudless sky, wondering if today's warmer weather would last, and she could soon plant her potatoes. "We want to pay our own way and not be beholden," she said with a proud tilt of her chin.

"Nonsense. I don't know what we'd have done without you, dear niece," Henrietta's smile was warm and her eyes misty. "Although I terribly miss Sally, you being here makes the hole in our family less obvious, not to mention everything you've done for us."

Alana's cheeks heated at the praise. "Ye must stop thanking me. In fact, I will not allow ye to do so any longer. I have received such pleasure in living with kin and being needed."

"You are as stubborn as my eldest daughter, who, of course, takes after her father."

Alana chuckled. "Aye, an O'Donnell trait. And speaking of stubborn…I know having the two of us here will crowd the house." With only one bedroom, Alana slept on Sally's pallet in the sliver of a loft with the other children. "As soon as Bridget and I have a profit from the potatoes, we can pay to add on another bedroom."

Henrietta shook her head. "Let's not get beyond ourselves. I doubt either of you will be living here long. Young women are scarce in the west, especially pretty ones. Some man will snatch you up as Harry did with my daughter. I will just enjoy your company while I have it."

Appalled by the thought, Alana shook her head. "I'm content to abide here. I've no wish to wed." Now that she was feeling better, she'd found comfort in planning hers and Bridget's next few years. She wasn't about to abandon her ideas.

Henrietta gave her a wise look. "You've undergone a lot of difficult changes in the past year, Alana. 'Tis not surprising that you don't want another big one. But life has a way of changing on us—for good or for ill—sometimes when we least expect it."

Alana opened her mouth to protest.

Charlie burst into the house, sending a gust of cold air their way. "There's a stranger riding up on a big black horse. A beauty!" He dashed back outside, slamming the door behind him.

"I want to see." Isleen bounced to her feet, dropping her sampler on her chair.

An odd feeling, almost like a premonition, curdled Alana's stomach. *Patrick Gallagher!*

Don't be foolish, she chided herself. *What would that man be doing all the way out here?*

Still, Alana knew she was right and wasn't sure if the shiver down her spine was dread or excitement.

In their brief meetings, the big, handsome horseman had rubbed her wrong, not only because of the assessing way he'd stared at Bridget, but because she could tell he was accustomed to women fawning over him. He'd obviously expected the twins to do likewise.

She lifted her chin at the thought. *Although I'm not outgoing like Bridget, neither of us is the fawning type.*

Not that the horseman had looked at Alana. Bridget was the sister who'd drawn his gaze, which was fine with her. *Not that I'd want him to court Bridget, either.*

Resolving not to move from her chair to gape out the window, she made another careful stitch in Charlie's stocking before glancing up.

Her eyes shining, Henrietta tucked away her knitting. "Perhaps he's come from the Thompson's ranch, bringing us word of Sally and Bridget."

With more energy than Alana had yet seen her display, Henrietta pushed from the chair to a standing position and removed her apron.

Her aunt wobbled as she tried to take a step. "Oh, dearie me."

With a gasp, Alana dropped her darning and rushed to Henrietta's side. "Let me help." She tucked a hand under Henrietta's elbow and snatched up the shawl that had fallen off her shoulders. Not for the first time, she wondered if missing her eldest daughter had made her aunt vulnerable to the influenza. *I can put up with Patrick Gallagher if he brings news that will lighten Aunt Henrietta's heart.*

The twins cracked open the door and peered out. The cold air blew into the room.

"Ye two close that door," Alana scolded. "Yer letting the heat out."

"Off with your aprons, girls, for company's here," their mother ordered. She flicked her hand in Alana's direction in a command for her to do likewise."

With an eye-roll she made sure her aunt wouldn't see, Alana complied.

Shifting from foot to foot, Isleen gave them an antsy look.

"Don your coats, and go on out," Henrietta said. "Or you can stay in and watch from the window."

Giggling, the girls looked at each other and grabbed for their coats.

Alana helped her aunt walk toward the window. Once there, she tucked the shawl around Henrietta's shoulders. "Let's get ye wrapped up tight. Ye are to stay out of the draft, hear?"

Her aunt laughed and rested a hand on Alana's. "You will make a wonderful mother someday, my dear. You already sound like one."

Alana plastered on a smile to hide the hurt her aunt's words inadvertently caused. In her daydreams, she'd thought to have a houseful of children with Timkin. *Not for me the joys of motherhood.* "Yer to stay inside," she ordered. "Ye'll meet this stranger soon enough."

"Spoilsport," Henrietta joked.

Patrick Gallagher or not, Alana couldn't deny how the stranger's arrival had lifted her aunt's spirits. "Don't be disappointed if this man is not from the Thompson's," she warned. "I'll allow no setbacks to yer recovery."

"You tyrant." Henrietta teased. "Even so, company is always welcome. You haven't been with us long enough to know how isolated our farm is. In the winter we can go for weeks without seeing any faces but our own." She peered out the window. "Why, that is a magnificent horse, indeed. The man has his back to me, so I can't see his face."

The twins scampered out the door.

Alana joined her aunt in looking out the window and fought to hide her recoil. *Patrick Gallagher.* Even from behind, she recognized the man's broad shoulders. He'd dismounted and stood talking to Uncle Rory and Charlie.

The twins darted over to them.

The visitor turned to welcome the girls.

The sight of his strong profile made her certain.

Mr. Gallagher glanced at the house.

He looked as handsome as she'd remembered, his dark eyes as bold.

Embarrassed to be caught staring, Alana ducked away from the window and set her back to the wall. "Yer in luck." She tried to sound matter-of-fact, but the tightness in her chest caused her words to wheeze out. "He's not one of Mr. Thompson's ranch hands, but he was visiting there when last I saw him. Patrick Gallagher, he is. And that black creature he rides is his Thoroughbred stud."

Henrietta clapped her hands like a girl. "Wonderful." She glanced toward the stove. "Do we have enough to feed him? Of course we do," she responded. "The rest of us will just have to eat less."

Alana shook her head. "No need for scrimping. I made plenty."

"Do you have water warming?"

"Aye, Aunt." Alana tried not to sound impatient. "Always."

"Listen to me." Henrietta shook her head and gave Alana a rueful glance. "As if, by now, I didn't know your competence. It's just that I so long to hear word of my daughter." She patted Alana's cheek. "And I know you miss your sister."

Alana did long for news about her sister, but she wished Harry or another cowboy had come instead. Something about Mr. Gallagher had made uncomfortable from the start of meeting him.

The girls tumbled back into the house, shutting the door behind them.

"Can we go to the barn, Ma, please?" Isleen glanced out the window before sending her mother a pleading glance. "That horse is so beautiful, and I want to pet him. Maybe give him a carrot."

"You two stop your gawking and act like young ladies." Henrietta gestured for them to sit. "We can't be wasting carrots on livestock."

Both girls made faces but reluctantly obeyed. They took off their coats and gloves and cast a longing glance outside. Slowly they picked up their samplers and sat, their silent rebellion evident in the stiffness of their movements.

"Charlie gets all the fun," Isleen muttered, her head bent over her sampler. She took a careless stitch that probably would have to be ripped out later.

Alana chuckled.

All three looked askance at her.

"Ye sound just like our Bridget," she explained. "If she were here, my sister would rush outside to see that creature and not ask permission, either. She'd want carrots to feed it, and our mother would have said the same thing about wasting food. But that wouldn't faze Bridget. No, she'd be finding a patch of sweet clover and picking it for the beastie."

"We don't have sweet clover," Isleen grumbled.

Idelle tilted her head. "Why do you call Mr. Gallagher's horse a creature and a beastie?"

"Why, 'tis a big black creature, indeed," Alana said lightly, having no desire to disclose her fear of horses. She'd taken enough teasing about her avoidance of them and would prefer her relatives didn't learn about her shameful weakness. Nor did she want to instill the girls with her fears. *Best have them keep their enjoyment of the great animals.*

Alana tilted her head toward Henrietta's chair. "Back down ye go, Aunt, before ye wear out yer energy. Mr. Gallagher will be in soon enough."

"Oh, dearie me. You're right." She allowed Alana to escort her to her chair and took out her knitting.

Alana sat, picked up Charlie's stocking, and positioned the

wooden darning egg at the heel. She began to stitch, hoping the familiar task would calm the fluttering of her heart.

Seemed almost half an hour passed with Aunt Henrietta and the girls in obvious impatience and Alana in dread before Uncle Rory opened the door and ushered in their guest.

Charlie walked behind them. All three held burlap sacks.

At the sight of Patrick Gallagher, standing taller and broader than her uncle, his black gaze sweeping the room, Alana's stomach dipped. The man was attractive with patrician features, but an air of something power, perhaps—made her shiver. She avoided eye contact, concentrating on her darning as if no acquaintance had entered the house.

"Ah, Mr. Gallagher, here's my wife up and about and able to greet you." Her uncle sounded the happiest since Alana's arrival. "Henrietta, here is Mr. Gallagher come all this way to bring us news of Sally and Bridget."

Henrietta made to stand, necessitating Alana to drop her darning and move to help her.

But before she could rise from her chair, Mr. Gallagher motioned her aunt to stay and took long strides to stand in front of her. He took Henrietta's hand and bowed. "Now I see where Sally gets her beauty." His tone was warm and flirtatious.

Pink rose in Henrietta's cheeks, lending her the attractiveness her illness had taken. "You flatter me, Mr. Gallagher."

"Call me Patrick. And I do no such thing. I can see you're pulled a bit from being sick, but I'm delighted to see you on the mend. I'm sure Miss Alana will have you back to your usual self in no time." He cast Alana a sidelong look.

Wondering if her color matched her aunt's, she slid her gaze away.

"You must be frozen and hungry, Mr. Gallagher." Henrietta waved for him to take her husband's seat in a worn leather chair. "Please join us for a meal." Her gracious tone showed no trace of her eagerness to ask questions about her daughter.

"Famished. But I'd best wash up first." Mr. Gallagher raised the burlap bag he held. "I couldn't descend on you empty-handed, so I paid a stop at the mercantile."

Henrietta touched his arm. "Why, Mr. Gallagher, how thoughtful of you."

"No need to be formal. Like I said, call me Patrick." He bowed again to Alana and looked her over with frank approval. "Miss O'Donnell, I'm glad to see you well."

"Mr. Gallagher," she said in a distant tone, giving him a regal nod, hoping to put him in his place.

"Patrick," he reminded her with a charming smile.

She ignored him.

Henrietta waved toward the back of the house. "Alana will bring you water to wash up. Please avail yourself of our bedroom to do so. And of course, it's too late in the day for you to be venturing out again before nightfall. So later, we'll make a pallet for you in front of the fireplace."

Alana wondered if the man was used to such poor accommodations. Judging by what she'd seen of the spacious Thompson house, he'd been sleeping in a fancy guest room for weeks. She wondered what his own house was like, then caught her thoughts and brought her attention back to her task.

Mr. Gallagher nodded. "Mighty kind of you," he said to Henrietta.

Alana peeked up at him from beneath lowered eyelashes to see his gaze lingering on her.

With a polite smile, she rose. Keeping her eyes averted, Alana moved past her uncle and into the kitchen area. She wrapped a potholder around the handle of the kettle and hefted it off the stove, and then headed toward the bedroom. Out of the corner of her eye, she could see their guest place his burlap bag on the table and then follow her.

Alana led him into the bedroom. Her shoulder blades twitched as if his gaze touched her back. She stepped to the side to let him enter, grateful that earlier today she'd taken the opportunity of her aunt being on her feet to change the bedding.

Although the once white sheets had yellowed with age and usage, she'd ironed the linens to crispness. She'd also folded fresh towels next to the washbasin and opened the window long enough to clear away the musty smell of sickness and let in fresh air.

This house must be too humble for his taste. Once again her imagination strayed to wondering about his home, which must be as fine as the Thompson's large two-story one.

Hoping he wouldn't notice the chips on the lip of the pitcher that she'd turned to the far side, Alana poured the hot water into the white ceramic basin. That done, she moved to leave the room.

Mr. Gallagher touched her arm in a gesture for her to remain and gazed into her face. "You're looking well, Miss O'Donnell. You have roses in your cheeks," he said in a gallant tone.

Roses wouldn't be the term she'd use to describe the heat flushing her face. Alana took a breath lest she give him a tart rejoinder. She wouldn't want to shame her family by making a guest feel unwelcome. "I've recovered from the long journey," was the best she could do. She pulled away her arm and edged toward the door.

"Ah." He lowered his hand. "Traveling from Ireland to Montana must have been an arduous experience."

Ye have no idea. Alana gave him a fake turn-up of her lips. "Well, today, 'tis ye who've had the journey," she said with artificial lightness. "By the time ye've finished washing up, we'll have supper on the table. I hope you like rabbit stew."

"Rabbit stew will suit me just fine."

With a little nod, she stepped out of the room, quietly shutting the door behind her.

Her aunt and uncle stood together just beyond the bedroom, facing each other in an obvious private moment.

Not wanting to disturb them, Alana shrank back against the closed door.

Rory brushed aside the bangs from Henrietta's forehead and planted a kiss there. "It does my heart good, *A ghrá geal*, to see you out of bed," he said in a low voice.

"I looked in the mirror and received quite a shock. I'm so thin." Henrietta touched her head. "And where did these gray hairs come from?"

"You are as beautiful to me as the day I first set eyes on you and vowed to make you my wife. I'm blessed to have you by my side, Henrietta. I want you to take care of yourself, so I don't have to fear losing you. I never want to live through such dark times again."

"We've weathered them before, dearest," Henrietta said, placing a hand on his chest. "And we will again."

"Aye, but I'd prefer to avoid them if possible. Promise me you'll take it slow and steady. Rest when you have need, else I'll be enforcing my husbandly authority." His tone sounded suggestive.

Henrietta's cheeks flushed.

For the first time, Alana could see the comely woman her aunt had been before her illness.

Henrietta reached up and touched Rory's cheek, her luminescent smile a promise.

Seeing her uncle look at his wife with such love in his eyes, Alana's heart ached. She suppressed the image of Timkin that rose in her mind, instead, for the first time, wishing for a different man—a husband who'd care as deeply for her as Rory did for Henrietta.

"No fussing over our visitor. Let our niece do that."

Henrietta stretched close to Rory, and he bent to listen. "The last man who showed up here with food aimed to court our daughter. I've no doubt Patrick is another such. I knew we'd lose Alana to a suitor, but I thought we'd have a little more time before she left us."

Alana froze. *Suitor?*

"Don't get ahead of yourself, *A ghrá geal.* Rory took Henrietta's hand. "As much as we might wish to, we mustn't be selfish about keeping our beautiful girls with us. They must spread their wings and fly. We who are left on the ground can only watch them with sadness and joy."

Henrietta leaned into him. "The Good Lord sent Alana to us when we needed her most. Now perhaps he and the Blessed Mother are sending her on to a man who needs her more."

Alana's stomach twisted at the thought.

Rory dropped a kiss on his wife's head. "I have no doubt."

Unlike her uncle, Alana had plenty of doubts, and she made a resolution to stay as far from Patrick Gallagher as possible and give him no opportunity to engage her in private talk.

Chapter Four

Patrick felt pleased with the view across the plank table. For supper, they all crowded on the two benches that lined either side. Alana, Henrietta, and the twins—identified by the color of their dresses—sat on one side, Charlie, Rory, and Patrick facing them.

The position gave him a good view of Alana O'Donnell, who to his surprise, had filled out since last he'd seen her, although she still was thinner than Bridget. She had the navy blue eyes that all the O'Donnell family members seemed to possess. Her curly hair, a color between chestnut and palomino gold, was pulled tightly back into a braided bun. Tendrils frizzed across her forehead and framed her face.

A sense of wellbeing filled him. He'd finally warmed up after the cold ride, and the rabbit stew was mighty tasty and seemed plentiful enough for him to eat his fill.

Unless he had company, he was used to taking meals—prepared by his housekeeper—alone. Dining with the Thompson family and now the O'Donnells reminded him of the comfort and affection of kinship, of conversing, telling stories, and laughing during supper, when the day's labor had ended. Patrick hadn't realized how much he missed having family ties, with his parents gone and an older married sister living in California.

Henrietta must have decided she'd politely waited long enough for Patrick to take the edge off his hunger, for she set down her fork with a decisive click. "Now, Mr. Gallagher, please tell us of our Sally."

"Patrick," he reminded her.

Everyone stilled, staring at him in expectancy.

Sally. He searched for the best way to politely discuss Sally's delicate condition without actually mentioning her pregnancy. "Uh, according to Bridget, your daughter is still ill in the mornings but feels better later in the day. Sometimes, she, Harry, and Bridget took supper with the Thompsons. On those occasions, I observed Sally's appetite to be fine, although not hearty."

For the first time, Alana looked directly at him and nodded in apparent approval. "As long as the nausea passes at some point, and Sally takes nourishment, she should be fine."

Patrick grinned and then glanced around the table at the family. "Harry is quite the besotted husband. So much so that he's often the butt of the other cowboys' teasing."

Rory chuckled.

Henrietta's thin hand lifted to her chest, and she sighed. "Young love." She exchanged a memory-filled glance with her husband.

Patrick tried not to notice how his stomach tightened at the obvious bond between the couple—the same he'd seen with the Thompsons and the newlywed O'Hanlons—the kind he'd begun wanting for himself. He caught Alana's eye and gave her a charming smile, determined to melt her iciness toward him as the next step in his courtship.

Her eyes widened. She glanced down at her plate and pushed her food around without taking a bite.

Undaunted, Patrick filled in the remainder of the tale. "But Harry takes everything they throw at him with a good-natured grin. Truth be told, I think the hands are all jealous of his wedded bliss." *I certainly was. But I also thought to soon have my own.*

Pleased smiles bloomed on everyone's faces.

Henrietta patted her chest. "You ease my mind, Mr., ah, Patrick."

Rory smiled at her before giving Patrick a nod of obvious approval. "My wife's fretted so about our darling girl, which I believe added to her illness."

Their comments made Patrick feel almost virtuous, as if he'd truly done a good deed, even though he'd come with an ulterior motive. He looked directly at Alana, sure his next bit of news would excite her, bitter though the words tasted in his mouth. "Your sister is newly betrothed to James Whitson."

Alana gasped. "Betrothed?" Her hand flew to cover her mouth. Eyes wide, she stared at him in apparent dismay.

Concerned by her reaction, Patrick rushed out the rest so Alana would be reassured about her sister's choice. "Before I left the Thompson ranch, I heard the cowboys were placing bets about whether Whitson's cabin could go up as quickly as Harry's, and I heard Thompson gave permission for Bridget to plant those potatoes of hers on a piece of land that's not good for grazing." Thankfully, he didn't have any other tidbit of information to offer. He'd escaped the ranch before learning anything more of the couple's plans.

Instead, the added details made Alana look worse—pale and drawn—as if the news of her twin's approaching nuptials had sucked the life out of her.

"James Whitson," Henrietta said slowly. "I'm trying to place him."

Isleen bounced in her seat. "I know Mr. Whitson. He has the pretty gray Appaloosa."

"I know that horse." Charlie straightened. "Dusty." At the family's puzzled looks, he added, "Dusty is the name of his Appaloosa."

Isleen waved for their attention. "One time after school when Idelle was still inside helping Mrs. Gordon, I was skipping down the street. Mr. Whitson rode by, and I was so busy looking at his fine horse that I tripped and fell to my hands and knees. My books and slate went tumbling down. Mr. Whitson jumped off his horse and helped me up, making sure I wasn't hurt."

Idelle frowned. "You never told me," she said, sounding put-upon that her twin would keep a secret from her.

With a pleased toss of her head, Isleen ignored her sister and continued the story. "Mr. Whitson was so nice. He brushed off my skirt and my hands. Then he gathered my books and slate, wiping them clean with his sleeve. My chalk was broken in two, and I was so upset." She dipped her gaze and then looked up again. "He took me into the mercantile and bought me a new one."

"Isleen Mary O'Donnell!" her mother scolded. "I cannot believe you allowed a stranger to purchase something for you."

"I protested, Ma. Really, I did," Isleen said in an innocent tone, her eyes wide and guileless. "But Mr. Whitson insisted, telling me it was his fault I fell."

Rory tried to turn a laugh into a cough but didn't quite succeed. "Well, because of your mishap, at least we know Mr. Whitson is a gentleman with a care for children and a generous spirit, which relieves my mind. But I still want to give my stamp of approval to my niece's marriage—make sure he's not taking advantage of her unsettled situation. After all, Bridget is under my protection."

Henrietta smiled at her husband. "I'm sure I'll be well enough to travel soon, and we'll see them on a Sunday. Then, as her uncle and protector, you'll be able to interrogate the poor man regarding his circumstances and intentions," she said in a teasing tone.

As much as Patrick couldn't abide a discussion about James Whitson, Alana's dismayed reaction worried him far more. He leaned forward. "Miss O'Donnell, my news seems to have come as quite a shock."

"A whirlwind romance." Alana forced a smile. "Mr. Whitson was quite kind when we met." She glanced at her uncle. "He was the reason, really, that we went to the Thompsons' instead of coming here. Now that I think of it, he was quite taken with Bridget." She flicked a narrowed glance at Patrick that said, *and so were you.*

Unable to meet her knowing gaze, Patrick looked away, wishing she hadn't seen his attraction to her sister. *Courting Alana might be more difficult than I thought.*

They lingered at the table long after the last of the food had been consumed, lighting the oil lamps when the sunlight failed. For the first time, Alana saw her uncle's family with an air of happiness, their bodies free of tension as they joked and laughed. They exchanged stories and listened to Patrick's tales of his horse breeding business. He acted at ease with her relatives and that impressed her.

Although upset by the news of her sister's betrothal, Alana wouldn't allow selfishness and fear to mar her enjoyment of the evening. *It's not that I don't want Bridget to be happy.... I just don't know what her marriage will mean for me.* She shoved the news to the back of her mind to ponder when she was alone and focused her attention on her relatives and their guest.

Her aunt and uncle had suspended the children-should-be-seen-and-not-heard formality, and the three young ones obviously enjoyed being part of the conversation. That Patrick didn't seem to mind was a point in his favor. *Not that I'm tallying him.*

Alana found herself softening toward the man. She couldn't deny the thoughtfulness of the gifts he'd brought. The food would help eke out the dwindling supplies in their larder until her uncle would be able to hunt farther afield from the house and the garden began producing.

The cinnamon cookies were a welcome surprise. She'd not made dessert the whole time she'd lived with the O'Donnells, for she hadn't wanted to exhaust Henrietta's small supply of sugar. The peppermint sticks he'd brought, usually a treat only for Christmas, had been an instant hit with the children, although they were shelved for a day when dessert wasn't already present.

This evening, the children were blooming in a way Alana hadn't seen before. She'd known how much their mother's illness had frightened them...the dread they'd carried—*that we all carried*—how in spite of all their efforts and prayers, Henrietta was slipping away. The extra chores had lain heavily on the children's young shoulders. But Charlie and the twins had worked hard without complaint. Under her supervision, they'd still kept up with their studies. Now that their mother was back on her feet, and the weather was better, the three hoped to attend school.

She kept an eye on Henrietta, at first alert to make sure her patient didn't overtire herself. But gradually, she relaxed her watchfulness. The evening was good for Henrietta, and Alana took satisfaction in seeing her aunt's face light up as laughter chased away the malaise caused by her illness.

Patrick recounted a time when he'd been bucked off an ornery horse he was breaking, who seemed to have deliberately aimed to toss him off right onto the biggest pile of horse manure around. "Definitely a soft landing," he finished.

Laughter welled from deep within her and bubbled up. Her sides ached—an almost foreign experience she hadn't felt in a long time. *I can't remember when I last felt so merry—when I last belly laughed.*

Alana remembered that she and Bridget had laughed the night before Alana left the Thompson ranch, but that was the first incident in ages. Before that... She rummaged through her mind, trying to remember a time of mirth. She'd struggled with so much...too much to bear, really—nursing her mother through her last illness, followed by the grief of her death; anxiously waiting for Timkin to propose; Catriona's elopement; their funds dwindling away despite their best efforts; Bridget's determination to move to a new land; Timkin breaking her heart. *Can a year really have passed since I last laughed?*

In her gratitude toward Patrick for bringing the gift of

laughter, for providing them with the opportunity to celebrate life, Alana found herself letting down her guard more. Watching him made unexpected sensations swirl through her. *Too bad he doesn't live here.*

As if he read her thoughts, Patrick looked at her. "What do you think, Miss O'Donnell?"

"Since we are being informal, call me Alana," she said, forgetting she'd planned to keep him at a distance. "Bridget and I have always been addressed by our given names. At home, being called Miss O'Donnell was a sure sign the speaker couldn't tell us apart, and we didn't take that well." She winked at the twins. "Unless we were purposely trying to confuse people."

Isleen giggled, while Idelle tried to look innocent—without quite succeeding.

"Ah, a test." Patrick leaned back in his chair, a mischievous grin on his face. "I don't see how anyone could mix up you and Bridget."

"Ye've only seen me thin," Alana hastened to explain. "Bridget and I used to be more alike. If I had a penny for every time someone mentioned we were *two peas in a pod*...." She sighed. "Well, let's just say I'd have more coins in my pocket right now."

Patrick crossed his arms and shook his head. "Your expressions are different. The way you move. Bridget has more determination in the set of her head, in her step."

Henrietta leaned forward. "You haven't seen her in the sick room, Patrick. I can assure you our Alana is *plenty* determined there."

The wryness in her tone made everyone laugh.

Uncomfortable with his admiring gaze, Alana appreciated her aunt taking Patrick's attention off her. "I'm *determined* to see ye well, dear Aunt."

"Our niece has been such a godsend," Henrietta said to Patrick. "I don't know how we would have managed without her."

Heat warmed her face, and Alana knew she must be blushing.

Patrick gave her a pointed look. "Outside the sickroom, where luckily I've no experience of you, for tonight *doesn't* count," he said firmly. "You have a gentler way about you than your sister."

How would you know? I've practically glared at ye since your arrival.

The appreciative look in his eyes flustered her. *So different from Timkin's friendly acceptance.*

Guilt swamped the pleasurable feelings, and she looked away from him. *How can I possibly compare Timkin to Patrick?*

Alana remembered the comfort she took in Timkin's presence, in the strength of their bond, their long familiarity, how well he understood her, and their silent ways of communicating. *No, Patrick is not at all like Timkin.* But for the first time, the shiny memory of her lost love seemed tarnished.

The change made her uneasy. *Grateful to him or not, the sooner Patrick Gallagher leaves, the better!*

Chapter Five

The next morning, Alana stayed in bed as long as her conscience would allow. She had no desire to see Patrick Gallagher before he left.

In a quiet moment last night, Henrietta had told Alana to sleep late. Her aunt intended to rise early to make breakfast and see the children off to school.

Although Alana had protested, almost to the point of scolding, she couldn't dissuade Henrietta from her determined position. When her aunt, with a wistful expression, commented how much she'd missed being a wife and mother, Alana had given in. But she'd taken the twins aside and whispered instructions, so their mother could *think* she was doing the work, but the girls would actually perform the tasks.

Unfortunately, she couldn't sleep past the time everyone stirred—the open loft meant she heard what was happening in the room below, including Patrick moving around and getting dressed in the semi-darkness.

But she waited until the men went outside to see to the livestock and the children dressed and climbed down the ladder before she rose, dressing hunched over to avoid hitting her head on the low slanted ceiling. She had to sit on her bed to brush her hair, plaiting a braid that she coiled into a bun by feel, and stabbing in hairpins, for no mirror hung in the loft.

The smell of frying ham and coffee drifted her way, and her

stomach grumbled. Her appetite had returned a few weeks ago, and now she looked forward to breakfast, especially since they'd gone through most of the provisions she'd brought with her from the Thompson ranch. All that had been available in the last week to cook for the family were eggs and porridge, for Rory had no success with hunting.

The sound of the front door opening and heavy footsteps on the wooden floor told Alana the men had returned.

"This ham you brought will sure be a treat, Patrick." Henrietta had a lilt in her voice. "We finished our last one right before I became ill."

Alana couldn't help but smile in satisfaction at Henrietta's return to health. With the children attending school today, where they'd see the Thompson children, the news of her mother's recovery would reach Sally before nightfall. She straightened the sheets and blankets on her pallet, and then climbed down the ladder.

The pink-gold light of dawn filtered through the frost-etched windows. The lamp on the table pushed back the shadows into the corners.

The men weren't in sight, but the sounds of masculine voices in the bedroom told her they were washing up.

Her aunt presided at the stove, scrambling eggs. Her color looked good, and her balance more stable than yesterday. But as soon as the children left for school, Alana intended for Henrietta to rest.

The girls were busy setting the table and gave her conspiratorial looks, secretly jabbing their fingers at the middle of the table, where a pot of porridge and a platter of fried ham awaited.

She smiled and nodded, proud of them for helping their mother.

The men emerged from the bedroom, and Rory sniffed the air. "You're cooking up a feast."

"That I am. And grateful to be doing so—both for my recovery and for the provisions Patrick brought."

Charlie nudged his father. "I think we should stay home from school another day in celebration."

"Oh no, you rascal. The celebration is you and your sisters going to school and giving us some peace and quiet."

Charlie made a comical face of disappointment, and everyone laughed.

That was Alana's opening. "Good morning," she said to her family and, with a glance, included Patrick.

They smiled and greeted her.

Her aunt tilted her head in askance. "Did you have a good sleep?"

"Aye, although I feel guilty shirking." With a mock frown, Alana gestured toward the stove.

"Nonsense. You've worked hard these last weeks and deserve a bit of a rest." Henrietta glanced down at the skillet. "Now, everyone, breakfast is ready. Sit yourselves down."

Alana helped her aunt bring the rest of the bounty to the table.

Unlike supper, breakfast was mostly a silent meal. Everyone tucked into the food, with obvious appreciation. As soon as they finished, Henrietta dismissed the children to do their chores before they left for school.

Rory turned to Patrick. "If you could spare the time, I've been needing the strength of another man. I'm building an addition to the barn. It's slow going, for I'm only making progress when I can afford more wood. I've a beam to put up that's too much for Charlie and me to lift on our own."

Patrick took a last slug of his coffee before setting down his cup. "No problem at all. Glad to oblige."

Alana didn't know whether to wish the man would take his leave or feel glad he was sticking around for a few hours. While she and her aunt cleaned the breakfast dishes and worked in silent harmony, Alana thought of Patrick, and of Bridget's engagement to James, and of her own beloved Timkin.

Strangely enough, her memories of Timkin had lost their

vividness. He seemed almost a shadow man compared to Patrick, who was so full of life—in a way that disturbed her, not at all like the secure connection she'd felt with Timkin. Concerned that her feelings for him might be fading, Alana made a concerted effort to remember cherished memories and felt again the familiar ache in her heart. Better the pain than to forget him.

The children rushed in to grab their books and slates, kissed Henrietta and Alana good-bye, and ran out the door. She didn't envy them the long trek to town, far colder and a greater distance than she and her sisters had to walk to the village school. But their neighbor Erik Muth, a dairy farmer who hauled milk to the mercantile, would give the children a ride in the wagon.

After the last dish was dried and put away, Henrietta smoothed down her apron. "I'm going to sit and see to the mending, which will be restful, so you'll have no need to hover over me." She made a shooing motion toward the door. "Go outside and get some fresh air."

"A walk sounds wonderful." Alana glanced out the window. The sun had appeared again, and it looked to be another mild winter day—*mild, that is, for Montana.*

"Rory always likes a cup of coffee about now, when we have beans to spare, of course. You can take some to the men. You go get ready, while I brew more coffee."

Not wanting to see either Patrick or his horse, Alana drew out donning her coat, scarf, hat, and gloves for as long as possible. Finally, she had no more excuses, for to linger would only make Henrietta curious. She took the two Mason jars of hot coffee, wrapped in towels, and left the house.

Outside, a chill wind whipped tendrils of hair into her face, and the breaths she took cut sharp with cold. Alana shivered, grateful for the warmth of the hot coffee jars pressed against her chest. *And they tell me this is unseasonably warm for the winter.*

After crossing the muddy yard, she reached the barn and wrenched open the door, stepping into the dim interior, grateful to be out of the wind. A single lantern hung from a beam in the roof, throwing enough light for her to see Patrick working on Thunder in a nearby stall.

Alana looked away from the horse and tiptoed down the aisle, lest she draw the man's attention. Following the whistling sound of "The Minstrel Boy," she found her uncle in the back of the barn, stacking odds and ends of lumber. Even in the shadowed light, she could see the haunted look Rory had worn so often since her arrival had vanished.

"Ah." He made a sound of pleasure and reached for a Mason jar. "I was just about to go inside and check on your aunt." He unscrewed the top and took a sip.

"She's fine, Uncle Rory. I left her mending one of yer shirts."

"I need to see my beloved with my own eyes." He winked. "And with everyone out of the house, I can do a bit of canoodling with my beautiful wife. Do you think you can give us a few minutes before you come back inside?"

A giggle bubbled out, surprising her with the girlish lightness of the sound. "I can give ye more than a few minutes. How about an hour?"

"I wish for such a long time, but there's work to be done. I'll take half an hour." Tossing her another wink and whistling the ballad, he sauntered out of the barn.

She glanced down at the jar of coffee and reluctantly walked over to the stall where Patrick was grooming Thunder. She could hear him crooning to the Thoroughbred while he worked. *Why can't he be doing something else like chopping wood, where I could bear to stop and watch, instead of having to approach that great beastie?*

Although why would I want to watch Patrick Gallagher?

Discomfited by the thought, Alana squared her shoulders and moved to give the man his coffee. She knocked softly on the frame of the stall, hoping Patrick would step out rather than continue working and make her come to him.

He looked up and smiled, his dark eyes warm.

Ignoring a flutter in her stomach, Alana held out the jar. "I've brought ye some coffee."

"Just what I need." He moved the currycomb over Thunder's back and jerked his head in an invitation to enter.

Her feet remained planted, while her insides still quivered.

His eyes narrowed, and he set down the comb on the crosspiece of the stall wall. "You can come in. Thunder won't hurt you."

Alana shook her head, refusing to look at the Thoroughbred.

"Is it just Thunder, or are you this way with all horses?"

"All." Only the single word slipped out. "But worse with Thunder."

He crossed his arms over his expansive chest. "Why are you so scared?"

Alana couldn't tell him. Her explanation of her fears would only sound ridiculous and make her appear superstitious and silly. Patrick, the avid horseman, wouldn't understand.

He uncrossed his arms and leaned closer, taking the jar of coffee from her and setting it next to the currycomb. "Did you have an accident? Fall off?"

She shook her head, not meeting his eyes.

"See someone else fall off or get hurt?" Although Patrick fired the questions at her, his voice was unexpectedly gentle—the same tone he used with Thunder.

The thought almost pulled a smile out of her. Alana gave Patrick a quick sideways glance but saw only concern on his handsome face. "Ye'll think me foolish."

"I already think you foolish," he teased. "For allowing your fear to keep you from experiencing the joy of horses."

Frowning, Alana stared at the ground. "I see no joy in the creatures."

"That's sad. Of all God's gifts to His people, horses are the biggest blessing."

She couldn't help laughing at that. "I think yer missing a few more important blessings…like family." *Like love.*

"Well, except for my older sister who is married and lives in San Francisco, mine have all passed away. So Thunder and my other horses are my family."

Compassion softened her rigidity. Alana sent up a quick prayer of thanksgiving for Bridget and for her uncle's family who'd become so dear. *And surely, someday, we'll hear from Catriona.*

"Tell me why," Patrick pressed.

She gave a quick glance upward to see the encouragement in his eyes. "I wasn't always so fearful. Not that I was ever horse-mad like our Bridget. As a young girl, I rode now and again."

"What happened, Alana?"

The man is certainly persistent. She sighed and gave in. "A wandering storyteller came to our village, and Da took the family to the pub to hear his tales. At first I thought them splendid. He told of the *Tuatha Dé Danann*, Darby O'Gill and the Good People, and of our last great king Brian Boru, then...." Remembering made her tongue freeze, and her body followed into paralysis.

"Alana." Patrick reached out and took her hand, giving her fingers a squeeze. "Best spit out the story, darlin'. Lance it quickly, as you would a boil."

The image made her chuckle in spite of his brazenness in touching her. The rigidity left her body, and the laughter gave her the impetus to spill out a few words. She pulled away her hand. "He told of the *Pooka*..."

"*Pooka*?"

"Ah, ye *American*! Don't ye know yer Irish history?"

"My grandparents came over from the old country, but they died when I was young."

"A *pooka* is a faerie."

"A fairy," he repeated, his eyebrow cocking in obvious amusement.

"Not—" Alana held her thumb and forefinger a few inches apart "—a sweet wee one with wings. But a dark *Unsídhe* shapeshifter. A sleek black horse with a long wild mane." She waved toward Thunder but didn't look at the horse. "Much like that one, I imagine."

Patrick waited, his gaze on her.

Something about the big, handsome man focusing on her,

listening with his whole being, made her feel protected. *If any human could stand fast against the wiles of the Unsídhe, that man would be Patrick Gallagher.*

"We'd always heard stories of the pooka being a mischievous sort. Apt to stop and have a conversation, or even do good deeds if ye treated him right. But the old storyteller told of a malicious *pooka*, who magicked a young girl into riding him—a beautiful horse, she'd thought. Then the creature turned into an evil beast with sulfurous yellow eyes. The *Pooka* kidnapped her and gave her the most terrifying ride of her life. Never again did the girl venture out of doors, even in bright daylight, for fear of encountering the *pooka*."

"The story frightened you?"

"Aye. Terrified me. The old man stared straight at me with a piercing glare, as if warning me I'd be next. That night, I had a nightmare...*nightmares*.... 'Twere those that did the worst of the damage. I'd wake up screaming after dreaming a pooka kidnapped me." She shuddered. "I couldna bear the sight of a horse, especially a black one."

"Do you still have nightmares?

"No.... I had some when we left Ireland. I guess, ye could say that the ship was a kind of *pooka* bearing me away from my homeland, so to speak. But I don't scream anymore. Even Bridget doesn't know. She thinks I outgrew them."

Staring at the stall wall, Alana waited for Patrick to make fun of her admission. Silence stretched out. Finally, she succumbed to curiosity and risked a glance at him.

He watched her, one hand on the horse's neck. An unexpected tenderness showed in those long-lashed dark eyes. "I'm honored that you confided in me."

Relief rushed through her, accompanied by another warm emotion—one she couldn't identify. "*Honored,* ye say? *Confided* is what ye call it, eh?" She spoke sharply to cover the emotion welling up from his words. "I think ye poked and prodded and *badgered* the story out of me."

"I did," Patrick said with a cocky grin and a lift of an eyebrow. "However, you could have refused to tell me. Even fled back to the house and left me standing here. But you didn't."

He's right. Alana didn't want to think what confiding in him might mean. *Why, I never even told Timkin of my nightmares.*

What is it about this man that made me open up to him?

Patrick smoothed a hand down Thunder's neck. "Come, Alana. Make friends with my boy, here. Unlike most Thoroughbreds, he's as gentle as the day is long—at least until you get him on a racetrack." He fished in his pocket and pulled out a carrot. With a challenging grin, he broke the carrot in half and gave her a piece. His hand extended, he waited for her to respond.

In a childish reaction, Alana tucked her hands behind her back, but she slid a glance toward the horse.

Thunder turned his head and looked at her reproachfully with soft brown eyes, as if she'd hurt his feelings.

Reassured by the horse's calm demeanor, she rolled her eyes and snatched the carrot from Patrick. "Fine. Then maybe ye won't be a pesterin' me anymore."

He laughed.

With a huff to hide her nervousness, she turned to face Thunder. Instead of jerking away her gaze, she looked at the horse—the intelligent dark eyes in a well-chiseled head, the long neck and deep chest. For the first time, she *saw* the Thoroughbred and not the creature from her nightmares.

Alana straightened her trembling hand. With the carrot resting on her flattened palm, she held out the treat.

Seeing Alana's pinched expression and the fear in her eyes bothered him. An unexpected feeling of protectiveness seized Patrick so strongly that he had to clench his jaw to keep from backing down. He'd seen her solicitous behavior toward Henrietta and the children, seen her laugh out loud, and admired her pretty looks and musical accent that reminded him of his grandparents. But her vulnerability tugged his growing affection into something perilously deeper.

Alana hesitated before extending a shaking hand toward the horse.

That a girl. He kept the words unsaid. She needed to do this on her own. He could only stand close enough to touch her and provide silent support, inwardly cheering her on. Not only did he want this accomplishment for her, but also because her terror of horses created an obstacle to his courtship.

Thunder stepped forward.

Alana stood her ground.

His admiration grew. *She has more courage than a man who's about to mount the wildest bucking bronco.*

The horse dipped his head and daintily lipped the carrot.

Alana's expression relaxed, although her shoulders remained stiff. "I'd remembered their big teeth but forgotten how velvety soft their mouths are." She spoke quietly, as if to herself, still focused on the horse.

Thunder crunched down the piece and checked for more, snuffling her hand and then becoming friendly enough to explore her arm, planting a horse kiss on her cheek—a familiarity he hadn't even allowed himself. *Someday, I'll tease her about Thunder gettin' in the first kiss.*

She giggled and touched Thunder's nose, petting him.

That little sound freed the tension inside Patrick. "I believe I heard a giggle."

With a shy smile, Alana cast him an almost flirtatious look from under her eyelashes.

"Shall I teach you to ride?"

Her smile fell away. "I know how to ride," Alana said stiffly, avoiding eye contact. "I just haven't done so since I was eight." She lowered her hand and glanced toward the barn door. "I must be getting back to Henrietta. She's full of vigor this morning, but I expect she'll droop any time now."

That she lingered instead of heading back to the house raised a hope that Alana wanted more of his company. Patrick decided not to push her to ride, lest he cause her to high-tail back to the house before he had a chance to discuss courting her. *Best gallop at the fence before she runs away.*

Having *badgered*, as Alana called it, the secret fear out of her and seen her soften to him, he felt confident enough to risk taking the next step. "I came out here to court you."

Alana's eyes went wide. This time she stepped back. "Be ye daft?" she asked, her tone sharp and breathy. "One conversation does not a marriage make."

Although startled by her reaction, Patrick figured he'd just surprised her. "I said *courting*, Alana. I'm not asking you to wed me this minute."

"I'm not looking to wed."

He raised an eyebrow, not really believing her. *Don't all women want to get married?* "Wed any man or me in particular?"

With a weary expression, Alana's shoulders slumped, and she shook her head. "Both, perhaps. I'm not looking to wed and—" she lifted her chin toward Thunder "—I don't think we would suit."

Figuring she just needed some extra persuading, Patrick pressed on. "While I think you have no need to fear my horses—they total about twenty—you should know that I own a fine house…have some money set aside. I can offer you a good life."

"My life is good as it is."

The sadness in her eyes belied her words.

"What is it, really, Alana, that you have against my suit?" Patrick coaxed, still confident he could get her to come around to his way of thinking. "Tell me?"

"Because I've spoken to ye about my *pooka* nightmares does not mean I'm willing to give up more to ye…." Her voice broke, and she seemed to crumple. Then she took a breath and straightened. "I thank ye for the honor ye do me," she said formally. "But, ye have not engaged my affections, so I must ask ye to respect my decision and leave." She waved a dismissing motion, spun, and strode from the barn.

He stared after her, unexpectedly feeling bereft.

Chapter Six

Once more rejected by an O'Donnell sister, Patrick rode towards Sweetwater Springs, his spirits lower than the mud ground under Thunder's hooves. *So much for my delusion that Alana would be less stubborn and more manageable than Bridget.*

The shamrock necklace burned in his pocket. *What a waste of money.* He was tempted to fling the piece of jewelry out onto the prairie as far as he could.

His chest ached. This time, he suspected his heart was more wounded from his failed attempt at wooing Alana than from his proposal to Bridget. *Ye have not engaged my affections.* Her words sent a bullet through his heart.

With Bridget, Patrick now knew he'd only felt a superficial attraction and a bond formed by their compatibility in regards to their love of horses. On the surface, Alana and he seemed to have nothing in common. Yet her sweetness—with just enough tart—had soaked through the hard shell of his heart.

For a long time, he rode with his insides frozen and his mind going over and over why he'd failed. The horse followed the road without his guidance. Then he conjured up images of Alana laughing at dinner last night and opening up to him this morning, bravely sharing her fears in spite of the potential for his judgment.

Now what? Patrick figured he'd retreat to his stud farm to lick his wounds, focus on work, and put all thoughts of courtship, especially with blue-eyed, Irish lasses, out of his mind. *Life will be just like it was before.*

He tried to believe the words, but Patrick sensed he'd be fighting loneliness. *Hopefully someday, I'll be ready again to court a woman—although not until the far future.*

Lost in his painful thoughts, he rode through a thicket of trees near a stream, budding limbs thrusting over the road. A rustle in the branches above yanked his thoughts to the present. At the corner of his vision, a shadow moved.

The hairs on the back of his neck stood up.

Panther! Fear stabbed him. Patrick cursed that his Colt was tucked in the holster under his coat. Leaning forward, he kneed Thunder. But the command came too late.

Something heavy landed on his back. *Man, not beast!* An arm wrapped around his throat.

A second man in a black coat dropped from a tree in front of Thunder, hat pulled low, scarf hiding most of his face. On the landing, he stumbled.

Thunder shied.

The robber missed his grab for the horse's reins.

Although unbalanced by his assailant, Patrick gripped Thunder with his legs. He tightened the reins and sawed the Thoroughbred around, fighting to stay upright in the saddle.

But the man's weight on Patrick's shoulders pulled him back over the horse's rump. He gripped tight with his legs, but the momentum proved to be too much, and he came out of the saddle.

With a final tug, his attacker jumped free, landing to the side of the horse, and staggering several steps away.

As he fell back, Patrick twisted to slap Thunder's rump and yelled, "Hah!"

The horse snorted and bolted back the way they'd come.

Relief flashed. *They'll never catch him.*

The outlaw cursed.

Patrick had only a second to realize he'd just put the

O'Donnells in danger before he thudded to the ground. The back of his head hit something hard, and his vision went dark.

After their visitor left, Alana stayed in the house. She chivvied her protesting aunt into bed to rest, and then surveyed the main room with an eye for a task that would take her mind off Patrick and his intentions. *I could scrub the floor.* But she knew from experience that her hands could tackle the familiar tasks of housework while her mind kept ruminating.

The walls of the cabin closed in on her. She wanted to escape, but there was no place to go. *I need to get outside.*

She grabbed her coat and shrugged into it, pulling on her cap. After winding the scarf around her neck, she tugged on her gloves.

Once outside, Alana breathed deeply of the cold, pure air and trudged along an icy path to the barn to locate her uncle and found him mending a harness.

Rory looked up and smiled. "I'm catching up on all the tasks I'd set aside while Henrietta was ill. I've quite a list."

"I'm going for a walk."

"Aye, it's a fine day for wintertime. Could almost believe spring was right around the corner. Good for you to get out in the fresh air and stretch your legs." He set the harness on his lap. "You've been cooped up too long. Might as well enjoy the weather while it lasts, because it surely won't. Montana has a fine way of a teasin' us into wishful thinking, then dropping a load of snow on our heads."

"I haven't had a ramble since we left home."

"Just follow the road, or if you go in a different direction, stay in sight of the house. If you're in mind for company, turn to the left when you reach the road. I'm sure Daisy Muth will be glad to make your acquaintance."

"Actually, I've a mind to be alone. I'll head in the direction of town."

Rory shot her a sharp look but only nodded. "Aye, sometimes one needs to be outdoors and under God's great spaces." He jerked up his chin in a gesture to the vivid blue sky. "Has a way of putting things in perspective, it does."

I hope so. "I'm looking forward to it, Uncle."

"Enjoy your walk." Rory smiled and turned back to his mending.

Once on her way down the road, the countryside stretching as far as the eye could see was white patched with brown and looked drab to her eyes. She headed down the track that led to the road, following the children's footprints and Thunder's hoofprints in the slushy mud. At the road, she turned right toward Sweetwater Springs, noting wagon tracks and more hoofprints. Erik Muth's milk wagon, she surmised. The footprints ceased, and she figured that was the spot the children must have caught a ride with their neighbor.

Once on the road, she stopped studying the ground and looked up, hoping to find the guidance she needed. Some clouds as fat and puffy as a flock of sheep before shearing drifted across the rich blue sky. *I made the right decision to reject Patrick's proposal.* Alana wasn't sure if she was speaking to herself or to God. *So why do I feel so strange?*

The heavens didn't open up with an angel appearing to give her an answer, but still she felt encouraged to continue the mental conversation. *I don't even like the man.* She paused. *Well, I didn't at first, but apparently, he grew on me.*

She walked farther in silence. *Why did he have to say he wanted to court me? Why couldn't he have let things be?* "He ruined everything." She tramped a few steps, mud squishing under her feet, as if pounding the dilemma into the ground.

Alana slowed and let out a sigh. *Too much change.*

She thought of Bridget's approaching marriage and wondered why her sister hadn't sent a letter with Patrick. She didn't even know if her twin wanted Alana to live with her after the wedding.

Emptiness gaped inside—in her heart, in her life. When they'd set out on this unwanted journey to America, Alana had thought at least she and her twin would be together. *Now I'll be on my own in a foreign country.* She let out a sigh.

She had no doubt her aunt and uncle would want her to live with them. They certainly could use her help. But now that her aunt was nearly well and able to do more, Alana felt at loose ends.

As she walked, Alana sorted through her feelings—everything from Timkin, to Bridget's upcoming marriage, to Patrick's sudden and surprising intentions, and now this inexplicable sense that she might have made the wrong decision. *Would I have accepted if he'd singled me out from the beginning and not focused first on Bridget?*

Alana didn't know the answer to that question, but figured she would have felt more willingness to at least consider his suit if he'd been drawn to her first. She hadn't reached any conclusion before movement made her glance up the road to see Thunder loping toward her, stirrups bouncing, saddle empty.

Something's happened to Patrick! Heart pounding in time with the hoofbeats, she glanced behind her for help only to see the farm was out of sight—too far to run for her uncle.

She bit her lip and faced forward toward the approaching horse, as big and black as a *pooka*. Her stomach tightened until Alana thought she might be sick. Her instinct was to flee, but she swallowed down the terror rising up to choke her.

Concern for Patrick overrode her fear of the horse. Instead of stepping back, Alana forced herself to slowly walk forward, hand extended. "Thunder," she crooned as the horse came to her, hooves crunching in the snow. She planted her feet to hold her ground.

The Thoroughbred slowed to a stop, snorted, and tossed his head. His nostrils were flared and his sides heaved. He took a step toward her.

"Easy now," Alana said, letting him grow calmer. "There ye be." She patted Thunder's nose, inhaling the smell of horse and stroking his neck, the smooth movement a contrast to her rapidly beating heart.

Thunder nickered, as if giving her encouragement.

"Thank ye, beautiful, boyo." Once more she glanced behind her, as if the farmhouse had magically moved closer. Only the image of Patrick lying injured on the cold ground somewhere drove her decision. *If I hesitate, he might die.*

Alana kilted up her skirt and petticoat, tucking them into her waistband. She gathered the reins, brushed her hand over Thunder's neck and shoulder, and grabbed the saddle horn, stretching her left foot to reach the stirrup. For a panicked moment, Alana realized the horse was too big, and she wouldn't make it without help.

Desperately wishing for a mounting block, she lifted her leg higher and hopped, finally thrusting her foot into the stirrup. With a bounce, she hauled herself up, landing in the saddle with an ungraceful thump. "Sorry, Thunder, sorry," she apologized, feeling sure the Thoroughbred had never felt such an ungainly mount in his life.

Once in the saddle, she couldn't reach her feet to the stirrups. Alana reminded herself of those times she rode bareback as a girl. But Thunder was no pony. *I'm so high off the ground.* Her hands shook.

Thunder shifted and danced a little, blowing out a breath.

She grabbed the horn and clung with her legs, keeping her seat.

If the Thoroughbred took it into his head to bolt, Alana would be off in a few strides. *I'll have a long fall to the ground. Hopefully, the snow and mud will cushion my landing.*

She took a deep breath for courage, released the horn, and evened out the reins. *Please, dear Lord, keep me in the saddle so I can find Patrick. Please keep him safe.*

She wheeled Thunder around and kneed him into a canter.

After sloshing in the too-big saddle, Alana caught a rhythm remembered from her childhood before the *Pooka* fears overtook her, and she settled into the ride.

As they moved, she scanned the road, searching for some sign of Patrick, to no avail. The way was open, but snowdrifts and small hills could hide him from view if he'd crawled away from the road. She slowed the horse to a walk to watch for signs, wondering if she was doing the right thing when speed might be of the essence. She followed Mr. Muth's sleigh rails and Thunder's hoofprints for about a mile.

Not until Alana reached some trees near a stream did she see Patrick sprawled on his back on the road. Her heart kicked, and she gasped, grabbing the saddle horn and urging the horse to a trot, uncaring of how she bounced in the saddle. *Please don't be dead.*

A few feet away, she reined to a stop and slid off the horse, looping the reins around a low tree branch and trusting the well-trained horse would stay. She rushed to Patrick's side and dropped to her knees in the snow-churned mud. Guilt gripped her. *This is all my fault. If only I hadn't sent him away!*

His eyes were closed, his skin gray.

Praying hard, Alana ripped off her mittens, stuffing them into her pocket, and touched the side of his neck. Feeling a pulse, she went momentarily weak as a wave of relief washed through her, then she checked him over.

Expertly, she ran her hands down his arms and legs, feeling for broken bones. Thankful not to find anything wrong, she studied the angle of his head. His neck didn't appear to be broken, but she had no choice but to move him and hope not to cause more damage. Gently, she slid her palm under his head and felt the stickiness of blood. Her fear deepened. A rock scratched the back of her hand. *Head injury.*

Alana glanced at the red blood on her palm and rose to her feet. She ran to the stream, the banks edged with ice, crouched and rinsed off the blood in the freezing water. Her fingers went numb. She yanked a handkerchief from her sleeve and dunked the cloth before standing. As she wrung out the cloth, she saw two sets of new hoof prints heading in the direction of town. Without giving them any thought, she hurried back to kneel by Patrick.

He hadn't stirred.

"Patrick," she said, running the wet handkerchief over his face, trying to bring him back to consciousness. "Patrick."

He didn't rouse.

Her throat tightened. Alana folded the handkerchief and left the cold cloth on his forehead. She reached to tug loose her petticoat, ripping a long strip from the hem, and then a larger piece, which she made into a pad. Gently lifting his head a few inches, she wiped the blood and dirt with the wet handkerchief, and then placed the pad over the wound, using the long strip to tie the makeshift bandage in place.

How long has he been unconscious? She patted his cheeks. "Patrick, please wake up. Patrick!"

He moaned but didn't open his eyes.

"Come on," she encouraged. "All the way now, ye great sleeping giant."

He blinked, showing unfocused eyes.

"That's better." She gave him a reassuring smile.

He stared at her without recognition.

"Patrick, it's Alana."

"Ah, there are two of you," he murmured. "Is Bridget here?"

"Ye have a concussion." Alana squeezed his gloved hand. "That's why yer seeing double. Ye've fallen from Thunder and hit yer head."

Her words seemed to penetrate, for he jerked as if to rise. "Thunder?" he asked in an urgent tone.

She pressed him back, slipping her other hand behind his head, taking care to make sure he missed the rock. "Thunder's just fine. He's right here." She gestured toward the horse.

"Outlaws," he croaked. "Jumped me. Take Thunder and ride to safety. Hurry."

With a gasp of fear, Alana snapped her gaze up, scanning the area. No sign of anyone. "They're long gone," she said, trying to assure both herself and him. "If they were still here, they'd have attacked by now. And I saw two sets of hoofprints heading toward town."

"Go," he ordered, grabbing her hand on his chest and pushing her away. "Leave me."

"I'm not leaving ye alone." She made her tone firm. "I don't know yet all that is wrong with ye, but I'd be more worried if ye didn't remember what happened."

He groaned.

"I wish we didn't have to move ye. I'd rather not risk it. But we've no choice. Ye can't stay here. The ground is cold, and I don't want ye catching a chill on top of yer head wound. The injury won't kill ye, but in yer weakened state, an illness could."

"Give me a minute." He took a breath and tried to lever himself up but only succeeded in rising a few inches.

Alana thrust an arm under his back to help.

The effort made the pallor in his face whiter still. Once in a sitting position, he paused, taking several panting breaths. "My head's spinning," he ground out, his jaw clenched. "I'm as weak as a babe."

"Shows what ye know about babies," she retorted, hoping to take his mind off his pain. "They are quite determined when they set their minds to something."

He gave her a half smile. "Hardly a gentle bedside manner, you've got there."

"*When* we get ye into a bed, *then* I'll show ye a gentle bedside manner." She nudged his back with her arm, encouraging him to rise. "Up with ye now."

Propping an elbow on the ground, he made as if to rise.

She helped him sit up.

"Can ye stand? Lean on me." She lifted his arm over her head, lowering it to her shoulders.

He sucked in a sharp breath. "Give me a minute. I'm dizzy"

"A minute is all ye have. I'm not wanting ye to catch cold,

and I've got to wash that head wound proper and stitch it up." His arm lay heavy across her shoulders, as if he didn't have the strength to hold it up. "Ye must be bruised from head to toe."

Patrick glanced at her, winced at the movement. His eyes still looked unfocused, but a wry grin pulled at the corner of his mouth. He tapped her shoulder. "Too bad I'm not in a condition to enjoy this."

"Oh, ye!" she scolded, becoming aware of their bodies pressed together, how close his lips were to hers. She tried to distance herself by donning the role of healer. *He's now my patient.* But the reminder didn't stop heat from flooding her cheeks. "If yer well enough to flirt, yer strong enough to get to yer feet."

Patrick winked. "Right now, it's much easier to flirt with a pretty lady than to move."

"Get along with ye, then, Patrick Gallagher," she said sharply to cover how his compliment pleased her.

He slowly turned his head in Thunder's direction and let out a shaky whistle to summon him closer. "Pathetic sound."

Thunder ambled over, ducking his head to snuffle Patrick's face.

"I'm all right, boy. Glad you escaped capture." He inhaled and tilted forward, pushing to his feet as she rose with him, and leaned heavily on her.

She stood pressed against him in an intimate embrace.

He bent and dropped a kiss on her lips, then gave her a wry grin. "This is definitely worth the pain."

Flustered, Alana leaned away. "Behave, or I'll leave ye to stand on yer own," she scolded. An idle threat, for she couldn't risk him toppling back to the ground. And truth be told, she didn't mind the kiss. *Perhaps under different circumstances....*

Patrick reached out to place an unsteady hand on Thunder's neck and wobbled forward, obviously trying not to lean much on her. He paused at the stirrup, patted his hip, checked his pocket, and cursed. "Those thieves stole my gun, holster and all. My money, too."

She sucked in a breath. "Wicked men!"

"I'm lucky they didn't strip me naked. Probably figured Thunder running loose would alert someone, and they needed to get away fast."

"Thank goodness Thunder did just that, else you'd have taken quite a chill and might have gotten very ill."

"If I get my hands on them…." He took a steadying breath. "I still have Thunder, and that's what's most important." Patrick rubbed a hand over the horse's neck. "Right, boy?"

The stud shook his head, as if agreeing.

"I'm glad I trained him to stand when I mount. But he's going to be surprised when I land in the saddle like a tub of lard."

"Thunder's recently had practice. The way I plopped onto the saddle, he must have thought a couple of sacks of beans dropped atop him."

He turned sharply, wincing at the movement. "You rode him?"

His eyes were clearer than she'd yet seen. A good sign. "Had to," Alana said dryly. "I found him wandering down the road with ye nowhere in sight."

"My brave girl," he said, staring at her lips as if about to kiss her again.

Alana wasn't sure if she wanted him to or not. "I had no choice. I was too far from the house to run for help."

"Still took courage to master such a deep fear, my brave Alana. You have my most sincere thanks."

"Thank me when we get ye safely home." She'd meant to speak tartly, but the words came out sounding breathless.

"Well, now that I have your permission, we'd best be gettin' on our way," Patrick drawled. He grabbed the saddle horn, slipped his foot into the stirrup, and with a grunt of pain, hoisted himself up.

Patrick looked about to lose momentum, so Alana gave his buttocks a push that toppled him into the saddle. She lowered her hands, still feeling the press of his hard muscles on her palms. "Ye made it."

Alana bent down and picked up her bloody wet handkerchief and used the clean edges to wipe her hands free of mud and blood. Wrinkling her nose at the state of the cloth, she bunched the handkerchief into a ball and slipped it into her free pocket. She wiped her hands on a dry spot on her coat, pulled out her gloves, and tugged them on.

"With some extra help." He extended a hand and slipped his foot out of the stirrup. "Your turn. Best ride astride instead of pillion."

She clasped her hands in front of her. "Oh, no. I'll walk." This time her reluctance didn't stem from mounting Thunder but because of how closely she'd have to ride pressed against Patrick. She lifted her chin in the direction of the road home, indicating he move along without her.

For the first time, an impatient expression crossed Patrick's face. "I'm not leaving you behind with outlaws on the loose. By the time you get home, night will have fallen. Either get on the horse, or I'll dismount and walk with you."

Alana bit her lip. *He's right.* "Don't look," she commanded, stooping to grab her hem. Once again, she tucked up her skirt and ruined petticoat. She placed her hand in his. "Here goes." Hefting herself up, she pulled on his arm to help swing her leg high enough to step into the stirrup, and swung her other leg over. Overbalancing, she gasped and grabbed Patrick's waist.

Patrick grunted.

Feeling guilty for causing him pain, she stayed still, her hands tight on his hips. The back of his coat was caked with mud, which she knew had just transferred to hers.

"You steady?"

No. Her heartbeat wobbled. With her legs on either side of him, her nose filled with his man scent, her breasts pressed against his back.... *How could I possibly be steady?*

"Go ahead," she urged, trying to calm her heart and eased away a few inches.

He placed a hand over hers to apparently keep her close and

kneed Thunder into a walk. "Gonna be a slow journey home."

"At least we're moving, and yer not lying dead back there." The thought made her throat tight.

"Guess that's one benefit of a hard head."

She couldn't bring herself to answer.

"I owe you a new petticoat." His hand gave hers a squeeze.

Heat suffused her face. "I told ye not to look!"

"I wasn't looking, at least not most of the time. I did have to peek to make sure you got on the horse without falling off."

She wasn't about to discuss her undergarments and hoped he wouldn't press the issue.

A wagon appeared in the distance drawn by a team coming toward them.

Alana squinted and made out her uncle driving his mules. Guilt stabbed her. She'd been gone a long time, and he must be worried.

Patrick released her hands. He guided Thunder to the side of the road.

Rory pulled up beside them, his expression tight. He set the brake and glanced from Patrick's bandage to Alana. "Are you all right?" he asked, his tone urgent.

"I'm fine, Uncle Rory," she hastened to assure him.

"I was attacked," Patrick explained in a bitter tone. "Two varmints jumped me from a tree. Trying to steal Thunder, I presume. Knocked me out, but the horse got away, thank goodness."

Rory let out a Gaelic curse. "You two keep going back to the house. I've left your aunt unprotected." He shot Patrick a sharp glance. "You have a gun?"

Patrick shook his head and then groaned. "They took my Colt. But I'll protect the women if I need to throw rocks."

He's in no condition to do any protecting.

Rory nodded. "I'm going after the children."

Alana gasped, thinking of her vulnerable cousins encountering the outlaws. After school, they'd catch a ride from their classmates' father who worked in town. Then they'd walk several miles from the friends' homestead to their own. *Oh, dear Lord, protect them, please. Mary, Blessed Mother, keep them safe.*

His expression grim, Rory tied off the reins. He reached under the seat of the wagon, flipped down the side of a long wooden box and pulled out a rifle, setting it across his lap. "Once I pick up the children, I'll keep going into town and inform the sheriff. Thank the Good Lord we have one now; she's new, only here since Christmas."

She? A female sheriff? That can't be. I must have heard wrong.

Rory narrowed his eyes, studying Patrick's face. "Do you need me to send for the doctor?"

"No, I'll trust in Alana's skill and capable hands."

"Aye, you are right to do so."

Patrick nodded. "Take care." He urged Thunder forward.

Rory flicked the reins, and the mules started up.

Alana leaned her chin on Patrick's shoulder. "Do you think the children are in danger?" She felt his hesitation in the way he drew a breath. "Tell me true, Patrick. Don't lie to make me feel better."

"If the girls were older, maybe, but since your cousins have nothing valuable to steal, they have nothing to interest the thieves. Possibly the robbers will leave the road when they get close to town. The children might not even set eyes on them."

The two fell silent on the rest of the way.

Alana grew more and more chilled. Kneeling on the damp ground had soaked through the front of her skirt and undergarments. But at least Patrick's body protected her from the worst of the wind. She fretted that the cold on top of his injuries might make him ill.

When they reached the farm, Sian ran out to greet them, barking, until Alana calmed the dog. He walked alongside them, wagging his tail.

When they arrived at the front of the barn, Patrick reined in. He twisted and took Alana's hand, aiding her to reach the ground. "Go to your aunt, let her know you're safe."

"I'll help ye first."

He held up a hand to stop her. "I can manage from here. I need to see to Thunder. Tell Henrietta what happened before she sees me with my head bandaged. She'll be terrified enough when she hears her family might be in danger."

He's right. Alana capitulated. Lips pressed tight, she nodded her agreement, doubting Patrick could manage the horse as easily as he made it seem. She'd give Henrietta the news and head right back to the barn. She pushed open the barn door for Thunder to walk through and rushed toward the house. She slowed to enter, not wanting to burst in and startle her aunt.

Henrietta stood at the stove, stirring something in a pot that smelled like ham and cabbage soup. Her aunt glanced up, and a relieved look crossed her face. Flour dusted her hands and arms. Two loaves of unbaked bread sat on a tray on the table to rise. She dropped the wooden spoon. "At last! Your uncle and I were so worried. You look frozen through." She hurried over and started to give Alana a hug before pulling back. "Why are you all muddy?" She held her at arms length to study her face. "What happened? Are you all right?"

"I am well, dearest aunt. But I have bad news. Patrick was attacked near where the road crosses a stream."

"Oh, no! Will he be all right?"

"Aye, with time. Thieves tried to steal his horse and knocked him unconscious. Luckily Thunder escaped. I found Patrick and tended to his wounds. The robbers were nowhere in sight when I arrived, but their tracks led back to town."

Henrietta gasped, a hand flying to her throat. "The children!"

"Uncle Rory has gone for them. He knows the situation and has the rifle with him." She repeated what Patrick had said about her cousins' safety.

Lines grooved Henrietta's forehead, and she didn't appear reassured. She crossed herself, her lips moving in prayer.

Alana eased her aunt away from the stove. "Let's get ye seated." She helped Henrietta to walk over to collapse into the nearest chair. "I'll make some tea."

Henrietta clutched Alana's hand. "Do you think they'll attack here?"

"Patrick's in the barn now but will keep guard." Alana released her aunt. She didn't mention the stolen gun.

"What about warning the neighbors?" Henrietta's voice quavered.

"We have no one to spare to go to them. But, remember, the outlaws' tracks were heading in the opposite direction toward town, so I think everyone out this way is safe for tonight. By tomorrow, maybe the sheriff will have caught the robbers, and they'll be sitting in jail."

"That will be a worry gone. But I'll be fretting and praying until my husband and children are safe."

I will be, too.

"Bring me my rosary, will you, dear? It's hanging by my bed."

"I know. I borrowed it a few times when I nursed ye and didn't want to climb into the loft for mine." Alana patted Henrietta's shoulder. "After I make yer tea, I'm going out to the barn to help Patrick."

"In that case, be sure to push the pot to the cool side of the stove. I can reheat it later. "I was just making egg noodles to go in the soup."

Alana glanced at the counter to the dough in the bowl and forced a smile. "My favorite." She grabbed Henrietta's hand before her aunt moved back to the stove."

"I might be a while. Patrick has a terrible concussion, and I don't want him to collapse."

"Oh, dear me. Fear for my children put the thought of his injuries right out of my mind. You must insist he come inside."

"I can insist all I want. That doesn't mean the stubborn man will listen," Alana said in an ironic tone.

"I'm sure you can persuade him."

I don't know about that. On the ride back, neither of them had mentioned their last conversation—specifically, her rejection.

Indeed, once she'd spotted Thunder running loose, Alana hadn't given Patrick's offer a thought until right now. They'd had more important matters to cope with.

Alana took down the canister of tea—the treasured beverage now replenished by Patrick's generosity—and scooped some leaves into a strainer. She pushed the pot of soup to the back of the stove and picked up the kettle, pouring hot water over the leaves. While she was at the task, she decided to brew willow bark tea for Patrick to help his headache and body soreness.

While both teas steeped, she fetched the rosary, pressing the cross into Henrietta's palm. Her aunt's face was still pale, and her eyes showed the strain of her worry. But Alana had done what she could to ease her fears.

She donned her coat and left the house for the barn. She glanced down the road, hoping for a sight of her uncle's wagon, even though she knew he couldn't possibly have made it to town and back.

We have a long wait ahead of us.

Please, dear Lord and the Blessed Mother, keep them safe and bring them home forthwith.

Chapter Seven

The moment he saw Alana enter the house, Patrick sagged in the saddle, grateful to no longer have to hide his pain. His head pounded, his stomach churned with nausea, and his side ached like the devil had stabbed him with a pitchfork. He suspected one of the horse thieves had taken out his ire over Thunder's escape by kicking him. He didn't think his ribs were broken, just badly bruised. Otherwise, Patrick suspected he wouldn't be able to move or breathe.

With a groan, he dismounted, leading Thunder into the barn and closing the door, all of which taxed his strength. Moving with leaden legs, Patrick led the stud into the stall he'd used last night and removed the bridle. Thank goodness the pail still held water.

Thunder drank thirstily.

Patrick managed to unbuckle the girth without leaning over too far, but he had to grit his teeth to lift off the saddle, hefting it on top of the stall wall. His head throbbed, and his stomach roiled. The move had him gasping and dizzy. He leaned against Thunder until the wave of pain ceased, and he was sure he wouldn't cast up his accounts.

He shuffled toward Thunder's head and picked up the pail, carrying it out of the stall and setting it down in the aisle. He staggered to the feed bin and scooped up some grain, making a mental note to replenish Rory's feed beyond what he'd brought, for he'd surely be staying a few more days with the O'Donnells until he healed.

He'd just poured the grain into the feed bin when he heard the barn door slide open. He turned to see Alana coming toward him. She had an air of determination about her, and Patrick figured he'd best not try to argue her back to the house because it wouldn't do any good. Instead, he grabbed a cloth and started wiping Thunder's back.

"What are ye doing?" Her voice rose.

He kept his gaze on his task. "Seeing to my horse like a man's supposed to." He couldn't help the bite to his tone.

Alana grabbed the cloth from him. "I'll do that!" With her hip, she shoved him aside.

He couldn't help a hiss of pain.

She stopped and stared at him, eyes wide in obvious consternation. "Patrick, I'm so sorry!"

Clenching his jaw, he held up a hand in a forgiving motion.

Her eyes narrowed, and she shook the rag in his face. "Ye shouldn't be doing this."

"Far worse would have to be done to me before I'd neglect my horse. Besides treating him right as a man should his faithful mount, the majority of my livelihood comes from Thunder—not just the stud fees for his services but also the purses he wins in races." He ran a hand down Thunder's sleek shoulder. "His loss would have devastated me."

The horse turned and snuffled at Patrick's arm.

"He's irreplaceable."

Her mouth formed into an *O*.

Patrick wanted to bend and kiss her but figured by the time he got his stiff body to move, she'd step away, and he'd be smooching air. Instead, he tried to recapture the rag.

Alana jerked the cloth out of his limited reach. "Oh, no ye don't." She placed a hand on Thunder's back and began to rub. "Ye stay there and tell me what to do."

Looking at her determined expression, he couldn't help but

marvel and feel her sink deeper into his heart. "Is this the woman who wouldn't even look at my horse this morning?"

"A lot has changed since then," Alana said tartly, running the cloth along the horse's sides.

She didn't look at him, but he could see a blush creeping into her cheeks, which gave him a sudden feeling of hope. *Does that include her feelings about eventually marrying me? Have her affections changed?*

Maybe this situation isn't so bad after all. It will give me time to court Alana. He opened his mouth to say so, but then had a sudden fear that her feelings had only softened toward him because he was wounded and she was his nurse. *No, I'll wait to speak until I'm healed, and she has no choice but to see me as a man, not as a patient.*

The eagerness he felt somewhat eased the pounding in his head, although Patrick couldn't help wondering how long his recovery would take.

Not until they'd entered the house and Patrick struggled to remove his coat did Alana realize far more was wrong with him than a head injury and general soreness from his fall. She took his coat, surveyed the muddy back, and hung the garment so it wouldn't touch anything. Later she'd drape it over a chair by the fire to dry, so she could brush off the mud.

She glanced down at herself. Her skirt was damp and dirty from kneeling in the mud. The front of her coat would also have to be dried and cleaned. *Later, after I see to Patrick's wound.*

Alana narrowed her eyes and studied his body, realizing he was favoring one side. She skimmed her fingertips over the area, only touching his shirt. "I want to see yer injury."

Henrietta, who'd joined them, waved toward the fireplace, where a fire warmed the room. "Over there, so Patrick can take off his shirt and roll down his long johns but won't catch a chill. I'll fetch the witch hazel."

Alana expected Patrick to protest, but she caught the thoughtful glance he gave her aunt and, as if she could read his mind, realized he'd figured out that if Henrietta was fussing over *him*, she wouldn't be fretting about her family. Sudden gratitude made a lump rise in her throat. *Not one man out of ten, no twenty, would act in such a thoughtful way.*

Why did I think him so arrogant?

She bit her lip. *Perhaps I was the arrogant one.*

Disconcerted by her realization, Alana walked briskly toward the bedroom. "I need to get out of this coat and wash my hands," she said over her shoulder.

"There's still warm water in the pitcher," Henrietta called after her. "I just used some myself."

Alana shed her coat and dropped it muddy side up on the floor in the corner. Then she removed her gloves, scarf, and hat and left them on the bed. She rolled up the cuffs of her sleeves, poured water from the pitcher into the ewer, and thoroughly washed her hands, drying them on a towel. Glancing down, she rolled her eyes at the condition of her skirt, but she had no time to change.

When Alana left the bedroom, she saw Patrick standing in front of the fire. She hurried over to him and tugged gently on his arm. "Come." She led him to the nearest seat—a wooden one that wouldn't take harm from his muddy clothes.

He obeyed, walking with her to the chair. Once Patrick sat, he let out a long breath, stretched out his legs, and raised his hands to unbutton his shirt, his movements jerky from pain.

"Let me." Alana caught his arm and lowered his hand to his lap. She reached for his top button, conscious of his dark eyes watching her, of the intimacy of her taking off his shirt. She couldn't help but be aware of an energy simmering between them. She'd removed clothes from injured and ill men before, but this time felt different—sensual. *What's more, he feels different.*

I've lost my normal healer's detachment.

Shaken by her reactions, Alana pulled his suspenders down over his shoulders, undid his buttons, and untucked the ends of his shirt from his pants. "Don't move." Relieved to sound normal, she slid the garment off his shoulders, draping the shirt over the back of the chair.

Patrick held himself rigid.

Alana reached for the buttons at the neck of his long underwear, and her fingers trembled. As she opened each one, more and more of a broad chest dusted with black hairs was revealed.

She became aware of the shallowness of her breath, the quiver in her stomach. Alana kept her gaze lowered, for she couldn't meet his eyes, afraid her expression might give her away. She eased the long johns from one muscled shoulder.

Patrick shrugged, trying to help.

"Let me." Alana looked at him from under her eyelashes.

He stilled, but his gaze didn't leave her face.

Henrietta bustled over, holding a glass bottle. "I've witch hazel and some clean rags."

Her aunt's presence broke their connection, and Alana felt an odd sense of loss. *But even a chaperone can't take away my awareness of this man.*

A spark burst in the hearth. Henrietta pulled over a small table, setting down the bottle and rags for bandages. "Let me help you, Alana. I'll take Patrick's right side."

Together, as gently as possible, they rolled down his long johns to his waist.

Henrietta gasped at the sight of the angry purple bruise spreading across his right side. "Oh, dear Lord."

"Ye must have hit another rock when you fell." Alana scrunched her brow, trying to remember if she'd seen the rock in question. "I didn't notice one, though." She crouched and gently traced the shape of the bruise, inhaling sharply when she realized he'd been kicked. Her gaze jerked up to meet his eyes.

He frowned and shook his head, flicking a warning glance toward Henrietta.

Alana bit her lip to keep from saying something that would cause her aunt to fret. Patrick was right not to add to Henrietta's worry about the type of outlaws Rory and the children might be facing. "Do you feel a sharp pain when you breathe?" Her voice sounded thin.

"It definitely hurts, but not as much as I think broken ribs would."

"We'll hope that's the case. But I'll still need to ascertain whether or not they are."

Patrick gave her a look of resignation, and his shoulders drooped an inch.

"Please soak a rag in witch hazel, Aunt, and bring the clean linen ye use for bandages," Alana directed, keeping her voice even. "Then if ye'd be so kind as to bring some ice for his bruises."

Henrietta obeyed, pouring witch hazel into a bowl and dropping in the rag to soak. "I'm going to the icehouse. I'll be right back." She whirled to don her coat and yank on mittens. She hastened out the front door, not even bothering to put on a hat and scarf.

Alana's legs started to feel the strain from crouching. She looked up at Patrick. "I must press on this area to check for any broken ribs. 'Twill hurt."

"Go ahead and torture me," he said with an obvious attempt at levity.

"Brave man." She matched his light tone and pressed her fingers against his side.

He hissed and then clenched his jaw.

"'Tis better to breathe through the pain than to clamp down on it," she instructed. "Pant like a dog on a hot day."

Patrick chuckled, and then winced. "Don't make me laugh."

"Breathe," Alana ordered, continuing her examination. She hated to cause him pain but knew she had to. Finally, she finished and stood, her legs aching. "Well, I don't think ye've broken anything."

"Told you."

"I'll apply witch hazel and then ice." As she spoke, Alana picked up the soaked pad, inhaling the astringent scent, and held it against his side.

Henrietta rushed into the house, the handle of a basket crooked over her arm. She shut the door. "I chipped off small pieces." She hurried over and wrapped the ice in a rag, handing the bundle to Patrick, then rubbing her hands along her hips to warm them.

Alana guided his hand over the bruise. "Hold the ice in place while I examine your head wound."

Henrietta left them to go take off her coat.

Patrick placed his hand over hers.

His touch sent warmth tingling into her, a contrast to the cold on her palm from the ice. She waited a few extra seconds before drawing her hand away and untying the makeshift bandage from around his head, catching the coppery smell of blood. "The hem of my petticoat," she said to her aunt, who'd moved close to peer over Alana's shoulder.

"Very resourceful of you." Henrietta picked up the strips by the clean edges. "I'll soak them in soapy cold water with a little baking soda. Later, you can sew them back on."

"I said I'd buy you a new one," Patrick muttered. "And I will."

"Hush now. There's no need." Alana parted his bloody hair to reveal a gash and swelling. "Yer going to need stitches," she said, in a matter-of-fact tone.

"So I figured." He sounded resigned.

Alana poured witch hazel on another rag and dabbed at his head wound. "Aunt Henrietta, Could you please bring me the scissors to cut his hair, and then uncle's razor to shave close to the scalp."

"Certainly."

"I'll need light to make sure I've gotten all the dirt out."

Henrietta moved from Alana's side. "I'll bring everything and hold the lamp for you." She quickly returned with the lit lamp, adding the smell of kerosene to the air.

Alana had stitched up plenty of head wounds before, and she deftly went about the business, knowing the quicker she finished, the better for her patient.

Patrick remained stoic, only growling at the first poke of the needle, then keeping his jaw clenched.

But even as Alana worked, she retained the knowledge that this man was so much more than an ordinary patient, although she wasn't ready to explore *what* he might be.

Leaning close, Henrietta studied the wound. "Such neat stitches."

"Plenty of practice." Alana knotted the last suture and snipped the thread. "There. I'm done." Stepping back, she smiled at her aunt. "Ye can set down the lamp now."

"Just in time." Henrietta lowered the lamp to a rustic side table. "My arms were getting tired. I still don't have all my stamina back."

"Ye'll get stronger every day," Alana assured her. "Now, if ye could fetch the willow bark tea for Patrick…."

"Good idea. That will help with the pain." Henrietta patted Patrick's shoulder. "And then I'd better get back to cooking supper. My husband and children will be wanting a hot meal as soon as they arrive." Although Henrietta said the words briskly enough, the anguish was back in her eyes.

Alana's heart twisted in fear, and she took a deep breath to soothe herself. *Don't borrow trouble.*

Once her aunt walked to the kitchen area, Alana selected some clean linen and bandaged Patrick's head. She made a second ice bundle. "Ye'll need to hold this on your head for a bit longer to keep the swelling down." She moved around to his front and studied his face, noting his paleness and the lines of pain around his eyes and mouth. "Have ye nausea?"

"I'm trying not to think about my stomach."

She frowned. "I'll add peppermint to the willow bark tea. Then ye should lie down in the bedroom and rest. I'll wake ye when everyone is home."

"I can't sleep until Rory is back to keep guard, and I know the children are safe."

Alana narrowed her eyes at him, torn between ordering him to bed or letting him be. But she figured if Patrick had the same kind of anxiousness gnawing at him that she did, he was better off where he was.

He quirked an eyebrow. "Well, Doctor O'Donnell, what's my prognosis?"

"Excellent." She leaned in to drop a kiss on his forehead and caught herself just in time, shocked by the naturalness of the gesture. "Provided…" She tried to sound stern to cover up her slip. "Ye take things easy for the next few days, mayhap a week or even more."

Even as she said the words, Alana couldn't help but feel a surge of pleasure at the idea of him being their guest for a while longer.

Chapter Eight

In a chair by the fireplace, Patrick stared out the darkening window, watching dusk settle over the prairie and hoping to catch a glimpse of Rory driving his wagon, the children riding in the back. Alana sat near him knitting, and Henrietta worked in the kitchen area by the light of a kerosene lantern hanging on a ceiling hook over the stove.

The tea had taken the edge off of his pain and nausea. His head no longer felt like an anvil to a blacksmith's hammer, and the spear pierced his side only when he shifted wrong. An inner restlessness made him want to get up and pace, but Patrick knew he was still too stiff and sore to move, even if space existed in the small home to do so.

He didn't like the heavy feeling of powerlessness weighing on him. *I'm a man who's used to taking control. Running my own enterprise.*

Patrick tapped his fingers on his thigh. *I have ranch hands and a housekeeper I can depend on. Money in the bank. I've pretty much arranged everything just the way I want.*

Until robbers crossed my path and unseated me.

No, before that, when neither O'Donnell sister fell in with my marriage plans. Now, to be sure, he was grateful for Bridget's rejection. *What if we'd married, and then I learned I'd chosen the wrong sister?*

Alana's healing instincts seemed still on alert, for at the sound of his drumming fingers, she looked up from her knitting and glanced over as if assessing his mental and physical condition.

Patrick flattened his hand on his leg, not wanting to show his inner agitation.

She gazed at his face as if searching for what he was thinking. When he didn't volunteer what was on his mind, she bent over her knitting, appearing fully absorbed in the task.

He studied her profile—the shape of her nose and firm chin, the curve of her neck. The firelight gleamed on her hair, deepening the hue of the tight curls fringing across her forehead and in front of her ears. An unfamiliar feeling of affection, no, more than affection, surged through him. Between this morning and now, Alana had come to mean so much to him. *Well, look what all took place in the space of those few hours.*

Patrick thought of the gold shamrock necklace, stolen before he could give it to her as a courting gift, and had to hold in his anger. Then guilt wracked him. *What if the outlaws spotted me in town and followed me to steal Thunder? By riding my Thoroughbred out to see Alana, I brought danger to her and her family.*

She's safe. Now if only I knew for sure Rory and the children were safe, too. He glanced at Alana again. *How can she look so calm when I know she must be even more anxious than I am?*

Just as Patrick thought he was about to explode from waiting, he heard the sharp bark of the dog.

Gasping, Alana tossed her knitting onto the side table.

A pot clanged as if Henrietta had dropped it on the stove.

Alana jumped to her feet, gathered up her skirts, and ran to the door.

Henrietta beat her to the door by a step, wrenching it open, and peering out.

Patrick gingerly pushed his protesting body to stand, clenching his jaw to hold in a groan. He moved like an elderly man, bent over, stabilizing his ribs with an arm until he was able to straighten.

Henrietta raised her hands to the heavens. "Thank you, Blessed Jesus!" she cried. "Blessed Mary, Mother of God, thank you!" She vanished through the doorway without stopping to put on a coat.

Alana gave Patrick a quick backwards glance and a tremulous smile. Happy tears made her eyes glow like sapphires. She followed her aunt into the gathering dusk.

Their joyful reaction eased the tightness in Patrick's belly. *Everyone must be fine.* He lumbered toward the door, mentally cursing the stiffness that made him so slow. Like the women, he didn't stop for a coat. Once outside, he saw the wagon and quickly counted heads. *One, two, three, four. All safe.* "Thank the Lord," he said, his tone fervent.

Rory tied off the reins, set the brake, jumped down, and opened his arms to catch his wife as she rushed to embrace him. He held Henrietta tight, and they kissed.

Alana hovered a few feet away, obviously giving the couple a private reunion.

Henrietta burst into tears. "I was so worried!"

Rory cradled her face with his hands. "I know, *A ghrá geal.* I know. Stop your crying now, for all is well."

The children jumped off the wagon and ran to their mother, tumbling into a hug, arms entwined around her sides and back.

"There's some bad men," claimed Isleen in a shrill tone.

Henrietta twisted to face them. In the middle of her brood, she laughed through her tears. "Oh, my dears, yes, and it's so *good* to see you." She pulled away from her husband to squeeze her children to her breast and rain kisses over their upturned faces.

Alana moved close to hug each family member.

Sian ran around them with happy barks and tail wags.

Never had Patrick witnessed such a joyous homecoming. Yet, he stood frozen in isolation, watching the happy family. Although so very relieved that everyone was all right, guilt held him in place, keeping him from moving forward and greeting them. His skin was hot, and even the wind couldn't chill him because inside he was colder than ice.

Rory waded through his family toward Patrick to hold out his hand and give him a hearty clasp.

Patrick gestured toward the children. "Glad to see everyone's safe. Your womenfolk have been on pins and needles."

Rory's eyebrows pulled together. "Couldn't be helped. I came as quick as I could."

"Any sign?" Patrick asked, keeping his voice low.

"Only tracks. The sheriff's on their trail now."

Henrietta stepped back to her husband's side.

Rory dropped an arm around her waist.

Feeling out of place in the face of their obvious fondness for each other, Patrick tilted his head toward the wagon. "I'll take care of the mules."

"Ye will not," Alana snapped, fisting her hands on her hips. "Charlie will take care of them."

Rory eyed his son. With a jerk of his head toward the barn, he signaled his agreement with Alana. "I'll lend a hand." He turned back to Patrick. "We'll be in as soon as we can and tell you everything."

Charlie kicked at a clump of dirt. "Nothing much happened, anyway." He glanced at Patrick's bandaged head and scrunched his nose. "We missed all the excitement."

Patrick shook his head, then bit back a groan at the drumming pain from the movement. "Not the kind of excitement you want, Charlie. I guarantee it."

Charlie scowled.

"Now, a good kind of excitement is…" Patrick deliberately trailed off to catch the boy's interest, waiting for Charlie's frown to change to a questioning glance. "Watching Thunder race. *Win.* Now *that's* excitement."

Charlie wore an expectant expression. "That would be just dandy, Mr. Gallagher. Except, I won't get to see Thunder race."

The exchange with the boy had melted some of the coldness inside Patrick. He mustered a grin. "Well, I guess Sweetwater Springs is as good as any place for a horse race. Might have to consider it for the future. But I'm thinking my Thoroughbred will need some exercise in the next couple of days, and I doubt your cousin the watchdog—" he winked at Alana "—will let me ride him."

Charlie's eyes lit up. "I have a good seat and hands. Mr. Sanders said so. He even let me ride his Appaloosa once."

Patrick had met Nick Sanders—a rancher who had a rare, fine way of taming horses. After church a few weeks ago, he'd lingered and spoken to the man about putting Thunder to one of his mares. "Well then, you'll ride Thunder around the paddock—at a walk first—under my watchful eye."

"Oh, thank you, Mr. Gallagher." With a bounce in his step, the boy headed toward the mules.

Patrick glanced at Alana.

She beamed at him with obvious approval. "In spite of the *watchdog* remark, that was well done. Just what we need to turn the children's attention away from what happened today."

We aren't out of the woods yet. Those outlaws are lurking out there somewhere. The thought made his stomach clutch.

Rory dropped a kiss on his wife's head and released her.

Smiling, Henrietta snugged a daughter to each side. Together, they walked to the house, squeezing through the door.

Once again, unfamiliar feelings of being excluded reared within him. *I've taken pride in my independence, but I've missed out on these kind of familial bonds and the deep love the O'Donnells have for each other.* He rubbed his chin. *I might enjoy my money and horses and belongings and success, but I don't possess what this family, so poor in worldly goods, has.*

Alana started to follow her relatives but stopped. She looked back, her eyebrows drawn in obvious concern. The soft glow from the doorway cast a fuzzy aura around her.

He forced a grin and lifted his chin in an *I'm fine, go ahead* motion.

She must have taken him at face value, for she flashed him a happy smile.

For the first time Patrick saw Alana had a dimple, although on the opposite side of Bridget's. The power of her smile made his heart stop. Warmth flooded him, melting the last of his frozen feelings.

Alana stepped forward to grasp his hand and squeezed. "I've said a lot of prayers the last few years that haven't been answered. But today...." She took a shuddering breath. "I prayed as hard as I did to save my mother when she was dying."

Patrick dredged up a long ago sermon from the depths of his mind. "How do you know your former prayers weren't answered?"

She wrinkled her forehead in puzzlement. "I think the answer was obvious."

He cocked an eyebrow before continuing. "Maybe they were, but you didn't like the outcome. Perhaps God's answer was *no*. And maybe *yes* answers will come in the future for you from prayers you didn't even know to utter."

As he spoke, Patrick realized this was true for him as well.

Alana's forehead smoothed. "Well, that was a fine priestly thing to say. But I suppose yer right, and I must think on yer words."

He gave her a slight bow, ignoring the jab of pain from his ribs, and raised her hand to his lips. A gust of chill wind made her shiver and brought his attention to the cold outside and their lack of coats. With a tilt of his head, Patrick signaled for them to go inside.

She nodded, not meeting his eyes, and pulled back her hand.

Patrick let go, wishing he had the right to keep holding on.

They went into the house, inhaling the welcome smell of soup and fresh baked bread. His stomach grumbled, the nausea having passed.

Henrietta, chivvying the girls to wash up and help set the table, looked over at them. "You two must be freezing." She made a shooing gesture. "Sit by the fire for a few minutes. The girls and I will have supper on the table in no time."

With careful steps, he followed Alana toward the fireplace.

"I didn't even notice how cold I was until now." Alana crouched to feed the fire with a log from a wood box near the hearth. She held her hands to the flames springing up around the edges for a minute before rising and turning to him, the color high in her cheeks.

Patrick wondered if she was flushed from the heat of the fire or from when he kissed her hand. The thought of the latter gave him hope.

Alana pointed to the cushioned wooden chair nearest the fireplace. "Sit. The heat will do ye good."

I might not be able to do much in my current condition, but at least I can see Alana is taken care of. He sank into a worn leather chair farther away, then reached over and patted the seat of the wooden one. "Sit close to the fire and warm yourself," he commanded. His small effort to overcome his previous helplessness made the words come out more strongly than the situation warranted. He strove to soften his tone. "I'm fine right here."

She narrowed her eyes at him, obviously not liking his imperious manner.

He raised his eyebrows and waited for her compliance.

With a toss of her head and a gleam of laughter in her eyes, Alana obeyed, daintily perching on the edge of the seat.

Although Patrick knew she was teasing him, still, the small victory restored his equilibrium.

Rory entered and lifted the rifle to the rack above the door. "Left Charlie fussing over your horse." He raised his voice so Patrick would hear.

"Thunder will enjoy the attention."

Rory removed his coat, scarf, hat, and gloves and hung them up before heading to the bedroom to wash up. When he returned, he stopped at the stove, put an arm around his wife's waist, and said something softly to her.

Henrietta nodded. "Girls, finish putting the food on the table." She handed the wooden spoon to Isleen.

Rory guided his wife over to Patrick and Alana, but he

remained on his feet, still holding Henrietta. "I followed the tracks to town," he said in a low voice. "Once I made sure the children were safe, I left them in the care of Mrs. Gordon—our schoolteacher. Then I went to the sheriff's office, told Sheriff Granger the story, took her outside, and pointed out the tracks."

Patrick had met the law woman one Sunday and, after he got past his initial astonishment that the sheriff was female, had been impressed with her air of cool competence.

"Sheriff Granger said since the tracks were headed through town and toward the railway, it would be safe to take the children and head home—to leave her to apprehend the robbers if they were still around. She knew the train had been and gone."

"Did she go after them alone?" Patrick asked.

Rory nodded. "She loaded up her guns.... Well, more guns—" he amended. "I've heard she usually always wears a gun belt except to church. In addition, she slipped a small derringer into her coat pocket and another into her boot. She grabbed a pouch of bullets, or so I think by the clink of them, and stuck them in her other pocket. She took a rifle out of her gun cabinet as well."

Patrick frowned. "That's as much as you know?"

With a tired exhale, Rory rubbed his forehead. "We parted ways."

Patrick wasn't reassured. "Then we should assume those robbers are still at large."

The alarm on Alana's face and Henrietta's gasp made Patrick regret he'd spoken his thoughts aloud. "I doubt they'll head back this way in the dark," he hastened to assure the womenfolk. "But we should still keep watch." His head ached at the thought. A sudden drop in energy made him want to collapse.

Rory must have seen his exhaustion. He lowered a hand to Patrick's shoulder. "Let's eat. Trouble always looks worse on an empty stomach."

With an inward brace against the pain, Patrick pushed to stand.

Charlie dashed into the house. A wave of cold air gusted in

his wake. He quickly shut the door and peeled off his outerwear.

"Come." Rory gestured toward the table. "After supper, we'll worry about what to do tonight." He walked to the door and lowered the bar.

They took seats on the two benches flanking the table.

Henrietta ladled a hearty soup into wooden bowls and passed them around. Then a platter with thick slices of brown bread made the rounds.

Charlie hurried from the bedroom where he'd gone to wash up and took a seat on the far end of the bench next to Idelle.

Rory clasped his hands and bowed his head in a silent signal to say grace.

Mostly from eating alone all the time, Patrick had fallen out of the habit of giving thanks before a meal. After a month with the Thompsons, saying a blessing had once again become familiar. But today, a petition to the Almighty felt not only right but important.

"Dear Heavenly Father, we ask for protection," Rory said, his tone fervent. "Please shield our family and our friend Patrick Gallagher from all harm. We ask for you to safeguard our livestock and possessions, as well as our fellow citizens of Sweetwater Springs. Guide our sheriff, gird her with your armor, and grace her with your wisdom."

Patrick snuck a peek at Alana, sitting across the table from him, her long lashes feathering her cheeks. *While you're at it, Lord, I, too, could use some of your wisdom.*

The joy and relief from the safe homecoming had ebbed. After Rory finished praying, the subdued family began to eat. The darkness of the interior of the house pressed dim and close, lit only by the lantern on the table and the small fire in the fireplace.

Knocking on the door startled them.

Patrick leaped to his feet, his heart thumping, his hand dropping as if reaching for his Colt. His head throbbed at the jolting movement.

Rory rose, motioning for his family to stay seated, while he stepped to answer the summons. He reached to take down the rifle from over the door, his body tense.

With an arm bracing his side, Patrick moved to join him, aware of his empty hands.

"Who's there?" Rory called, his words clipped.

"Sheriff K.C. Granger."

Rory's shoulders relaxed. He returned the rifle to the rack, flipped up the bar, and opened the door. "Come in, Sheriff. You're just in time for supper." He made a sweeping motion into the house.

A breath of relief squeezed out of Patrick.

The sheriff, a tall woman dressed in men's clothing, stepped inside, bringing in a chilly breeze. She unwound the wool scarf wrapped around her neck and part of her face, and then took off her wide-brimmed hat. Two brown braids dropped down her back. "Glad to hear that. I'm right starved. I could wrestle a grizzly for his supper."

Henrietta's smile was welcoming. "We have plenty."

Patrick realized he'd have to take the law woman aside to secretly tell her of the stolen necklace.

"Sheriff Granger, I'd like to introduce my wife Henrietta to you." Rory gestured to her. "We haven't been to town since Christmas, so you haven't met her yet. Then there's my niece Alana, who's too newly come from Ireland for you to know. Have you met my children?"

The sheriff shook her head. "But I've noticed them, especially your girls. That they are identical twins caught my eye when I saw them once after school."

"My daughter Isleen wearing the green hair ribbons is next to her mother." Rory swept a hand toward each one. "Idelle is across the table, with my son Charlie next to her."

Everyone nodded and smiled a welcome.

Rory tilted his head toward Patrick. "So you two have met?"

"Two Sundays ago," the sheriff said, eying his bandaged head and doing an apparent visual sweep of his body, as if checking for other damage.

"I'm surprised you remember." Patrick was a bit taken aback by the recognition. "I've heard you've only lived in Sweetwater Springs for a few weeks. Must be plenty of people for you to get to know."

When Patrick had met the woman, K.C. Granger had a watchful air, her cool gray eyes surveying her surroundings as if making sure all within her territory remained on the side of law and order.

Now, the sheriff looked tired, with fine lines fanning out around her eyes. She untied her scarf and shrugged off her coat before turning back to them. "I have good news and bad news. The bad news is that the varmints got away. The good news is they caught the train out of town. Hopefully, they won't be back to bother us."

Patrick took the coat from her hands and hung it over his. "How do you know?"

The sheriff tilted her head in Rory's direction. "He trailed the tracks into town, and then came straight to my office. One of the horseshoes has a distinct dent on the right side. I just had to follow where the print led. Wasn't easy to track them through town with all the foot and horse traffic we have, but I searched the whole road. Stopped in at the saloons to check just in case, but no one had seen any strangers." She grimaced. "I'm too new in town to discern strangers from most of the regular inhabitants. But I've been spending a lot of time making the rounds of the saloons, and I knew everyone I saw today."

Patrick hadn't visited the saloons in Sweetwater Springs, and he wondered what kind of reception the female sheriff had encountered.

"I checked at the depot. Stationmaster Jack Waite said that a stranger had bought two tickets and planned to stay with their horses in the boxcars. Since Jack keeps his finger on everyone in the area, he knows who belongs here. He gave me a good description of the man. After he left, Jack went to the window and spied another man with him. Didn't recognize him, either. But that one kept his hat pulled low and wore a black coat and same-colored scarf wrapped around his neck up to his chin. For all we know, he could have been from here."

Fear made Patrick's stomach clench. His thoughts raced. *How soon can I get to a telegraph so I can let my people know to stay armed and keep watch? Especially over those valuable mares in foal by Thunder.* "Did they head for Crenshaw?"

The sheriff shook her head. "Opposite direction."

Patrick relaxed, letting out another slow breath. "If they'd targeted Thunder, wouldn't they head in the direction of Crenshaw, looking for another opportunity?"

"Seems to me they would," Sheriff Granger said slowly as if thinking. "Have your men been with you a long time? Are they trustworthy?"

"Known my foreman from my cradle. He was a friend to my Pa. Some of my other hands have been around almost as long. The rest of my cowboys have worked with me at least five, six years." A corner of his mouth turned up. "I pay them well. Bonuses even. Treat them like family. Don't think any of them would stoop to horse thieving." The more Patrick talked, the more reassured he felt by his own explanation. "In fact, my men have won quite a bit betting on Thunder's races, with more to come in the future. They wouldn't risk their winnings and their necks to steal the horse."

"What can you tell me about the robbers?"

"Didn't even see the attack coming," Patrick said bitterly, cursing himself for being a fool to ride Thunder over the prairie without paying a lick of attention to his surroundings. "One jumped me from a tree and landed on my back. The other landed in front of the horse, but I was already falling off backwards, so only caught a glimpse of a man in black like Jack saw. That's all I can tell you."

The sheriff shrugged. "Can't be helped. At least they're gone, and you weren't terribly hurt."

"Are we safe now, then?" Isleen asked in a small voice, her shoulders rounded with tension. She leaned against her mother, who placed an arm around her. On the other side of the table, Charlie and Idelle huddled together, the boy's arm protectively around his sister.

The sheriff's expression softened. She smiled at Isleen and then at her two siblings. "Those men made a foolish mistake today—besides trying to steal a horse, that is. Jack Waite saw what one looked like. From now on, our stationmaster will be on watch, and if that scalawag ever shows his face in town again, Jack will let me know. I'll write up a report and will be sending out a description of the attack and the culprits to the towns and cities around here and along the train route." She flashed a wolfish grin that didn't bode well for the criminals. "So don't you worry now."

"Yes, ma'am." Isleen's shoulders relaxed. "Thank you, ma'am."

The sheriff nodded and turned back to Patrick and Rory. "Must have been a crime of opportunity. Perhaps they simply were after your money and valuables."

Patrick didn't believe that for a moment. *And even if those two only meant to steal from a chance traveler, once they set eyes on my stud, they'd have gone for bigger stakes.*

"Or for some reason, they were in the area and heard about your fine horse or perhaps saw the stud for themselves."

"Could be," Patrick agreed, thinking. "I only rode Thunder to the Thompson ranch, and then from there directly here. But I don't usually stay so long in one place. I ride to a ranch, give the owner a chance to check on Thunder while I look over his mares. Stay a couple of days before moving on, returning when the mare's in season. I've been in Sweetwater Springs a month, and word could have gone out to whatever local outlaws you have around here."

The sheriff frowned. "That's just it. I've been told there are no local outlaws, and I've done a lot of casual questioning of all types of people—nosing out their concerns, so to speak. So I don't know if someone who lives here got a bug up his—" Glancing at the children, she cleared her throat. "Or if those two men came from elsewhere on purpose to steal your stud."

Henrietta gestured to the bedroom. "Sheriff Granger, let me take you to wash up. Isleen, bring some hot water, and, Alana, if you'll get a bowl for our guest and dish her up some soup?"

The two hurried to obey.

Charlie bounced up from his seat. "I'll see to your horse while you eat, Sheriff."

She gave the boy a nod. "Much obliged, Charlie."

A few minutes later, they all resumed eating. Out of respect, no one pestered the law woman to talk until she'd obviously sated the worst of her hunger.

Then, from both politeness and curiosity, they asked the sheriff several questions about her life before she came to Sweetwater Springs, and she told a few humorous stories that made them laugh.

When everyone had finished, the sheriff smiled at Henrietta. "Sure was good to eat a home-cooked meal. The food at the saloon is adequate, but it's not the same."

Henrietta's thin cheeks pinked. "I didn't expect company, or the meal would be more than soup and bread. Please return sometime, perhaps dinner after church, when I can feed you a fine meal."

Sheriff Granger nodded. "I'd like that." She folded her napkin and set it next to the plate, let out a tired breath, and glanced from Rory to Henrietta. "If you'd be willing to put me up for the night, I'd be obliged."

"Of course!" Henrietta stood. She looked to the area in front of fireplace where Patrick had slept on his bedroll the night before. From her thoughtful expression, she was wrestling with the dilemma of propriety.

As a female, Sheriff Granger shouldn't be bedding down on the floor next to Patrick, but instead should sleep in the loft near Alana and the children. Then again, she was the sheriff in a role in which her behavior was masculine, and she obviously expected to be treated like a man. "You can sleep in one of the girl's beds. The twins can bunk together."

Patrick raised a hand to stop Henrietta. "No need. I plan to bed down in the barn anyway." He saw Isleen's sudden look of fear and caught himself from adding—*so I can nab the outlaws if they return.* Not that he expected they would. His gut told him Thunder was safe. But just in case, he'd sleep light tonight. "Thunder's had quite a day, and so have I. We should be together, don't you think, Isleen?"

Her eyes brightened. "Can I bunk in the barn, too, Mr. Gallagher? I love lying on the hay in the loft."

"Certainly not." Henrietta shook her head. "But—" She laid a finger on her daughter's pout. "—to give you something to look forward to, you children can have one night this summer in the hayloft."

"Take my rifle with you, Patrick," Rory offered with a wave toward the Winchester. "The sheriff probably has enough guns to hold off an army. So we won't need it."

"Just about." The sheriff smirked. "And, if you're keeping watch in the barn. I'd rather stay warm in the house. I'll have a long, cold ride tomorrow, backtracking those hoofprints to see where they came from."

"Let's hope the weather stays dry." Patrick squirmed, trying to find a position on the hard bench that didn't hurt, but to no avail, for the effects of the willow bark tea had worn off.

Silence followed the comment. They all knew how often snow came at this time of year.

Sheriff Granger covered a yawn. "I need to hit the hay."

"No, that's me hitting the hay," Patrick quipped with a grin.

She winked at him.

Tonight, they didn't linger at the table after Henrietta and Alana had cleared away the dishes.

Patrick's body had stiffened, and, as he slowly rose from the table, he suppressed a grunt of pain.

Alana must have spotted his discomfort, for without him asking, she pressed him to drink more of the willow bark tea she'd made.

Patrick was sore enough to comply. He sipped the bitter drink and grimaced. Even though she'd sweetened the brew with some honey, the taste was still nasty.

Later, bedded snuggly with extra quilts in the hay in the barn, with the tea having taken away enough of the pain, he fell asleep.

During the night, the sharp sound of sleet on the barn roof woke him. With dismay, Patrick listened to the drumming sound and knew there'd be no way the sheriff could backtrack and find the outlaw's lair.

Chapter Nine

The next morning after breakfast, Patrick sat on a straw bale near the front of Thunder's stall and waited for Sheriff Granger to finish saddling her chestnut gelding so he could have a private talk with her. The women were in the house washing the breakfast dishes, and the children had already left for school.

Sian sat beside him, the dog's head on Patrick's leg.

A single lantern, hanging from a low beam in the center, cast a fuzzy yellow light. Across the barn, Rory tended to the mules.

Patrick rested his head against the wall and closed his eyes. The storm had passed, leaving a clear dawn. The barn, redolent with the smell of horse manure and hay, was cold, but warmer than waiting outside in the wind.

Thunder leaned his head over the door and chuffed Patrick's left shoulder, the closest part of him the horse could touch.

Without opening his eyes, he reached up and curled his hand around the Thoroughbred's nose. Raising his left arm hurt less than raising his right. Earlier, Thunder had given Patrick a puzzled glance when he didn't performed the usual morning feeding. But the horse settled in to eat as soon as Charlie had poured a measure of grain into the feed bin and added a flake of hay.

Alana had made Patrick promise to do nothing but greet Thunder and allow Charlie to do all the work. He didn't like idleness, but his body had stiffened up worse than yesterday, and every movement hurt. So he'd only put up a token protest about her bossing him around before he gave in.

"Ready, Big Red?" Sheriff Granger patted the neck of her gelding.

Before she could lead the horse from the stall, Patrick rose, wobbling like a creaky old man, and caught the woman's eye. He beckoned her to follow him to the shadowed corner of the barn. He hoped Rory wouldn't overhear their conversation. The bulldog trailed him, taking a seat at Patrick's feet.

Wearing a bulky black coat, with a scarf wrapped high around her neck, and her braids tucked under her hat, the woman could, indeed, pass for a man. She turned to face him and waited.

"I, um…I had something else stolen," Patrick said in a quiet voice. "A necklace with a gold pendent in the shape of a shamrock."

She cocked a feathered eyebrow. "And you're telling me this privately because…?"

"I bought the jewelry at the mercantile in town to give to Alana."

"I wasn't aware you'd met her before."

Heat burned across his neck.

The eyebrow didn't lower. She squared her shoulders. "You seemed rather attentive to Miss *Bridget* O'Donnell when I saw you at church. Yet I heard yesterday the young lady is now engaged to James Whitson. Did you decide to court the other twin, sight unseen?"

Patrick mentally cursed the speed of the Sweetwater Springs grapevine. "I met Miss Alana when she first arrived," he said smoothly. "She stayed for a night with her cousin on the Thompson ranch before leaving to come here."

"One twin is as good as the other, ah?" The sheriff's gray eyes gleamed, although she remained straight-faced.

"The situation wasn't like that," he protested. *Well, it was. But I'm not about to admit the truth, even if she threatens to string me up.* "I've become fond of Miss Alana. More than fond. They're fine folks, the O'Donnells.

"Sounds like you had marriage in mind."

"I thought a ring might be a bit much to offer on such short acquaintance," he said stiffly, and then realized he'd answered a question that was none of her business. *Guess the sheriff's a woman at heart, after all—nosing into matchmaking matters.*

Her mouth quivered as if she tried to hold in a chuckle. "I 'spect you're right about that. Although, if it's a convenient wife you're wanting, I could point you in the direction of women who'd grab a ring from you, and you'd barely have to say hello."

Narrowing his gaze, Patrick started to cross his arms over his chest, winced at the pull from his sore ribs, and lowered his hands. "When you're done amusing yourself at my expense…."

"In my job, I have to take humor where I can get it."

"Glad to provide the opportunity," he said with a sarcastic bite.

Her expression sobered. "Actually, you might have just given me a good clue. Unlike money, a necklace is distinct. If I come across it again, your shamrock might lead me to the men who assaulted you. I'll ask the Cobbs to keep an eye out, too. They'd recognize the piece if someone tried to sell it to them."

"That's true." He felt a little better. "I have a favor to ask." He reached into the pocket of his coat and pulled out a piece of paper. Last night before falling asleep, he'd itemized what he needed from the mercantile. Luckily, the outlaws hadn't valued his stud services notebook, maybe because they'd had a hard time reading his cryptic notes—if they could read at all. "I need to ask a favor." He handed her the list. "Unless I miss my guess, Miss Alana will take a firm stand against my riding any distance until I'm in much better shape. So I can't get to town the way I'd like."

"Maybe you're not in a hurry to leave."

"Maybe not." Patrick wanted to maneuver the conversation away from his feelings for Alana and back to his topic. "As you know, the robbers took all my cash. I'm forced to buy on credit. If need be, I'm sure Wyatt Thompson would vouch for me. I'm certainly good for the money. Once I can get to town, I'll go straight to the bank."

The sheriff waited, her expression unchanging.

Bet she has a great poker face. "Under those circumstances, do you think the Cobbs would extend me credit? I need a gun—several guns, in fact—and a few supplies, so my staying here will be a help, not a hindrance, to the O'Donnells."

"I'll make it happen." The sheriff glanced down to read the paper, and a smile pulled at the corner of her mouth.

Patrick knew what she saw—a list far beyond basic necessities. He'd included fabric dress lengths for the women and girls, flannel shirts for Rory and Charlie, a petticoat for Alana, trimmings and lace, four new shawls, a pocketknife for the boy, exotic fruits such as oranges and lemons, a jar of honey, maple syrup, sausages, popcorn, more flour, sugar, and other staples. Perhaps the sheriff would think he'd gone overboard, and Patrick knew he probably had. But not too much so—not as much as he wanted—for he sensed the O'Donnells would be too proud to accept any gifts of larger value, such as a cow.

Sheriff Granger looked up with a humorous glint in her eyes. "Quite a list you have here. A *few supplies*, eh?"

"I owe them *everything!*" Patrick fired back, keeping the volume in check so Rory didn't notice. My *life,* for who knows how long I'd have laid there unconscious…if I'd even been able to find shelter by nightfall moving on my own tottery legs. And my *horse*—anything could have happened to Thunder roaming around loose." The thought made his stomach clench. His fingers curled against his palms. "I want, *need,* to show my gratitude."

"I think you'll succeed."

Her quiet tone went a ways to settling him. Patrick took a deep breath to be able to speak calmly. "If you don't mind picking out a Colt and bullets, a gunbelt and holster. And a Winchester with a saddle sheath."

His shoulders tightened, waiting for her to quip about the guns—maybe saying, "That's a lot of firepower," or "Too late to do any good."

"I'll choose well."

Patrick relaxed. "Also any supplies Mrs. Cobb might add to the list. She would know more than I what the family usually orders. Money is no object—provided, of course, I have that credit."

"Knowing Mrs. Cobb, you could find yourself in possession of considerably more."

Henrietta entered the barn, carrying what looked like a bundle of rags. She glanced around, spotted them, and headed over.

The dog greeted his mistress by sniffing her legs.

"Here's a jar of piping hot coffee for you, Sheriff." She extended the bundle. "Won't stay that way long, I know. But I thought you'd like to have something to drink along the way. And I rolled up the leftover buckwheat pancakes and filled them with applesauce. In case you have stops to make before you reached town."

The sheriff tucked the paper into her pocket. "Mighty fine of you, Mrs. O'Donnell." She reached out to take the bundle.

Henrietta handed over the provisions. Her curious gaze rested on the sheriff's pocket.

Now is a good time to somewhat prepare my hostess for the arrival of the supplies and such. "I've asked Sheriff Granger to pick up a few things from the mercantile."

A shamed look crossed Henrietta's face, as if she were too embarrassed to admit that the family didn't have enough food on hand for the kind of hospitality she'd like to extend. "You've already brought plenty," she said hurriedly. "We'll make do."

Patrick shook his head. "Don't make me feel beholden," he chided, knowing he was manipulating her into agreeing. "I'm already in your debt as it is."

By the expression crossing her face, his hostess obviously

struggled with not wanting him to feel obligated, but also wanting to preserve her pride. Henrietta's concern for his feelings won. She nodded. "Very well."

Patrick smiled, pleased he'd surmounted the first hurdle. "Since I'm not riding into town, I just need to figure out how to get them from the mercantile to here."

"Mr. Muth will pick up everything on his next milk run. He does such for us from time to time. I'd often had him over for Sunday dinner in return." Henrietta's brow wrinkled. "Now that he's married, though, we don't see him as much. Daisy Muth is quite a good cook."

"What would be a good gift to thank him for lugging everything I ordered to your house?"

"There's no need to repay him. We all help our neighbors whenever we can."

"I'm a stranger, not one of your neighbors," he pointed out. "I'd rather not feel beholden." Patrick wondered if she'd notice he'd twice played the obligation card.

"Well…Daisy Muth is partial to peaches. A can of them would be a fine treat."

I'm sure the O'Donnells would also like peaches. He glanced at the sheriff. "Add canned peaches to the list." He turned his head so Henrietta wouldn't see his face and winked. From her slight nod, he could tell the sheriff had caught his message.

Sheriff Granger tilted her head toward the horse. "I'd best be going. Unless they've already hitched a ride with Mr. Muth and his dairy wagon, I'll catch up with your children and escort them."

Smiling, Henrietta placed a hand on her chest. "I'd appreciate that, Sheriff Granger."

"Thanks for your hospitality." The sheriff moved toward the stall, opened the door, and led out her horse.

Seeing her about to leave, Rory propped his rake against the wall and walked over to join them. Once outside the barn, they all said quiet good-byes.

The sheriff mounted, pulled her scarf higher about her face, and flicked a hand in farewell. She nudged the chestnut gelding down the track.

Sian trotted after the horse, only stopping when Sheriff Granger headed right onto the main road. Then, his duty done, the dog turned and loped back to join them.

Henrietta shivered. She pulled the ends of her scarf tighter and turned back into the house.

Rory returned to his work in the barn, the dog at his heels.

But Patrick stayed and watched the sheriff ride in the direction of town. She had an easy way in the saddle. Mounted astride, hat tipped low to shield her face from the wind, she appeared like any man. But something about her posture called to mind loneliness.

Patrick wondered if he looked the same when he headed out from places where he'd briefly stayed. His isolation had never bothered him before. He had a full and busy life, and his decision to go wife-hunting had only sprung to mind when he'd met the O'Donnell twins. *I'm not courting because I'm lonely.* But he didn't quite believe his protestation.

The figure on the horse dwindled, until she faded into the distance and became lost over the horizon.

Patrick turned from the road toward the house and saw the yellow glow of lamplight in the window. Suddenly, he became aware of the icy wind whipping around him and tugged up his collar. Knowing he no longer wanted to be a solitary rider, Patrick strode toward light and warmth and Alana.

Two days later, as the setting sun gilded the frosty windows in gold and pink, Patrick kept his ears pricked for the sound of horses' hooves and wagon wheels, hoping Erik Muth would deliver the supplies from the mercantile today. He couldn't wait to see the delight on the women's faces—especially Alana's.

Preparations for supper were made—the salt pork parboiled and floured, the cornmeal mixed and ready to fry in cakes, the stewed pumpkin in a pot to heat before serving, the beans and greens simmering on the stove, and the watermelon rind pickles set out on the table. He'd helped with cutting the salt pork into strips, mixing the cornmeal, keeping the stove fed, and setting the table.

All women's work. But neither Henrietta, or Alana, nor the girls teased him about his lack of expertise, although he often saw a twinkle in their eyes or heard a giggle, quickly suppressed.

Soon the children would arrive from school, and Rory would return from hunting the rabbit whose tracks he'd seen earlier. When everyone was home, Henrietta and Alana would finish cooking the meal. But until then, the women and Patrick had a bit of a lull to sit.

Not that the women were resting. Henrietta mended the torn sleeve of Rory's shirt that caught on a nail yesterday, and Alana knitted lace from pale-blue thread. He could tell by the aprons they still wore that he was no longer considered a guest, else they would have removed the protective garments when they left the kitchen area.

Instead of feeling restless and irritable from being cooped up to recover from his injuries, Patrick found the quiet company of Henrietta and Alana soothing and calming. Two words he wouldn't normally have applied to his life but needed now because his head and ribs continued to ache, although his headache didn't hurt like the dickens any more.

Patrick suspected he'd be going stir crazy were he anyplace other than here on this little farm in the middle of nowhere. If he'd been home, he probably would have done his best to push through his pain to take care of his normal responsibilities—directing the care of the horses, seeing to their training, corresponding with the owners who wanted Thunder's services for their mares.

Although annoyed by his limiting injuries, he also blessed them, for they provided the opportunity to spend time in Alana's presence, getting to know her, as well as quietly court her. *An unusual courtship to be sure.*

Amazing all the ways they touched when working together. He'd stroke her fingers when holding wide loops of yarn while she formed them into balls. She molded her hands over his when teaching him to grind the beans into coffee or to peel potatoes. When they folded laundry, their hands would brush when bringing together the edges of heavy clothing and sheets.

Best of all was the feeling of her hands on his bare skin when icing his bruises and changing the bandage binding his ribs. From the way her eyes lowered or color rose in her cheeks, Patrick knew Alana was just as aware of those moments as he was, and he took hope from her attentiveness.

At loose ends without a newspaper to read or something to occupy his hands, Patrick leaned toward Alana, feeling the pinch of pain in his ribs, and admired the fine lace forming in delicate scallops. "Beautiful."

Giving him a sideways glance, she tossed her head, causing the wispy curls framing her face to dance. "This is for the hem of my petticoat to hide the mended places," she said in a defiant tone.

Thinking of his secret, Patrick almost laughed. But with great forbearance, he refrained. *She'll have a new one soon enough, maybe within the hour if Muth arrives today.* "When you're finished—" he said with mock gravity "—I'm sure there'll be no sign that your petticoat once suffered from being made into bandages."

Alana rolled her eyes, but a smile played about her mouth.

From outside, Patrick heard Sian bark. Then came the sounds he'd been waiting for. *Yes!* He fisted his hand. *The way I'm excited, you'd think Thunder was about to race for a hefty purse, instead of my anticipating the arrival of supplies and a few gifts.*

Henrietta lowered the shirt. "That must be Mr. Muth. I can't imagine anyone else coming around at this time. He must have brought the children from school. So thoughtful of him."

Slowly, Patrick pushed to his feet. "I'll go help your neighbor unload," he said in a casual voice.

Alana narrowed her eyes at him. "Unload what?"

"Some supplies I ordered from the mercantile."

Her brows dipped. "Are they heavy?"

Henrietta beamed at the two of them. "I'm sure Mr. Muth will carry in anything that's too much for Patrick."

Good manners kept him from growling at the woman. But by the gleam in her eyes, he could tell she was teasing him. "I can manage," he ground out.

Alana bundled up the lace, yarn, and needles, placing them on the side table. She stood and removed her apron. "Never mind. I'll go with you and supervise." She folded her apron and set it next to her lace before taking quick steps to the door.

"You do that, dear," Henrietta encouraged, setting aside the shirt. "I'll make some tea." She stood. "I'm sure Mr. Muth will enjoy something warm." She sent Patrick a grateful look. "Having tea to serve a guest is such a treat."

Warmed by the compliment, he moved toward the door.

Alana, already in her outerwear, held his coat open.

Patrick eased his arms into the sleeves.

She hefted it over his shoulders and moved around to his front to do up the buttons, as if he'd broken his hands instead of bruising his ribs and knocking his head. "Best not wear a hat and disturb the bandage. You'll only be outside for a few minutes." She took his scarf and wrapped the length around his neck, her fingers brushing his chin. Her gaze met his. Color rose in her cheeks, and she lowered her eyes.

Even through the wool of her gloves, Alana's touch sent a tingle down his spine. *Is it my imagination that her hands are lingering, as if she's enjoying touching me?*

Charlie burst through the door and skidded to a stop. "Mr. Muth has a huge load of things. He says they're for *us*." The boy's eyes were as big and bright as silver coins. "He's brought almost the whole store!" He didn't wait for a response, but popped back outside, slamming the door behind him.

Patrick stooped to let Alana pull his woolen hat over his head, wishing he could give her a thank you kiss. *If only we were married.* He imagined the pleasure he'd take in giving and receiving kisses in the midst of performing ordinary tasks—provided no one was around, of course, actions that would be much easier in the privacy of his big house. With that wistful thought, he followed Alana through the door, the cold wind chilling his face.

Outside, the winter dusk spread purple and blue shadows over the prairie. The twins swarmed about Patrick, their eyes excited, noses pink from cold. "Is everything in the wagon really for *us*, Mr. Gallagher?"

"Well, I doubt Mr. Muth will part with his milk cans." Patrick teased, and then shooed them toward the wagon. "Start unloading the parcels." He took a few steps to meet the neighbor, who'd removed his rabbit fur hat to greet Alana, exposing shoulder-length pale hair.

She greeted him and then performed introductions.

The men nodded and shook hands.

The dairyman was about Patrick's age and size, perhaps burlier, although he couldn't tell with the bulky fur coat the man wore. Muth had bright blue eyes, a ruddy face, and a blond beard. Patrick had imagined a somber German or Scandinavian, so the man's wide grin caught him by surprise.

Muth jerked his head toward the wagon, hitched to a pair of brown horses, one with white stockings. "Have a heap of parcels, bags, and crates back there for you."

"What?" Alana hurried to the wagon, placed her hands on top of the side, and looked over, her expression curious. "Oh, my Lord!"

While Patrick would have preferred to keep watching her reaction, politeness made him focus on Erik Muth. "Mrs.

O'Donnell has some hot tea for you, and Charlie will see to your horses if you step inside for a bit."

"No need for that. I won't say no to tea, though, but I'll help you unload first and then be on my way. I'll have Mrs. O'Donnell pour the tea in a jar and take it with me. My *wife*—" he favored the word "—frets if I'm too late. Daisy seems to think I'll be attacked by a grizzly or such."

The fatuous look on the man's face told Patrick that Muth didn't mind humoring his wife.

"Daisy expected me to be gone longer than usual, because I delivered milk to some far locations. But the horse on the right—" he tipped his chin to the horse with white stockings "—threw a shoe. Turns out to be a good thing. I was late enough that I could haul the youngsters back from school."

Charlie passed them, carrying a flour sack in one hand and a parcel tucked under his other arm. "I'll tell Ma you can't stay, Mr. Muth, and to put your tea in a jar." He hurried toward the house.

"My Daisy is with child," Muth explained, with a proud smile. "She's never taken to the *wild wilderness*." He emphasized the two words as if quoting her. "But in her condition, she frets more. I'm sure, she'll settle soon."

Patrick hoped for Muth's sake that was true. The isolation and sheer brutal labor of breaking the untouched prairie land into a prosperous farm beat down far too many women. He strode to stand next to Alana, grinned at her, and then leaned over the side of the wagon and rummaged through a wooden crate of cans of food to find one of peaches. He straightened and extended the can to Muth. "Maybe this will sweeten the delay. I hear your wife's partial to peaches, and I'm appreciative of you acting the teamster for my goods."

Muth gave the can a bewildered glance. "No need for that. Mighty glad to help out."

"And I'm *mighty glad* to send you home with a surprise for your wife."

From the glint in his eyes and the sudden grin breaking over his face, the man foresaw a pleasurable evening with a happy wife. With a nod of thanks, he accepted the can.

Rory trudged up, the rifle over one shoulder. He saw Patrick eying his empty hand and shrugged. "Eagle or fox got to the rabbit first." He greeted the dairyman and then looked back and forth from the children running to and from the house carrying the brown-paper parcels and burlap or cotton bags. "What's this about?"

"Muth delivered a few supplies I ordered." Patrick made himself sound matter-of-fact.

Rory's eyes bulged. "You call this a *few*?"

"I have a big appetite," Patrick said deadpan, although sure the glee in his eyes gave him away. "Now put up your gun and help with the unloading so your neighbor can get home to his wife."

His mouth tight, Rory looked about to argue but then shook his head, grabbed a heavy sack, and headed to the house.

Muth glanced from Patrick's ribs to his bandaged head and met his eyes. "Heard what happened. I'm keeping the news from Daisy, though, else she'll not let me out of her sight." He set the can of peaches on the driver's seat. "She'll learn soon enough, but 'til then, I'd like some peace." Moving to the side, he leaned over the wagon and hefted the crate containing the cans. "Looks like we've got all you ordered."

Seeing Patrick hadn't lifted a thing, Alana gave him a satisfied nod and moved toward the house.

Mr. Muth raised his eyebrows and looked from Alana to Patrick but said nothing.

Alana held open the door for the men to file through.

Inside, Patrick saw the laden table, although the bowl of watermelon pickles had been removed to make way for bags, a crate, and the packages. The children had taken off their outerwear and stood around the table with expectant expressions.

Henrietta moved around them to hand Mr. Muth a Mason jar wrapped in a towel. "Are you sure you won't stay?"

The dairyman shook his head. "If we have a day that's clear and warmer, I'll bring Daisy for a visit. She's not up to driving over by herself."

"We'd love to have her," Henrietta said warmly. "I haven't seen her all winter."

"When the baby comes, I know we'll need your help—at least until Daisy's mother arrives, which she's bound and determined to do." Mr. Muth rolled his eyes, as if indicating he wasn't looking forward to his mother-in-law's arrival, and raised the jar in a thank you. To a chorus of good-byes, he opened the door and walked out.

Isleen danced close and tugged on Patrick's arm. "May we please open up everything?"

"Go right ahead." He raised his arms to unbutton his coat, only to have Alana forestall him by pushing down his hands and doing the task herself.

Her color was high, and she didn't meet his eyes. But a smile played about her lips. She turned from him to hang up their outerwear.

As if to embrace the whole table, Isleen spread out her arms. "This is better than Christmas."

Rory frowned at Patrick and seemed about to voice a protest.

Patrick held out a hand to forestall him. "You all saved my *life*. A few supplies and presents aren't enough to repay that. Not to mention that you are forced to put up with me for a while."

Rory shot him an exasperated look, followed by a wry shake of his head.

"Allow me to express my appreciation." Patrick found himself almost pleading, so he took a breath. "I don't have a family to indulge and planning this surprise has given me great pleasure and taken my mind off my troubles. I certainly can afford it."

Shifting his weight, Rory studied Patrick's face, then his gaze roved over the pleading expressions of his children, at last locking with his wife's gaze in a silent communication.

Henrietta nodded and smiled, as if in encouragement.

Rory grinned. "Guess we're about to experience Christmas in February. Not much different than December, anyway. Still cold and snowy."

The children cheered and scooted to sit on the benches at the table, the twins together on the kitchen side, and Charlie opposite them.

By tacit agreement, the adults stood back and let them explore. They made quick shrift of poking through the staples, such as beans and flour but stopped to exclaim over the oranges and lemons.

Standing behind the girls, Henrietta reached over Isleen's shoulder to pick up a lemon. She sniffed the rind and smiled. "This brings back memories of Virginia—those afternoons of sitting on our porch and drinking lemonade."

"Surrounded by your beaus," Rory cut in with a playful scowl.

She met his gaze. "But I chose you."

Rory moved around the table to join her. "And I had to whisk you away to Montana to escape your other suitors."

Her cheeks pinked, and she glanced at Patrick and Alana, shaking her head. "Don't you believe him. We didn't move here until years later."

"To escape your swains," Rory repeated. Then he winked at Patrick. "They kept coming around, 'til it was either shoot 'em or head west." He reached Henrietta's side and, with a casual arm around her waist, pulled his wife near, until they stood hip to hip. Although they turned their attention to their offspring, a bond resonated between them.

Living intimately with this family in a small space had given Patrick an opportunity to observe the O'Donnells' relationship—unlike his parents' more reserved one. Henrietta and Rory had opened his eyes to the affection possible between a husband and wife. He enjoyed the couple's sense of humor and obvious love. His gaze slid to Alana, who watched her young cousins with a fond expression.

As if sensing his regard, she glanced at him, a soft look in her eyes.

Warmth settled heavy in his belly, rising to fill his chest. Their gazes held, and only Henrietta speaking drew their attention.

"Children, mind you be careful with that paper and don't tear it," she warned. "We'll find plenty of uses for it later."

Obediently, they untied the string and unwrapped the packages before handing the brown paper to their mother to fold into neat squares.

Charlie had the first one open, exposing a pile of fine white cotton and some glimpses of blue embroidered flowers and frothy lace. "Eww!" he exclaimed, holding up Alana's new petticoat.

Isleen giggled, her shoulders bouncing.

"You can have it." Charlie threw the undergarment across the table at his sister.

"Charlie!" his mother reproved.

He flashed her an unrepentant grin and waved the paper in Henrietta's direction for her to take.

Isleen caught the petticoat and spread out the hem, fingering the row of blue flowers and machine-made lace. "This is so pretty."

"That—" Patrick told Isleen "—is for your cousin Alana to replace the one she ruined by making bandages for my wound."

"Oh," Isleen half stood so she could reach over the table and hand Alana the petticoat. "I want one like that when I grow up. I'd wear it to parties and to church on Sundays."

Red flooded Alana's face. She crumpled the petticoat between her hands.

Patrick enjoyed her blush and waited for a happy smile, even if she was too embarrassed to admire the undergarment in front of the men.

Instead, Alana dropped the petticoat on the table, not even

bothering to look at it. With an annoyed expression tightening her face, she turned to him and fisted her hands on her hips.

Uh, oh. Patrick's throat went dry. *This isn't turning out the way I expected.*

"Mr. Gallagher, I told you *not* to buy me a new one," she snapped.

The rest of the family stilled, obviously startled by her uncharacteristic behavior.

Patrick couldn't figure out why Alana was stirred up over a gift, even if the item was a feminine undergarment. Blushes and embarrassment, he could have understood. But not anger. *If she's this upset over the petticoat, which I think good manners would indicate I replace, how will she react to the dress material and the shawl?*

He realized Alana might be viewing the supplies and presents as courtship gifts. *Which, to be honest, they were. What if she's angry about my pursuing her if she's not interested.* Heat prickled the back of his neck.

"You didn't *listen* to me." This time her tone wasn't as sharp.

He swallowed, feeling he was walking down a manure-strewn road, stepping carefully to avoid any pungent piles. "You're right," Patrick said in the tone he used to calm a fretful horse. "I didn't listen to your *words*."

Her expression remained implacable.

"But I listened to what I thought were your *wishes*." Patrick imbued what he was saying with sincerity, hoping if Alana could discern his *intentions*, she'd stop being angry. "That, like most women, you'd like a pretty new petticoat." He gestured toward the garment.

Alana's head drooped and her shoulders rounded, as if the act of staying upright took too much of her energy.

He wanted to kiss the vulnerable spot on her exposed slender neck, feel the delicate white skin under his lips. But now Patrick feared he'd set back any progress between them and wondered if he'd ever have an opportunity to touch her so familiarly.

He waited on tenterhooks for her response. His heart

pounded so hard Patrick thought the sound would give away how much this conversation meant to him. He sent up a prayer for divine help.

As if in inspiration, a more rational argument came to him. "You ruined your petticoat for me, Alana," he said in a soft tone. "If the situation was reversed, and I'd torn up a shirt to bandage you, wouldn't you want to fix that shirt for me in the best way you could?"

Alana finally raised her head. "You're right." Although she smiled, her eyes appeared sad. "Thank you for such a thoughtful gift."

As if to draw attention away from her niece, Henrietta rattled the brown paper she'd taken from Charlie. As she was in the process of folding it, she paused. Holding up the paper, she tapped some lettering. "These parcels are labeled with names. This was obviously meant for Alana to open." She glanced around the table. "Children, stop everything until we sort this out."

Charlie picked up a package. "This one's for me!" He hefted it. "Can I open it, Ma?"

"Wait until we check each one." Henrietta reached for a package near her and read the name. "Oh." With a startled look she glanced at Patrick. "This one's for me."

"I didn't leave anyone out." He grinned at her. "Even Sian can gnaw on the hambone after you've made soup with it."

"Well, that certainly is generous of you."

Rory gestured toward the package. "Show us what's inside."

Everyone watched Henrietta undo the string and unfold the paper to reveal the emerald fabric.

She gasped and held the swath of material to her chest. "Why, this is so beautiful!"

Isleen fingered the edge of the fabric. "Ma, you'll look so pretty in this. Can I use some for new hair ribbons?" She held up the end of one of her braids. "I can wear them on Sunday."

"I'm sure there'll be enough to spare."

Idelle bounced in her seat. "Ma hasn't had a new dress in *years,*" she said to Patrick. "She said it's better for us to have something new because we're growing."

"Very practical." Patrick glanced at Rory to make sure he hadn't rubbed the man's poverty in his face, but he was beaming at his wife, as if imagining her wearing the dress when it was finished.

He relaxed and enjoyed as each one took turns opening their gifts. The girls squealed over the flower-sprigged fabric in pale blue, and Charlie, although liking his new shirt, levitated off the bench, brandishing his pocketknife.

"Something extra for taking such good care of Thunder," Patrick told him, even though he knew the boy felt working with the horse was enough of a treat.

"Gee willikers, Mr. Gallagher!" Charlie glanced at Patrick before examining the knife.

"Charlie," his mother cautioned. "No using slang. Thank Mr. Gallagher properly."

"I'm mighty appreciative, Mr. Gallagher," Charlie said, his eyes shining with sincerity. "I'll make you a present of the first thing I carve."

Patrick gave the boy a solemn nod. "I'd like that."

Charlie returned his attention to the knife, snapping the blade open and shut several times.

Patrick loved watching the children's faces light up and seeing their happiness reflected in the pleased glow of their parents' expressions. This occasion certainly was better than Christmas at his place, which tended to be a fairly subdued holiday. After breakfast, he'd hand out presents to his stablemen and his housekeeper, and he received one in return that everyone had chipped in for. Once the presents were opened and admired, the workers finished their chores, only to later come together and sit down to enjoy a Christmas feast. A pleasant day, but nothing compared to the energy and excitement buzzing in this room.

Patrick had never given much thought to children, beyond

having a son or two to someday step into his boots. But after these days of close contact with Charlie and the twins, he'd come to want children of his own.

Paper crackled as Alana opened her parcel to reveal navy blue broadcloth, sprinkled with a pattern of pale blue and gold ribbons.

Whether it was Mrs. Cobb or the sheriff who'd chosen the fabric, she'd fulfilled expectations that had been printed on his list. *Miss O'Donnell, dress material (navy blue, if possible)*

Patrick hoped Alana would like the fabric, but after her reaction to the petticoat, he braced for a protest, for anger, as with the petticoat but dared to hope for a more positive response.

Her only reaction was a widening of her eyes. Then, as if reading his thoughts, Alana looked at him. Her mouth turned up at the corners. "Thank you, Patrick. This will make a fine dress for Sundays."

"And parties," he echoed, thinking of Isleen's earlier words.

"And parties," she agreed. The smile remained, although the sadness in her eyes seemed, if anything, to deepen. "I will think of you when I wear it." She glanced at Idelle. "You can have some of mine for hair ribbons," she said gaily, acting perhaps too cheerful.

With an uneasy feeling, Patrick watched Alana. Although she was saying and doing all the right things, something was wrong, and he couldn't quite put his finger on what.

He glanced around to see if anyone else had noticed something odd about her, but the others were caught up in the thrill of their presents. The family seemed as happy about each other's gifts as they were about their own.

He couldn't figure out a way to talk privately to Alana tonight, but he'd try tomorrow.

Chapter Ten

That night after supper, the family gathered around the fireplace. They'd arranged their chairs in a semi-circle to catch the heat and light from the flames. Rory seemed content to stare into the fire, while Henrietta darned a sock. Only Charlie, working arithmetic problems on his slate, remained at the table.

The twins were waiting until their brother finished so they could use the slate for their schoolwork. In the meantime, when they couldn't convince their mother to immediately begin making their dresses, they coaxed Patrick to hold the finished end of the rag braid they plaited to make into a rug. A battered cardboard box near their feet held a pile of rags cut into strips. When one twin came to the end of her piece, she'd rummage through the box, select one, stitch it on, and continue the braid.

The girls chattered to Patrick, telling stories of each rag that had once been a piece of clothing. He seemed to enjoy helping the twins, arbitrating when they bickered over which color to choose next, and even appearing gratified when Idelle remarked how much faster their braid grew with his help as the anchor.

Since the girls focused on their guest, Alana could remain silent, continuing to knit the lace once destined for her old petticoat. Now that she had a new one, she could consign the damaged undergarment to be worn only when doing the messiest of chores and use this lace on something else.

Alana had positioned herself so her hands moved in the light of the second oil lamp, but her face remained in shadow. If she were to make sense of the thoughts churning in her mind, she didn't want her expression to give anything away.

After becoming upset with Patrick, Alana had worked hard to pretend all was well with her—something she had plenty of experience with since leaving Ireland. Her family seemed fooled by the show of normalcy, but she suspected Patrick wasn't, for he sent studied glances her way far too often for her comfort.

Thinking back to the moment she'd held the new petticoat, Alana tried to trace the origins of the surge of emotion she'd experienced. Now the strength of her reaction seemed ridiculous, but at the time, she'd practically shaken with anger. *Why?*

Such behavior was unlike her. The only two occasions Alana could recall ever feeling so angry, she'd also been acting protective. Once she'd railed at William Doody because he refused to refrain from marital relations, even though his wife had borne a babe a year and then miscarried three more. She'd harshly told him that if he didn't want to be a widower raising ten children on his own, he'd better be more considerate of his wife. Another time, Granny Gogerty attempted to drown her cat because she feared the animal would suck the breath from her infant grandson. Luckily the cat clawed its way to freedom. Alana bandaged the daft old woman's hands and arms and gave her a sharp scolding to set her right. Cat and baby both thrived.

The memories made her think of Timkin, her confidant, in whom she'd confided both experiences. He'd always been such a good listener—something she'd loved about him.

Alana had left Ireland with a broken heart, knowing her life would completely change. What she hadn't realized was how much *she* had changed as a result of Timkin's rejection, and, she reflected in dismay, in ways she didn't like. *Will I always become angry when a man doesn't do what I want? As if I'm some spoiled beauty needing her every whim indulged.* The idea almost nauseated her.

Perhaps I just needed to be angry, instead of sad and mopey, and Patrick became the target. She took a deep breath. *He didn't deserve the lambasting. Too bad I didn't have a chance to express my ire to Timkin.* She imagined scolding him like a fishwife, shaking a finger in his face. The image almost made her laugh, and, suddenly, she felt better.

She peeped at Patrick from under lowered eyelashes. Although as different from Timkin as could be—both in appearance and personality—his big body and bold, handsome looks had grown on her sensibilities.

He is, indeed, a fine figure of a man. The more she was around him, the more attracted she became, something that just a week ago, she wouldn't have believed possible. *But attraction isn't love.*

"Finally!" Charlie threw down his chalk and then had to grab the piece before it rolled off the table. "I never thought I'd get that last one right. I had to go through the problem three times before I found my mistake," he said in a long-suffering tone. He waved at the slate. "Your turn," he told the twins.

Isleen made a face at him.

Slumping, Idelle let out a sigh.

Charlie swung his legs over the bench and jumped to his feet. He picked up a piece of pine and a page from the newspaper that he'd set on the table and walked over to take Isleen's chair. He spread the paper on the floor near his feet, took out the new knife from his pocket, threw Patrick an appreciative grin, and began to slice shavings off the middle of the wood.

Patrick raised his eyebrows. "What are you making for my present? Or is it a surprise."

"A horse like Thunder. I've carved one before using Pa's knife."

"Came out looking like a three-legged dog," Isleen teased.

Her mother sent her reproving look. "That's enough out of you, young lady. You two, get going on your schoolwork."

The girls knotted the end of the rag braid and neatly coiled it into the box on top of the rags before slowly rising to their feet.

Isleen, obviously dawdling, stopped to look out the window into the darkness. "It's snowing."

Idelle joined her. "Maybe we won't have to go to school tomorrow."

"We could work on our dresses," Isleen said in a wistful tone.

Henrietta glanced up from her darning. "When you two are finished with your schoolwork, if it's *not too late,* I think we can have some of that popcorn Patrick brought us."

"We won't be long," Idelle assured her mother, while her sister hurried to the table. "We did most of the schoolwork on the way home. We read the history chapter about the Battle of Lexington and memorized two stanzas of Longfellow's "Paul Revere's Ride"."

"*One* more than we need to know for tomorrow," Isleen interjected before plopping onto the bench in a most unladylike manner that, luckily, her mother didn't witness.

As if her twin hadn't spoken, Idelle continued. "As well as our spelling words. Now all we have is our arithmetic problems."

With the girls no longer claiming Patrick's attention, he began watching Alana in almost the same way Rory gazed into the fire, as if her moving hands and the inches added to her lace trim mesmerized him. She suspected he kept trying to see her face, and she was grateful for the shadows.

Unable to bear his scrutiny, Alana wracked her brain for something to occupy his attention until she hit on an idea. She set her handwork on the table and rose, skirting the chairs to reach the ladder of the loft. She climbed up and, without her feet leaving the rung, she stretched to pull her satchel from beside her bed. The heavy volume of Shakespeare's plays laid on the bottom. She fished out the book and climbed back down, walking to Patrick and handing him the volume. "Make yerself useful, boyo," she said in a playful tone. "Pick a play and read to us."

"What a lovely idea, Alana," Henrietta exclaimed. "It will be nice to listen to a different voice."

"What, are you tired of me Irish accent?" Rory said with a sly look and an exaggerated lilt to his words.

Henrietta merely smiled and shook her head. She placed her darning into her sewing basket and stood. "Let me first make the popcorn." She motioned for Alana to come help.

Alana had never eaten popcorn—a distinctly American food—so she was eager to see how it was made. She followed her aunt into the kitchen.

Henrietta spooned lard into a kettle on the stove. "The trick is heating the oil just right. Too quickly and the kernels only partially explode. Too slowly, and they don't pop at all." She smiled at Alana. "Those are the old maids." She poured a handful of popcorn into the kettle, resulting in a low sizzle, and then set on the lid. "We need to make sure the kernels don't burn, so we need to often shake the kettle, and slightly lift the lid to release the steam. As soon as a bunch pop—" She lifted her chin toward the ladle "—your job is to remove the ones that are ready."

Alana nodded her understanding.

After a few minutes, the first kernels crackled, and, with a popping sound, burst open into white puffs. After that, they quickly exploded, keeping Alana busy scooping out the snowy pieces and dropping them into a big wooden bowl.

When they finished, Henrietta sprinkled salt over the whole batch. She poured a portion into a bowl that she placed on the table for the girls to share. Then she distributed the rest into five other bowls, so everyone could have their own. She gave two to Alana. "Hand these out. Make sure to pass out napkins, as well. I'll make us all some chamomile tea with honey."

After Alana handed Patrick his bowl, with a thumb and forefinger, he grasped a kernel and held it up. "You realize I can't eat and read at the same time."

"I'll eat yours," Charlie offered.

"Don't even try. My knife is bigger." Patrick winked at the boy and ate the piece. "Perfect."

Alana went back for hers and Henrietta's bowls and set them on the side table, while Henrietta brought tea for everyone. She took a seat and gingerly put the first fluffy kernel into her mouth. The popcorn was airy and crispy. Each piece crunched and melted at the same time and tasted like salty goodness. She wanted to gobble up her share and, at the same time, savor each one. When her mouth became too dry from the salt, she took a sip of the hot tea, enjoying the sweetness of the honey. "This is wonderful!"

"You realize you're a full-fledged American now," Patrick said in a teasing tone. "Baptism by popcorn."

Heat rose in her face. Unknowingly, Alana had shifted into the light of the oil lamp. Although not entirely averse to the idea of becoming an American, she wasn't ready to open herself to Patrick's scrutiny. She slid the chair left a few inches and leaned back so the shadows once again enveloped her.

Patrick finished his share, set the bowl on the side table, wiped his hands on the napkin, and picked up the book. He paged through the thick volume before looking up. "Any suggestions?"

Alana absolutely did not want to hear *A Midsummer Night's Dream.* Puck reminded her too much of Timkin, but she didn't want to say so. What reason could she give for not liking the play? She braced herself for the wave of grief that inevitably came when she thought of her lost love, but when the emotion hit, the feeling seemed more wavelet than wave.

Before Alana could figure out what that change meant, Isleen bounced up from the bench and came a few steps closer, her hands clasped in front of her chest. *Romeo and Juliet,* she said, in a dreamy tone. "The older students are studying the play, and I've been listening when they read aloud. But mostly Mrs. Gordon talks to them about the meaning of the words and character roles, and they answer questions. I haven't gotten to hear the whole story."

Patrick grinned at the girl. *Romeo and Juliet* it is."

With raised eyebrows, Henrietta sent Isleen a stern look and pointed toward the table.

Patrick glanced at Rory and Henrietta. "Unless someone else votes for another choice." His gaze lingered on Alana.

She shook her head, relieved by her cousin's choice.

"Very well." Patrick moved his chair closer to the oil lamp, held the book near the light, and began to read the opening lines. In the poetry of words and cadence only The Bard of Avon could produce, the first paragraph laid out the story and drew the listener in.

Two households, both alike in dignity,
In fair Verona, where we lay our scene,
From ancient grudge break to new mutiny,
Where civil blood makes civil hands unclean.
From forth the fatal loins of these two foes
A pair of star-cross'd lovers take their life....

As he read, Alana couldn't help but admire Patrick's smooth voice and how he brought the characters to life, making her appreciate Shakespeare in a way she hadn't before. Even though she kept her focus on her handwork, from time to time she glanced up and observed him.

Alana hadn't read the play for several years, and, at first, she found her sympathies lying with Romeo as he spoke of loving a girl who didn't love him back. When he lamented, "*Oh teach me how I should forget to think,*" Alana remembered all the times she'd had the same wish about Timkin. Somehow, lately, that wish had started coming true.

With that realization, she sucked in a sharp breath. *Why, since Patrick was attacked, I've barely given Timkin a thought until earlier tonight.*

Her chest expanded, as if filled with lightness and air. *My heart is healing.* The sense of relief at the insight brought tears to her eyes.

"*My bounty is as boundless as the sea, my love as deep....*" Patrick raised his gaze to lock with hers. "*The more I give to thee, the more I have, for both are infinite.*"

Desire stirred in Alana, different from her former longing for Timkin and an emotion she'd never thought she'd feel.

The sensation brought up a question from the depths of her heart.

Can I, like Romeo, fall in love again?

The next evening after supper, the dishes dried and put away, Alana donned her coat and slipped outside, needing some private time. She left Henrietta contentedly knitting by the fire, with the men working in the barn. She headed out to the prairie, trudging through the thin layer of snow, the breeze tugging the curls from under her cap to blow every which way. Her goal was a low hill on the edge of the horizon, where she could perform the ritual that she hoped would finally set her free.

When Alana crested the hill, she took a deep breath of brisk, clean air. The exercise and solitude had done her good, as if her blood now flowed throughout her body with renewed energy.

I must say goodbye to Timkin—a proper good-bye. Alana wrinkled her nose, realizing mayhap *good-bye* wasn't quite what she meant. Perhaps, instead, what was needed was a gentle blessing, a soft and loving opening of her hands to release into the wind the man—now seen as a beloved friend—whose memory she would always treasure.

Alana faced what she imagined was the direction of her homeland and used Juliet's line, although she altered the last bit. "*Parting is such sweet sorrow*, my dearest Timkin. That I shall say farewell…."

She searched her mind for the perfect send-off of her message. With a sense of rightness, Alana settled on an ancient Irish blessing and closed her eyes. "May the road rise to meet ye. May the wind be ever at yer back…."

Pausing, she stretched her arms toward the old country; behind her eyelids moisture gathered and spilled over. "May the sun shine warm upon yer face." Her voice grew thick with emotion, and she swallowed before continuing. "And the rains fall soft upon your fields."

Alana hesitated and then added one more wish for him. "May ye find a love that fills yer heart." She smiled, imagining a joyful expression on her friend's face instead of the tormented one he'd worn at their parting. "And until we meet again, dearest Timkin, may God hold ye in the palm of his hand." Sighing, she lowered her arms and felt warm wetness on her cheeks.

With a smile, Alana wiped away the tears and opened her eyes, looking around her as if seeing everything afresh.

The snow-covered, low hills were broken only by a distant smudge of brown trees, perhaps lining a stream. Layered blue-gray clouds edged in pale gold floated above faraway purple mountains.

So beautiful! She stared at the horizon, unable to even find words to describe the sight. With an ache of loneliness, she wished her sister were here. *I'll have to absorb everything about this moment so I can tell Bridget.* Yet Alana wondered if she could possibly render the visage into mere words.

Now, too, Alana knew she could unburden her heart to her twin—reveal the pain she'd carried and how she'd finally made peace with her feelings for Timkin. She could also admit the secret resentment she'd harbored toward Bridget for dragging her from their home, for forcing her into this new life. "I forgive ye, sister."

Under the clouds, as the sun dropped toward the mountains, the bottom of the golden ball cast pale heavenly light toward the earth. Rays streaked above the clouds and across the sky like a corona.

She tilted her face upward. "What color are ye?" she murmured, not quite able to put a name to the beautiful hue of the sky.

"Indigo," said a voice from behind her.

Alana hadn't realized she'd asked the question aloud. She

whirled to see Patrick holding Thunder's reins. Somehow, man and horse had managed to sneak up on her. Heat flooded her cheeks, but she didn't look away.

"My sister had a dress that color, and she called it indigo." His eyes intent, he gazed down at her. "Indigo," he repeated, his voice husky. "The color of your eyes."

Patrick saw Alana's motionless figure on a hill facing west. He rode Thunder in a sweeping angle that placed him toward the front right of her, giving him a close-up view.

She stood with her eyes closed and hands outstretched, her body elongated as if about to soar like an angel into the heavens, and didn't hear his approach.

Patrick propped an arm on the saddle horn to watch. His elbow nudged the gun holster at his hip. He'd taken to wearing the Colt whenever he left the house, even for short rides.

A smile crossed Alana's face, although her eyes remained closed.

Not wanting to interrupt her silent reverie, he quietly swung down from the horse, and, holding the reins, led Thunder closer, pausing a few yards away.

Too absorbed in her conversation with the sky, she didn't see him. The setting sun illuminated her face, gilding her curls and the faint freckles on her nose.

His heart clenched at the sight. *How could I have thought her interchangeable with Bridget?*

When he answered her question, and Alana spun to face him, Patrick was relieved to see she'd come back to earth. By the animation in her countenance at the sight of him, she seemed to have worked through whatever had been bothering her.

He let out a breath, a silent prayer of thanksgiving.

With a dimpled smile that made her eyes even bluer, she held her skirts a few inches from the ground, walked over to him, and stopped to pet the horse, as if the stallion had never frightened her.

"Communing with the sky?" he asked.

"I guess ye could say that. But I was really saying a proper farewell to my former life." She glanced from Thunder to Patrick. "Promisin' to find a way to root myself here in America, to face forward and not look behind me."

I like that idea just fine. "Are you still annoyed with me for the petticoat?"

She flashed him a gamin grin and pointed a toe forward, exposing a worn brown boot. Slowly, she lifted the hem of her dress a few inches to reveal white lace and blue-embroidered flowers. "I should save wearing it for good and not risk dirtying or tearing the lace while doing chores. But I couldn't resist today." Dipping her chin, she released her skirt.

"How about risking your petticoat while taking a ride on Thunder?"

"Patrick," Alana chided with a shake of her head. "As much as I'd like to take a turn on this boyo—" she ran a hand over Thunder's neck "—I can't ride astride with my dress kilted up. The other day was an emergency."

He rubbed his chin. "I don't know if Thunder would take to a sidesaddle, so I guess you'll need a gentle mare, a ladies saddle, and a riding habit."

Alana let out a sigh. "Might as well wish for the moon."

If she were mine, I could give her the moon. "Is that your real wish, Alana?"

"More my sister's," she retorted. She glanced toward the sun dropping behind the mountains. "Speaking of the moon, we'd better head home before it gets dark."

They fell into step, Patrick leading Thunder.

"As for me…." Her forehead crinkled, and she remained silent for a few minutes. "My moon dreams have changed. Now I suppose…." She slid him a sideways look, as if expecting a critical response.

"Go on," he encouraged.

"I'd like to study medicine." Her words lingered on the evening air.

"You certainly have the gift of healing. Would you want to become a doctor?"

She shook her head. "That's not the moon, that's wishing for the stars."

"A nurse, then?"

Alana shrugged. "In Ireland there were no other opportunities for learning beyond what my mother taught me. So why waste my thoughts on such dreams?"

"Let's pretend for a minute…that you could have whatever you wanted. Would you focus just on people? What about animals?"

"Small animals, aye." She glanced over her shoulder at Thunder. "I never thought to work on horses, because I wouldn't go near the creatures. But, now…maybe."

"It can't hurt to figure out what you want to be, Alana. A wife and mother, of course. But also a nurse, doctor, veterinarian, or something in between. You're capable of achieving any of those."

Frowning, she shook her head as if not believing him.

He stopped and set a hand on Alana's shoulder, turning her to face him. "The more you focus on the obstacles—how far away the moon and stars are—the greater they'll become. But if you keep your eye on the goal, then life or God or your own will or however you want to describe it, has a way of helping you to make that happen."

Her brows drew together. "Do ye really think I could?"

He smiled. "I have no doubt."

A cold gust blew tendrils of hair across her face. He reached up to tuck them into her cap.

She shivered and pulled her scarf tighter.

Patrick released her. "Let's get going before you freeze." He held out his elbow, hoping she'd allow him to escort her.

Alana wrapped her hand around his arm, glanced up at him, and smiled. "I will think on what ye've said." She gathered up her skirts with her free hand and tugged to get him moving.

As they strolled toward the house, twilight deepened. The moon peeked over the edge of the horizon and began to rise, milky-pale against the indigo sky, a beacon of hope and promise.

Chapter Eleven

Three days later, Patrick stood at the window of the house, washing the glass with crumpled newspaper dipped in a solution of diluted vinegar, as he watched for Alana to return from her walk. Since their last private conversation, she'd had a thoughtful air about her, as if she'd taken his words to heart and was pondering her future. Yet she'd also acted cheerful and seemed in good spirits, so he figured she wasn't worried or distressed.

The energy between them had changed—becoming more comfortable—with, on her part he dared hope, an obvious growing attraction to him. Mostly, he'd stepped back, wanting to give Alana time to sort through what was on her mind, hoping that whatever she decided about her future, he'd be included.

As Patrick healed, she allowed him to do heavier tasks, usually assisting her and Henrietta, although she'd still declared he shouldn't ride too far. Truthfully, Patrick had enjoyed being pampered a bit, even though his headache had dulled and the pain in his ribs lessened. If he were well, he'd have no excuse to stay, and he was far from ready to leave.

To keep from feeling like a malingerer, he helped out as much as he could. This time of year, Rory had little need for an extra pair of hands since the man had exhausted his lumber supply for building the barn addition. So Patrick assisted the women by doing such chores as scrubbing the floor, ironing clothes, chopping vegetables, blackening the stove, scouring pots and pans, cleaning and refilling the kerosene lamps, kneading bread dough, and, now, washing windows.

From this time at the O'Donnells', he'd developed a new appreciation for women's work. Not that he hadn't seen women laboring before—hanging up the wash, cooking, ironing. But he'd been ignorant of the multitude of the steps, many of mind-numbing drudgery, that went into keeping a family fed and clothed, and the home efficiently run. This new awareness left him feeling humbled and somewhat ashamed. He remembered his mother and, with regret, wished she were alive so he could express belated thankfulness for all she'd done for her family.

In fact, from this experience, Patrick had started forming a whole new political philosophy beyond his primary belief that the less the government interfered in a man's affairs, the better. Watching Henrietta and Alana go about their tasks prompted him to give serious thought to the issue of women's suffrage. He'd concluded that not only should females have the right to vote, they should probably be governing the whole darn country. He had no doubt a petticoat government would run more efficiently and far more peacefully than the one men had cooked up.

He crumpled another section of newspaper to dry the window, peering sideways through the glass to catch a glimpse of Alana. *What in tarnation is taking her so long?*

Although he knew worry was unreasonable, Patrick couldn't help a niggling doubt about Alana's safety that had overturned his peace. He tried to calm his thoughts and check his gut, seeing if his concern stemmed from his intuition or just the conjured vision of his beloved running afoul of robbers or some other danger. *I just want to know she's safe.*

Well…if I'm honest, I want to be taking that walk at her side.

"Patrick."

A hand touched his shoulder. Henrietta—the only other person in the house.

"Do not fret yourself."

He patted her hand and then shifted to face her. In this last week, with her health and appetite returning, his hostess had gained some weight and had more color in her face. He liked knowing the supplies he'd purchased had tempted her appetite. Patrick gave her a rueful smile. "Am I that obvious?"

She tilted her head and studied him. "I've come to know you well in this past week, and I believe you've fallen in love with my niece."

The directness of the statement took him aback, and he responded just as bluntly. "Alana rejected my offer to court her."

Henrietta drew her eyebrows together in a frown. "Perhaps Alana doesn't know her own mind." She paused, bit her lip. "My niece hasn't spoken a lot about Ireland…but I have a feeling she left behind a man she cared deeply about."

The thought made his stomach twist.

As if anticipating his reaction, Henrietta raised a hand in a stopping motion. "At the same time, I believe Alana isn't as indifferent as you might think. Tell me, when did you ask to court her?"

"Before I left. After she rejected me, I was so lost in gloomy thoughts and not alert to my surroundings that the robbers were able to attack." He shrugged off a prickle down his backbone at the memory and attempted a smile. "But I can't complain, considering I've had a chance to remain here longer."

A smile curled her lips. Henrietta shook her head in an amused, *Oh, Patrick* gesture. "I thought you meant you'd *recently* proposed. A lot has changed in a week—including, I believe—my niece's view of you."

"At times, I think that's true," he admitted. "But then doubt creeps in. With each day that passes, my love for her grows so much more…." Patrick searched for a description but couldn't find one that quite matched his feelings. He shrugged and abandoned the attempt. "*Real*, for want of a better word."

Henrietta's smile widened. She reached up and pulled his

head down to kiss his cheek. "I couldn't think of another man I'd rather have as a nephew-in-law." She stepped away, her eyes filling with happy tears. "Even though you'll take our Alana to live with you, I hope you'll bring her back for a visit from time to time."

The picture her words painted made his heartbeat race.

She pointed at the door. "What are you waiting for, *nephew*? Go to her."

Anticipation spurred him. Patrick leaned down to kiss Henrietta's cheek. "Thank you, Auntie." He grabbed his coat, threw his scarf around his neck, and shoved his hat on his head. Not taking the time to button up his coat, wrap the scarf tight, or pull out his gloves from his pocket, he strode out the door, determined to saddle Thunder, track down his beloved, and ask for her hand in marriage.

Patrick found Alana were he'd thought he would, on the same hill as before, her back to him, a hand shading her eyes as she watched a red-tailed hawk float in the vivid blue sky. He reined Thunder to a stop. *If we lived here, I'd build her a bench in this spot.* He imagined sitting with his arm around her, talking or silently observing the natural beauty of their surroundings.

This time she sensed his arrival, lowering her arm and slowly turning. She waited with a smile for Thunder to reach her. "Have ye come to tempt me to ride yer beastie?" she teased, her accent richly Irish and charming.

"What, ride with your skirts kilted up and showing your legs?" Widening his eyes, he pretended to sound shocked. "Of course."

Alana chuckled, showing her dimple, and patted the stallion. "Hello, me beautiful boyo," she crooned. "Sorry I am for calling ye a beastie. I was only jokin' with yer master."

Happy to hear her laughter, he swung down from the horse. "You've been doing a lot of thinking?"

"I feel I've lived a lifetime in this last week. I've learned. I've changed. I've had much to mull over."

Patrick let his admiration, no, his *love*, show on his face, without daring, yet, to speak and risk another rejection.

With her palm on Thunder's neck, Alana peeked at him before lowering her gaze. "Ye were quite taken with my sister."

Something about the way the skin tightened around her eyes made Patrick think he'd hurt her by singling out Bridget. Caught off guard by the comment, he tried to explain. "I'm just a rough rancher. Mostly, I'm focused on my horses. I've never courted a woman before. No wonder I've fumbled my way through the whole thing. Yet, Alana, I've come to care deeply for you."

When she lowered her gaze, apparently giving Thunder her full attention, Patrick knew he'd missed the right answer—the *tricky* answer. *I could dodge or admit the truth.* "I was taken with Bridget, yes. Since then, I've done a great deal of pondering on the subject to figure out why. I think my instincts were leading me in your direction. But you hid behind your twin. You never talked to me. In fact, you avoided me. Bridget was more outgoing, and she shared my love of horses, so she was the obvious choice. And she was *there*, Alana, and you were *gone*."

She glanced up, a guilty look in her eyes.

Ah, I'm right. Although best not rub that in. "If I'd put the two of you side by side, I'd have focused on *you*, not Bridget."

Alana raised a skeptical eyebrow, looking about to argue.

He lifted a hand in placation. "All right. I might still have focused on her at first, but if I had been around both of you for long, I *know* my heart would have chosen you."

Will she believe me?

Does it matter? Even if she cares, her heart might not be free. "Your aunt hinted that your affections might already be engaged…a man in Ireland."

A sad emotion crossed her face. "Timkin, my closest friend from early childhood, is…very *dear* to me."

His stomach clenched as if trying to absorb the blow.

"Like ye with Bridget, my heart led me to another man," she said, her expression earnest. "I thought the feelings I had for Timkin were the same as what he had for me, because I knew I was dear to him, too. But he didn't feel the same…*depth*. Didn't want to wed, which devastated me."

He lifted his hands as if to embrace her, to give comfort but reined in the impulse, not sure yet if she'd welcome his touch. "I do understand. Bridget's rejection hurt mostly because it hit my pride, especially since, at the same time, she chose another man instead of me. But I didn't feel deeply enough for her to be *devastated*."

"I wish I could say the same." Alana sighed and inclined her head. "I must be honest. I was at the point of not wanting to go on. Without Bridget at my side almost every moment of our journey to America, with her forcing me to live, I might have sunk into a decline and not recovered." The emotion behind her words lingered in the air.

Patrick sucked in a breath, not wanting to think of a world where they'd never met, where Alana had died of a broken heart.

"I can see that I wove a fantasy around Timkin that wasn't really love, but a picture in my mind of what love is supposed to be." She touched her chest and rubbed a circle there. "Now, I can allow his place in my heart to be merely that of a dear friend."

Has she space there now for me? Patrick had never wanted anything, not even a win from Thunder's biggest races, like he wanted to be Alana's true love. "I've had my share of wild times and wasn't ready to settle down until I came to Sweetwater Springs. But even then, it was *you*, my dearest Alana. You, with your sweetness and goodness, your care for my well-being, have gentled me to your hand." Knowing he'd laid out his feelings, he waited anxiously for her response.

Alana couldn't resist teasing Patrick about his analogy. "Gentled to yer hand? Like Thunder?"

He rolled his eyes. "I'm being serious here. I want to marry you."

She sent him a mock demure glance from under her lashes.

"I know living away from your sister will be hard. But Crenshaw isn't far by train, and you could visit often. When I bring Thunder to service mares in the ranches around Sweetwater Springs, you could accompany me. Or I could hire James, and he and Bridget could move to live near us."

The extent of his thoughtfulness deeply touched her, making her tumble the rest of the way into love. But Alana wasn't quite ready to say yes. She had a sense that he'd value her all the more for having to work for her acceptance. Besides, she wanted to tease him a bit. Picturing the Thompson and Cameron homes, Alana asked, "Does yer house have a washroom with indoor plumbing?"

"Of course," he said with a shrug of obvious impatience. "What does that have to do with anything?"

"Then, I will consider marrying ye."

"You'll consider my proposal because I have indoor plumbing?" he asked in an exasperated tone.

"Not that *ye* have indoor plumbing. All humans have such," she said playfully, touching his stomach. "But because yer *house* does."

He scowled, but his eyes showed a hint of vulnerability.

Alana clasped Patrick's arm, feeling the hard muscle under her hand. "Nay, love. 'Tis only an extra blessing, for I'd live with ye in a humble homestead and be grateful to do so."

His scowl smoothed out. "Alana," he said, her name a sigh of relief. "'*The more I give to thee, the more I have.*'"

The line from *Romeo and Juliet* that he'd read while gazing at her four nights ago sounded pleasant to her ears.

"'For both are infinite.'" A gleam lit his eyes. "Including my home's indoor plumbing," he added.

She chuckled.

"You're going to keep me on my toes, aren't you?" Patrick pulled Alana into a hug and lifted her off her feet.

Alana squealed with laughter, a sound she couldn't recall ever making, and playfully smacked him. "Set me down, ye oaf. I'm not done talking."

"As her majesty commands." He slid her down, but didn't entirely release her, keeping a loose grip around her waist.

Nor did she release him. Instead, she splayed her palms over his upper arms.

"Is there something else you need to know? If you're wondering whether the barn has an indoor washroom, the answer is no."

Alana pretended to pout, but she couldn't maintain the expression, for the joy bubbling up made her smile.

His expression grew serious. "As important, if not *more* important than indoor plumbing, are your medical studies. If you wish to work with the local physician or veterinarian…go away to school, then I will back you one hundred percent, even if that means living apart with only visits for a few years."

Happy tears misted her eyes. She'd never felt so respected and adored. "If I hadn't met ye, I might have missed what it really is to love. I wouldn't have thought that a big rough rancher with a scary horse would understand me so thoroughly. That he'd feel safe enough for me to become unjustly angry with." She squeezed his arms for emphasis. "That he'd coax my secret dreams into words and guide me through my fear of horses. Whereas Timkin *indulged* my fears, ye helped me *face* them. I didn't appreciate yer interference at the time, but now that I've ridden Thunder, I've freed myself."

"I can tell," he told her with obvious pride.

"I've realized how much more important it is to have a partner to help me be the best I can be as a woman and a wife." She gave him a shy smile. "And I can be a helpmate to him in that same way…to *you* in that way."

Patrick's eyes watered. He took a shuddering breath, roughly rubbed an arm across his face, and gathered her to him.

The intimate feel of his body, his strength, made her feel cherished and protected.

His eyebrow angled up. "Now can I kiss you as I've wanted to for *days*, or do you have more talkin' to get out?"

Alana chuckled and sent up a silent prayer of gratitude for all that had brought her to this moment. Filled with blessings and bliss, she tilted her face to his.

With the tender touch of his hand, Patrick cupped her cheek and stared into her eyes—into the very depths of her soul. Then he leaned down and tentatively brushed his lips against hers, as if fearing she might still pull back.

The brief contact of his mouth sent a shiver through her. Alana rose on her tiptoes to press against him and returned his kiss with all the fervor in her heart, wanting him to know she'd finally found her way home.

A Rolling Stone

Chapter One

SWEETWATER SPRINGS, MONTANA
Spring 1895

Catriona O'Donnell shifted on the hard seat of the train transporting her across America to a reunion with her twin sisters, searching for a comfortable spot. She placed a hand over the curve of her stomach, covering the bastard she carried in her womb. *Baby Flea probably rides far more comfortably than I do,* she thought resentfully.

Discovering her sisters had left her behind still stung. Four months ago, while Catri was gallivanting around Ireland with Bartley Crogan, Bridget and Alana had emigrated to live with their uncle's family in Montana. Catri had returned home, thinking to find a refuge after her ill-judged elopement—only to find their croft occupied by new people.

Logically, Catri couldn't blame the twins. *I'm the one who abandoned them first when they needed me the most, the one who didn't contact them once during the five months I was away.* Pain had driven her from her home into the arms of the peddler. *Pain I'd thought to outrun.* But instead she'd taken the pain along, adding a further burden of guilt and shame. *And I've acquired a child for the world to bear witness to my disgrace.*

She wiggled again, trying to squeeze some life into her numb buttocks, and uttered a low-breathed curse she'd learned from Bartley. *Mama would wash my mouth out with soap for even knowing such words.* The memory of her dear mother made her heart feel heavy as a stone.

If Mama were still alive, I wouldn't be in this situation. Then she thought of Godfrey Ainsworth, in his shining glory. *I would have still ended up in disgrace.* She'd paid a heavy price to learn the handsome son of the squire was just another man, with a man's selfish needs.

Throughout the journey to America, Catri had hoped to miscarry—to lose this unwanted child, so when she arrived in Sweetwater Springs, Montana, she could pretend the whole shameful escapade had never happened. But instead, her stomach had only grown larger.

Escapade. Hardly the way to describe the six-month liaison she'd had with the peddler. The memory of Bartley Crogan left a sour taste in her mouth. She tried to swallow from a throat gone suddenly dry.

She reached for the Mason jar on the seat next to her for some water. Although she wanted a long drink to quench her thirst, Catri restrained herself to only a sip. The baby's weight on her bladder had already caused her too many trips to the toilet, a long embarrassing walk through swaying cars with everyone knowing where she was headed. Even if she'd needed to relieve herself, over the past hours, her energy had drained. She was too tired and weak to move.

Soon she'd be with her sisters, and they'd make a home together—the three of them and the baby. Their own little cloister, although she supposed Bridget would want to be out and about working with horses, and Alana would be healing the whole neighborhood. Just as well those two were capable of earning a living. Catri could keep house for them and take care of the baby. After the last tumultuous year, all she wanted was a peaceful home, without a man in sight.

Please, God, may this child be a girl! She didn't want a son who would remind her of either Godfrey or Bartley. She didn't want a boy who'd grow up to be a man.

The connecting door opened, sending a gust of smoky air into the compartment. A portly conductor stepped through and strode down the aisle. "Sweetwater Springs coming up."

Catri didn't bother looking out, for she didn't care what she'd see. She'd viewed enough American frontier towns through the train window to have a good idea of what she'd find. They all looked pretty much the same: rickety, unpainted buildings with rising front panels that held store names, one church with a steeple, and more saloons than necessary, flanking a muddy main street.

A bitter smile pulled at her mouth. So might it be said for Irish villages, although perhaps stone cottages appeared more picturesque and tidy in comparison to the press of false-fronted wooden buildings thrown up on dirt lots. Traveling with a peddler had given her a chance to learn of the wider world—even if that only meant a corner of Ireland—although the journey hadn't been the escape she'd craved. *One place is just like the other when you're with the wrong lover.*

With clanks, metallic groans, and a screech of brakes, the train jerked to a stop.

If Bridget and Alana had known of her arrival, if they awaited her, Catri would have peered eagerly out the window. She had no desire to see the empty platform, or even worse, other travelers being welcomed by loved ones. *Who would have thought I'd miss my annoying younger sisters so much?*

An ache of loneliness shuddered through her body. But she'd come to know well the hollowness echoing inside her, and Catri squashed down the emotion, as she had done these many months. Instead, she held her head even higher, looking straight ahead, as if, by refusing to look out the window, she could postpone the moment when she'd find herself alone outside the train station.

With a grimace, Catriona pulled out the single hatpin that

anchored her misshapen and dusty hat to the bun of her hair. It didn't help that, somewhere along the way, she'd lost her other hatpin. Consequently, the hat often slipped to the side of her head.

She twisted her grandmother's *claddagh* on her finger, the heart on the ring facing her fingertips to symbolize her supposed marriage. The ring was too big and tended to slip sideways. *Mary, Mother of God, please may it not be a sign of what's to come.* She'd already had her life turned upside down, and wanted nothing more than a simple, straight future.

Catri smoothed a wrinkle from her skirt, dyed black to lend credence to the lie of her widowhood. She'd let out the seams as far as they'd go, but still, her bulky belly strained against the fabric. Soon the garment would no longer fit, and she had no idea what she'd do to acquire a dress to wear through the rest of her pregnancy. Another problem to add to the dozens she already carried. Perhaps when she finally caught up with her sisters living at her aunt and uncle's farm, she'd find solutions.

Please, dear Lord and the Blessed Mother, let that be so.

Moss Callahan rode Traveler, his white gelding, down the dirt track leading from the Thompson ranch to Sweetwater Springs. He'd left at daybreak, just in time to escape the bustle of the O'Donnell twins' wedding, carrying all his worldly possessions in two saddlebags and a bundle wrapped inside the bedroll, strapped behind the saddle. The wanderlust tickle in the soles of his feet this past month had grown to a fierce itch, too acute to ignore—not that he'd intended to do so. He'd just had to wait out the winter weather. A ludicrous self-delusion. In Montana, snow could still fall in the summer. Spring, more often than not, brought one rainstorm after another.

But today had dawned sunny and bright. Wedding weather,

the Thompson's housekeeper had proclaimed, a wide grin crinkling the wrinkles of her face.

Traveling weather, Moss contended. But he hadn't said so aloud.

After a hard winter cooped up with a bunch of stinkin' cowboys, or out riding in freezing weather, Moss was more than ready to cut out for someplace warm. Wyoming was the farthest south he'd ever traveled. Texas beckoned, for he had a hankering to see the ocean.

The *real* reason he was scootin' out as quietly as he'd arrived nine months ago—the one he didn't really want to think about—was his fear of *wedding fever*. Yes, a highly susceptible outbreak of the illness, caused by proximity to the pretty O'Donnell girls—the twins and their cousin Sally—had driven Moss away from gainful employment made more than tolerable by the fairness and generosity of his boss, Wyatt Thompson, and his beautiful wife Samantha. He certainly had some regrets about leaving Thompson's employ, which wasn't usually the case. Bosses always looked sharp-eyed at the new hand—and Moss was always the new one—and assigned him the worst jobs.

But the marrying epidemic had infected two of Thompson's cowboys and also one of the male guests—a horse breeder from a neighboring town—striking the men like lightning. Moss wasn't sure if susceptibility to the sickness was caused by nearness to a pretty O'Donnell girl in particular, or just from loneliness in general. But he wasn't of a mind to stick around and become victim number four. *Not, God be thanked, that there are any more O'Donnell girls of suitable age to infect vulnerable males.*

But I'm not taking chances.

The train had just arrived when Moss reined in by the brown clapboard station. He'd almost cut the time too close. He swung down from the saddle, tossed the reins around the hitching post, and took the stairs two at a time to the platform, racing to buy a ticket for himself and a stall in the horse car for Traveler.

The door to the depot stood open, probably to let in the fresh spring air.

A young woman in a loose gray coat and carrying a bag came around the corner of the building. Something about her seemed familiar, although Moss knew he'd never seen her before. Even showing the ravages of a train journey, he'd have remembered her ethereal beauty—the blue eyes that stared past him as if he weren't there, the hair of glorious red-gold showing from underneath a once-blue bonnet that had since seen hard usage.

Out of gentlemanly reflex, he touched a respectful finger to his hat but caught himself before he could flash the patented Moss Callahan grin. No sense allowing the lure of a woman to make him linger and risk catching the deadly disease. However, a partial smile slipped his control—just enough to bring the woman's focus to him and the faintest tinge of peach into those alabaster cheeks before she looked away.

The woman faltered a step. "Oh," she said in a weak voice, raising a dainty hand to her forehead. Her bag fell from her fingers to thump onto the platform. She started to crumple, as if her knees buckled.

With a curse, Moss leaped to grab her, catching the woman just as she fainted into his arms. He scooped her up. Holding her close, Moss could feel she was waif-thin beneath her coat. Helplessly, he glanced around. Not seeing anyone nearby, he carried her inside. "Jack!" he yelled for the stationmaster. "Jack!"

Moss tossed a glance to the left. Jack wasn't behind the counter, and the door to the office was closed. He hurried over to the nearest bench and gently laid down the woman. Long eyelashes the same auburn as her hair swept her cheeks. Her pale skin was almost translucent, with the faintest dusting of golden freckles over her nose. *Angel kisses,* his mother had called them, and the heavenly description suited her.

His chest tight, Moss pulled off his gloves and thrust them into a pocket. He touched her neck for a pulse, relieved to feel a flutter under his fingertips. "Miss, Miss, please wake up." He brushed back the hair from her face and patted her cheeks.

Her eyelashes fluttered and then lifted, showing beautiful eyes of dark sapphire blue. At first she stared blankly at him, and then awareness returned.

Once again, he was struck by a sense of familiarity, but he couldn't place her.

"Oh," she murmured, shifting as if to rise.

"Careful, now. Can't have you going off again." Moss slid an arm under her shoulders to assist her to a sitting position. Once she seemed steady, he reluctantly removed his arm.

"I 'spose yer right. Fainting away once can be excused." She sounded almost amused. "But not twice."

Her musical Irish accent smacked him upside the head. Moss suddenly knew who she was. Well, not precisely *who.* Dread weakened his limbs, and he folded to his knees in front of her. "You're an O'Donnell."

She raised a fine red-gold eyebrow and gave him a faint smile, a mere upturn of pale pink lips. "How do ye know?"

"You look like Bridget and Alana and their cousin, Sally. You all have the same beguilin' blue eyes." *Although her eyes have a slight upward tilt at the corners, making her appear even more dangerous.*

What have I done? I've put myself square in harm's way.

Flirtation sparked in those eyes. She gave him a coquettish flick of her eyelashes.

Moss tamped down a wave of lust. Climbing to his feet, he held up a hand as if to ward her off. "Don't even think about turning those eyes on me. You save those pretty wiles for all the other men around here who'll soon be falling at your feet."

Those lovely eyes narrowed. "Better than *me* fallin' at *theirs.*" The O'Donnell siren held up her left hand to reveal a gold band with a heart and crown on her ring finger.

Moss should have felt relief that she was married, but instead he experienced an inexplicable sense of disappointment, as if he'd just lost something very dear.

"So ye see, boyo, yer very, *very* safe with me."

Moss didn't feel safe with her at all. Quite the contrary. His skin felt flushed, his chest ached, his throat was tight, and his head spun—all recognizable signs that he'd caught a sickness. If he weren't in the presence of a lady, he'd turn the air blue with his curses, even if that meant his sainted mother rising from the grave to take a switch to his behind.

Moss gestured toward the door of the depot. "I need to get you to the doctor." *And be done with you.* Only vaguely did he hear the tooting whistle of the train signaling a departure, for he was too mesmerized by the beguiling creature.

"I don't need a doctor. I'm fine."

"I beg to differ, Miss…um, Mrs?"

"I'm Catriona O'Donnell. Well, ah, Catriona O'Donnell *Crogan*." She patted her rounded stomach. "And this is Flea."

Moss had been so focused on her lovely face that he hadn't noticed she was with child. "Flea?" he asked, bewildered.

"For the saying, 'If ye lie down with dogs, ye'll get up with fleas.'"

Moss cocked his eyebrow. "Would that be a boy's name or a girl's?"

His teasing coaxed a reluctant smile from her lips.

Then the deeper meaning of her statement sank in. Mossed hissed in a breath. "Your husband mistreated you?" He rose to his feet, fisting his hands, as if to throw a punch at the man. Realizing the ridiculousness of the impulse, he forced himself to relax his fingers.

The woman scowled. "I won't be speaking ill of the dead. Just as well. Else ye'd be hearing a sermon equal to the best haranguing a priest could give ye. But ye probably get enough of that on Sundays, anyways."

"No," he answered automatically. "Father Fredrick only comes once a month or so on his circuit." Hearing she was widowed made his feverish symptoms increase. Moss forced himself to continue speaking, attempting to sound somewhat coherent. "Well, to be fair… Reverend Norton, the Protestant minister, and Father Fredrick are both apt to preach the kind of sermons a man's disposed to listen to."

"I suppose that's one good thing about this town."

"Only one?" He removed his hat, dropped it on the bench next to her, loosened the scarf around his neck, placed a hand over his heart, and waggled his eyebrows. "You're forgetting me. Moss Callahan, the man who rescued you."

"Callahan. A fine Irish name," Mrs. Crogan said thoughtfully, ignoring all his antics. "Are ye related to the—"

Moss held up a hand to forestall her. "I don't know my father's people. He left us—my mother and I—when I was just a little shaver. A traveling man, he was, just like me."

"Ye don't look like a traveling man. Ye look like one of them cowboys."

"I *am* one of *them* cowboys. I just like to work a spell and then move on. There's always work for a man who's good with horses and cattle."

She flicked a graceful hand in the direction of the train tracks. "Is that why yer here? Moving on?"

"I find myself delayed."

"Ye've missed your train."

"That I have." Moss had a feeling he'd done far more than missed his train.

Chapter Two

For a woman who'd sworn off men, Catri was possessed by quite an annoying case of disappointment when she heard Moss Callahan was leaving town, for he was a fine figure of a man. Indeed, he was one that prior to golden Godfrey Ainsworth blinding her and leaving her to the likes of Bartley Crogan, she would have sought out as worthy of flirtation. Of course, Catri thought most men worthy of flirtation, although some were far more so than others, and this man was definitely one of the former.

Mr. Callahan was tall, with a mop of curly brown hair waving to his shoulders, laughing hazel eyes, and a long nose. His wide mouth looked quite capable of smiling with deadly charm and kissing a woman into forgetting all her hard-won resolutions.

Annoying to find her feminine responses to a handsome scoundrel weren't deadened, after all. Catri stiffened her resistance to the man's charms. *I'll only have to hold out against him for a few minutes more. Just until I get my bearings.*

A small man with bushy hair hobbled over, holding a tin cup. "I saw you carrying the lady inside, Moss. Before I could get out from my office and come to your aid, I saw her revive. And since I was in the midst of brewing some tea." He extended the cup to Catri. "I've brought you some, with plenty of sugar stirred in. Hot, but not too much so. You can safely drink without burning your tongue."

Catri glanced up at the old man, smiled her thanks, and took the cup from him, inhaling the fragrant scent. "Wouldn't that be just perfect now? I haven't had tea with sugar in ages." Her chilled fingers began to warm. She took a sip, closing her eyes and savoring the sweetness. She sighed in satisfaction and opened her eyes. "I think that will do the trick, Mr….?"

The man colored. "Jack Waite, stationmaster and postmaster. But you can call me Jack. Everyone does." He stopped talking and tilted his head, looking like an inquisitive bird. "Don't tell me, let me guess." He laid a gnarled finger aside of his nose. "You're an O'Donnell."

Delighted by the man, Catri burst into laughter. "Not ye, too? Is Sweetwater Springs so cluttered up with O'Donnells that ye can be picking us out so easy? Must be an awfully small town."

Jack chuckled. "Oh, no, Miss O'Donnell." He straightened his shoulders. "I know everyone in the vicinity of Sweetwater Springs. It's just that you have such distinctive eyes, as do your twin…sisters?"

She flicked a glance at Mr. Callahan. "So I've been told."

Moss Callahan smirked.

Annoying man. She turned her attention back to Jack. "Yes, my younger sisters set out before me."

"Ah." He tapped his chin. "Then you'd be Miss Catriona O'Donnell."

Catri chuckled, amused by Jack's obvious pride in his perception.

"Miss Bridget sent you a letter not one month past," he explained. "She told me that Miss Alana had included a note that she enclosed to save on postage."

"I left before then, so I missed all their news." She smiled up at the stationmaster. "And ye are right about me being Catriona. I'm a widow. Mrs. Crogan. My sisters didn't know of my marriage, nor my husband's death."

"My condolences on your loss, Mrs. Crogan."

"If I'm to call ye Jack, ye must call me Catri." She didn't want to be burdened with answering to a false name any more than she had to. "I wasn't married long, so I never became accustomed to being Mrs. Crogan. She gave Moss Callahan a cool glance. "Both of ye." She turned her attention back to Jack in time to witness his moonstruck expression—a not uncommon reaction of the male species upon meeting her—and took a sip of her tea.

"Ah, Mrs. Catriona…." Jack nodded his hoary head. "I had the honor of welcoming the Misses O'Donnell when they arrived here. A cold day that was, thick with snow." He gestured toward the inner door. "I invited them into my office to warm up and, also, they'd just learned of your Aunt Henrietta's grave illness and were quite concerned."

Catri gasped.

"She's recovered," Moss interjected, shooting Jack an exasperated look. "Your sister Alana nursed your aunt back to health."

Catri let out a sigh of relief. "Aye, Alana has the healing touch." *Like our mama*, she almost said aloud, but sorrow closed her throat on the words.

Jack thumped his chest with his fingers. "Did I not say to your sisters that they'd be married before Valentine's Day?" He beamed, looking like a wise old gnome. "And I was right. Well, maybe not about the *date* of the wedding, which is today."

What? Her chest pinched.

"But on Valentine's Day—" he went on without a breath "—Bridget became engaged to James Whitson, a cowboy who works at the Thompson ranch. Patrick Gallagher, the owner of a stud farm outside of Crenshaw, claimed Alana a week or so later."

Catri reeled as if from a physical blow. "Married? Both of them? Today?" Shock made her lightheaded.

Moss Callahan sat on the bench next to her and took her arm, as if fearing she'd swoon again.

While annoyed at showing vulnerability, Catri appreciated the man's perceptiveness and protective reaction. She took a deep breath and nodded at him that she was all right. "Did I hear correctly? They married today?"

Moss released her, pulled his watch from his pocket, and checked the time. "Not yet. The ceremony's not for a few more hours."

"Is there time for me to make the wedding?" she asked with sudden hope. *Perhaps I can talk Bridget and Alana out marrying, for surely they couldn't have fallen in love in such a short time.* Remembering Alana's infatuation with Timkin Walsh and Bridget's total absorption in horses and in growing potatoes, she relaxed. *Once I talk to them, reveal my plan, they'll see no need to wed.*

"Nope," Moss Callahan said again. "You're not going to the Thompson ranch. I'm taking you straight to the doctor. *He'll* determine what you do from there."

Jack cleared his throat. "Doc Cameron's at the Thompson's. He and Mrs. Cameron are attending the wedding."

Catri seized the information to further her cause. "Ah, well, then—" She widened her eyes and gave Moss Callahan her most appealing smile. "The sooner we reach the ranch, the sooner I can see the doctor."

If that don't beat all. Moss choked down a groan, for he well knew who'd end up escorting the O'Donnell siren back to his former employers.

Catriona perked up. "Will ye be takin' me, then? Please, Mr. Callahan?" She made big, beseeching eyes at him.

Moss knew he should resist—to keep to his resolution to head away from Sweetwater Springs—but somehow the apprehension that had driven him from the ranch had turned into a feeling of anticipation that swirled in his belly. *The woman has no need to work her wiles. I'm already a goner.*

"Might as well call me Moss," he grumbled, and then he

looked at Jack. "Has anyone rented the livery's surrey to drive to the wedding?" Even as he asked, Moss realized the irony of seeking information from the man who ran the *train station* about what was happening at the *livery* and *the Thompson ranch.* He hadn't met Jack Waite but a couple of times, but he'd heard plenty about the stationmaster's proprietary interest in the people of Sweetwater Springs—a benign concern, rather than a need to gossip.

Jack shook his head, a regretful expression crossing his face. "The Misses O'Donnells, sweet ladies that they are, invited me. But with my rheumatism, traveling for more than twenty minutes is beyond me. Too painful, although I'm better in the summer. Tomorrow when Mr. and Mrs. Gallagher depart Sweetwater Springs, she's promised to come early before the train leaves, so she can tell me about the ceremony. And Miss Bridget promised to stop by the next time she's in town and do the same."

"Sounds just like my sisters," Catri said with a wistful expression. "They are kind girls." She took another sip of her tea, tipping back the cup.

Moss leaned over to glance into the mug, saw she'd finished, and studied her face. While still pale, her skin had lost the translucent quality that earlier had concerned him.

"The wedding is rather small." Jack reached to take the cup from Catriona. "The girls haven't been here that long to form many friendships."

"They've been here long enough to form relationships with fiancés," Catriona said in a petulant tone.

Amused by her crankiness, Moss suppressed a smile.

"That they have." Jack chuckled. "I just meant your sisters don't know many people in Sweetwater Springs. They haven't really been to town much, what with being cooped up by the winter weather, which keeps most far-flung folks at home. Then also with Miss Bridget living on the Thompson ranch to see to your cousin Sally, who's with child and feeling poorly, and Miss Alana nursing her aunt at the O'Donnell homestead on the prairie, and all…."

"How do ye know so much about my sisters?" Catri asked, obviously bewildered by all the family information Jack dropped on her.

The stationmaster radiated pride. "Your O'Donnell cousins and the Thompson brood go to school unless the weather is too difficult. The children take your sisters' letters and exchange them. Also, when people come here to pick up their mail, they tell me what's going on."

"Well, now that I've learned the answer to my question about renting the surrey in a few pithy words—" Moss interjected in a playfully sarcastic tone, anxious to move along the conversation "—I'll be moseying over and renting the vehicle, if it's to be had." The thought of pregnant Catriona riding pillion behind him wasn't to be born. "Good thing my horse Traveler can pull a surrey. We wouldn't want to miss the wedding would we?" he said.

Apparently undaunted by his tone, Catriona wrinkled her nose at him, a glint of amusement in her eyes.

From out of nowhere came the notion to pull her to him and drop a kiss on that pert nose. Alarmed, he avoided her enticing blue eyes.

Jack patted the woman's shoulder. "You probably haven't eaten. Come with me to the back, and I'll give you some bread and butter while Moss, here, arranges transportation."

"Yer so kind." She cast a dazzling smile at the stationmaster.

Jack shifted the cup to his left hand and crooked his arm toward Catriona. "Allow me to escort you to my office."

Watching the stationmaster's reaction to the woman, Moss shook his head. He guessed few men could remain unsusceptible to the woman's charms.

I wish I were one of them. He scooped the hat from the bench and set it on his head, before spinning on a boot heel and heading toward the door. He tugged at his neckerchief as he went out, aware that with the arrival of Catriona O'Donnell Crogan, a noose had just dropped around his neck.

Chapter Three

The morning of their double wedding dawned as fresh and bright as both Bridget and Alana O'Donnell had hoped and prayed. The twins had slept in the same guest room they'd occupied on their first night in Sweetwater Springs and intended to stay in seclusion until the ceremony. They'd already made the big four-poster bed covered by a green and pink quilt.

Earlier, the Thompson's housekeeper Mrs. Toffels, had brought them breakfast, setting the tray on the marble top of a small circular table near the window. She'd taken their wedding dresses to iron out the wrinkles, leaving them wearing only a chemise and drawers. They were under firm orders from their hostess, Samantha Thompson, to remain out of sight in the guest room until the ceremony.

After partaking of the flapjacks, bacon, and eggs and indulging in two cups of sweetened tea, Bridget sat in the light of the window, stitching blue lace to the hem of her best petticoat that Alana had knitted and bestowed as a wedding gift. Alana sat in the other chair, brushing her hair. Earlier, the two had exchanged handkerchiefs that each had embroidered, with a shamrock for luck in one corner and the new initials of the bride in the other.

From time to time, Bridget glanced up and drank in the sight of her identical twin, restored in body and spirit. Gone was the gaunt, dead-eyed, ashen-skinned ghost of a sister. Alana had filled out, although she wasn't yet back to her normal weight. Her curly red-gold hair crackled with life, and her pale skin looked dewy. Best of all was her sister's vibrant expression. Bridget's heart filled with joy to have Alana returned to health and vigor.

A knock sounded on the door. "It's Mrs. Toffels, my dears."

"Come in," Bridget called.

Mrs. Toffels, a plump woman with a good-natured expression, carried a gown draped over each of her widespread arms, so the fabric wouldn't touch the floor. One was silvery-blue and the other a soft peach. She twisted sideways to enter the room without narrowing her arms and walked over to carefully lay the gowns on the bed. "You'll both be as pretty as a picture in these."

"Thank ye, Mrs. Toffels," they chorused and then looked at each other and laughed.

It wasn't uncommon for them to say the same thing at the same time, but after having been apart for several months, Bridget felt good knowing they still had their special connection.

Mrs. Toffels's chuckle followed her out of the room.

Bridget hadn't seen Alana's wedding dress yet, and she gasped and walked over to examine the satin material.

Alana set down the hairbrush, rose, and moved to touch the lace on the sleeve. "This gown is a gift from Patrick. He had a dressmaker in Crenshaw make it to my measurements."

"We've never worn this color." Bridget admired the gown. "But the hue will be stunning with yer blue eyes."

Bridget couldn't envy her sister the elegant garment, for her own dear James had chosen the fabric for her dress—a peach silk scattered with blue violets. He'd surprised her with the present, telling her he'd wanted her to make a special new dress for the wedding. *Well, both James and Patrick knew we come to them with only potatoes as our dowry.*

Alana could have far out-shown Bridget by choosing an elaborate white wedding gown—the kind never to be worn again and eventually passed down to her daughters. But she'd chosen a color and a dress style that would see future use, just like Bridget's gown, which would be worn for parties and other special events for the next several years.

"Look—" Alana slid a hand over the top of the bodice of her gown. "I left the neckline plain, so today, I could still wear the collar Mama crocheted for me. Later, when I wear the dress again, I'll add the same lace that's on the sleeves around the neckline. But for today, I needed—"

"Something from her. I did the same." Bridget sniffed, touching her white lace collar. She stiffened her spine against the longing for her mother. "Ye'll look as beautiful as can be wearing such a gown."

"We never had different dresses until we came here to Sweetwater Springs."

Bridget laughed. "Aye, no more buying a piece of fabric and patterning it out just right so the length makes two."

"We'll never have similar dresses again," Alana said wistfully.

Bridget shrugged. "Ye and I were never much concerned about clothes. What with me mucking out the horses, and ye with yer healing and both of us in the garden. Three dresses sufficed—one for good and one for every day and one for mucking about."

"Aye, that's true."

"Catri was the one always longing…" Bridget stuttered to a stop at the wave of sadness that tightened her throat at missing those gone to heaven or run away. Then she scolded herself for thinking of her older sister. *Today is a day for happiness.* She swallowed and continued on. "Catri always wanted a new gown."

"Aye, to attract the attention of Godfrey Ainsworth, foolish girl," Alana said tartly. "And then she compounds her foolishness by running off with Bartley Crogan." She gasped and held her hands to her cheeks. "Listen to me! I sound so catty."

Bridget grinned. "I *am* listening to ye, and glad I am that sweet Alana is *finally* showing a bit of anger. Catri deserves it."

Alana clasped her hands together. "If only I knew Catri was *happy*. Safe, and warm, and well-fed, with a husband who loves and cherishes her as Patrick and James do us. Then perhaps I'd not be so upset with that sister of ours."

"If I knew all those things, I'd still take Catri by the shoulders, shake her 'til her teeth rattled, and ring a peel over her. She deserves that and more." Bridget waved a hand back and forth between them. "Just look at us. Instead of being all excited about marrying our two handsome, adoring men, we're fretting about that reckless sister of ours. No matter that she's the elder, we've been worrying about her for years, what with her discontentment and wild ways." Bridget saw Alana frown in protest. "Ye know that's true, so don't even try to defend her."

Alana glanced away, but not before Bridget saw moisture in her eyes. Although tempted to follow her twin and cry, they'd already shed too many tears for their wayward sister. "Enough about Catri." She put on a mock upper-class accent. "We were discussing the far more important topic of our wedding dresses."

Alana rewarded her with a smile that went from wan to wondering. "Aye."

"And now I have *four*, and ye have *five* dresses! Such luxury," Bridget teased. "Although, I suspect ye will be acquiring a larger wardrobe. I'll have to content myself with four. That's what I get for choosing a poor cowboy over a rich horse breeder."

Alana chuckled. "Need I say how grateful I am for yer choice of James over Patrick? I can't imagine secretly falling in love with my brother-in-law. I would have been miserable for the rest of my days—first longing for my childhood love Timkin and then Patrick. I'd have carried a doubly heavy heart. Instead, I'm so happy. I never want to pine for a man again!"

Bridget lifted her eyebrows, impressed by her gentle sister's impassioned response. Her twin seemed happy enough with Patrick, but Bridget hoped she wasn't settling because the horse breeder was handsome and wealthy. Bridget liked Patrick *and* his

Thoroughbred, Thunder. Seeing him dote on her sister last night had been enough to convince her that the man truly loved Alana in a way he hadn't loved Bridget.

Up until now, Bridget hadn't dared ask the question in one of her letters to Alana, for she didn't know what information her sister had shared with the rest of their relatives. "Does that mean yer done mooning over Timkin Walsh?"

"Timkin will always be a dear friend, the love of my girlhood. But Patrick holds my heart, and I his." Alana hesitated, a grave look on her face. "I need to apologize to ye...."

"Oh, and without Mama even making ye?" Bridget quipped.

Alana's expression didn't change. "I fought ye dreadfully about coming to America, and sorry for that I am. Then I was so unhappy about Timkin and leaving home that I wanted to die."

"I knew, oh, how I knew." Bridget released a sigh, remembering their dreadful journey, her constant fear. "Why else did I never let ye out of my sight on the ship? I knew how easy it would be to sneak upstairs and throw yerself overboard."

"I was tempted a time or two."

"That's why I made ye sleep between me and the wall, else I'd never have been able to catch a wink of sleep."

Alana clasped Bridget's hand. "I knew ye were worried, but I couldn't seem to care. But ye were right, Bridget, about coming to America—to Sweetwater Springs. Thank ye for being so farsighted and loving me enough to *punish* me by dragging me along with ye." She chuckled.

Bridget gave their joined hands a little shake. "Our lives will grow apart. I felt it the morning after ye left—that we'd come to a fork in our lives, and from now on our paths would take us different ways."

Alana became teary-eyed and hugged her. "Patrick has promised we will visit often."

"Are ye *sure* about him, Alana? Ye two are *so* different. Are ye marrying Patrick for security?" Bridget looked down. "Because I'm marrying James, and ye don't want to be alone or dependent on us or our relatives? I don't question *Patrick's* feelings. That man never looked at *me* like he does *ye*."

"Ye and I haven't had a chance to talk privately, and I didn't want to put this in a letter." Alana raised her chin to a proud angle. "Turns out Patrick and I are not so different, after all." She waited a beat. "I've found I rather like horses. What would ye say if ye knew I'd ridden Thunder?"

Bridget gasped. "*Ye* rode him? The girl who was so afraid, she wouldn't even look at a horse? Did ye not call that black Thoroughbred a *devil* horse? I heard ye with my own two ears."

"Aye. A devil horse, a great beastie, a creature."

Shaking her head, Bridget laughed. "Poor Thunder. That boyo is really as sweet as sugar."

"So I've learned."

Bridget glanced out the window. "The morning is running away from us. Let me help you into yer dress, and ye can tell me the whole story." Bridget walked over to the bed and ran an appreciative hand over the silver-gray satin, she asked. "Did ye ever think to wear a dress this fine?"

"Never, and I'd gladly give the gown to Catri and wear my work dress if only she were here."

Straightening, Bridget slashed the air. "Stop, sister, will ye?" She tempered the unaccustomed anger to pleading. "Let us speak no more about Catri. We have each other and James and Patrick. We have our aunt and uncle, cousins, and our new friends, do we not? We have *no* need for anyone else today."

Alana nodded in obedience but still looked unhappy.

"I'm a wretch." Bridget threw her arms around her sister. "I didn't mean to sound like such a shrew. I guess it's inevitable we'd think of our loved ones on our wedding day."

"Aye." Alana returned the embrace. "And that we'd be so jittery." She pressed a hand to her stomach. "Maybe I shouldn't have eaten the flapjacks, but they tasted so good with that strawberry jam."

"Ye'll need your strength for the whole day and…." Bridget

grinned. "The night." She picked up Alana's corset, handed it to her, and made a twirling motion with her finger. "I'll lace you up."

Alana hooked up the front of the corset and then raised her arms.

Bridget pulled the strings in the back far tighter than Alana usually wore them, even for Sundays and special occasions. "Bend slightly." She tugged on the laces. "Reach in and cup your bosoms."

"Really, Bridget," Alana protested.

"Just follow orders. Sally taught me this. She said it was a trick of Aunt Henrietta's."

They chuckled at the thought of their aunt when she was a young Southern Belle.

Bridget gave another tug. "Uncle Rory said she had so many suitors and some didn't stop flirting with her even after she was married."

"Do you think Aunt Henrietta wore hoopskirts when she was a girl?"

"I don't know, they might have gone out of style by then. She probably wore a bustle. We'll have to ask her."

Alana wiggled her hands down the front of her corset and lifted her breasts.

"Well then….when I tell you, let go," Bridget directed. "Now!" She gave the laces a final yank and tied them off. "Can you breathe? We can't have ye fainting away."

"Yes. It's tight, but comfortable enough."

Bridget stepped back and surveyed Alana's figure. "I believe Aunt Henrietta's trick has shrunk yer waist another inch and raised yer bosoms. I'll bet Patrick, with his big hands, will be able to span your waist. As for your bosoms—"

Color rose in Alana's cheeks. "Bridget O'Donnell, not another word!" She motioned toward Bridget's corset. "Your turn."

The sisters continued helping each other to dress. The familiar ritual was made unique by the excitement fluttering inside them, but leavened by the heavy awareness of this being the last time they'd helped each other in such a way.

When they'd finished dressing, Bridget sat in front of the mirror, while Alana did her hair. Yesterday, they'd bathed and washed their hair using Mrs. Thompson's rose-scented Castile soap. Today, their hair was clean and shiny. Luckily, their mass of curls made for a perfectly fashionable coiffure, without them having to resort to using heated tongs to achieve the waves and curls. Their short bangs frizzed naturally on their foreheads. The longer hair, when pulled back, displayed lovely side waves.

Today, Alana chose to coif a French twist rather than Bridget's usual coiled braid. As a final touch, she slipped in tortoiseshell combs on either side of her sister's head. The combs—a gift from the Thompsons—had stylized silver mountings. Flowers scrolled across Alana's, and Bridget's had a pattern of *fleurs-de-lis*. As a final touch, Alana shaped the frizz on Bridget's forehead to form three proper curls.

"Perfect," Bridget said on a breath, turning her head each way to admire the sides. "Now if only they'll stay that way."

"As long as no rain threatens, we'll be fine."

They both looked out the window, as if fearing to see a last minute storm blowing up. But all looked clear, at least from the direction they could see.

"Sunshine for good luck," Bridget said with a sigh of relief.

"Now for your veil." Alana picked up the lace veil that Samantha Thompson had lent Bridget, the tiara covered in white artificial flowers, and anchored the attached combs, so the veil fell softly from the top of Bridget's head. Alana fluffed the lace, which almost reached the floor. "We'll pull the front piece over yer face right before the ceremony."

As a final touch, Bridget took her grandmother's gold locket and clasped the chain around her neck. The gold complimented the peach satin. She stood. "Yer turn."

Alana took a seat before the mirror. "I think I'll have a Newport coiffure," she said in a hoity tone.

Bridget rolled her eyes. "Ye would." She obediently brushed her sister's hair into a high switch, then twisted and wove the tail into a coil, part bun and part twist. She added the combs and styled Alana's bangs.

Alana wore their mother's wedding band on her right hand and a diamond engagement ring on her left. She picked up a shamrock necklace in white gold from inside the top drawer of the chest. "Patrick gave this to me last night. I didn't know it at the time, but he'd bought me a gold one that was taken when those robbers tried to steal Thunder."

Bridget reached for the pendant. The delicate piece would be a fitting touch to the elegance of Alana's silver-blue gown. "A perfect present for ye. I'll put it on." She clasped the delicate chain around her sister's neck. "James and Patrick are both generous men. We are so blessed."

"Aye, indeed."

Bridget picked up Alana's veil, lent by Aunt Henrietta for the occasion. A few months earlier, Sally had worn the veil when she married Harry O'Hanlon. Gauzy netting hung from a circlet of artificial flowers. She placed the headpiece on her sister's hair and lowered it over her Newport twist until the circlet centered on Alana's forehead. With light touches, she smoothed out the netting.

"Come." Bridget took Alana's wrist and tugged her twin over to the chest of drawers until the two stood side-by-side in front of the mirror over the chest of drawers, their heads tilted toward each other. Now that Alana's face had filled out, the two looked almost identical again, even with the differences in their clothing.

"Remember when we did this on the night we first arrived?" Alana asked.

"You were so thin then. I was afraid ye'd wither away to nothing, and I'd lose ye."

Alana turned and hugged Bridget. "Ye never have to worry about losing me again. Well—" she wrinkled her nose. "Except for childbirth, illness—"

"Enough!" Bridget laughed and held up her hand. "No need to list every situation that would cause me to worry about ye."

A heavy tread sounded outside. "Are you ready, my dears?" came a man's voice from outside their door.

Alana checked with Bridget and, on her nod, called, "Come in, Uncle Rory."

Rory O'Donnell opened the door and stepped inside. With his dark hair and blue eyes, he looked enough like their late father to have caused a pang to Bridget's heart when she first met him and, at the same time, immediately rendered their uncle familiar and dear. He even sounded like Da, only his years in America had smoothed out his Irish accent, even though he hadn't completely lost the voice of their homeland.

Rory eyed Alana first, then Bridget. "Two more beautiful brides I never did see."

Bridget swept him a playful curtsey.

He winked. "And I can make that compliment in all truth because when I married my Henrietta and then later walked my Sally down the aisle, I only had one beautiful bride to behold at a time."

The twins laughed.

"If only my brother could be here this day to see ya." Rory's voice grew thick, his accent stronger. "But it's sure I am that he's lookin' down from heaven to see his sweet girls wed. Aye, indeed he is."

Bridget felt a lump rise in her throat. Bad enough that they missed their mother and older sister, but to grieve for her father, gone these three years, was even harder. She'd been closer to Da than Alana was. As soon as she was old enough, she had shared his work with their horse and the labor of the garden and their small potato field. She'd also helped him with cutting peat, both for their own fires, and to barter with their neighbors and sell to the squire.

In contrast, Alana was a healer like their mother. From an early age, she'd gone with Mama to harvest herbs, tend the sick, and birth babies. She'd learned all that their mother could teach.

Not for the first time, Bridget wondered if Catri's problems had stemmed from feeling excluded by the closeness of the twins with each other, as well as with their parents. *Well, it wasn't as if Catri had lacked attention. Our home, although poor, was filled with love.*

"You're *sure* you both want to go through with the ceremony, even though Father Fredrick couldn't make it?" Uncle Rory asked.

Bridget laid a hand on her uncle's arm. "It's not Father Fredrick's fault that he's tied up in Honey Grove with people dying of influenza and needing Last Rites and burials. I like Reverend Norton, and Alana trusts my judgment. Father Fredrick can give James and me his blessing later, and Alana and Patrick will go to the priest in Crenshaw."

"Well, then." Rory held out his arms to Alana. "Come give your old uncle a hug. I'll be careful not to muss your gown."

She smiled. "Gladly."

He gathered Alana to him in a gentle hug and kissed her forehead before stepping back with a hand on each of her shoulders. "You could not be more dear to me than my own child. Aside from being my flesh and blood, with your skillful nursing, you gave me back my beloved wife."

"With the help of the Good Lord and the Blessed Mother," Alana murmured.

"Now, Uncle..." Bridget grinned. "I must be as dear to ye as Alana, for 'twas I who dragged her kicking and screaming from Ireland to Sweetwater Springs so she could heal Aunt Henrietta."

Rory laughed. "So I've heard. Aye, and you have a bit of spunk in you. Like your mother that way, God rest her soul."

"There's no greater compliment ye could give me." *Perhaps*, Bridget mused, *sharing sorrow wasn't such a bad thing on a joyous day, after all.*

"Ah, Bridget, my dear one. It's not fair that James scooped you up before you had a chance to live with us. But I must console myself by remembering how you brought my wife peace of mind during her illness. Knowing you were there to help our Sally meant Henrietta didn't fret about our darling girl."

Bridget smiled. "Well, Sally's morning sickness has passed, and she's fine now. She and Harry need some time alone without a cousin cramping them."

"Aye, our Sally's bloomin'. Gave me quite a start to see her." He patted his stomach.

Alana chuckled. "Just ye wait. She's going to get a lot bigger."

"To think that less than six months ago I couldn't have imagined the changes—that before many months passed, my daughter would be married and soon to present me with a grandbaby, and my two nieces would be here in Montana with us. Why, who knows what surprises the next year will bring?"

Bridget exchanged a smile with Alana. *Who knows, indeed?*

Chapter Four

Catri spent the first part of the surrey ride fighting sleep. With a meal in her stomach and a fur of some sort snugged around her, she was warm and drowsy. In spite of Moss being a man and a stranger, she felt safe with him, like she could relax for the first time in ages.

In a reverse from her attitude on the train, she eagerly studied the town that was to be her new home. As she suspected, Sweetwater Springs was small, although not as small as others she'd seen on the way, and less primitive than she'd expected.

In addition to the false-fronted wooden buildings, the brick mercantile, the white-steepled church, and the saloon, they passed an ornate three-story brick mansion—the type that in Ireland would belong to the gentry, although the house was as unlike the squire's ancient manor as could be. Catri also spotted some nice two-story clapboard homes with fenced-in yards, any one of which she'd gladly call her own. She squashed that thought. *The only way I could have such a house is through marriage, and I've sworn off men.*

Catri glanced at Moss, noting the slope of his nose, his firm chin, and the strength of his hands holding the reins. *Oh, yes, I've definitely sworn off men.*

He caught her gaze and flashed her a knowing grin.

Her stomach fluttered, and she turned away, hoping he hadn't seen the tale-tell color flushing her cheeks. *Some temptations might be stronger than I anticipated.*

They passed the last of the scattered homes and entered a forest, driving along a trail strewn with dried pine needles and mulched leaves. Moss managed to avoid the worst of the ruts, some filled with muddy water. When he hit one and the buggy jolted, Flea kicked, as if protesting being disturbed.

After one such reaction, she placed a hand on her distended stomach and patted. *Not that I'm trying to calm the little bug or anything maternal like that.*

Without the houses and buildings to distract her, Catri's drowsiness won. She descended into sleep, barely aware when her head tilted toward Moss, and he shifted closer so his shoulder made an inviting pillow.

In such deep sleep, even the jolting of the surrey didn't awaken her, only now and then pulling her from dreams, leaving her with fragments—walking hand-in-hand through a meadow with a man who looked like Moss, although without the cynicism in his eyes. Laughing. Playing with a small child—girl or boy, she couldn't tell.

"Wake up, Briar Rose."

With Moss's amused voice rumbling in her ear, Catri became aware of her head resting on his muscled shoulder. With an exclamation, she pushed herself upright, raising a hand to rub the side of her neck that ached from the strain of being in a tilted position. She touched her hat, finding it askew.

Moss cast her an amused smile. "You snored."

"I did no such thing!" she said indignantly. *Did I?* Flustered, Catri straightened her hat, causing the hatpin to prick her scalp. She didn't usually snore; her sisters would have complained. But maybe something about the trip or being pregnant or her awkward position....

"You snored louder than old Sid. His bed is in the farthest corner of Thompson's bunkhouse. But since I was the new hand, I had to sleep nearest him. I forced myself to fall asleep before he did, that's for sure."

Seeing the gleam in Moss's agate eyes, Catri became sure he

was teasing her. "I didn't snore," she said with conviction. She pulled out the offending hatpin and pushed the needle back in, anchoring her hat.

"When you started snoring, you scared off a covey of quail." Moss transferred the reins to one hand and lifted his arm, flapping his hand in the air. "Too bad I didn't have my gun handy. Could have brought dinner with us. Not a bad wedding gift, eh?"

She looked up into the trees. "I don't see any quail."

"That's cuz you scared them all away."

Catri leaned closer to him so she could elbow his side.

He chuckled. "Briar Rose, you're so prickly."

Catri ignored the fairytale name. She certainly was no sleeping beauty, prickly or not. She'd never looked worse in her life—travel-stained, too thin except for her protruding stomach, clumsy instead of graceful.... But a part of her, that womanly part she was trying so hard to suppress, couldn't help but flutter.

Moss winked before turning his attention to driving, unsettling her even more.

Now fully awake, she became aware of the uncomfortable need to relieve herself. "How long before we arrive?"

"'bout another hour or so."

Catri held in a groan, knowing she'd never make it that far, and regretting drinking the tea Jack had provided, good though the beverage had tasted at the time. Although embarrassed to admit her need, there was nothing else she could do. She cleared her throat.

He glanced at her with raised brows.

"I, um..." Catri bit her lip and glanced down at her lap. "I need to—" She waved a hand toward the outside of the surrey.

"Whoa!" he called to the horse and reined-in. "I think we should stretch our legs for a few minutes," he said tactfully. "Give Traveler a short rest."

Relieved by his understanding, Catri nodded. She reached into her satchel to pull out a piece of the old newspaper she'd torn into rough squares.

"Wait and let me help you down." At first, Moss didn't move. Instead, he studied the area with narrowed eyes and then jerked his chin to the right. "There's a nice wide oak. Go behind that." He set the brake and tied off the reins, climbed down, and went around the surrey to help her clamber out.

Once on the ground, she avoided meeting his eyes. Perhaps seven months earlier, Catri would have been even more mortified, for she'd always privately used a chamber pot behind a screen or an outhouse and had never needed to relieve herself in nature. But traveling the countryside with Bartley had worn away some of her fastidious ways.

He patted the side of the surrey. "I'll stay right here and keep an eye out to make sure no bears come to bite you," he teased.

Catri sent him a quick upward glance and a small smile. She pressed her fists into the small of her back, trying to ease the ache lodged there, and waddled toward the oak. Once behind the tree, she looked around to make sure of her privacy, gathered up the bottom of her coat, skirt, and petticoat, and reached up for the ties of her drawers and tugged them down.

Luckily one of the gnarled tree roots made for a lumpy seat, for Catri wasn't sure she could squat in her condition without wetting her clothing. Holding up her garments with one hand and the trunk with the other, she lowered herself to gingerly perch on the root and relieved herself. Once she finished, she used the newspaper square to wipe off, then crumpled the paper and tucked it under a rock.

Getting up was almost more difficult than going down and involved muttering some unladylike curse words she'd learned from Bartley. Once on her feet, she panted to catch her breath. Then she pinned the kilted bundle of fabric against her side with one elbow and pulled up her drawers with her other hand. Freeing her garments, she used both hands to tie the drawers closed. Although she wished she could wash her hands, Catri had to settle for brushing them off on her coat.

She leaned against the oak for a moment, feeling

immeasurably weary, and sought strength from the tree, as if she lived during the time of the druids. One of the good things about Bartley was the ancient tales he'd collected on his travels, and he'd spin them out on the long drive between villages.

"You all right back there?" Moss called.

Pushing away from the tree, she trudged around the oak.

Moss was propped back against the surrey, one foot tucked behind him on the wheel, and his arms crossed in front of him.

Catri gave him a tired smile.

He straightened and held out his hand. "Your traveling days will soon be over."

The kindness in his tone almost made her cry. Catri nodded and gathered up her skirt, leaning on him more than she'd like as she climbed to the seat. *Only another hour.*

Moss settled in beside her, took up the reins, released the brake, and urged the horse forward.

"Tell me a story," she asked.

He slanted her glance. "A story, eh? What kind of story?"

"Any kind."

"How 'bout I tell you the story of the Thompsons. They own the ranch we're heading to."

"I'd like that."

"They're good people." He paused, apparently thinking. "Wyatt and Samantha. Not been married long. Was a time when we wondered if they'd be married at all, although anyone could see they had sparks. My boss… He can sure be a stubborn cuss. Has high standards, though. A fair man. Actually, more than fair. Good to work for."

"Then why are ye leaving?"

Moss shot her a look of mock reproof. "If you want a story, you've got to let me tell it as I see fit." He flicked the reins. "Now, where was I? Ah. The boss has a half-grown daughter, whom he dotes on. He's very protective of Christine. Her ma died in giving birth."

"I can see why he'd be that way," Catri murmured.

"Now, Mrs. Samantha...Rodriguez, she was then. Well, she inherited the neighboring ranch and moved here from Argentina with her son Daniel, who's about Christine's age...."

The twists and turns of the Thompson's tale kept her engrossed, and the hour of traveling flew by.

Moss lifted his chin to point ahead of them. "We're just about out of the trees, and then it won't be long."

Once again, Catri pulled out the hatpin and lifted the disreputable hat from her head, setting it on her lap so she could smooth her hair. She felt his stare and glanced over, peeking from underneath her eyelashes.

Moss watched her with a hawk-eyed, hungry gaze, much like the slack-jawed expression that often came over men's faces when they looked at her. But unlike with most men, she didn't have to suppress a shudder. Instead, the heat in his eyes set a corresponding warmth swirling in her chest in the place that had been cold for so long—ever since Godfrey.

No. Don't think of Godfrey! She'd often given herself that command over the last six months, to no avail. But Moss Callahan wasn't Bartley Crogan, who'd failed as a distraction from her pain over Godfrey. Today, Moss had drawn her attention from her past to the present.

She flicked her eyelashes in a flirtatious response before once again remembering that she'd sworn off men. *Old habits die hard. I'll need time before I can reform to nun-like habits.*

Pleased with her mental pun, she brushed dust off the worn velvet of her hat and placed it on her head at the proper angle, then poked the hatpin through the crown into her knot of hair. *That's the best I can do.* Catri straightened, wishing she could look more presentable, especially knowing everyone at the wedding would be wearing their finest clothes.

"Not far now. Just around those trees." He transferred the reins to one hand and pointed.

They emerged into wide pastures fenced with barbed wire. A brisk breeze ruffled the tips of grass, feathering through the dried foliage covering the ground and stirring up the scent of soil and plant life. Reddish brown cattle, bigger than the milk cows in Ireland, grazed undisturbed by their passage.

After about ten minutes, buildings came into sight. Catri straightened in her seat to get the best view.

She caught her breath when she saw the house—two-story, white, a wide porch, surrounded by beds of red tulips. Lilac bushes grew in one corner of a picket-fenced yard. Two red barns, one bigger than the other, loomed even larger than the house.

Moss headed the horse toward the first barn, passing a corral full of horses. "We'll go in through the side door of the house that takes us directly into the kitchen." He parked near a group of vehicles—several surreys and a wagon—and pointed to a low white building beyond the second barn. "That's the bunkhouse. After that, the first log cabin is Sally's.

"I see."

"Her husband Harry roped us all into building the darn place in a week so he could rush her into marriage." Moss shook his head. "I've never seen a man so smitten. It's been four months, and Harry still walks around with a shi—um, *silly* grin all the time."

Catri knew all about impulsive decisions regarding men and wondered if Sally felt as happy with her husband as he was with her, or if her cousin was regretting her hasty marriage. *Probably the latter.*

"We do our best to wipe that grin off Harry's face." Moss let out a long-suffering sigh. "But no amount of poking fun at him does the trick. Our teasing rolls off him like water from a duck's back. Guess in some cases love works better than wearing a slicker."

Catri rolled her eyes at his falsely mournful tone.

"Harry just says he feels sorry for the rest of us bachelors."

Men. They never grow up.

Moss glanced around. "Looks like even the cowboys are at the ceremony. We were all invited, but I thought some of them might have the same aversion to weddings that I do. Old Sid has a marked aversion to people. But if he's in the barn, he'll come out to take care of the horse."

The derogatory comment about weddings hurt, even though she agreed with him. *Why should I even care what this man thinks of marriage?*

"I'd best go in with you, and then I'll come out and see to Traveler."

At least I rank higher than the horse.

Still, she'd rather not go into a strange house by herself. Ashamed of her appearance, unsure of her welcome, and nervous about her ability to stop the wedding, Catri would take whatever support she could get. She forced a polite response. "I'd appreciate that."

After Moss came around and had settled her on the ground, he touched her cheek. "Even in all their finery, you'll be the most beautiful woman there. That's saying a lot given some of the women who'll be in that parlor. Just hold your head high, as if you wore the dress of a queen."

The warm feel of his hand on her cheek lingered. Touched by his sensitivity and understanding, she found herself able to smile.

Without waiting for Catri to speak, Moss placed a hand on the small of her back and guided her up a brick walkway flanked by beds of the red tulips.

As she walked through the flowers, Catri marveled. Even the squire's garden didn't hold so many of the expensive bulbs imported from Holland—something she knew from glimpsing the gardens through the windows when the squire and his wife threw parties and hired extra help.

During those occasions, Catri helped with the preparations, aided the serving maids, and assisted in the clean up afterward. Once during her secret affaire with Godfrey, they'd strolled through a part of the garden that was sheltered from sight of the house. But that had been in autumn, and she'd admired the dahlias and asters.

Moss helped her up the steps to the house and opened the door for her.

Catri entered a big, comfortable kitchen; the smell of fresh bread and roasting meat made her stomach grumble. The kitchen was as large as the squire's, dominated by a big black stove and a long table covered in a red-and-white checked cloth that matched the curtains at the windows. Platters of food covered by netting were set out on the table. A white-frosted cake sat in the middle, flanked by two brown whiskey cakes, a tradition at Irish weddings.

Alana and Bridget certainly would have had a grand wedding feast. Guilt stabbed her for what she was about to do. Catri hadn't thought of the work that had gone into preparing for today's event—how the Thompsons, their workers, and the others who'd gathered for the celebration might feel when the wedding was called off. *Well, they won't be robbed. Even without a ceremony, everyone can still eat all this food. They'll have a party instead of a reception.*

The kitchen felt so homey, Catri would have loved to settle into the rocking chair near the stove and relax.

"There's a bathroom upstairs. But—" Moss pointed at the sink "—if you want a quick wash-up."

Without even removing her coat, Catri rushed to the sink and pumped some water to wet her hands, and then used a bar of brown soap, marveling at the ease of indoor plumbing. She splashed some soapy water on her face, careful to keep her eyes closed, and then rinsed. She groped for the towel draped over the edge and dried off.

Hearing the strains of piano music, Catri knew there was no time to linger. She took off her coat and gray woolen muffler and straightened her bonnet, hands shaking from nerves.

Moss took the coat and muffler and hung them on a peg. He held out an elbow to escort her and then paused, staring at her with concern. "You're not going to faint on me again, are you?"

"Don't be ridiculous," she snapped, mortified by the reminder of her earlier weakness.

"It's not ridiculous when you've done so already."

The heat of embarrassment flooded her chest, although her hands grew cold. Catri preferred to forget she'd fainted, much less that this man had caught her. She lifted her chin in a signal for them to move on.

He led her from the kitchen into a hall that crossed with a wide entryway, where a staircase ascended to the second story.

She saw the opened double doors of the parlor, people gathered inside. "So many," she murmured.

Moss leaned to speak low in her ear. "A mere handful. People crammed the whole parlor during the boss's wedding. Standing room only. I was jammed into the corner. Luckily everyone had bathed."

She put a hand over her mouth to stop a chuckle.

They crossed the entry to the doorway.

Catri's heart pounded so hard she could feel the pulse in her ears. She wrapped a shaky hand around his arm.

"Ready?" Moss shifted to usher her into the room.

She shook her head, squeezing his arm in a signal to wait and surveyed the parlor. A white-bearded minister in a shabby suit, holding an open book, stood in front of two couples.

No priest? Her spirits rose. *Maybe my sisters aren't serious about their marriages.*

On each side of the room, leaving an aisle in between, well-dressed adults sat in chairs lined up in three rows. Behind them, several men and children perched on benches.

Relief shuddered through her. *I'm in time to save Bridget and Alana from making a big mistake.* The two mistakes, both wearing black suits, stood with their brides. The twins, who were next to each other, wore beautiful dresses that Catri had never seen before. To her consternation, from behind and cloaked in long veils, she couldn't tell which sister was which. The one in the silvery-blue dress was thinner, but not by much.

The realization unsettled her, as though she'd stepped out expecting firm ground, but instead sank into a bog. Then Catri realized that she'd never seen the twins from behind, standing side-by-side, unmoving, and her world stabilized. *I'll know them by their faces*, she reassured herself.

"If any man can show just cause—" the minister intoned "—why they may not lawfully be joined together, let him now speak, or else hereafter forever hold his peace."

That's my entrance. Catriona glided a few steps forward, pulling Moss along. She took a deep breath to project her voice throughout the room. "I protest my younger sisters gettin' married without my knowledge and approval."

With gasps and surprised exclamations, everyone turned.

Her knees shaking, Catri kept her gaze on Bridget and Alana, although she clutched Moss's arm, as if drawing on his strength to keep her upright.

The twins both whirled, and then froze in wide-eyed disbelief.

Catri smiled at their reaction, although her throat tightened at the sight of their beloved faces—as she'd suspected—easily recognizable.

Alana screamed in high-pitched delight.

Bridget moved first. She dropped the arm of her groom. "Catri!" She thrust her wildflower bouquet into the man's hands, pulled up the front piece of her veil and tossed the lace over the flower crown of her headpiece. Grabbing up the skirts of her peach colored gown with one hand, she flew down the aisle, extending her other arm.

Alana, having given her groom her bouquet of tulips, also pulled back her veil before rushing right behind her twin, her gown billowing around her.

Catri released Moss's arm just in time to receive Bridget's fierce hug, which almost knocked her over. Only his hand on her back kept her upright. She opened an arm to gather in Alana against her and Bridget, crushing them in a three-sister embrace. *We haven't hugged like this since the day of Mama's funeral.* She hadn't realized how much she'd missed their affection.

Alana let out a sob and kissed Catri's cheek. "Yer alive! Yer *here*. Thank you, Dear Lord! Thank you, Blessed Mary!"

Bridget grabbed Catri's shoulders and shook her. "How could

ye do that to us? Run away like that! Do ye know how worried we've been?" Then she, too, started to cry.

The tears of her sisters brought forth her own. Catri hadn't wept when her mother had died, when Godfrey had broken her heart, when she'd found out Bartley was already married—to three other women—when she'd discovered her pregnancy, or when she'd left Ireland behind forever. But now, cheeks pressed together, feeling the deep love between the three of them, Catri's tears flowed freely, mingling with those of her sisters'.

She felt a light touch of comfort on her back and, without looking, knew Moss had remained close to offer support. Vaguely, she was aware of her sisters' men doing the same for them. While she found Moss's touch comforting, the intrusion of the two grooms on this sacred moment annoyed her, which in turn stopped her tears.

People stared, but she didn't care.

Bridget was the first to sniff and pull away a few inches. "How like ye, Catri, to interrupt our wedding so dramatically!"

Alana patted Catri's cheek. "Perfect timing. We so wished for you to be here for our wedding ceremony." She hugged her again, and then pulled back abruptly, her eyes wide. "Catriona Siobhan O'Donnell, yer with child!" Her voice was quiet but fierce.

Bridget's eyes widened. "Bartley Crogan?"

I don't know. "Of course," Catri said airily. Then, remembering her deception—that she was posing as a widow—modified her expression to one of grief. "But I'm afraid my dear husband passed away of a sudden illness."

Bridget's eyes narrowed in apparent disbelief.

Catri never had been able to fool Bridget. Alana, with her tender heart, was the gullible one. She shook her head in a silent message. *Not now.*

Bridget nodded her understanding. "We'll speak more of this later," she said in a low voice.

Alana's hands fluttered to her chest. "I'm going to be an

aunt!" She glanced back at the tall, attractive man behind her who must be Patrick Gallagher. "And ye'll be an uncle."

The man reminded Catri of Bartley Crogan—handsome, with bold, dark looks. She took an immediate dislike to him.

He grinned at Alana. "A husband and a brother-in-law and an uncle in the same day. I'm certainly acquiring a lot of family." He slipped his arm around Alana's waist. "I think you should introduce us, my dear."

"Oh my." Alana shook her head. "Where have my wits gone?"

Bridget chuckled. "Catri's surprise appearance has scattered yer wits to the wind."

Alana tapped Catri's arm. "My errant sister, Catriona O'Donnell *Crogan*." She frowned at Catri when she said Bartley's name. "I'd like ye to meet my fiancé, Patrick Gallagher, who, in a few minutes, will be my husband."

Not if I can help it. Catri thought quickly about what she could do to prevent the wedding. *I need to get them alone so we can talk privately.* "Alana, I'm feeling a bit weak after my journey." She pressed a hand to her bulging belly.

Moss, who'd been hovering in the background, but within earshot, moved to her front. Frowning, he surveyed her face. "She fainted earlier," he said to Alana. "The doctor should see to her. Dr. Cameron!" He raised his voice and waved for the doctor's attention. "You're needed here."

A redheaded man in a frock coat nodded and began to make his way over.

"Ye fainted?" Bridget gasped.

Alana grabbed Catri's wrist, checking her pulse. "Ye must lie down."

"If ye wouldn't mind postponing yer wedding for a bit." Catri made herself sound wistful. "So ye could see to me…check if the baby's all right."

"Of course." Alana exchanged a glance with Bridget, who nodded. She looked up at Patrick Gallagher.

The man's tender smile made Catri want to gnash her teeth. With effort, she kept a tremulous expression on her face.

Patrick gently touched Alana's cheek. "My love, you must see to your sister's well-being. I'm sure Reverend Norton and the guests won't mind waiting."

His willingness to support Alana, and thus Catri's scheme, should have endeared him to her, but she still disliked him.

Bridget's groom also hovered behind her, and Bridget quickly introduced James Whitson. With his boyish good looks—kind brown eyes, snub nose, and wide, dimpled smile, he seemed milder than Patrick. Catri didn't dislike James on sight, but the fact that the man was about to bind her sister to him in matrimony certainly made a black mark against him in her book.

A beautiful woman with auburn hair and an air of calm command moved to take control of the situation. She wore a cornflower blue silk dress that matched her eyes. "I'm Mrs. Thompson," she said to Catriona. "But you must call me Samantha. You are a lovely surprise for your family and a welcome guest to our home. Your sisters will take you to their guest room. Dr. Cameron can see to you there."

"Thank ye." Catri smiled sweetly but envied the woman her gown. And not just the gown, the whole house. *Her husband is probably paunchy and old like the squire. There is always a price to pay when you marry a man with money.*

But when Samantha Thompson looked up at a tall, gray-eyed man with no paunch in sight, moving toward them, Catri's envy only increased. Although the man wasn't as classically handsome as Patrick Gallagher, he was certainly attractive. *Some women have all the luck.*

Alana tugged Catri's wrist. "Come with us."

Moss's eyebrows jutted together. "Are you going to be fine to walk on your own? You don't want your sisters to have to catch you."

"Did ye really faint?" Bridget asked.

"Oh yes," Moss answered, with a dramatic sweep of his arm

to his forehead. "She swooned into my arms. Probably overtaken by my good looks. I do have that effect on women." He threw Catri a wink and a charming grin. "I must say, your Catriona made quite a play to get my attention."

The rogue. Catri could only frown and shake her head at his antics.

Bridget laughed out loud.

Alana chuckled.

"I'd say she succeeded in gaining your attention, Moss," Wyatt Thompson commented in a wry tone. "Early this morning, you hightailed it out of here without saying good-bye to anyone but me." His stern glance said he didn't approve. "Seems only a pretty woman could stop you, much less make you return."

Moss rolled his eyes and shook his head, evidently not willing to admit the truth of the man's statement.

Samantha took her husband's arm, and they moved on to talk to their other guests.

Catri hadn't paid any attention to the people who'd formed a second circle around the sisters until an older man nudged his way between Bridget and Alana. With one look, she didn't need to be told who he was, for the resemblance to their da was enough to make her catch her breath and tear up. "Uncle Rory," she said softly.

"Aye." Rory enfolded her into a hug. "I see I have another lovely niece to welcome to Sweetwater Springs." He stepped back and surveyed her face. His eyes wet with obvious emotion, his gaze briefly dropped to Catri's stomach, then back to her face. "You've had a hard time of it, my girl," he said, his tone warm and loving, and sounding so like Da. "But you're with family now. All will be well, you'll see."

A traitorous tear spilled over. Catri wiped away the tear before it could streak down her cheek. *Here I'd thought I was resigned to my fate.*

Uncle Rory beamed at the twins. "Was I not saying just

before the ceremony that who knew what other surprises the year would bring? I must have a touch of the sight. Now, Catriona, my dear, you must meet the rest of your family." He turned to gesture a woman closer. "Henrietta, my lovely wife."

Gray liberally sprinkled her aunt's thick red hair. Her careworn face showed signs of a hard life. But, at her husband's compliment, her eyes lit and her cheeks pinked, showing her faded beauty. She smiled and clasped Catri's hand in welcome.

Warmed by her aunt's smile, Catri leaned forward to hug Henrietta. "I heard ye've been ill, and my sister was nursing ye. I'm so relieved yer better."

"My dear Catriona. I'm so glad you've come to us, both for your sake, and because your sisters have been fretting for you. Now we'll have peace of mind knowing you're safe with us."

Catri wasn't sure how much peace of mind she'd provide for her relatives—at least not at first. *But surely, they'll feel better later on when they see how well my scheme has worked.*

"Make way for the rest of the family." Rory chuckled and urged forward his children—all with blue O'Donnell eyes and his dark hair. "Your oldest cousin Sally and her husband, Harry O'Hanlon, my son Charlie, and our twins Idelle and Isleen."

"Welcome, Cousin Catriona," Sally spoke with an American accent. Her pregnancy was just beginning to show. Although she had her father's coloring, her features resembled her mother's. She had the glow of a woman who was happy with her lot in life.

Feeling old before her time, Catri wondered if she'd ever have a glow about her. She dropped a hand to her stomach. *Probably not.*

Sally's husband, Harry, a rugged-looking cowboy of medium height, stood with his hand protectively in the small of his wife's back.

Sally leaned in toward her husband.

Their obvious love match made Catri feel relieved for her cousin's sake, yet also envious of her good fortune. *Not that I'd want to be married to a poor cowboy.*

Moss, who'd remained standing behind her, leaned forward. "I believe Mrs. Crogan has expressed feeling weak and needing her sisters. I suggest you all postpone more of the family reunion until the doctor has a chance to examine her."

"Moss, I told ye to call me Catriona," she chided, speaking more for her relatives' sake than as a reminder to him. She smiled at everyone around her. "I don't want to stand on ceremony in my new community."

Uncle Rory gestured toward the parlor door. "Be off with you, *mavourneen*, and let your sisters and the good doctor tend to you. We'll catch up later."

Catri smiled at him, remembering all the times her father used Gaelic endearments with his wife and daughters. Impulsively, she rose on tiptoe and kissed his cheek, although she had to grab his arm because carrying the weight of Flea threw off her balance. "Thank you, Uncle Rory."

"Ach, I'm blessed *and* bedeviled to have so many beautiful lasses as kin." Rory's Irish accent deepened. He grinned at Harry and the two bridegrooms. "Good thing it is that I have you three to share my blessings."

"Rory," Henrietta chided. "*Bedeviled*, indeed. Good thing Reverend Norton didn't hear you. He'd be assigning you a penance for saying such."

Laughing, Alana and Bridget linked arms with Catri—one on each side. The twins guided her from the room to the foot of a wooden staircase.

Once he watched Catriona go upstairs, Moss turned and headed toward the barn, thinking to take care of Traveler. Outside, he found someone had unhitched his horse. He glanced at the corral and didn't see his pale gelding, and he continued into the barn. The windows and doors stood open, providing light, and the hands had been up early cleaning out the stalls—so the place smelled about as good as a barn could—of straw and horse.

Deuce, the gangly, carrot-topped youngest cowboy was grooming Traveler in the horse's stall. The boy looked up and nodded.

Moss flicked him a wave of thanks and headed over to a group of male wedding guests, standing in a circle and passing around a jug. He spotted the boss talking with the two bridegrooms, as well as Harry, Rory O'Donnell, and Nick Sanders, another rancher in the area whose wife Elizabeth had made friends with Alana.

Sauntering closer, Moss realized one wasn't a man, but K.C. Granger, the female sheriff of Sweetwater Springs, who dressed like a man. Today, she wore her brown hair in a long plait down her back, instead of hiding her braids under a hat.

When she noticed him staring, the sheriff met his gaze with a cool look.

She's probably used to that sort of scrutiny. Never knowing quite how to treat her, Moss touched his hat, like he'd respectfully acknowledge any other woman.

Sheriff Granger gave him a faint smile and turned her attention back to the conversation.

Mr. Thompson handed Moss the jug. "The hard cider Mrs. Toffels makes," the boss explained. "Enough to wet your whistle but still keep you sane. My wife would shoot me if we all returned to the wedding inebriated."

"But after the ceremony…well, that be a different story," Rory joked, his Irish accent thick. "I've brought whiskey, made from me own potatoes. We can all lift a dram as is tradition at an Irish wedding."

Moss shook his head and took a swig, enjoying the fermented apple taste. The Thompsons and their cowboys were a mighty temperate bunch, and, even with a double Irish wedding and Rory's whiskey, he doubted today would be much different. Truth be, while he liked an occasional drink as much as the next man, he'd learned that imbibing too much alcohol only caused problems. Drunk men did stupid stuff, and as much as possible, he stayed away from stupid. He passed the jug to the sheriff.

Alana's fiancé, Patrick, looked at James, his fellow bridegroom. "I was waiting to discuss this with you in person, but since our arrival last night, we've been too busy to talk, and now seems as good a time as any. You gentlemen and—" he bowed slightly to Sheriff Granger "—one lady, of course, can weigh in with your opinions."

James tilted his head in askance.

"I know you and Bridget are planning on living here," Patrick said, waving an arm to indicate the ranch. "But I wanted to suggest that you and your bride move to my place outside of Crenshaw. You are more than welcome to work for me."

James gave him a bewildered look. "But?"

"Let me finish." Patrick held up a hand. "I'll build you and Bridget a house on my property—one with two bedrooms. That way Catriona can choose whether to stay with you or with Alana and me. Or she can go back and forth between us."

James grimaced. "I don't know."

"Think of it this way." Patrick crossed his arms. "If you live at my place, our wives won't be pining for each other. They'll be happier."

James looked thoughtful. "There is that. If Bridget's happy, I'll be happy.

Nick Sanders chuckled. "Isn't that the truth."

The man should know. Although younger than Moss by a few years, Sanders had an air of quiet competence. He'd married a woman about Moss's age—a wealthy Boston beauty. Now the two had a baby, and their unlikely match looked loving and happy.

"Not always easy to pull up roots, even if they're newly planted." The sheriff's husky voice could pass for male. "Best take that into account."

"That's true." James glanced at the boss, his forehead

crinkled in evident concern. "We'd leave the new house I've built standing empty."

Wyatt chuckled. "Don't let that concern you. With the way things are around here lately, I'm sure we'll soon need the cabin for another couple. Old Sid, perhaps. I think he has his eye on Mrs. Toffels."

Harry guffawed and slapped his leg. "That'll be the day."

Rory crossed his arms over his chest and with lowered eyebrows shot a stern look at Patrick and James. "I don't like the idea of you men taking my nieces away to where I can't keep my eye on you…make sure you're being good to them. Or else…." He smacked a fist into his palm.

James glanced at Patrick. "Sold!"

Everyone laughed, including Rory.

"I think that's a fine idea." Harry reached over to snag a piece of straw from the stack of bales behind him. "Although Sally will miss her cousin Bridget. Those two have become fast friends. On second thought, better stay, James. Can't be upsetting my wife, especially in her delicate condition." He twisted the straw into a knot and flicked it at his friend.

James batted the knot away and turned his attention to Patrick. "Bridget, thank goodness, didn't arrive with many possessions except those potatoes of hers. I think we could pack up and leave when you do." He cast an uneasy glance at the boss. "What do you think? You be shorthanded."

Wyatt shrugged. "We'll figure something out."

Moss crossed his arms over his chest. "You're forgetting Catriona. I doubt the doctor will allow her to travel tomorrow."

"That's true." James rubbed the back of his neck. He lowered his hand. "I can't make the decision alone. Bridget and I will need to discuss moving, although I'm fairly sure she'll want to go with Alana. We'll see what the doctor says about Catriona. Give her time to rest up and for the boss to hire some new help."

"Speaking of help—" Wyatt shot Moss a wry glance. "I'd ask

if you're back to stay, but something tells me that you're heading wherever Catriona's going."

Moss hadn't even thought of trailing after the woman, but as his former boss spoke the words, he realized he wasn't leaving for the south just yet. He intended to make sure Catriona O'Donnell Crogan was safe and settled. "When a woman faints into your arms, you become sort of responsible for her. That's all it is."

Harry chuckled. "That's a lie if I've ever heard one. Once a pretty O'Donnell lady casts a blue-eyed glance at you, your heart is caught."

Patrick nodded. "Even if it takes a while for your head to figure out your heart."

"Might as well give up now," James chimed in with a wide grin.

"But she's not at all the type of woman who interests me," Moss fibbed.

"Another lie." Nick chuckled. "I only caught a glimpse of her, but any red-blooded man—" he cleared his throat "—who wasn't, of course, happily married or about to be so—which is every man in this circle but *you*—would be interested in the lady." He reached for the jug, hefted it toward Moss in a congratulatory salute, and took a swig.

Wyatt joined in the knowing laughter. "I know the feeling. Samantha poleaxed me when first we met, though I tried my darnedest to see her through critical eyes, hoping to save my heart. But to no avail. Marrying her was the best darn thing I've ever done." His expression sobered. "Except for marrying my first wife—Christine's mother. I count it among my greatest blessings to have loved two such fine women."

Wyatt and Samantha Thompson enjoyed one of the best marriages of any couple Moss had been around. Although a second marriage for both, the couple had an obvious bond that spilled over to all the folks around them. The boss could be hard at times, as a rancher needed to be. But he showed a tender side to his wife and children—both his daughter and the mixed brood of four boys, three of them adopted—who'd come with Samantha upon her marriage.

Such a marriage might not be so bad after all. Shocked by the traitorous thought, Moss strove to banish any idea of matrimony from his mind. *Just as I feared—wedding fever is contagious.*

The boss gave Moss a direct look. "I've learned that you can love a child sired by another man as wholeheartedly as you love your own. You love them differently, of course, as you do each of your offspring. The child or *children* become part of your family."

Moss grimaced. "If you wouldn't mind, I'll stay around and keep working for a *few days*—" He didn't meet Thompson's gaze. "I want to make sure Catriona is well. I'll work for my keep."

James's mouth crooked a wry smile. "Those O'Donnell women are irresistible, aren't they?"

"I'm resisting," Moss said fervently.

Everyone laughed and gave him knowing looks.

"You stay for a few days," the boss said with a quick nod. "There's always room in the bunkhouse." He dropped a hand on Moss's shoulder. "Something tells me your wandering days are over."

Moss shook his head and held up his hands in a warding-off motion. "No, once she's settled in, I'm heading south."

Although Patrick Gallagher remained straight-faced, the glint of humor lurking in his eyes made Moss think he had the same attitude as the boss. "And—" Gallagher said, as if not hearing Moss's protests "—you can follow Catriona to my place."

Chapter Five

Dr. Cameron followed the three sisters to the stairs. "I'll give you a few minutes together." His blue-eyed gaze was shrewd but kind. "Mrs. Crogan, if you could partially disrobe…?"

Catri didn't like the thought of the doctor examining her. But then again, she didn't like anything about being pregnant, and this was just another item to add to the list.

Alana nodded. "I'll see to it."

They ascended the staircase, pausing on the landing to allow Catri a moment or two to catch her breath. "Climbing stairs never used to be hard," she said between panting breaths.

"When have ye last eaten?" Alana asked in a solicitous tone.

"The stationmaster gave me a cup of tea at the train station. He added a lovely heap of sugar."

"*Eaten*?" Alana's tone took on an edge. She swung around to stare into Catri's face.

No sense in trying to evade Alana's questions when she turns into a bossy healer.

"Jack also fed me some bread and butter."

"And before then?"

Catri wrinkled her nose, not wanting to admit she'd run out of money. "I had a bit of bread yesterday."

Alana sighed in obvious exasperation. "That's probably why yer out of breath. Ye need to eat."

"Mrs. Toffels always has a pot of soup simmering on the

stove." Bridget stepped in as peacemaker—usually Alana's role. "We'll have a bowl brought up."

"Do I have time for a bath before the wedding?" A much-needed bath would serve two purposes—getting clean and causing more of a delay with which to convince her sisters to fall in with her plan.

The twins looked at each other in apparent communication.

Catri wiggled out of their grip and crossed her arms against the familiar feeling of being shut out by her sisters. Although Bridget and Alana were only a year and a half younger, she'd never been as close to them as the two were to each other. The strong bond of the twins always seemed to exclude other children, including Catri.

The emotional distance between her and the twins hadn't changed as they'd grown. By that time, Catri also was to blame, for she'd focused her attentions on charming the men around her, searching for the most advantageous match possible. But when Godfrey Ainsworth returned from the university, she'd tumbled into infatuation and set her sights on him, even if he was far above her station in life. The odds were slight that he'd offer marriage. But she'd been so determined and let her heart rule her head. *For all the good that did me.*

Bridget touched Catri's arm. "I'll go ask for some soup and be right back." She hurried down the stairs and disappeared into the kitchen, returning a moment later. She glanced around, probably to make sure no men were in sight, drew her skirts above her ankles to avoid tripping on the hem, and raced up the stairs. "Mrs. Toffels will bring up a tray."

The three continued into the bedroom that showed evidence of the twins' occupancy, from Bridget's shawl tossed over the foot of the four poster bed, to two worn satchels leaning against a new portmanteau. On a chest of drawers, tulips filled a crystal bowl next to the dresser set the twins shared. Catri wondered how they'd divvy up the comb and brush after their marriage.

As soon as the door shut, Catri whirled on the twins. "I can't believe yer getting married!"

"Why not?" Bridget challenged. "Ye did."

The lie about her marriage kept Catri silent.

Alana fisted her hands on her hips. "Ye ran off, Catriona Siobhan O'Donnell, and without a word. Ye left us behind."

This discussion wasn't heading in the direction Catri wanted. She could see the anger in Bridget's gaze, the hurt in Alana's eyes, and knew she needed to make amends as best as possible before the three of them could move forward. But she certainly couldn't tell them the whole shameful truth. "Do you remember the Bible story of the prodigal son?"

Bridget's scowl didn't abate.

Alana nodded.

Forcing a smile, Catri spread her arms. "Behold the prodigal *sister*. I left for much the same reasons the prodigal son did—wanting a more exciting life, to see more of the world than just our little village." *Running from Godfrey's rejection.* She left that out, ashamed their warnings about him had come true, and sighed. "But unlike the prodigal son, I was all churned up with grief from Mama's death. I couldn't bear to be home when she was not."

Bridget grabbed Catri's shoulders. "Do ye think we felt any different? We missed her every day." She shook Catri. "Even worse, we missed *ye*, too. Mama didn't make the choice to leave. It was her time. But *ye*! Ye chose to leave us."

"Bridget," Alana said sharply. "Let be. Catri is with child, and yer not to be shaking her."

I'd just as soon ye shake this baby loose from me. But she held in the words, knowing the truth would shock and wound her sisters.

Bridget drew her hands from Catri's shoulders and, stiff-backed, strode to the window. She placed her fingertips on the sill and leaned forward until her nose was an inch from the glass. Staring out, she evidently pretended to be engrossed by the view.

Alana cupped Catri's cheek. Her eyes filled with tears. "To have ye here is a miracle."

Bridget pushed away from the window. "An answer to prayer."

Catri was relieved to see the anger had left Bridget's face, and her sister sounded more conciliatory.

"*More* than our prayers," Alana responded. "I only prayed to *hear* from ye, to know ye were well and happy." She glanced at Bridget in apparent inquiry.

Bridget smiled. "Same for me."

Alana patted her chest. "God saw the desire in our hearts—for the three of us to be united."

Catri seized her chance. She grasped Alana's hand, and then reached for Bridget's and squeezed. "I've prayed for the same outcome. Now that we are together, there's no need for ye two to rush into marriage. I think we could manage to be comfortable, just the three of us." She sketched out her plan. But instead of the relief she expected to see on their faces, Catri only saw dismay. As she sensed what she was about to hear, her heart grew heavy.

Bridget shook her head. "Ye don't understand. We're not marrying to have someone take care of us—to be *comfortable*, although that is important. I love James and *want* to be his wife. Alana feels the same about Patrick."

"I know the timing seems fast," Alana said, in a soothing tone. "I'm told courtship moves quickly here. Men outnumber the women, and those who are available are quickly snatched up. The only reason we've waited this long to get married was because we wanted Aunt Henrietta to be fully recovered and for the days to warm a spell. We didn't want to tax our aunt's strength by a long journey in the cold. Although—" she amended "—in Montana, at least what we've seen so far, the weather is always cold."

Catri shook her head. "Ye barely know these men, and ye two never had much doings with suitors, or even paid attention to the boys. Well, except for Alana with Timkin, and he really doesn't count. He's like one of the *sidhe*—a changeling—rather than a real man."

Alana gasped and then laughed. "I wish ye'd said that before."

"I did once to Mama, and she told me to keep such thoughts to myself."

"Aye." Alana grew misty-eyed. "Mama was fond of him."

"I spoke with Timkin when I went home before coming here," Catri told her. "He misses you and sends ye his regards."

"I miss him, too," Alana said in a wistful voice. "He was my best friend." She glanced at Catri. "Did he seem happy?"

"He's taken in an orphaned youth to help with the farm. Well, maybe Mac's not so young. He's about eighteen. The two have become quite…close. Ye know even with yer friendship, Alana, Timkin always seemed so isolated. But now I think he's happy."

Alana tilted her head, obviously thinking. "Well, now, that answers some questions. I'm glad to hear he's happy."

Back to the topic at hand. Catri made one more attempt to change their minds. "Men turn ye up sweet to get their way with ye, but once they have ye, things change, and ye'll be trapped. Ye need to make your men court ye for a year or two to be sure."

Both of the twins looked at her, wide-eyed.

"I'm trying to save ye," Catri said in desperation, practically begging.

Alana's eyes filled with pity. She placed a tender hand on Catri's arm. "Is that what happened to ye?"

Catri stiffened against the urge to spill out all her troubles. "This isn't about me. It's too late for *me.* This is about ye two staying safe."

Alana gave her a sad smile. "*Life* isn't always safe, dearest. Loving brings a risk of pain and grief. Ye can't stop living and loving out of fear. A few months ago, I couldn't have told ye how wonderful it feels to give yer heart to someone and take his in exchange."

"Don't quote Sidney to me." Catri realized her tone was snappish and softened her words. "Please, don't."

Alana's brow crinkled.

"Who's Sidney?" Bridget asked.

Too late, Catri remembered her sisters wouldn't know the poem. Their village school had only taught the basics. Godfrey had read the poem to her in those heavenly days when she'd believed his courtship to be true. "Sir Phillip Sidney was a poet who lived in the time of Shakespeare. He wrote a poem that started with, 'My True Love hath my heart and I have his.'"

A dreamy smile banished the sadness from Alana's face. "Sounds lovely, and ye've just given me an idea for a gift for Patrick. I'm sure he'd enjoy a volume of Sidney's poems—if there is one. His birthday is in two months."

Catri wanted to shake some sense into Alana. Instead, she twisted away from her sister's touch and turned to Bridget, hoping the sensible twin would agree with her.

Bridget shook her head. "*Think*, Catri," she urged. "Our parents had a love match. And Uncle Rory adores Aunt Henrietta." She swept her arm wide. "Here on the ranch… Why, ye should see the way Harry cossets our cousin Sally; and Wyatt Thompson, for all he can seem so stern, why, his face lights up at the sight of Samantha. Just because ye've had a bad experience doesn't mean all men are like Bartley Crogan."

"Bartley was a *peddler*, Catri," Alana interjected. "He appeared for a few hours or a day every few months."

"Not to mention how persuasive salesmen are." Bridget shook her head. "And that one certainly had a golden tongue, the way his wares flew from his cart."

They couldn't know Catri wasn't thinking only of Bartley.

"No one in our village knew that man's character," Alana said. "No way to see him in day-to-day interactions. So ye couldn't know what kind of man Bartley was."

Oh, I knew all right. He was exactly what I needed. That's why I ran away with him.

"We didn't want to leave home without ye knowing—without saying good-bye." A haunted look in Bridget's eyes told of the pain of that decision. "But we couldn't afford to stay. We were running out of money. As it was, we sold everything to buy our tickets."

Everything? Catri thought of some of the dear possessions that she'd missed when traveling and living out of a peddler's wagon. *But I missed my sisters far more.* She comforted herself. *They did what they had to.*

She looked at Bridget and Alana with new eyes—as people in their own right, not just family members. In a few short months, the twins had changed—grown from girls into women. Clad in their wedding finery, with their hair in stylish coiffures, they were not just pretty but elegant, looking mature and wise. They were twenty-three to Catri's twenty-four, but in their presence, she felt both aged and childish.

A knock sounded on the door.

"Just a minute, Dr. Cameron," Alana called. She quickly began to undo the buttons on Catri's dress.

"There *will* be a wedding today, Catri," Bridget said with an earnest expression. "But we won't abandon ye and the babe. We'll figure something out, ye'll see."

Deflated by how they'd punctured her dream, all Catri could do was stand there like a doll while the twins undressed her down to her chemise and drawers and chivvied her onto the bed, covering her legs with the quilt. She was too disheartened to make another attempt to stop the wedding, for she could see the twins were set on their course, foolish or not. But remembering their happy expressions, a niggle of doubt made Catri wonder if *she* was the foolish one.

The doctor had a rumpled look to him, as if he'd run a hand through his curly red hair, and the pockets of his frock coat sagged. The leather of his black bag was scuffed and worn. He gave them all a friendly glance with his kind blue eyes. "Between you three, my wife and I, and Samantha Thompson and your aunt Henrietta, and the cowboy Deuce, I believe redheads might almost outnumber the other shades today," he said in a joking tone. "You might think we were back in Ireland or Scotland." His smile revealed crooked teeth.

The doctor's teasing made Catri feel more comfortable.

He walked over to the bed and set his bag on the side table. "Now let's see what's going on with you. I've heard you prefer to be called by your given name. Is that correct?"

"Please."

"Well then, Catriona, are you normally this thin?"

"No," Alana answered in disapproval, with a sharp glance at Catri.

Catri rolled her eyes at her sister. "No," she echoed, as if they were six instead of grown up.

The doctor tried not to react to their sisterly scuffle, but a smile played about his mouth. He opened the bag and took out a long, cylindrical instrument made of metal, about the width of a finger with a trumpet shape on the end.

"What is that?" Catri asked, unable to stop herself from leaning away.

"A stethoscope. This allows for diagnosis by auscultation."

Catri wanted to roll her eyes at the doctor but made herself act her age. She looked at Alana for clarification.

"It's a way for him to better hear yer heartbeat." Alana tapped her chest. "Mama used a wooden tube, but this is far finer." Her expression was bright with obvious fervor. "Dr. Cameron allowed me to use it on Aunt Henrietta and practice on the rest of the family. Fascinating."

This time, the doctor didn't suppress his smile. "First, I'm going to listen to your heart, and then the baby's. If you would please lie flat."

Alana hastened to take the pillows from behind Catri, so she could lie down.

The doctor held up a hand. "Now, if I could have quiet please?" He pulled a watch from his vest pocket and flicked it open. Then he slipped the trumpet of the stethoscope just inside the neckline of her chemise and placed it on the left side of Catri's chest.

The metal rim was cold. She made herself hold still.

Dr. Cameron tilted his head and bent over to place his ear over the end of the instrument. Then he looked at the watch and remained still. His lips moved slightly as if he were counting for what seemed like a long time before he straightened. "Your heart is beating just as it should. Now for the babe's. I'll reach under your chemise and lower your drawers to below your belly." He waited for her permission and at her nod, loosened her clothing and gently prodded her stomach. "Ah."

"What?" Catri asked, fascinated in spite of herself.

He took her hand and moved it over the baby. "Feel this smooth hard area? That's the babe's back. It's the best location to hear the heartbeat."

"Ah." Over the last months, she'd tried not to feel the baby inside her, not wanting to become attached. She couldn't believe—didn't want to believe—that this little being under her hand was her child.

The doctor repeated the procedure he'd used to hear her heart, putting the trumpet end to her stomach and bending over to listen, although this time, he didn't look at his watch. He straightened, keeping his hand flat on her stomach. "There's a kick," he said with a grin. "And that might be a thrown elbow. I think the wee one didn't like my stethoscope."

Catri searched his expression, but he seemed calm and unalarmed.

Dr. Cameron handed the stethoscope to Alana. "Would you like to hear your niece or nephew?" He moved out of the way.

She eagerly grasped the instrument, tossed her wedding veil over one shoulder, bent over Catri's stomach, and listened. A look of apparent awe came over her face, and her smile was blissful.

In that moment, Catri envied her sister being able to listen to the baby, being able to love….

Alana straightened, her eyes misty. "Such a beautiful sound! I wish ye could hear yer baby, Catri." She handed back the stethoscope. "The sound is so much better with this than the one my mother used."

"Now for your lungs. If you'd sit up, please, and turn this way." This time, the doctor held the stethoscope to her back and instructed her to breathe, and then moved the end of the instrument to another area, followed by a third.

The doctor straightened and looked at Catri with a reassuring smile. Then he glanced to the twins and back. "The good news is you're healthy, and so is the babe."

Catri saw the looks of relief on her sisters' faces, and in spite of not wanting Flea, she couldn't help a feeling of relief that he or she was healthy. *Well, if I'm going to actually have this child, best that it's healthy.*

"But—" Dr. Cameron held up a cautionary hand. "You're far too thin and drawn. Your condition is not good for the child."

Alana nodded in obvious agreement.

"I do na know where you're planning on ending up, lass. Whether you're going with Alana to Crenshaw, or with your aunt and uncle or staying here with Bridget or Sally. But regardless of your plans, I want you resting, getting your health back, and gaining some weight. His eyebrows drew downward. "The next time I see you, I'll expect you to be plumper with color in your cheeks."

"Complete bed rest for a while, Doctor?" Alana asked.

"Nay, I don't think that's necessary. Catriona, you can attend the wedding and such."

"Oh, good!" Bridget clapped her hands.

"No imbibing spirits today," Dr. Cameron ordered. "Nor for the remainder of the pregnancy and while you are nursing. Despite what some people believe, I don't think it's healthy for the babe. Tonight and for the next few nights, go to bed early. I want you to sleep in the morning until you naturally awaken and take a nap or naps during the day, if need be. Eat plenty of Mrs. Toffels's good food, even if you don't have much of an appetite, and get out in the fresh air. Take some gentle walks—the exercise will be good for you. No riding a horse, but a short buggy ride might be just the thing. I'm sure one of the cowboys, Moss Callahan, for instance, will be glad to drive you." He winked at the twins.

Her sisters chuckled and exchanged knowing looks.

With the heat rising in her cheeks, Catri suspected the doctor might already be seeing the color he'd demanded.

He gave her a penetrating gaze. "I want you to stay put at the ranch for at least a week, maybe two. Then I'll visit and see how you're doing and decide if you're free to travel."

The need to make decisions about her future settled like a weight around her shoulders.

What will become of the babe and me then?

Chapter Six

A knock sounded on the bedroom door. "I've brought food for Mrs. Catriona," an unfamiliar voice said.

Bridget moved to open the door.

A plump, full-breasted older woman carried in a tray to the small table by the window and set it down. The smell of beef broth wafted in the air. "I'm Mrs. Toffels, the housekeeper." She wore an apron over a black silk dress. A pearl bar pinned a froth of lace to the collar. "This soup should hearten you right up, dearie, if I do say so myself." She beamed at Catri, her broad smile scrunching all the wrinkles on her good-natured face.

"Thank ye," Catri murmured, wiggling to sit up against the bed pillows and pulling the quilt to cover herself.

Samantha Thompson, Sally, and Aunt Henrietta followed the housekeeper into the room.

"Dr. Cameron gave us the news," Samantha said, a blue garment draped over her arm. "Sally and I are quarrelling dreadfully to see who gets to keep you for the next few days." She offered up a warm smile to Sally. "Neither of us has yet conceded defeat."

"And I—" Henrietta fisted her hands on her hips with a smile "—as your aunt and standing in the stead of your mother, want you to come live with Rory and me when the doctor gives you permission."

Catri stared at the women, unable to believe her ears. *They all want me?* Shame curled within her. *If they knew the truth—that I'm a fallen woman, they'd not be so eager to welcome me into their homes.* She could depend on her sisters, even if they knew the truth. They wouldn't forsake her. But other respectable women—even if they were relatives—might not feel so generous.

Samantha gestured toward the door. "In a few minutes, I'll turn on the water in the bathtub. A hot bath is just what you'll need to feel quite yourself again. I brought you my dressing gown to wear to and from the bathroom. She eyed Catri's dress, draped over a chair by the table. "Given your circumstances…." She waved toward her bulging middle. "I must ask…."

Catri braced for some pointed questions, prepared to tell whatever lies necessary.

Samantha's cheeks colored. "Do you have a clean dress that fits? Mrs. Toffels can launder this one for you tomorrow, but until then…."

Dumbfounded by the woman's unexpected question, Catri needed a few extra seconds for the meaning to penetrate her brain. "Ah, no. I've only altered the one."

Samantha frowned. "Oh, dear. I don't have anything to lend you."

Sally exchanged glances with Alana and Bridget. "I haven't let out my dresses yet, although I need to. This one—" she waved a hand down her body "—is almost too tight. I'd planned to buy some inexpensive fabric and make one to wear until the baby is born."

"Well…." Catri tried to put on a bright smile. She hadn't expected anyone to lend her a gown anyway. "After I bathe, I'll just put this one back on and sit in the back corner, where no one can smell me."

"I believe I have a solution." Mrs. Toffels had lingered near the door. Her plump hands tightened on the sides of her apron.

Samantha titled her head and surveyed the housekeeper appraisingly. "Hmm. If we pin the waist…."

Mrs. Toffles chuckled, even though sadness lingered in her

gaze. "We don't have enough pins to make a dress of mine fit Catriona." She glanced at Catri in askance. "If I may be so free with your given name?"

"Please do."

Mrs. Toffels's expression sobered again. "I have a gown without a waist put away in my cedar chest from when I was a young woman. The dress is in good condition, which is why I've kept it all these years. I'll go fetch it right now." She gave the soup a pointed glance. "And while I do, you eat up, Catriona. We need to put some meat on your bones, and we have a wedding awaitin' downstairs."

The housekeeper bustled out the door, closing it firmly behind her.

Samantha stared after her in obvious concern.

Alana eyed Catri and silently pointed at the tray.

Samantha handed her the blue robe. "I'll be right back." She left the room.

Still bemused by the kindness she was receiving, Catri moved to obey by climbing out of bed, donning the soft robe, tying the sash over the top of her stomach, and taking a seat at the small table. The tray held a bowl of soup, a plate with two golden rolls and a pat of butter, along with a cup of tea.

The soup was more like stew, thick with beef—a rare treat—and carrots, onions, peas, potatoes, and herbs. Catri hadn't thought she was hungry until she tasted her first spoonful, when the rich flavor hit her mouth. She almost groaned with pleasure and devoured the food at a fast, but still ladylike pace.

Bridget fluffed out her veil. "Catri, I wish there was time for me to show ye our dear little house. Wyatt has given James the day off tomorrow. Samantha is going to give us a basket of food, so we can be undisturbed, although, of course, we'll emerge for a few minutes to say goodbye to Alana and Patrick. But the following day, ye must come visit me."

Sally lifted her chin in a haughty tilt. "You may come visit me tomorrow. You'll present your card," she said in a mock hoity-toity tone.

The others dissolved into laughter.

Alana's expression sobered. "I'm nervous about going to live in Crenshaw. It was one thing to travel to my aunt and uncle's by myself. We knew them through their letters, and Bridget, ye weren't far away. Of course, I'll have my own dear husband, and I hope to make friends with his housekeeper. But there are no other women living on the stud farm, and I won't know *anyone.* Ye must come to Crenshaw, Catri. Otherwise, I'll be lonely, even with beginning my medical studies."

"Studies?" Catri couldn't imagine what her sister meant. She took a sip of tea.

"Patrick has arranged for me to study with the local doctor. At some point, I'll need to decide if I want more formal schooling, or just keep working with Doctor Byron."

"Do ye want to be a nurse, then?" Catri asked. "How's that different from what ye already did in Ireland?"

"Or a doctor." Alana smiled. "There are medical colleges in America that accept women."

A doctor! "But…" Catri said faintly. "What about your husband?"

"Studying medicine was Patrick's idea. I'm not set on doing so, probably because I can't even wrap my mind around the possibility. Nor do I want to be away from my husband and my home for long periods of time. I just want to gain more knowledge about healing. The more I know, the more I can help people."

"And if ye have children?" Catri asked.

Alana face colored. "Patrick and I want to wait on having children."

Catri glanced down at her bulging belly. "Ye won't have a choice. Children come once you're married." *And even if ye are not.*

"There are ways to prevent conception, even if the idea goes against the Catholic prohibition on birth control." Alana's lips tightened.

Catri remembered how angry Alana had been with William Doody for almost killing his wife with baby after baby. Her gentle sister had raised her voice to the man and told him some pointed truths.

Alana let out a breath. "A man can wear a sheath," she said in a matter-of-fact tone. "Or, a woman can use a small sponge inside her with a string tied around it—or even a rag if a sponge isn't available—and soak it in vinegar and insert it inside. It's not foolproof, mind, but it increases the chances of preventing conception."

"Alana O'Donnell!" Catri exclaimed, more intrigued than shocked. "Where did ye learn such a thing?" *And why did ye never tell me?*

"From Doctor Cameron. One of my regrets is not being able to remain here and work with him."

"I wish I'd known that when I married," Sally said wistfully.

Catri gave her sister an admiring glance. "Ye've changed so much and have truly become a strong, independent woman."

Alana was silent for a minute, her lips pursed. "I have. Between Bridget's dragging me to America, living with our relatives—feeling needed and loved by them.... But mostly—" she gently thumped her chest with her knuckles, "—it's because of Patrick. He encouraged me to face my fear of horses, and from that, I know I can overcome other fears like getting married and moving away."

Catri gasped in disbelief. "Never say ye are riding again? Why, ye've been deathly afraid of horses for half yer life."

"I am," Alana said with a proud smile. "Choosing yer partner in life makes all the difference. Most men only want women to take care of them, the children, and the house and garden. But there are men who'll encourage yer dreams and help ye overcome yer fears. That kind of man will bring out the best in ye, as ye bring out the best in him."

Alana might as well have been speaking a foreign language for all Catri understood her. *Of course, when a woman is starry-eyed with new love, she believes the best about her man and is blind to the worst.*

Alana must have read her mind, for she took Catri's hand. "Our parents had such a match. Mama couldn't have done the works of midwifery and healing without Da's support. Think of all the times he took care of us when she was gone.... How he saved all year to buy her Alasdair Grey's *Anatomy* for Christmas." Her voice wavered, and she swallowed before continuing. "They were a good inspiration for a fine marriage—one I intend to take to heart."

Sally sighed. "I wish I'd known my aunt and uncle. They sound so wonderful."

"They were," Bridget said in the fierce tone she tended to use to hide obvious emotion.

"Yer parents are wonderful, too," Alana told Sally. "So very loving."

"Living isolated as my family did, we only had each other," her cousin said. "I can't imagine the horror of familial discord or lack of care between a husband and wife. I didn't realize the difference until I came to live at the ranch and saw both the stresses and the comforts that living among other people can bring. Harry and I are less dependent on each other than my parents are, but that doesn't mean we love each other less, but...."

"I understand," Catri told her. "The ranch is like a village, and Mr. Thompson is the squire. Too bad he doesn't have sons of marriageable age," she quipped.

The others laughed. Only Catri realized the bitterness that lay beneath her words.

"Guess ye'll have to wait a few years—" Bridget teased "—until one of the older boys grows up."

Maybe by then I'll be ready to try men again. Catri thought about her attraction to Moss, and her stomach churned.

Probably not.

Mrs. Toffels didn't knock, but instead she entered the room with a black gown draped over her arm.

Samantha followed and shut the door behind her.

Mrs. Toffels held up the garment. "Forty years old. As I said, out of style, but the dresses one wears when one is with child are similar, despite the fashion."

Samantha touched her housekeeper's arm, her expression sad. "I didn't know you had a child."

Mrs. Toffels clasped the dress to her chest. "And how could you, then, if I never spoke of my Angel, for that's what I called her. My first husband and the love of my life, even though I later married and buried two good men, was taken from me when I was eight months along. The shock and pain of his death sent me into a decline. I didn't eat, did nothing but cry." She shook her head. "Foolish girl that I was. The greatest mistake of my life."

Samantha made a shocked sound. "I know that kind of grief. If I hadn't had Daniel to look after, I'd have done the same when Juan Carlos died."

The housekeeper sighed. "I'd like to think that if my daughter had already been born, I would have focused on her and not on my pain. But I didn't realize what a treasure I carried inside me, that she'd be my only child.... I went into labor not long after. Too soon. My Angel only lived a few precious moments."

Flea chose that moment to kick.

Catri placed a hand over her stomach, for the first time wondering if she could love this baby as Mrs. Toffels had loved her Angel. *Mrs. Toffels was happily married,* she reminded herself. *Her baby was conceived in love. That's different.*

Mrs. Toffels sniffed and obviously forced herself to go on. "I held Angel and kissed her and was a mother for the shortest time. But I never will forget the love I had for her, still have and always will. My only consolation all these years was the knowledge that I'll see her again in heaven."

Blinking back tears, Samantha rushed over to hug Mrs. Toffels. "And your Angel will be beautiful and welcome you."

Aunt Henrietta brushed tears off her cheeks. "You never forget the loss of a child, no matter the age he or she died, or how much time has passed. I, too, think every day of my Paddy, who left us when he was five, and I long to see him again. But not—" she glanced from Alana to Sally "—for a long while, for I still have children to raise and soon grandchildren and hopefully great-nieces and nephews to love."

Alana kissed Henrietta's cheek and then reached to take Mrs. Toffels's hand and squeezed. "You are an admirable woman," she told the older woman before releasing her hand. "To lose yer only baby and not succumb to bitterness and despair like so many women would do."

"Not so admirable," the housekeeper said wryly. "Still stupid with grief, I married quickly again. A good man, but I didn't love him. He died suddenly soon after. I seldom mention that marriage. I waited five years before I married again."

"Then we'll keep ye to two husbands." Bridget moved to Mrs. Toffels to also give her a hug. "But I know the thought of reuniting in heaven isn't yer only consolation. Ye mother everyone on this ranch, even Old Sid. Ye've certainly been as kind and wise and helpful with me as my own mother was."

"You're right, my dear Bridget. I've had a good life." Mrs. Toffels waved a dismissive hand. "After my third husband died—why, coming to work for Mr. Thompson when he was married to Alicia was the best thing I could have done. I consider Christine my own, for didn't I raise her from the hour she was born? And don't I have a whole bunkhouse of cowboys to keep in line? Now…." She clasped Samantha's hand. "I also have your dear boys."

"And they're quite a handful." Samantha's expression of pride belied her words.

Mrs. Toffels's smile at her employer, who obviously was a dear friend, made her look like her good-natured self again. "If my husband Clark and my Angel had lived, my life would have been much different. I wouldn't have been *here*, where I'm needed. I wouldn't have my Christine. My daughter is not forgotten; I talk to her every night in my prayers. I know now that her death led me to where I'm supposed to be. And I'm at peace."

Silence followed, as each of the six other women absorbed her story.

Mrs. Toffels moved to Catri and held out the gown. "Listen to me nattering on when we have a wedding awaiting on us."

Standing, Catri took the dress from her, inhaling the smell of cedar.

"I wore it briefly after Clark's death and before Angel was born." Mrs. Toffels wiped away a tear. "This is yours now. See that you treat yourself and that baby you're carrying differently than I did!" she said in a fierce tone. Without waiting for a response, she turned and left the room.

Catri stared after her, feeling guilty that she couldn't do what Mrs. Toffels had ordered and find love and longing for Flea. Then she held up the dress to examine it. With the lace at the neck and sleeves and designs of jet beading on the bodice, the dress was far nicer than anything she could have afforded. She turned the gown around and held it up to her body, glancing down to see where the hem hit.

Samantha scanned the dress. "Looks as if it will fit. Mrs. Toffels must have been a bit taller when she was younger."

Bridget reached for the dress. "I'll iron it while ye bathe."

Samantha glanced at the tray. "Since you're finished eating, Catriona, I'll go start the bath. You'll find everything you need in the bathroom. The day is fine enough that I think you can wash your hair. Then, towel your hair, but go ahead and twist it up, even though it won't be dry. We can't wait any longer than that for the ceremony; otherwise, people won't make it home before dark." She left the room.

Catri glanced from the twins to her aunt to her cousin Sally. "I never expected this."

"Welcome to Sweetwater Springs, Cousin Catriona." Sally leaned over to embrace Catri. "This is how we do things here. Is it not the same in Ireland?"

Catri shook her head. "A member of the upper class like Samantha would be treating ye—" she lifted her chin at Sally "—like a servant because yer married to one of her workers. She'd perhaps give ye a meal in the kitchen. Let ye dry yer clothes there if ye were wet. Actually, the lady of the house probably wouldn't even know about ye. It would be the cook or housekeeper who'd allow ye a meal and some warmth by the stove. But there'd be no dresses or baths or guesting."

"I suppose you're right," Sally said slowly.

"In America, or at least in the West, everything is new," Bridget said. "While some people like the Carters—one of the foremost families in the community—have been here two generations, most are newer than that—carving a living out of raw land."

"There aren't the class distinctions in the West that are present in the East and the South, where I'm from," Henrietta added. "Not that you can tell because I've lost my accent from living here so long. In the North, the Irish often are looked down upon, because of the massive wave of poor immigrants after the famine who became cheap labor. Pointed remarks were directed at me when I married Rory. My parents weren't pleased that I'd chosen a poor Irishman instead of a wealthy Southern planter. But Rory, as is his way, soon charmed them and won their consent."

"We need each other in order to survive," Sally added with a sage nod.

"And the history is different," Alana added. "People in America come from many countries to settle here. Yer neighbors might not even speak English, but ye will lend them a hand, and they will do likewise. There isn't the bitter hatred against the English—especially after they left us to die during the famine. Some people might feel that way about Indians, but the Indians aren't the ones in power here like the English are in Ireland."

Sally suddenly grabbed Alana's hands. "This is so lovely to be together, the four of us. I wish you all could stay at the Thompson ranch."

"That might be hard on Patrick," Alana said wryly. "I think he'd like his wife to live with him."

"Well, I'll have to be content with two of you," Sally sighed. "And to think, why just a few months ago, I was restless—loving my family, but wanting more. I couldn't have even imagined how much my life would change." She released Alana's hands and placed hers over her stomach. "A husband, a move, new friends, a baby, and three cousins. I'm so blessed!"

Catri had to look away from Sally's glowing face, familiar bitterness stirring within her. She, too, couldn't believe how much her life had changed. *And not for the better.* She glanced back at her sisters, at the healthy color in their cheeks and the sparkle in their eyes, at their new gowns. *Well, I can't really say that it's not for the better. Alana and Bridget are happy. We are together, even if not the way I'd desired.*

Somehow, I'll have to figure out a new plan.

Moss came upon Catri sitting at a bench situated along the side of the stairway in the entry hall. She was dressed in black—a finer gown than she'd been wearing, with damp hair up in a bun, although the curly fringe along her forehead was dry. In contrast to her spruced-up appearance, her expression looked bleak.

"Why are you so downcast?" Without asking permission, he took a seat next to her. "I'd think you'd be ecstatic. You're with your sisters and your family. Everyone's happy."

"I can't believe they're getting married."

"You don't sound pleased."

Catri sighed. "I don't know how I feel. I guess I'm still in shock that my little sisters will have their own lives—that the inseparable twins will be apart."

"Apart from you as well."

"The twins are closer to each other. Why, we used to tease Alana and Bridget that they'd have to marry brothers so they could live together all their lives. And there was some comfort in that. No matter what happened in their marriages, they'd still have each other."

Moss frowned. Much as he didn't like the idea of matrimony, James Whitson was as good a man as could be. While he'd known Patrick Gallagher a much shorter time, the wealthy horse breeder had dug in and worked side by side with Thompson and the cowboys when—as a guest—he could have stayed warm and relaxed in the house. There was no reason why either man wouldn't make a good husband. "Are you concerned your sisters are choosing the wrong men?"

"I just wish they weren't in such a hurry."

The apathetic expression on her face concerned him. "I don't know about Patrick and Alana, for I haven't seen them together until yesterday. He was around for about a month, living with the Thompsons." *Perhaps I shouldn't mention Gallagher's pursuit of Bridget. That wouldn't reassure Catriona.* "The Thompsons are good judges of character and the boss is very protective of those he loves. He wouldn't have had Gallagher stay so long—far longer than need be—if he didn't like him."

Catriona shrugged.

"But I do know James Whitson, having worked closely with him. I can assure you he's a good man. He's head over heels for your sister. Brought your sisters home from the train station and let it be known to the cowboys that he'd already staked his claim on Bridget."

She frowned.

Perhaps 'staked his claim' wasn't a good way to word things. He hurried on. "I've observed James and Bridget together for months now. Their relationship is as solid as a rock."

Catri let out a long sigh. "I'll just have to resign myself."

"I suppose you're disappointed," Moss said, thinking through what this must be like for her. "You expected to be together—to find your sisters living with your uncle's family. I'm sure you planned to join them. This wedding must have you as—" he caught himself before he could say "ass on the ground." *No rough cowboy talk around a lady.* Moss lifted and circled a hand. "What's that teacup saying, handle over spout?"

That phrase coaxed a smile from her. Not a big smile, but at least her eyes didn't look so dejected. "Tea*pot*, not tea*cup*. I guess that describes me perfectly."

From what little he'd seen, Moss sensed normally Catriona O'Donnell was an animated woman. He wondered what she'd look like if she fell in love and glowed like her sisters and cousin. *I want to be the man who puts a sparkle in her eyes.* He caught himself on that thought. A sparkling Catriona O'Donnell might infect him with the wedding sickness he'd worked so hard to avoid. But somehow that idea didn't set him running like his tail was afire.

"Do you know what you're doing after today?"

"The doctor said I could attend the wedding and reception, but then he wanted me to have bed rest for the next few days." She wrinkled her nose. "Well, not complete bed rest. I'm allowed to get up for meals and such. Take walks. Go for a buggy ride."

"I guess you won't be leaving for Crenshaw with Mr. and Mrs. Gallagher."

Another shrug. "I've decided not to worry about it. Seems everything I've tried to plan has been like—" she cupped her hands and then spread her fingers "trying to hold sand. Guess it's better not to plan."

"You sound like me."

She raised her eyebrows.

"I don't make plans, either. I like to ride where the wind takes me. Although, I had sort of formed a plan to let the sun take me south to the ocean, but now…."

Boot heels clicked on the floor. "He's like a tumbleweed that way."

Moss looked over at Buck Buchanan, his closest friend on the ranch, and grinned. The stocky blond cowboy had slicked himself up, which made Moss realize that he should go wash up and don his own fancy duds.

But no friendly look answered him back. Instead, Buck swept Moss a frosty glance that made his pale blue eyes look like ice. Then he looked at Catriona, his blunt features still set in a disapproving expression. "Don't get attached to this one," he told her, jerking a thumb at Moss. "Callahan don't care about anyone but himself."

"Now that's a harsh judgment, Buck," Moss drawled, knowing he deserved every word of the accusation. Not that he didn't care about *anyone*, but that he didn't care *deeply*.

The man ignored him, focusing on Catriona. "Yep, you'll think you're friends, good friends, and then he'll up and leave without a word—not even a good-bye."

"Easier that way." Moss leaned back on the bench, until his shoulders rested against the stair wall, and crossed his arms.

"For you, maybe," Buck retorted. "Not for the ones you leave behind."

Moss ran a hand over his neck, which had started heating up.

Buck turned to Catriona. "Do you know why he's nicknamed Moss?"

"I thought it was because of his hazel eyes."

"Are you familiar with the saying, 'A rolling stone gathers no moss?'"

She nodded.

"That's our boy, Moss, although I guess he could be nicknamed stone. Stone-headed. Stone-hearted."

Moss really didn't have anything to say in his defense. Not even an apology could make this better. Buck was right. He just wished his friend—former friend—had picked a different place for the confrontation. "Your beef is with me, Buck."

"Just warnin' the lady."

Moss glanced at Catriona, seeing the wary expression in her

eyes. *Well, perhaps this is for the best, after all. Now Catriona knows the truth about me, and no wedding sickness will infect either of us.*

Well... Wedding sickness might infect her.

Moss didn't like the idea of Catriona marrying another man, which begged the question: *What am I going to do about her? Or should I continue what I set out to do and move on?*

Chapter Seven

Before the ceremony, the twins stood outside of the parlor and introduced their sister to the guests as they filed back inside and returned to their seats.

Alana held her bouquet of tulips, which looked a bit worse for wear from their earlier mistreatment, bound together with a ribbon made from the same fabric as her dress. Although she'd been nervous before the first ceremony, now she was just excited and eager to become Patrick's wife.

Beside her stood Bridget, carrying her wildflowers, the stems tied with a peach ribbon. If some blooms were missing or drooping, Alana couldn't tell.

Catri stood between Alana and Rory, the rest of the family having gone into the parlor. Now clean and fed, her elder sister appeared far more composed than earlier. Although still pale, she seemed stronger. Even the black color of Mrs. Toffels's dress couldn't detract from her fragile loveliness, as evidenced by the admiring glances of the cowboys passing into the parlor.

The children moved in a group. Catri's three cousins came first, followed by Wyatt's daughter, Christine, who looked just like the portrait of her blonde-haired, blue-eyed mother hanging over the fireplace in the parlor; Samantha's son, Daniel, who had his mother's blue eyes, but dark hair and olive skin; the oldest son, Hunter, an Indian boy with his black hair in a long braid; and a set of male twins, looking as indistinguishable as Alana and Bridget when they were children.

Beautiful Elizabeth Sanders, whom Alana had met on her second day in Sweetwater Springs, came toward her carrying her baby girl. The woman wore a ruffled silk dress with an aproned overskirt in a shade between lilac and blue that was the most elegant Alana had ever seen and made the most of her blonde hair and blue eyes. She was from a wealthy upper-class family and had come to Sweetwater Springs from Boston a few years earlier. But even with Elizabeth's riches and social status, she was warm and gracious to everyone.

Her husband, Nick, followed her. He was a stocky man with blue-green eyes and a nose that had once been broken, who owned a small ranch and specialized in taming and training horses.

Elizabeth introduced her husband to Alana and Catriona before leaning closer. "Just as you predicted, Carol's colic has finally passed." She displayed the sleeping baby for Alana to view.

"She looks like an angel," Alana said with genuine admiration.

Nick cast a glance of pride at his wife. "Thank goodness our daughter takes after her mother."

Elizabeth shook her head at his praise, but a smile lingered in her eyes. "Alana, thank you so much for your kindness to my baby that day I met you in the doctor's office. Your suggestions really helped."

"My pleasure."

"I'm only sorry you'll be leaving our town. Once the weather improves, I'd planned to take Carol and start calling upon my friends."

Nick placed a hand in the center of his wife's back. "You'll have a chance to visit again soon. I want to put Patrick's stud Thunder to Diamond Jane. He and I've discussed it already."

"Wonderful." Elizabeth smiled at Alana with great charm.

"I'll look forward to you and Patrick visiting us." She transferred the baby to Nick and moved into the parlor to take her place at the piano in the corner. She began to play the beautiful strains of Mendelssohn's wedding march.

Until today, Alana had never heard the piece. Elizabeth had suggested the music as a processional.

But the music certainly made for an impressive start to the ceremony, and goose bumps broke out over her skin. She'd had the same reaction to the stirring music earlier during the first ceremony.

Catri leaned in to hug and kiss Alana and then Bridget. The scent of Samantha's rose-scented soap clung to her skin and hair. "My beautiful little sisters," she said, her voice trembling. "May good fortune go with ye both all the days of yer lives."

"Good fortune has attended us," Alana smiled, thinking back on her grief at leaving Ireland and Timkin and how different she felt now.

"But I'll take more," Bridget interjected with a laugh. "Ye can never have too much."

Catri left them to enter the parlor and take a seat next to Aunt Henrietta.

Uncle Rory held out his hands to the twins. "Well, my darlings. We've had our practice round. This time's for real."

Bridget chuckled and went on tiptoe to kiss his cheek. "We've already embraced and been misty-eyed about things changing and sad about Catri not being here. Now our lost sister has joined us, and I can't wait to be my Jamie's wife! No sadness at all!"

Alana smiled, still feeling as misty-eyed as Bridget described. Catri's surprise arrival and attendance at the wedding had, indeed, changed everything. She, too, lifted up on tiptoe to kiss her uncle's cheek, inhaling the scent of apple cider on his breath. *The men must have already started their celebrations.*

Alana reached behind Bridget for her veil. She drew the lace over her twin's face. Then she turned so Bridget could do the same for her.

Uncle Rory extended an arm to Bridget and another to Alana. "I think it's time to get the two of you off my hands," he teased. "I'm setting a record—marrying off three of my girls within four months." He winked at Catriona. "And I have a feeling that, in no time, I'll be giving away Catri, too."

May the Good Lord and the Blessed Mother make it so, Alana prayed. She knew there was more to the story than Catri had revealed. But they didn't have time to pry the truth from her sister. She'd have to trust things would work out for her in the same way they'd done for the twins.

Bridget started to tuck her hand around Rory's arm, and then stopped. "Wait. When we three walked up the aisle earlier, I had eyes only for James. I'm sure that will happen this time, as well. But I missed seeing what was happening with Patrick and Alana."

Alana realized she'd had the same experience. "Me, too."

Bridget gestured toward the front of the parlor. "How about Uncle Rory takes one of us up the aisle, and then comes back for the other?"

"Sounds like a plan," Uncle Rory said. "Who wants to go first?"

"Yer the eldest." Bridget made a shooing motion toward Alana.

"Ye met James first," Alana retorted. "So ye go to him now."

Bridget smiled and took their uncle's arm, nodding for him to proceed.

Her hands clasped to her chest, Alana watched from the doorway. The sun streaming through the lace curtains on the windows gilded the bride's hair. She couldn't see Bridget's face, but James's eager expression was all she could want for her sister. A lump rose in her throat. She could not have parted with Bridget to a lesser man. *James deserves my twin and she him*

James held out his hand to Bridget and tenderly drew her toward him.

Uncle Rory turned to walk down the short aisle to Alana, crooking his arm toward her. "Your turn, *mavourneen*."

She swallowed down the emotion for her sister and took a steadying breath.

Patrick had briefly watched Bridget's advance up the aisle but now turned his attention to Alana, waiting in the doorway, and kept his dark-eyed gaze on her.

He looked so handsome and imposing in his suit. If Alana didn't know Patrick so well, she would have felt intimidated by him—and indeed, had, when first they'd met. Now, she could barely recall those feelings, so full of love was she for him.

Alana had come far—both in distance and in the healing of her emotions—to find him. *I'll be forever grateful to the Good Lord and the Blessed Mother for bringing us together.*

As Uncle Rory escorted her up the aisle, Alana had eyes only for Patrick. This time moving toward him was the same and yet different—lighter because of no lingering fear or sadness about Catri.

Her groom had already had his first sight of her as a bride, but his expression was just as loving and proud. Patrick held out a hand to her. "'My bounty is as boundless as the sea, My love as deep,'" he quoted from Romeo and Juliet.

Patrick's use of Shakespeare's words was more than him proclaiming his love. During their courtship, he'd read the play aloud while visiting the O'Donnells, using the bard to send Alana hints of his feelings. Listening to him read the age-old, magical words had led Alana to fall in love with him.

Now the double meaning in Patrick's greeting filled her heart with joy. Alana eagerly placed her hand and her life in his.

Patrick guided her to stand at his side.

Reverend Norton, with his austere features and wearing in his rusty black frock coat, looked every inch the strict minister. "Who gives these two women to be married?"

"I, their uncle, stand in the place of my dear, departed brother." Rory's voice rang throughout the room. "I give my cherished nieces into the keeping of God and their husbands-to-be."

Alana suppressed a giggle. The first time around, Uncle Rory hadn't waxed so eloquently. *Nothing like some hard apple cider to bring out the Irish gift of gab.*

Reverend Norton gazed at Rory. The twinkle in his blue eyes contrasted with his stern expression.

When weather permitted, Bridget had attended the Protestant service with the Thompson family, Mrs. Toffels, and the ranch hands. She'd grown fond of the minister, whose caring heart belied his appearance. However, Alana hadn't met the man until today when he'd taken her aside for a spiritual talk about marriage. The O'Donnell homestead on the prairie had been too far from town, the winter weather uncertain, and Aunt Henrietta's health still weak, to afford the family a chance to attend church.

One of the questions Reverend Norton had asked Alana was if she wanted to exchange a kiss with Patrick at the end of the ceremony, saying the gesture wasn't part of the ritual, but was sometimes included in a Protestant ceremony, although, as far as he knew, never in a Catholic one. Both she and Bridget had opted for having the kiss included.

Uncle Rory smiled at each of the twins, and then he moved to take a seat in the front row between Henrietta and Catri.

"Dearly Beloved," Reverend Norton intoned. "We are gathered together here in the sight of God and in the face of this company to join together this man and this woman—" he nodded at James and Bridget "—and this man and this woman—" he inclined his chin to Patrick and Alana "—in holy matrimony."

Alana tried to concentrate on Reverend Norton's words, but the rapid beating of her heart and the tender light in Patrick's eyes made tears threaten. She concentrated on breathing deeply, trying to hang onto her composure.

Reverend Norton, thankfully, skipped the line about the impediments to marriage and had Bridget and James go first.

Their hands clasped, Alana and Patrick turned slightly so they could witness the other couple's vows.

Between the tears blurring her vision and the cloudy netting of her veil, she had to keep blinking to see. Bridget's face was turned away from her, but from the moisture pooling in James's eyes, Alana suspected her twin was crying, too.

She pulled a handkerchief from her sleeve and mopped her eyes, discretely blowing her nose.

Once James and Bridget were finished, Reverend Norton turned to Patrick and Alana. "Having just heard the vows, you two know what comes next," he said, breaking away from the ritual with a teasing gleam in his eyes.

Patrick chuckled. "Best prompt us, anyway, Reverend."

The levity between the two men amazed Alana, so different from the strict conformity to the Catholic ritual she was used to. But she appreciated the warmth and simplicity of this service. She listened to Patrick's vows and repeated her own, meaning every promise.

Reverend Norton joined James and Bridget's hands. Then he moved to Alana and Patrick and did likewise. He stood between the two couples and stretched out his arms so his fingertips rested on the clasped hands of each pair. "Those whom God hath joined together let no man put asunder." His gaze swept the room.

"I pronounce that they are man and wife—" Reverend Norton gestured to James and Bridget "and man and wife—" he indicated Patrick and Alana. "In the name of the Father, and of the Son, and of the Holy Ghost." The twinkle returned to his eyes. "You may kiss the brides." Shaking his head, he held up a hand. "Let me reword that. "Each husband may kiss his bride."

Laughter broke out, and Patrick and Alana both chuckled.

Her new husband lifted the front of her veil over her head. "You're so beautiful," Patrick said so only she could hear. "'Shall I compare thee to a summer's day? Thou art more lovely and more temperate,'" he quoted one of Shakespeare's sonnets.

Alana and Patrick hadn't had as many chances for kisses as she would have liked—given he'd gone home to his stud farm not long after they'd become engaged and had only a chance to visit once in the intervening months. But they'd still had some practice.

This kiss was different from any other they'd exchanged, for it was their first as a married couple. She felt the brief touch of his lips right down to her very soul and hungered for the intimacy to come.

A few moments later, the minister had them face their family and friends. He introduced Mr. and Mrs. Whitson and Mr. and Mrs. Gallagher.

To everyone's cheers, Bridget and James strode hand-in-hand down the aisle, followed by Alana, her hand on Patrick's arm.

As she passed, Alana snuck a glance at Catri.

She alone of their audience wasn't smiling, and her eyes looked sad.

Concern stabbed Alana, but she firmly pushed away the feeling, not willing to let any apprehensions about her older sister and the baby shadow this glorious day. *As long as Catri is here, everything will turn out all right,* she told herself. Yet she couldn't help feeling a niggle of doubt.

Watching the loving exchange of vows between the two couples was enough to make Moss's feet start itching, a reaction that usually started his stone a rollin'. But this time, a boulder seemed lodged in his stomach and weighed him down on his seat on the wooden bench, as if saying, *You're not going anywhere, cowpoke. You've met your match.*

Met my doom is more likely.

He'd already heard that, per doctor's orders, Catriona had to reside at the Thompson ranch for a week or two. *It won't hurt me to stick around for a few days.* Moss tried to convince himself he'd be fine.

Who am I kidding? Sticking around might very well hurt!

Buck, sitting next to him, gave him a nudge that was harder than usual. "Git a move on, Tumbleweed." He glared at Moss. "We've got some mighty fine vittles awaitin'."

In the old days—the before-today old days—Moss would have shot back a sharp or witty quip. *Since meeting Catriona, my wit seems to have spilled out of my brain.*

Moss pushed to his feet, feeling suddenly ancient. Without a backward glance, he stalked out of the parlor, following the crowd. The cowboys and children split off to head to the kitchen. The other guests—the O'Donnells, the sheriff, Reverend and Mrs. Norton, Nick and Elizabeth Sanders with their baby girl, and Dr. and Mrs. Cameron—headed to the dining room, walking behind the wedding couples and Wyatt and Samantha Thompson.

Catriona hovered uncertainly in the background, watching people flow in two directions.

Moss stopped before her, catching the scent of roses, and nodded toward the dining room. "Your place is with your sisters."

"I think I've had all I can take of wedded bliss. Can I sit with ye?" She shivered and suddenly looked exhausted.

He wanted to fold her into his arms. "We're eating in the kitchen. Not fancy but more comfortable, perhaps. You're welcome to join us. But you'd best tell one of your sisters so they don't worry." He held up a hand and shook his head. "Never mind. I'll do it."

After striding across the entryway to the dining room, Moss went over to Alana, who stood with her new husband talking to the Sanders. "Catriona is tired and cold. I think it's best she sit in Mrs. Toffels's rocking chair near the kitchen stove so she can rest and warm up. I'll see that she eats."

Alana gave him an assessing glance. "I appreciate ye taking care of her."

"Just doing my job, ma'am." He meant doing his job as one

of Thompson's ranch hands to provide service for their guests. But even as he spoke the words, Moss realized they had a more personal connotation.

Alana smiled and placed a hand on his arm. "Thank ye."

Only two words, but her eyes, so like Catriona's, conveyed much more—a sense of trust in him that his *job* really had become taking care of her older sister.

The responsibility felt right, in fact more right than anything ever had before, which in itself frightened Moss more than riding the fiercest bucking bronco.

Chapter Eight

That evening after supper when the guests who were not staying the night left for their homes, Catriona and Moss joined the other adults in the dining room. Moss was part of the group only because out in the yard after everyone said their good-byes, Mrs. Thompson had insisted he come inside with them, saying in an undertone that Catriona had known him longer than anyone else here besides her sisters, and she already seemed comfortable with him.

Moss still wasn't sure how he felt about that responsibility, but he trotted along behind the missus as if on a lead rope, taking Catriona's arm to help her up the steps to the kitchen. The look of gratitude she threw him as she lumbered up each one warmed his innards.

In the dining room, Wyatt took his place at the head of the table. The brides and grooms sat on one side and the O'Donnells, Harry and Sally, Moss and Catri found seats on the other side. After passing around cups of fragrant hot chocolate, Samantha and Mrs. Toffels left for the kitchen, refusing offers from the other women to help clean up.

Candles burned in the silver candelabra on the table and in silver candlesticks on the mantle of the fireplace, where a cheerful fire lent warmth to the room. The sweet scent of cocoa filled the air.

While Catriona enjoyed drinking the rare beverage, she really wanted to go to bed, not just to rest, but because she craved the solitude to *think*. She needed to sort through the events of the day.

Henrietta took a sip and exhaled a sigh of delight. "What a treat. I can't remember the last time I had hot chocolate. In fact, this whole day has been so wonderful."

With the candlelight bringing out the auburn glints in her aunt's hair and softening the lines on her face, Catriona could see the beautiful Southern belle Rory had written home about. Her grandmother and mother had saved all his letters, and Catri wondered what had become of them.

Henrietta looked at Wyatt, who sat at the head of the table. "You and Samantha have thrown a beautiful wedding for our nieces. We're very grateful."

"Didn't do much," Wyatt said in a depreciating tone. "Mostly provided a place and some grub. Seems everyone who attended brought food. We had a chance to be neighborly and spend time with good friends."

"Still, Rory and I—" Henrietta waved around the table "—all the O'Donnells, including those by marriage, thank you from the bottom of our hearts."

The other family members nodded and murmured their agreement.

Aunt Henrietta reached over to pat Catri's hand. "Now, before our newlyweds head off for some private time, we really must make plans for our Catriona."

Everyone's attention turned to her, making Catri feel guilty for intruding on such a festive day, for being a burden.

Flea started moving, as if wanting to be part of the conversation.

"Catriona is welcome to stay with us," Wyatt said. "We have room tonight, even with extra guests. The children are sleeping on pallets. She can take my daughter Christine's bed. After tonight, the guest room will be free for her use."

Sally jutted her chin. "Catriona must come and stay with Harry and me."

"Nay, daughter," Rory said gently. "You and Harry have gladly housed Bridget these months, and you two deserve some time alone before the babe arrives. Catriona must come with us," he said firmly.

"No, she must live with Patrick and me," Alana insisted. "Catri can't be climbing up and down a ladder into the loft, which is where she'd sleep at Sally's house, or Bridget's, or our aunt and uncle's."

Catri suppressed a shudder at the thought of clambering up and down a ladder each time she had to use the chamber pot, which was far too often the bigger Flea grew.

Alana's eyes lit with healing fervor. "Then, when it's time, I can deliver the baby."

Catriona had avoided thinking about labor and delivery in the belief—no matter how silly—that if she didn't think about it, the birth wouldn't happen. Somehow the baby would magically disappear from her body and her life.

"I add my invitation to my *wife's*." Patrick seemed to savor the title as if realizing he'd spoken the word for the first time. "My—" He stopped and smiled at Alana "—*our* house has plenty of rooms."

Alana beamed at her husband.

"But you and Patrick are leaving tomorrow," Bridget pointed out. "Dr. Cameron doesn't want Catri to travel for the next few weeks."

"Then Catri must come to us—" Alana waved between her and Patrick "—when Dr. Cameron allows her to travel."

"Or," James interjected with a glance at Bridget. "We can build on a bedroom. We'd planned to do that in the future, anyway. Would only take a few days. What do you think?"

"Why, that's fine, James." Bridget gazed lovingly at her husband.

Catri listened to them talking about her as if she weren't there, and she didn't like any of the solutions. It was one thing to plan a life with her sisters, but quite another to also live with their husbands' or to reside with her aunt and uncle's family without her sisters. She desperately longed for a home of her own.

Beside her, Moss leaned forward. "I think not. You all have been talking about Catriona as if she isn't sitting right at this table." He looked at her. "What would *you* like to do?"

Not be with child. She shrugged and sent him a smile, wondering if everyone else could see how false the expression. "Any of those plans are fine with me."

Catri saw in his eyes that Moss could tell she was lying, but since everyone seemed to take her words at face value, he didn't challenge her.

She made herself smile at everyone around the table. "I thank ye all for yer kind offers. It's a blessing, indeed, to be so loved and wanted." Her gaze settled on Wyatt. "I will take ye up on yer offer of staying here until Doctor Cameron approves me to travel."

Wyatt gave her a solemn nod. "That sounds wise."

Catri chose the best option, but not without a pang at the thought of leaving Moss behind—the man she'd known only for a single day. "After that, I'd like to go stay with Alana and Patrick since it sounds like they have the most room."

"But you'll have to travel alone," Henrietta objected in dismay, her eyes wide.

"I did so all the way from Ireland to here," Catri reminded her.

"But you fainted today." Her aunt's lips firmed. "I won't hear of you traveling alone. In addition to your own safety, you must think of the baby."

"I'll escort her." As he made the offer, Moss didn't meet Catri's eyes.

Her heart gave a little leap. She wanted to press her hands to her chest to hold her heart still, not let foolish wishes take root, but that gesture would reveal too much of her inner turmoil. Instead, she fisted her hands in her lap.

Patrick tapped the table. "As the men discussed earlier…I

have something you three sisters might want to consider, and even Sally and Harry…." He sent the couple a glance. "I'm about to expand my herd and had planned to hire more men. James, you could come work with me. Harry, too. There's no houses for you now, but they could be built."

"So," Wyatt interjected, raising one eyebrow. "You're offering to deprive me of another of my best cowboys, eh?" His tone turned teasing. "You come here under the subterfuge of checking out my mare and leave with four lovely ladies—and Sweetwater Springs already suffers from a deficit of women—and three of my cowboys." He shot a pointed look at Moss, obviously including him in the cowboy count.

Patrick crossed his arms and gave Wyatt a mock superior smile. "That's about right."

Clasping her hands together, Henrietta made a noise of protest.

Harry glanced from Henrietta to Sally, who both looked distressed, as if they weren't sure if the men were serious. Obviously, not for the world would Harry make his wife unhappy.

Catri envied Sally such a man.

"That's a tempting offer, Patrick, and much appreciated." Harry clasped Sally's hand. "But I've already turned you down once, and now I'll do so again. I can't take my wife away from her family. I know my mother-in-law thinks Sally already lives too far from her."

Both Sally and Henrietta's expressions relaxed.

Bridget reached for her husband's hand. "We just finished building our little home and putting in special touches, like the cabinets James made. I don't know if I could bear to leave. But even more so, I don't know if I could live far away from both Alana and Catri." She glanced at her new brother-in-law. "There is the matter of my potato field, Patrick. Wyatt has set aside some land for me to plant—an area that's no use for grazing."

Patrick looked thoughtful. "There are some possible areas at my place. That is, if you wouldn't mind having several plots and not just one."

Bridget's shoulders relaxed. "That would be acceptable."

"How about this?" Patrick laid his hand flat on the table. "James and Bridget can stay here, live in their home while a new one is being built at my place." He turned to Bridget. "That would give you some time to enjoy your home here. Once the new house is finished, you and James can join us—in time for planting those potatoes of yours."

For the first time, Bridget's eyes lit up. "I believe that would work just fine!" She clasped her hands to her chest. "Why, thank ye, Patrick, for making it possible for us all to be together!"

Rory pulled a face. "You're going to deprive Henrietta and me of all our nieces. We will sorely miss them."

"You can always come visit," Patrick assured the older couple. "Perhaps for Christmas. I'll pay for the train tickets for your family. Sally and Harry, too. And of course provide transportation from the train to the stud farm."

Rory leaned back in his chair. "Well, you've fair caught me out. I don't like to be beholden for the tickets, yet I can't say no when I've just complained about not seeing my girls."

"Well then," Patrick said with obvious satisfaction, folding his hands across his stomach. "That's settled." After a moment, he took Alana's hand. With an eager gleam in his eyes, he said, "Now, wife, I think it's time we bid everyone good night."

Before going to bed, Moss was alone in the barn saying good night to Traveler and using the solitude to think. The only light came from a lantern hanging from a hook on a nearby pillar. After such a tumultuous day, the quiet of the barn and the small restless sounds and aroma of horses calmed him.

Wyatt Thompson pushed open the barn door and entered. He carried his own lantern and still wore his suit from the wedding. "Looked for you in the bunkhouse, but you weren't there." He strolled over to the stall. "I've just had a conversation with my wife."

Conversations with the missus didn't usually lead to the boss having a talk with Moss. In fact, this was a first.

Wyatt leaned his arms on the top of the stall door. "When I told her about the probability of James and Bridget moving to Crenshaw, my wife became upset. She's enjoyed having two young ladies close by. Samantha, Sally, and Bridget have become dear friends."

"That's understandable," Moss murmured, running a hand down Traveler's neck. "Until Sally and Bridget came here, only she, Mrs. Toffels, and Christine lived among twelve men and four boys. Guess you'll have to marry off more of your cowboys." He caught himself and raised his hand. "Not me, of course."

"Of course," the boss echoed dryly. "You're already spoken for."

Moss choked.

The boss's expression sobered, and he drew a hand over his chin. "My wife's moved around a lot in her life, and one of the things she enjoys now is how rooted she feels here. Samantha has the large family she's always wanted, and, indeed, views everyone else here as her extended family."

Moss could see how the missus would feel that way—in fact everyone on the ranch seemed to feel the same, which was one of the reasons he'd decided to leave. The idea of being part of a family made his feet itch. His leg gave a reflexive twitch.

"So naturally my wife's care and concern for Bridget and Sally is spilling over to Catriona. Samantha is troubled about her, and I don't want my wife to be distressed."

Moss didn't want *Catriona* to be distressed either. "What can I do to help?"

The boss tapped the wood of the stall door. "I think

tomorrow's going to be hard on our new guest. She'll have to watch one of her sister's leave, right after they've been reunited. With Bridget and James taking the day for a honeymoon, and Samantha already committed to making a charity call with Mrs. Norton, Catriona will be alone."

"She has Sally."

"Catriona barely knows Sally. I have orders from my wife that our guest is supposed to be taken care of and made as happy as can be under the circumstances. I know that's hard, given that she's grieving her husband, as well."

Moss was pretty sure Catriona was *not* grieving Crogan's loss, but he didn't say so. Catriona's feelings about the man who'd fathered Flea were no one's business.

"Tomorrow Samantha wants you to introduce our guest to our little horses and take her out in the buggy. She's convinced the Falabellas will work their magic on Catriona."

Moss was afraid Mrs. Thompson might be right. The Falabellas had aided in several courtships. "Why me?"

The boss raised his eyebrows. "You'd prefer that one of the other hands take her riding?"

"I'll see to it," Moss said hastily. He might not know if he wanted the lady, but he certainly wasn't giving one of the other cowboys a leg up.

Chapter Nine

Although she'd wanted to stay awake and do some thinking, Catri had fallen asleep almost as soon as she'd settled into Christine's comfortable bed. Following a restful night, she woke early the next morning and heard sounds of people stirring outside the room. Feeling more optimistic than she had for a long time, she quickly donned Mrs. Toffels's dress, brushed and braided her hair into a tail, coiled the plait, stabbed in hairpins, and went down the hall to use the bathroom.

Minutes later, she emerged, smelling of roses from using Samantha's soap. Downstairs, she entered the dining room and found the adults arranged in the same configuration around the table as the night before, finishing up their meal. None of the cowboys and children were there, and she surmised that they were in the kitchen or had already eaten and gone.

Everyone greeted her, and she didn't receive a scold from Alana about not sleeping in, which surprised her. Then, in amusement, she realized her sister was obviously too starry-eyed after a night of marital intimacy and not her normal self. Both Bridget and Alana were absorbed in their husbands, exchanging glances and secret smiles. The two men seemed just as bemused, only politely making small talk with the others.

After a sumptuous breakfast, the likes of which Catri had never seen or eaten—flapjacks, eggs, sausage, bacon, biscuits and gravy, and butter and several kinds of jam, she tried to help Mrs.

Toffels with the dishes while her family went to gather their possessions. But the housekeeper made her sit in the rocker by the stove, which Catri appreciated after such a big meal.

Afterwards, Catri waddled to the bathroom to use the toilet again and donned her outerwear to join everyone in the yard outside the kitchen to say good-bye. She planned to remain as calm and contained as possible so her family could leave without worrying about her. Or, at least, not worrying too much.

A quick glance around told her no cowboys were in sight—the only men being Uncle Rory, James, Patrick, and Wyatt. *Not that I'm looking for Moss.* She wouldn't let herself feel disappointed.

Dawn was just breaking, and the top of the sun's golden disk peeked over the edge of the horizon, casting yellow, pink, and rose streaks across the sky. A cold breeze blew, making Catri draw her coat tighter around her, for she couldn't button it over her protruding belly.

Uncle Rory came over for a farewell hug. "You send word if you have need, *mavourneen.* Alana and Bridget developed their own postal system, using the children to exchange letters at school. Send a note with one of the Thompsons for Charlie or my twins. If need be we will come to you."

Too moved to speak, Catri squeezed him back as tightly as she could over the bulge in her belly before stepping back with a nod of understanding.

Aunt Henrietta came closer to place a hand on Catri's shoulder and kiss her cheek. "You're a brave woman, Catriona."

Me? Catri thought the opposite. *Didn't I run away rather than face my troubles and pain?*

"Hold to your courage, my dear niece, for you will need it in the months to come. We will keep you in our prayers."

Charlie and the young O'Donnell twins exchanged hugs with her before climbing into their wagon.

For all that she'd been at the ranch for less than twenty-four hours, Catri had already grown attached to her relatives. She hated to see Rory, Henrietta, and her three cousins heading out for the long ride home, although the children would be dropped off in town for school. She wondered when she'd see them again.

Another breeze gusted, making her shiver. Catri felt sorry for the Thompson children, leading their horses from the barn for the ride to school. At least her cousins could stay warm burrowed in the straw at the back of the wagon and covered with animal pelts, while her aunt and uncle, on the seat, had a blanket wrapped around their legs.

Christine tied her horse to a post near a mounting block. She kilted up her pink dress and blue coat, before climbing into the saddle, exposing the boy's pants she wore underneath.

Samantha saw Catri eying the girl's attire and leaned in to say, "Riding astride is safer than the sidesaddle. Warmer, too. Christine will remove the pants when she gets to school. Of course, she's only ten. When she's older, I'll have a divided skirt made for her."

"My sisters and I always rode astride," Catri told her. "Although not where people could see our legs. In the village, we drove the cart instead of riding."

The West seemed a place with more freedom for women—the knowledge of preventing conception, a female sheriff who wore men's attire, a girl who could ride astride into town for everyone to see her legs, even if they were clad in pants. Catri pondered what else might be different in Montana, and—she glanced down at her belly—wondering if Flea's illegitimacy would matter to the child as much here as back home. *Would he or she always be branded a bastard?*

Does being an unwed mother carry the same heavy disgrace in Sweetwater Springs as it does in Ireland? If I reveal the truth about being unwed, will I be dishonored and scorned as a fallen woman?

If only there was someone I could ask.

With shock, Catri realized that she'd thought first of the baby's welfare, and only after that had she speculated about her own. *Maybe I'm starting to think like a mother—putting my child first.*

Wyatt, James, and Patrick disappeared into the big red barn.

Bridget and Alana had their heads together, probably exchanging stories of last night. Catri had seen by the way they carried themselves and the secret smiles they'd exchanged with their husbands that her sisters had delighted in their initiation into marital relations. With a fierce stab of longing, she envied them.

While Catri had enjoyed her encounters with both Godfrey and Bartley, she'd sensed there should be much more to the experiences—a loving, soulful connection that translated into a physical one. She longed to experience that type of intimacy for herself. Yet, at the same time, she never again wanted to open her heart and body to a man. The consequences were too painful. She placed a hand over her belly. *Far too painful.*

As if on a signal, all at once the Thompson boys looped the reins of their horses over the hitching rail and ran to slide open the doors of the big red barn.

Samantha watched her sons with narrowed eyes. "Whatever are they doing?"

A brown horse with white ribbons braided in his mane and tail trotted from the barn, pulling a shiny black surrey. Catri recognized the driver as Patrick, sporting an ear-to-ear grin. He held a whip, the tail curled around the long handle, which he flourished at the group of ladies, and drew the horse to a stop in from of them. "Well, my dear wife." He leaned down to ask Alana, "What do you think of your new equipage?"

"Mine?" Alana squealed. "Really?" Both hands flew to cover her mouth.

"Well," Patrick said. "You're going to need a way to get to Dr. Byron's office for your medical lessons and to travel to your patients. I'll teach you how to drive when we get home."

Alana clapped her hands together. "I can't wait!"

"I thought having the surrey delivered here would be a nice surprise and ensure we had a comfortable ride to the train station."

"But how will we get it home?"

"The miracle of modern transportation," her husband said. "The surrey will ride in a boxcar of the train. Nipper here—" Patrick gestured with the whip toward the horse "—serves as a dependable mount for you to ride, as well as to pull the surrey. He will travel in a horse stall."

"Ye've planned well," Alana said in admiration.

Patrick climbed down and handed her the whip. "Your wedding present, my dear."

Apparently uncaring of the spectators, Alana went on tiptoe and threw her arms around his neck. "Yer the best, most generous husband!"

Patrick's hug lifted his wife off her feet.

The O'Donnell wagon party, the five Thompson children, and all the adults burst into applause and cheers.

Even Catri found herself clapping.

Patrick grinned and set down his wife.

In that moment, Catri realized she no longer disliked Patrick—quite the contrary. He'd won her regard. Aside from the superficial resemblance in their bold, dark attractiveness, he and Bartley were entirely different. She could see her new brother-in-law genuinely loved Alana and, just as important, he understood and supported her dreams.

"Children, get going!" Samantha called. "If you don't leave now, you'll be late for school."

Catri exchanged laughing glances with Bridget, for their mother had often told them the same thing, matching Samantha's exasperated tone. She wondered if someday she'd be chivvying Flea to school in a similar way. But she couldn't imagine the inconvenient babe nestling in her womb would someday grow big enough to walk or ride to school.

James silently approached his wife. He looked into Bridget's face. "Do you like Patrick's surprise?"

His wife leaned into him. "Alana's so happy with the horse and buggy. Nothing else could show how much she's changed. How she's overcome her fears. Seeing my dear twin—" Bridget's voice thickened, and she shook her head, obviously not able to go on.

James placed an arm around his wife. "You don't mind not having such things for yourself," he asked in a low voice.

Bridget turned to cup his face. "I'd not trade ye, my Jamie, for all the horses and possessions in the world." She lowered her hand and tilted her head toward Alana. "Let us make our farewells and return to our home for the rest of our honeymoon."

James's expression grew so bright with love Catri had to look away, for such vulnerable emotions belonged only between a husband and wife.

The wagon moved off, giving Catri a pinch of regret. Next, the Thompson boys mounted their horses and, with Christine alongside them, called and waved good-bye as they rode past.

Samantha walked over to Catriona. "I'll be leaving soon to drive to town to meet with Mrs. Norton. We've several charity calls to make. They are important, so I didn't feel I could cancel our plans."

Catri made a negating motion with her hand. "No need to even think of canceling on account of my unexpected arrival. I'll be just fine, resting up as the doctor ordered."

"Go to Mrs. Toffels if you need anything." Samantha smiled, moved to say a few words to Patrick and Alana, and then went back into the house.

As Patrick loaded the surrey with their possessions, Sally hugged Alana and moved to allow Catri and Bridget to crowd close. The sisters remained quiet, for, indeed, everything had already been said. But they lingered in the embrace for a few extra seconds. Then they kissed each other's cheeks, and Catri and Bridget stepped back.

Eyes burning, Catri bit her lip to keep her emotions in control.

Bridget took her husband's arm. "I've watched Alana leave me once before, and I don't want to do so again." She tugged James toward their house, flipping Catri and Sally a little wave as they went. "I'll see ye two tomorrow."

Sally moved to stand next to Catriona and linked arms. They watched Patrick help Alana into the shiny new surrey, and then walk around to climb in next to her, with his mount tied behind.

"Safe travels," Sally called.

A lump choked Catri's throat. With her vision blurring, she could only wave.

Alana fluttered her handkerchief.

Together, the cousins stood and watched until the surrey headed out of sight.

In spite of Catri's best efforts to remain stoic, a solitary tear spilled over and raced down her cheek.

"Well, that's that." Sally sounded matter of fact. "They'll be happy, and there's no sense in us moping because we're missing their company. Come to my house and spend some time with me, Cousin Catriona."

A thread of resistance ran through Catri. *Just don't talk about babies. Then I can relax and enjoy the visit.*

Sally pulled on their linked arms to head them in the direction of her house. "Or, should I call you Catri like your sisters do?"

"I'm Catri to my family and close friends."

"Well, I'm family, and I certainly hope we'll become close."

Catri liked looking at her cousin, who, with her dark hair and certain expressions, actually appeared more like their fathers' family, even though she had Henrietta's features.

They walked past Bridget's home to one that looked just the same—a small log cabin with a covered front porch that ran the width of the house, and two windows on either side of the door.

"Harry and some of the men just built the porch last week," Sally said with pride. "We waited until Bridget and James's home was finished before adding the porch. We're saving up to buy a rocking chair before the baby is born. I'm sure as long as the weather is fine we'll be sitting out here all the time." She opened the door and ushered Catri inside.

Catri looked around the single room, taking in everything. The cabin was smaller than the three-room croft she'd grown up in, but she liked the coziness.

The bed was tucked under a loft and a bureau stood nearby, with a comb and brush and a basket holding several colored balls of wool on top. In the kitchen area, a two-burner stove emitted some heat, which provided welcome warmth after the cold air outside. A table and two chairs sat in the corner. Four crates nailed to the wall held supplies, dishes, and pots. A crude icebox, judging from the pan underneath, must hold perishables. Catri wondered if, when needed, the pan did double duty as a washbasin.

"I've a present for you." Sally whirled to the bureau and opened a drawer, snatching up a navy blue scarf. She went to Catri and unwrapped her worn woolen muffler, replacing it with the new knitted one. "O'Donnell blue to match the color of your eyes. I knit them to sell in the store in town. I made some for the twins, too."

"But you didn't know I was coming."

"Sure an' I must have a touch of the sight, then," Sally said in a mock-Irish accent.

Catri laughed and rubbed her cheek along the scarf. "This is beautiful. I'll wear it with pleasure."

Sally stepped back and surveyed Catri. "Perfect! You are the fairest one of all of the O'Donnell girls. I envy you your red hair. I always wanted Ma's color instead of inheriting Pa's."

Seeing the irony, Catri laughed. "And I always wanted my da's, and the twins and I got our mother's."

"I hope my baby has Ma's hair."

Discomfort made Catri want to squirm. Ever since she'd started to show, other women had tried to engage her in talking about pregnancy, delivery, and babies. She'd managed to cut short such talks or avoid them all together. She'd purposely thought of Flea as little as possible, which was hard to do with all the changes in her body. But she couldn't see any way to divert the topic with Sally, for Catri didn't want to hurt her cousin's feelings. Nor did she want to slip with what she said and reveal her loathing for her circumstances.

She tried to herd the conversation along a more comfortable path. "Yer so pretty, Sally, and ye glow with happiness, which makes ye far more lovely than I." Catri had seen her haggard face in the bathroom mirror this morning and knew she was no longer the same beauty that she'd been. "Your Harry adores you, which—" in spite of herself, wistfulness seeped into her tone "—is a blessing beyond measure."

Sally blushed. "Well, take off your coat, cousin. You can hang it there." She pointed to a row of pegs by the door. "Then sit yourself down, and I'll make us some tea." She bustled around her small kitchen with evident housewifely pride. "We received the tea as a wedding present, and I serve the brew to Bridget and Samantha when they come to call. There's not much left, but I consider the leaves a gift well used."

"Then don't use it up on me."

"And why not?" Sally turned from the stove and put a hand on her hip. "What else could be so special than a newly arrived cousin—one that we've been fretting about?"

Catri's chest ached. All her life, she'd been surrounded by love that she hadn't acknowledged and appreciated. It had taken losing her mother, separating from her sisters, and throwing away her future chance at a relationship with a husband, to appreciate the riches she'd possessed. She'd left Ireland with a bleak heart, only to find a welcome in Sweetwater Springs such as she'd never dreamed of and certainly didn't deserve.

Leaning over, Sally added some wood splits to the stove. "Do you take milk and sugar in yours?"

"Just sugar."

Sally took a Mason jar from one of the crates and set it on the table. She laid a spoon next to the jar. Next, she placed two tin mugs of tea on the table, and then took a seat. "Wasn't that hot chocolate last night just marvelous? The Thompsons often consume the beverage, although Samantha also drinks a tea imported from South America, which she calls *yerba matte*."

"A real treat." *So far, we're on safe topics.* Her shoulders relaxed. Catri spooned some sugar into her tea—just a tad because she could see there wasn't much left. She held the mug, warming her cold fingers, before taking a sip. "Lovely, thank ye."

Sally's smile blossomed.

"Yesterday, I thought of a question for ye. Uncle Rory wrote letters home, and I wondered if the twins brought his correspondence to your parents." Catri smiled at a memory. "Sometimes, on long winter nights, we'd get the letters out and read them aloud. Better than a book, because the stories were about people we knew. Well, knew of."

Sally spooned a sprinkling of sugar into her mug and stirred. "We've saved the letters from Ireland, too, and we do just the same!"

They exchanged smiles, and Catri could feel a connection growing between them.

"To answer your question. Alanna and Bridget brought a few of the letters. They selected the ones they thought would have the most meaning for us—the news of when we were born, for example."

"I know just the ones," Catri took a sip of her tea. "I'm glad they weren't lost."

"Family ties." Sally leaned forward. "Will it sound selfish if I say I hope Dr. Cameron makes you stay here until your baby is born? I'm sure I'll love him or her and can practice being a mother." She frowned. "That is, if you're all right with sharing."

Oh dear, babies again. "I think a child can never have too many relatives who love and watch over her."

"Do you think the baby is a girl, then?"

"I'm hoping so."

Sally set down her mug and leaned forward. "Will I shock you, Catri, if I confess that I didn't want my baby at first?" She took a deep breath, as if nerving herself up. "In fact, I resented the wee thing." She pressed both hands to her stomach. "Does that make me a bad mother?"

"Well if it does, then I'm a bad mother, too." *A wicked mother, in fact.*

Sally's eyes widened.

"I suspect it's not-uncommon for pregnant women to not feel happy about a baby—for various reasons." *Mine will remain secret.*

Her cousin let out a sigh. "It's not that I don't want children, but I was dismayed to become pregnant right away when I wanted to enjoy time with my husband and adjust to this new life. Then I became so sick. My poor Harry."

"I'd say, poor Sally," Catri said wryly.

Sally laughed. "Yes, I did feel sorry for myself. But my husband has been so loving and supportive through everything, which has taught me what a wonderful man he is."

Finally, a different topic. Catri raised her brows. "Ye didn't know that before?"

"I *knew* so from the beginning. But we'd barely been acquainted for two weeks before we got married."

Catri's jaw dropped. "Two weeks? My sisters told me that marriages happen quickly out here, but...." She shook her head, too flabbergasted to speak.

"Now you can see why I wish I'd known about preventing pregnancy. I'd have waited at least six months, maybe a year." She shrugged and again placed a hand on her small bump. "But when my morning sickness passed and my energy returned, I also became excited about this little one. She patted her belly. "I love imagining what he or she will look like, how cuddling my child will feel, seeing Harry as a father."

Sigh. Back to babies. "Boy or girl?"

"Neither Harry or I care if we have a boy or girl as long as the baby is healthy. Why, I can't wait until I can feel him or her move. Ma used to let me put my hand on her stomach and feel the twins and my brother Paddy—the one who died." A sad expression crossed Sally's face before she perked up. "Maybe Alana will have a baby boy who's named after his father. We can call him Paddy. I think Ma would like that."

Catri picked up her mug, inhaling the fragrance of the tea.

"I'm such a chatterbox, aren't I?" Sally grinned. "You see, we lived so isolated on the prairie. We could go weeks without seeing another soul. I've had so little interaction with girls near my age."

Catri was four, almost five, years older than her cousin, but Sally's high spirits made her feel like a crone in comparison.

Sally chuckled. "I have a lot of talking stored up inside me that needs to come out."

Charmed, Catri echoed her laughter. *I can see why Harry scooped her up so quickly. Perhaps it wouldn't be so painful, after all, to talk babies with this cheerful, loving woman.*

Since Flea had been doing acrobatics the whole time the two women had been talking, Catri reached out and took her cousin's hand, placing Sally's palm on her belly. "There. Feel the baby kick and move."

Sally's eyes grew wide, and she placed her other hand on Flea, inching both around. With a swift intake of breath she asked, "The head?"

"Yes," Catri smiled."

Sally lowered a hand. "A foot?"

"I think so." *I haven't explored that much to be sure.*

Her cousin's eyes filled with tears. "Such a miracle."

Of all the things Catri had thought of Flea, the idea of the baby being a *miracle* had never crossed her mind. For a moment, she allowed her cousin's awe to seep into her heart. *Maybe there will come a time when I look upon Flea as a miracle.*

Chapter Ten

Later, when Sally took a nap, Catri, too restless to do likewise, wandered toward the barn instead of returning to the big ranch house. After being left to her own devices, she felt lost. The last month, she'd been so focused on getting *here*; now that she'd obtained her goal—but learned her plans for her and her sisters wouldn't come to fruition—she found herself at loose ends.

Catri soaked in the sunshine on her face. *Surely a few minutes won't hurt my complexion.* She wondered where the rest of the cowboys were—one in particular—and realized his absence made her spirits flat.

In the corral, which yesterday had been full of horses, she saw a single man lunging a brown horse and quickened her waddle in that direction, only to learn the cowboy wasn't Moss. She fought a stab of disappointment and walked over to the fence to watch. The horse had white spots splashed over his hindquarters—a breed she'd never seen before.

A few minutes later, as if conjured by her thoughts, Catri sensed Moss before he came into sight. Maybe it was his scent—soap and horse and man. Or maybe it was the shiver running down her spine. Or maybe it was just his *presence*—how something inside her *knew* him.

Her fingers trembled. Not liking her reaction, she pressed them hard against the wooden rail and straightened her shoulders to control any betraying weakness.

Moss came up beside her and rested his arms on the top rail, keeping his gaze on the horse. His hat shaded his face, hiding his expression. "I know something that will brighten your mood."

His voice reverberated through her, making her stomach do a fluttering curl, something she wouldn't have thought possible with carrying the burden of Flea. "How do ye know my mood?" Catri asked in her lightest tone, manufacturing a fake smile so bright it should blind him.

He looked at her, his hazel eyes concerned, wide mouth pressed firm. "There's a cloud around you." Moss gestured with both hands in a circular motion around his head.

Catri knew her wide smile wobbled. But she forced her lips up before it slipped entirely. Her fingers, which had loosened their grip on the wood, tightened again, and she locked her knees against their maddening tendency to wobble.

"Come with me." Moss placed a hand under her elbow and waited, obviously giving her time to make up her mind.

His thoughtfulness only made her irritable. Still, Catri released the fence and allowed him to guide her toward the barn. *What could possibly be in here that would cheer me up?* "I'm not horse-mad like Bridget," she said peevishly.

"I didn't think you were."

"And how would ye know?" Catri asked, her tone sharper than she intended. She wasn't sure why she was out of sorts with him. Moss wasn't responsible for her current predicament.

He cocked a grin. "Your claws are out little cat." He gestured toward the big barn. "This is the new one. Best I've ever worked in." He pushed open the barn door, swept her a theatrical bow, and gestured toward the interior. "After you, milady cat."

She rolled her eyes and stepped into the dim interior, lit only by sun streaming through the high windows, and inhaled the smell of hay and horse. The barn was massive, with an ample open space before rows of stalls led away to the back. Stacks of straw bales lined the aisles, and hay was piled in the loft overhead.

"Tack room on this end." He pointed. "Grain and medicine storage on the other. The wagon, surrey, two sleighs—one big and one little—and a tiny buggy are parked in a big shed out back when they're not in use."

Quite a contrast to the small stable tacked behind our croft that housed our horse. She had a moment of nostalgia, remembering her father seeing to the needs of their horse, young Bridget his willing stable hand. *Who could have known then what was to come of us?*

With his hand under her elbow, Moss guided her up the broad aisle. Their footsteps sounded on the plank flooring, another difference from the packed dirt floor of the stable back home.

Most of the stalls were empty. *The cowboys probably have most out working.* The remaining horses peeked curious heads over the top of their doors. Some nickered a greeting.

Moss stopped in front of a stall, the first in a row of ones with short doors. "Here we are. Look inside." Mischief danced in his hazel eyes.

Wary of what she might find, Catri leaned over the door to see a tiny black horse and was struck dumb. "Why, 'tis a fairy creature, all the way in the wilds of America."

She looked up and smiled at Moss, thanking him with her eyes. The man had, indeed, sensed what would cheer her up.

Catri didn't know if his understanding pleased or worried her. *Probably both.*

Midget magic, the boss called the Falabellas. If his wife was in earshot, the words were accompanied by a teasing grin.

Mrs. Thompson would always toss her head and smile back, the two of them sharing a secret memory.

As appealing as the little critters were, Moss had remained skeptical about any magic being involved. But now, he couldn't help wishing they'd cast a spell on Catri to lift her spirits.

A navy blue scarf wound about her neck, and the color brought out the sapphire of her eyes. He'd thought she was beautiful yesterday, when fresh—or not so fresh—off the train. But seeing her then couldn't hold a candle to the vivid loveliness she displayed now, igniting a flame inside him.

She angled in front of him and leaned over to see inside the stall.

Moss noted the delicate curve of her cheek, the short tendrils of red hair curling against the slender nape of Catri's neck. He wanted to lift the wispy twists with a finger and press a kiss to her soft, white skin. Instead, he leaned forward to watch her expression.

Catri's eyes grew wide, and she sucked in a deep breath before slowly letting out air. "What a little darling!"

"This little guy is Chico. He'll be taking us for a ride later."

"Surely not." Throwing him a frown, Catri unlatched the door and moved inside. "He's far too small." She shut the door behind her, not seeming to notice she'd left Moss on the other side. She leaned down to pet the Falabella. With the size of her belly preventing from bending far, her fingertips could only touch Chico's head.

"By himself perhaps. But he's not the only Falabella here. Mrs. Thompson has a whole herd."

He pulled a carrot from his pocket and handed it to her. "Feed him this, and he'll become your lifelong friend."

"Well, Chico, me dear," Catri murmured in a musical accent, stronger than usual. "I'm in sore need of friends. Will ye be mine?"

Ask me. I will indeed be your friend and more.

"If you go down the line, you'll find more of the little critters. Their nameplates are on the door. I'm taking Chico and hitching him to the buggy."

Moss led the Falabella outside and around the back to where the little buggy was stored. He'd already attached the harness but not hitched up the stallion. Next, he returned for gray Mariposa and led her to her place alongside Chico. The mare was in foal, but wasn't as far along as the other mares, which was why he'd chosen her.

He drove the buggy around to the front, reined in, set the brake, and tied off the reins. "I'll be right back, little ones." He strode inside and called, "You ready?"

Catri emerged from Pampita's stall and walked over to the buggy. "Ye expect me—" she patted her stomach "—Flea, and all, to climb into *that*?"

"You'll manage. If worse comes to worst, I'll use a hoist."

She laughed and allowed him to help her into the seat.

Moss walked around and climbed inside. Pressed close to her, he could smell the rose scent of the soap she'd used today and had to refrain from leaning over for a good sniff. Releasing the brake, he flicked the reins. "Giddy-up, you two." He guided the buggy down the track to town, careful to avoid ruts. The vehicle wasn't as well sprung as the surrey, and he didn't want to jostle his precious passengers.

Catri placed a hand under her belly.

Concern jabbed him. "You all right?"

"Flea's enjoying this. Bouncing up and down."

"Want to go back?"

"I want to drive forever," she said with a happy sigh. Her eyes sparkled, and her cheeks were pink with color.

Here was the animated Catriona he'd wanted to see, and his attraction deepened. "Can't do that. Together we weigh too much for the Falabellas to pull us very far. 'Bout another five minutes is all we can do before turning back."

"Still, this is a fine treat. Just what I needed."

"I'm glad my idea worked." Tactfully, he didn't mention her initial opposition.

Catri studied him for a moment. "Yer a good man, Moss Callahan." She tsked. "For a rogue."

His neck heated. *I should warn her against forming such an optimistic opinion about me.* But with her looking at him in flirtatious admiration, Moss had a hard time summoning rational thought and a change of topic. Finally he grasped one. "You're not really naming the child Flea?"

"Just till it's born."

"You could come up with a new nickname. Something that would suit either a boy or girl." Moss thought for a moment, running through several possibilities before settling on a familiar one. "How about Bobbie? Would work for Robert or Roberta."

"I'm not referring to *Flea* as Bobbie."

"That's all right, Cat." He gave her a smug grin just to rile her up. "I'll call him Bobbie."

"She's a girl."

"Fine. I'll call *her* Bobbie."

Something sparked in her eyes, and her cheeks flushed. But the emotion wasn't anger, for a smile played over her mouth. He wanted to drop a kiss on those pretty lips and, since no one was around, he did—a quick, sweet press of his mouth to hers. Just enough to surprise his Cat and get her to think about maybe kissing him back.

She let out a sigh of pleasure. Her gaze lingered on his mouth, as if wanting him to kiss her again.

He was just about to take her up on the perceived invitation when she shook her head and leaned away.

"Best be getting back home," Catri said with a teasing flick of her eyelashes. "Yer five minutes are up."

Chapter Eleven

Moss went back to work thinking everything would be the same between him and the other ranch hands. Instead, he found the cowboys were angry with him—their feelings expressed in the tension in the air. A stranger working with the men wouldn't have known the difference.

Cowboys as a whole tended to be a quiet bunch, often relying on hand gestures and jerks of the head to communicate. While the men used as few words as possible, they weren't above playing some pranks and teasing each other. Although, certain times brought out their loquaciousness, such as when a blizzard kept them in the bunkhouse. Then they'd sit and play poker and tell tall tales, with even Sid contributing a few.

But their anger with Moss showed more in the *way* they didn't say anything. No nod of hello. No half smile before someone turned to mount up. No joking with him, although they joshed with each other plenty. In fact, there seemed to be more of that going around than usual, and he didn't think the fine early spring weather, with the skies withholding the usual rain, had anything to do with the mood.

No. The cowboys, all the way down to young Deuce, who was always as friendly as an overgrown puppy, were pointedly excluding him.

Moss had never felt so isolated. Yes, every time he started a new job, he lived a period of waiting to be accepted. But that never took long. He was personable, clean, respectful to women, hard working, knowledgeable about horses and cattle, good with a jest and a quip, and in making people laugh.

As the newest hand, Moss *expected* that sense of isolation until he'd proven himself. This situation, however, was different. These were men he'd bonded with—worked with day in and day out in the roughest of conditions.

So he hadn't expected the cowboys' treatment of him to *hurt*. If anyone had said to him a few days ago, 'Hey, Moss, if you go back to the Thompson ranch, the hands won't talk to you,' he'd have laughed off the idea that he'd even care. But *experiencing* the shunning was another thing entirely.

He'd always been the one to leave—ever since he was six when his father had abandoned him and his mother. Ma cried, heck, they'd both cried. Moss had clamped his arms around Pa's legs, hanging on for dear life, while Ma clutched at his arm and pleaded for him to stay. They might have been talking to a rock for all their impact on the hard-hearted man. He shook them off, and, stone-faced, went about the business of packing, as if he was blind and deaf to his wife and child. Only when Pa walked out the door, possessions in a bag thrown over his shoulder, had he said, "I've stayed long enough. I can't be tied down."

In the void caused by the men's isolation of him, the memories of his past rose to crowd Moss's mind. As if caught in a never-ending stage play, his brain couldn't stop mentally reenacting the scenes from those childhood years. Only thoughts of Catri had the power to break his painful ruminations.

Finally, three days later, after a long day of moving cattle to farther pastures, Moss couldn't stand the silence and isolation any longer. The cowboys left the horses in the barn and started toward the door for supper. "Won't be keeping the horses in here much longer," he commented, seeing if he could get a response. "The grass is almost sprouted enough for grazing."

No one grunted or nodded in agreement.

Moss stepped in front of the gang and crossed his arms. "All right. Spit it out." He jerked a thumb at his former friend, standing a few feet away. "Buck has already given me his two cents worth. Might as well let the rest of you have at me." He bent his knees slightly, bracing himself.

They all avoided eye contact, staring at the wooden floor.

"Go ahead," Moss taunted, his gaze skimming over the group. "Take your best shots."

Sid was the first to raise his head and look Moss in the eyes. The wiry old man had tangled gray hair and was missing a few teeth. His skin was dark and wrinkled from being out in all weathers. "You didn't say good-bye."

Moss blinked, surprised that the taciturn man actually took the lead in confronting him.

"T'wasn't ya leavin'." Sid scowled. "A man's got a right to mosey on whenever he pleases. T'was not saying good-bye. Wasn't respectful, like."

Gangly Deuce pulled off his hat and rubbed at his head until his carrot hair stuck out. "Ya didn't give us a chance to wish ya well."

The oldest and the youngest have spoken.

Now Moss was the one to look down, avoiding their eyes. He slapped dust off one of his pant legs.

"Ain't how a good man behaves," Sid added.

Moss looked up, expecting someone to make a teasing remark about Sid—the most withdrawn and cantankerous of them all—waxing practically garrulous.

But no one spoke. Their silence—heavy and critical—said more to him than any words.

Moss sighed and kicked at a small rock that had found its way into the barn. *Time to own up and take my licks.* "I was wrong to leave without a word."

"*Sneak off* without a word," Buck said snidely.

"Sneak off," Moss repeated. "I won't do it again." He made eye contact with each man. "You have my word. I'll take a proper leave when the time comes."

Nods came from all around him, and the atmosphere lightened. Not enough for the men to smile, but he saw Buck's lips twitch, and that was enough. Moss felt better for the trial, confession, and absolution.

The group dispersed to the house.

Moss turned back to hide in Traveler's stall and do some serious thinkin', only to see Catri lurking in the shadows. His heart beat as hard as the cadence of a horse's hooves on the wooden barn floor. "Did you hear all that?" He sauntered over to her.

Catri wore the dress she'd arrived in, now clean and pressed. She gazed into his eyes. "After our mother died, I left my sisters without saying good-bye. I just left, fled, really. I had good reasons." She paused and shook her head. "I *believed* I had good reasons. But I was thinking only of myself. I didn't want to see the sadness and pain on their faces. I didn't want to hear them tell me I was abandoning them, because as long as nothing was spoken, I could pretend what I was doing—running away—was right."

He stared back in shock, hearing her express feelings so close to his own. Without conscious volition, his mouth opened and the whole story came pouring out—what happened to devastate that six-year-old boy, and in response, how the grown man had lived his life.

Catri listened without judgment or pressure in her eyes. She reached out and placed a hand on his arm, conveying her understanding.

Because of her closeness and support, he dared to linger in the memory instead of pushing it aside as he'd always done whenever the past dared intrude into his thoughts. He experienced again the pain he'd felt when his pa left. In that moment, Moss realized that perhaps he'd never wanted to see that expression of grief, which *he'd* caused—on another person's face. In fact, he'd held back from connecting with a woman to the point her heart would be broken if—no, *when*—he left.

Superficial relationships are all I know.

"Do ye think—" Catri said slowly "—there might be more to yer tendency to leave? That maybe ye decided to be like yer father—one who *leaves,* the one who has the *stronger* position—instead of the one who's left behind, helpless and hurting like ye and yer mother?"

The truth of her words made Moss realize he'd been blithely galloping down a trail through the forest of life, when a low branch came out of nowhere and knocked him out of the saddle. He'd just smacked onto the ground—hard. Winded, his head reeling, Moss needed to pick himself up and get away. He moved aside from Catri's hand and took a step back but, unbalanced, he had to grab the top of a stall to stay upright. "You'd think I was drunk," Moss mumbled.

Not wanting to see her face, he turned to the door and lowered his head to his hands, fighting not to be six years old again—not to feel vulnerable. *I've been running from this feeling all my life.*

A tentative touch on his back penetrated through his coat, shirt, and long underwear, burrowing into his skin and going even deeper to reach clear to his heart.

Reflexively, he shook Catri off. Then he heard her footsteps—quick, as if she fled from him—*as she should.* He wanted to call her back but was too confused to…he didn't know what. But her desertion—no matter how justified—hurt more than he could even admit.

Moss's rejection stayed with Catri for the rest of the day, tying her insides into a knot of shame. Over and over again, she berated herself for breaking her vow. *How could I be so foolish as to fall under the spell of a man, especially one who made it clear from the beginning that he wasn't intending to stay?*

Catri wondered if this weakness was inherent in her makeup, if she lacked the strength to stick with her convictions about what she needed to do and *not do* to provide a safe future for her and Flea. *Am I doomed to continually be drawn to attractive men—to form connections—only to be hurt over and over again?* The thought of such a life seemed unbearable.

In spite of her inner preoccupation, Catri tried to set aside her hurt, even if she had to put on an act of everything being fine. She had no desire to inflict her unhappiness on the host and hostess who'd been so kind. She helped Mrs. Toffels in the kitchen, doing light tasks. At supper that night, she joined in the lively discussions between bites of an excellent beef stew and blueberry pie.

Wyatt and Samantha's interaction with their five children fascinated her. They listened, participated in the teasing, offered advice, and, if need be, chided. By the end of the meal, Catri had started to learn about mothering a brood of boys, and a girl who gave as good as she got. *Not that I'll ever need to know how to mother a boy, much less a bunch of them.* Even though she had no control of whether Flea turned out male or female, she *could* insure only giving birth to one baby.

Catri enjoyed the boisterous Thompson children. She felt grateful that the couple allowed their offspring to speak freely at the table instead of remaining seen and not heard.

Hunter, the Indian boy, was the quietest, but his dark eyes were alert with interest and intelligence. She wondered how he'd come to be part of this family and looked forward to hearing his story—all of their stories.

Her gaze settled on the brown-haired, green-eyed, freckle-faced twins, Jack and Tim, whom she could tell were mischievous lads—in the kindhearted, not mean sense. Catri guessed their ages at about eleven or twelve. She suspected they'd be devilish brothers, quick to play a joke and full of teasing but just as swift to lend a helping hand. As with her own sisters, each had distinct personalities. Jack seemed similar to Bridget—outspoken and, at times, bold—while she suspected, Tim, like Alana, might be the gentler twin.

Pretty Christine was the princess of the family, and everyone obviously adored the girl. From what Catri could tell, the child was sweet-natured and not spoiled.

Samantha finished eating and laid her knife and fork across the plate. "Seems we are to have a social whirl this year. First, your sisters' wedding—" she smiled at Catri "—now there's an ice cream social planned in three days."

Daniel, of a similar age to Christine—nine or ten—bounced in his chair, his slanted eyebrows raised. "Oh, good." He paused and tilted his head. "What's an ice cream social? Whatever it is, if there's ice cream, I'll like it."

Samantha laughed. "I haven't been to one either. But Mrs. Norton said it's a party where everyone comes and eats ice cream. Some of the dairy farmers are donating the milk and cream. Other people are supplying toppings. We can take several jars of Mrs. Toffels's stewed cherries." She turned to Catri. "We're so isolated in the winter that come spring, we're more than eager to socialize."

Wyatt glanced at Catri and then back to Samantha. "Where'll this event be held?"

"The schoolhouse." Samantha frowned. "Oh, dear. That's too far for Catriona to travel."

Catri wasn't sure how she felt about not attending the ice cream social. If she'd lived here a year ago, she would have eagerly refurbished her best dress and anticipated going to a party, hoping to have fun, make new friends, and meet handsome, eligible gentlemen. But now? She glanced down at her big belly. *I'd just as soon stay out of sight.* "I'll be fine. Don't worry about me at all."

Samantha looked around the table. "Since everyone is done, children, take your dishes to the kitchen and start your homework." She waited until all five had left the room before turning to Catri. "I don't want you staying here alone."

"Why is that?" Catri bristled inwardly. *I traveled alone all the way across an ocean and half of America.*

Or maybe they don't trust me. Do they think I'd steal from them? The thought made hot shame twist tight.

Wyatt took a sip of his tea. "It's not that you're not capable, my dear Catriona. You've more than proven you're able to take care of yourself. I wouldn't want any woman at your stage—" he nodded toward her belly "—to be alone for too long."

"Not everyone will go to the ice cream social," Samantha assured Catri. "Sid, certainly, will remain here. Not that he counts, because that old codger won't go near any woman. But perhaps he can be bribed to check on you. If not, then maybe Sally or Mrs. Toffels will be willing to stay with you."

Embarrassed by the thought of someone missing the ice cream social to hover over her, Catri clenched her hands in her lap. *My obligations to this family—strangers to me until yesterday—are increasing by the minute.* Some of Catri's feelings must have shown on her face.

"Oh, my dear." Samantha reached over to pat Catri's hand. "Everything will be all right, you'll see."

"I don't want to put anyone out. Or make someone miss a lovely event."

"This is Montana," Wyatt said wryly. "A blizzard may come up, snowing in the whole area, and the ice cream social will be postponed. Bad weather could actually happen for weeks, until the end of May, even. Perhaps June, too. You might have the baby before we have the social."

Catri stared at him aghast.

"Wyatt!" Samantha shot him a look of wifely reproof. "You'll make her want to turn around and head back to Ireland." She looked at Catri and rolled her eyes. "My husband exaggerates. Don't pay him any mind."

Wyatt winked at Catri.

She couldn't help but be startled by such familiarity coming from a man who'd given her the impression of being rather stern. *Kind, but stern,* she amended.

Shaking his head, he raised his eyebrows. "Good thing

neither of you were here in '80-81 or '86-87. The kind of weather I described was exactly what those winters were like."

Samantha shot him a mock glare.

Wyatt pretended to ignore her, but a smile threatened to shatter his grim expression. "In fact, we owe our current prosperity to Jonah Barrett. In '86, he suspected we were headed for a hard winter. His first wife was an Indian, and he traveled to her tribe for confirmation of the signs he'd seen in nature foretelling what was to come."

Catri listened in fascination.

"Luckily, John Carter, a rancher who plays quite a leadership role in these parts, believed Jonah's warning and made sure to get the word out to everyone to prepare. I hauled in extra hay, packing the barns to the rafters, and paid for several shipments of grain. We also ordered food supplies from the East. Those in more affluent circumstances created a temporary store to share food with the families who couldn't afford to increase their provisions. If not for those advance preparations, the ranchers in this area would have been decimated, as happened elsewhere. Farmers, business owners, indeed, everyone would have suffered. And, likely, the loss of life would have been tragic."

"Now you've done it," Samantha said tartly. "You'll scare Catriona to the deserts of Arizona or Nevada Territories." She tsked. "And I'll go with her."

Catri swallowed down the fear of living through a year like Wyatt had described. "I can't imagine such a winter. But, even more, I can't imagine a town pulling together for the benefit of all."

Wyatt grimaced. "Sometimes a little less involvement would be nice."

She swallowed down the rising pain and banked anger that most Irish felt about *an Gorta Mór*, even many years later. "In my country during the potato famine, it's believed a million people died of starvation. The English government *knew* of our people's plight, yet they *withheld* food. Many of the rich landlords did the same. What did it matter if a few of their crofters died? Plenty more to take their place."

Samantha shook her head, her gaze sad, mouth downturned.

Catri swallowed hard, and then forged on. "Neighbors couldn't share, although some did, for doing so meant their own families might starve. Those were harsh years. We haven't forgotten the injustices, and the bitterness from that time will linger for generations."

Samantha reached over to take Catri's hand. "Bridget was marked by this tragedy, too. Thank God things are different in Sweetwater Springs. We must not take that for granted." With a pat, she released Catri's hand. "Bridget has promised me some of your blight-resistant potatoes for our garden."

Catri loved the notion of her family's treasure ending up feeding the Thompsons and all who worked on the ranch. The idea took away some of the sting of being beholden.

Samantha glanced at Catri, a playful expression on her face. "I'm sure if Dr. Cameron were here, he'd say, "Do na fret yerself, lass," she mimicked in a deeper Scottish brogue than the good doctor actually used. "Worra about the ice cream social three days hence. Aye, lass?"

"Aye, Doctor, if ye say so," Catri teased back and actually meant her words. *For now, I won't worry.*

Even more importantly, this conversation made Catri realize that, in spite of the possibility for horrible weather in Montana, she wanted to be part of a community that looked out for the welfare of everyone. *This is where I want to grow roots and raise Flea.*

Chapter Twelve

The day of the ice cream social, Catriona stayed busy. She started by altering Sally's best silk dress. She was a better seamstress than either of her sisters and had always been the one to make the family's clothing.

Originally, the navy blue dress had belonged to Henrietta, who'd made over the garment, removing the bustle, as a Christmas present for Sally. Shortly thereafter, Sally had worn the gown for her wedding.

Luckily, Henrietta had saved the extra fabric that originally draped over the bustle. Catri inserted gussets that she basted into tucks. Sally could expand them as the baby grew.

When she tied and cut off the last knot of thread, Catri examined the gown and smiled in satisfaction. Only close scrutiny would show the alterations.

Both Bridget and Sally had offered to stay home with her tonight. Catri firmly rejected the notion, pointing out the two women needed to spend the evening with their husbands because neither had attended social outings during their courtship.

The bathroom in the Thompson house stayed busy as a parade of four women and one girl took turns to bathe. The men used the bathing area outside the bunkhouse—a fenced-in horse trough—and had to import hot water. Deuce and the Thompson boys were kept busy fetching pails heated on the stoves in the kitchen, bunkhouse, and the Whitson and O'Hanlon cabins.

After Catri finished Sally's dress, she insisted on helping Mrs. Toffels. The housekeeper allowed her to iron what seemed like an endless stack of men's shirts, but deemed the women's good dresses too heavy for Catri to work on and ironed them herself.

Catri ironed shirts, one after another, enjoying the luxury of using two irons. So much easier to have one heat on the stove while she slid the other over the cloth, instead of stopping and waiting for the iron to heat before continuing. She could finish each shirt in half the time. When she completed four, Mrs. Toffels made her sit down and rest, while she took over and worked on a dress. Then Catri took a turn again until they'd finished all the clothes.

After a hasty early supper consisting of soup and sandwiches, everyone dispersed to get ready. At that point, Mrs. Toffels ordered Catri to her room to rest.

Catri was glad of the chance to lie down, for her back and feet ached. She removed her shoes but stayed fully dressed, climbing onto the bed and remaining on top of the pink and green quilt. She positioned two pillows to slightly prop her up.

A knock sounded on the door.

"Come in," she called, pressing a hand to the mattress.

Samantha swooped in, clad in the cornflower gown she'd worn to the wedding. She raised an imperious hand before Catri could struggle to sit up completely. "Don't you move an inch!"

With a sigh, Catri relaxed against the pillows.

Smiling, Samantha moved to the side of the bed. "Thank you for all your help today. You kept Mrs. Toffels from being overwhelmed."

Catri doubted the housekeeper overwhelmed easily, but she appreciated Samantha's attempt to make her feel useful. "I was glad to be able to do so."

"With the full moon, we'll probably be home late. You'll have the parlor all to yourself, so enjoy your quiet evening without a dozen people around to disturb you. Browse through any of the books."

Catri exclaimed in pleasure. “What a treat! I can’t remember the last time I could just sit and read, especially a new book.”

“We have all of Jane Austen’s.”

“Our blacksmith’s wife owned a battered copy of *Pride and Prejudice*—” Catri told her “—which was passed around our village…and then made the rounds again. The twins, my mother, and I took turns reading the story aloud.” She smiled at the memory, glad to recall her mother without feeling a stab of grief.

“Well, you can choose between rereading an old favorite or trying something new. And we have plenty more than Jane Austen, if your reading tastes take you farther afield.”

As far as Catri knew, no one was remaining home to keep her company. Had Wyatt twisted Sid’s his arm and forced the old cowboy into checking up on her later? She didn’t want to ask in case—hopefully—the Thompsons had forgotten to appoint a caretaker.

After Samantha bade her good-bye, Catri relaxed into a nap. When she awoke, anticipation made her rise from the bed; she was eager to peruse the Thompsons’ books. She straightened her hair, used the bathroom, and hurried downstairs.

Without other occupants, the Thompson’s parlor seemed far more spacious. Her footsteps echoed on the polished wooden floor, and she was glad to reach the hooked rug so she could waddle soundlessly to the small round table positioned between two rose velvet wing chairs. She took off the fluted chimney of a lamp with a cut-glass base, set it on the table, and then opened a hinged brass container, removing a box of matches. She struck one and touched the flame to the wick.

Once she set the chimney in place, she moved to light the two matching lamps on the mantle, pausing a moment to study the portrait of Wyatt’s first wife in a pink bustled dress. *Christine will look just like her someday.*

Next Catri moved to light the lamp on the piano in the corner, reflecting a soft glow onto the bookcase. The Thompsons didn’t stint on lamp oil, and so much light was a luxury.

With a thrill of anticipation, she held the lamp aloft and examined the four shelves filled with books. Catri had never seen so many in her life. She took her time reading through the titles, seeing novels, children's stories, and tomes on agriculture, animal husbandry, and science.

Her hand hovered over fine leather-bound editions of *Pride and Prejudice*, *Sense and Sensibility*, and *Persuasion*. Remembering the village schoolteacher once mentioning *Sense and Sensibility* was her second favorite Austen novel, she chose that one and settled in one of the wing chairs.

Catri paused before beginning to read. The silence in the house pressed down on her.

She, who loved parties, now sat alone. *I'll force myself to appreciate tranquility. Surely learning contentment can't be that hard.* To begin practicing, she took a deep breath, or as deep a one as Flea's presence allowed. The two months until she'd be able to breathe freely seemed like years away. Catri tried for another deep breath, imagining herself serenely reading.

Her thoughts drifted to Moss. At this very moment, was he flirting with a pretty girl at the ice cream social? Or maybe more than one? She imagined him charming a circle of admiring women.

With a determined huff, Catri opened the book and began to read. At first, concentration took effort. But the travails of the Dashwood sisters soon drew her into the story, and she found herself relating to the younger sister, Marianne. So deeply was she in Regency England that she hadn't registered the sound of footsteps on the floor.

A knock on the doorframe startled her. She looked up and gasped when she saw Moss standing in the doorway. His hair was slicked back, and he wore a suit, looking handsome and rakish.

Flea kicked, as if happy to see him.

"How long have you been there?" Her accusation came out sounding breathy.

"Not long *enough*." Moss drew out the word, implying that he'd enjoyed staring at her and would have watched for longer.

Warmth rose in her cheeks.

"Ye're going to be late to the party."

"I've arrived at the party I wanted to attend."

Not quite able to take in his meaning, Catri shook her head. "What are ye doing here?" She closed the book and set the volume on the table.

"I'm the shepherd in charge of watching the flock."

"Really? Yer likening me to a flock of sheep?"

"A lamb?"

She laughed. "Hardly." On the surface, their banter relaxed her, but her insides coiled.

"Cat, then. An orange marmalade, one that will curl up on my lap and purr." Moss prowled toward her, his gaze intense, a predator about to pounce. "Shall I make you purr, my dear Cat?" He held out his hand.

Mesmerized, all she could do was place her hand in his and allow him to draw her to her feet.

He leaned forward to touch his mouth to hers. The tip of his tongue teased her lips.

A thrill shot through Catri. Her mouth parted, allowing him access. The kiss deepened. Passion whirled through her, warm and enthralling. She'd been kissed before, enjoyed pleasure before. *Or so I'd thought.*

He pulled back to study her face.

Catri's heart thudded. She couldn't catch her breath, feeling as if she'd walked up a flight of stairs. But mere exercise couldn't account for the desire swirling deep within her.

With a wicked light in his eyes, Moss smiled and leaned forward. His wooing resumed, gentler now. His hands spanned her stomach, caressing the child within her, and then moving upward, stopping just below her breasts.

A burst of energy spread throughout her body to her very core. Familiar heat flooded her, carrying an urgency she'd never before experienced, sucking her into a whirlpool of desire.

Afraid to lose control and go too far, Moss broke off their intoxicating kiss. They drew apart, but they stared into each other's eyes.

His breathing ragged, every muscle taut, Moss shifted Catri to his right, the side of her belly pressing against his side, so he could better reach her mouth. "Cat," he murmured before, once again, setting his lips to hers and deepening their kiss.

In response, she placed her palms on his chest.

He stilled, fire shooting through him.

Catri slid a hand from his shoulder to the back of his head, fingers threading into his hair.

Moss had been touched by other women before, but their hands hadn't spread this warmth, this sense of *wanting* through him.

Catri made a tortured sound, burrowing upward as if they weren't close enough.

"I thought I never wanted to do this again," she whispered.

"I've wanted to do this since the day we met." Moss found her mouth again and covered her lips with his, tasting, holding nothing back. He'd never before been intimate with a pregnant woman; the lack of a corset gave his hands freedom to rove up her sides and over her ripe belly.

He nuzzled her neck. "You smell so good."

She shivered. "Samantha's soap. I smell the same as her."

Moss grinned. "Darlin', I beg to differ. Samantha smells like herself wearing her soap, and you smell like *yourself* in her soap. Not that I ever got this close to the missus to tell." He kissed her neck.

She inhaled a shuddering breath, and then exhaled before easing out of his arms. As he reached for her, Catri put up a hand to touch his cheek and caught his other hand between them. She lowered her gaze. "Ye need to know."

"I need to know what?"

"The truth."

Moss brought his attention to their conversation, a difficult task when his brain and body wanted only to lose himself in her. He wrestled his desire into submission. "Tell me," he said, his voice husky.

"I'm trusting ye with my reputation, with Flea's future."

"I wouldn't do anything to hurt you or Bobbie."

Catri rolled her eyes at the name, partially turned away, and held up a hand to stop him from coming closer. "I need to reveal my secret." She took a deep breath. "I'm not a widow. I was never married." She swallowed, refusing to look at him, color rising in her cheeks. "I'm a fallen woman."

As if she'd driven a fist into his gut, a whoosh of air left him. Yet a strange sense of hope made Moss want to hear her story.

"I'd tell ye that the squire's son seduced me, but that wouldn't be entirely true. I was *willing*, taking a gamble that Godfrey would love me. I lost."

"Go on." Two words were all he could manage.

"Our affaire lasted only one week. Afterwards, I was too ashamed, too afraid of what would happen if I was with child." Eyes downcast, she tugged on the hem of her sleeve. "Bartley Crogan was a peddler who often sold his wares in our village. He'd flirted with me for years and many a time had tried to coax me into traveling with him. He'd never offered marriage, though, so I didn't take him seriously. He was passing through our village one day, so I eloped with him." She said everything in a rush.

He stayed quiet, waiting for the rest, and feeling pity for her suffering. *My poor Cat.*

"So you see," Catri said, her tone sharpening. "I don't know which man is Flea's father."

Moss thought through what he'd learned of the O'Donnell sisters' timeline. "Didn't your mother pass away about then?"

"I see James has filled ye in on some family history."

"He could tell I was interested." Moss placed a finger under her chin and tilted it up. "Am I right about your mother?"

Catri looked into his eyes and nodded. "She died not long before."

Compassion filled him. "Then I imagine you weren't yourself."

"I was *exactly* myself," Catri said in a cutting tone. "My sisters will tell ye that I was wild, a flirt, a hoyden."

"You're definitely a siren." He tenderly brushed a wisp of hair off her cheek. His hand lingered to cup her face. "Cat, you can't tell me your mother's death didn't impact your decisions."

"No." Her shoulders slumped in defeat. "I can't. I was hurting, guilt-ridden for not being a better daughter. I missed her so much, especially her wise counsel. Without Mama as the heart of our home, the house seemed empty—just a shell. My sisters had each other, as always. I had no one. So I did what I wanted, rather than what was right."

"You're too hard on yourself."

Catri flung wide her arms. "Who else will be hard on me? How will I learn my lessons? Not make the same mistakes?"

"A few days ago, you showed me some kindness when I needed it the most. You listened and pointed out a home truth that shook me to my core." He gathered her close. "I'm sorry how I acted then. I didn't mean to reject you."

She searched his face, brows crimping as if looking for the truth.

Moss saw the pain in her eyes. "I hurt you, and I'm sorry for that. You helped me then. Let me do the same now."

"The situation isn't the *same*." She broke away and took three quick steps, pivoted, and paced back. She put a hand on her stomach. "I made my own hell and, thus, am suitably punished."

Moss didn't let Catri finish. He took her by the shoulders and gave her a little shake, but that didn't stop her.

"I lied about being married for Flea's sake." She shook her

head. "No. I'm still lying." Her hands fisted at her sides. "I hated Flea. Hoped to miscarry. The truth is, I lied to hide my shame. To be respectable. To start a new life."

"Sounds logical to me," Moss said in a reasonable tone. "Do you still hate Bobbie?"

Her head tilted, and she rested a hand on her middle. "I don't love *Flea*."

He smiled. "You're making progress."

The statement seemed to enflame her. She took a breath, and her chest swelled. "I'm a *fallen woman*, Moss. A fallen woman who's *with child*. I'm no longer decent and certainly not fit to be a good man's wife—"

"Don't say it!" he commanded, again taking her by the shoulders. "If you're a fallen woman, I'm a fallen man. I've lain with women. Certainly more than the two men you've been with."

A shoulder rose and fell. "Men are allowed to."

He fired up, hurt and angry that she'd distrust his support. "According to the Bible, men *aren't* allowed to. Both sexes are supposed to wait until marriage and then to remain faithful unto death."

She shrugged off his hands. "That's not the way of the world."

"Cat." Moss caught her hand and brought her fingertips to his lips, surprised by how adamant he felt. "You can't punish yourself for loving a man."

She pulled back her hand. "What's worse is I don't know that I did love Godfrey. I felt yearning, yes, but love…?"

"What you thought *at the time* was love," he amended.

She let out a sigh. "That's true."

As he spoke, Moss realized that he, too, had been punishing himself for loving the father who deserted him. That punishment extended to never allowing himself to trust, to love anyone—woman or man—again.

In that moment, Moss realized something inside had shifted.

For the first time, he could allow himself to feel compassion for the child he'd been. He imagined stepping between the boy who'd desperately loved his Pa and the father who callously walked out the door. He'd seen Wyatt wrap his arms around Daniel when the youngster was upset. No one had done that for him. *Ever. Maybe I'd best imagine hugging that six-year-old.*

As he comforted that boy inside him, Moss reached for Cat and gently drew her into his embrace.

Those other men don't matter, my Cat. You are mine, and mine alone. I'm staying.

Moss sensed now wasn't the time to share his newly discovered feelings. He was still sorting out his emotions, and Catri wasn't ready to let him in. *But I can at least get one foot in the door.* "I have something to say but you don't have to decide now. I promise not to press for an answer. There's time before the baby comes."

Moss led her to the sofa and had her sit. He angled himself next to her and took her hands. "If you marry me, then by law, Bobbie will be my child and not illegitimate. 'Course we will have to tell Reverend Norton you were never married and your name's not Crogan, so the marriage will be legal."

"Marriage?" Frowning, Catri shook her head.

He placed a finger across her lips. "Just think about my proposal."

She sighed, and her shoulders went limp, as if the air had gone out of her body.

Moss wrapped her in his arms and leaned against the back of the sofa.

She rested her head on his shoulder.

All he did was hold her close as time flowed into the late hours, and the oil in the lamps grew low.

Chapter Thirteen

Outwardly, Moss returned to the work on the ranch as if the evening with Catriona had never happened. But inside him, everything had changed. He felt lighter and freer—both free to leave and free to stay. The compulsion for wanderlust no longer ruled him. In fact, nary an itch twitched the soles of his feet.

Barriers he hadn't even known he'd erected between him and other people, especially the cowboys, crumbled. Now when he joked with the men, enjoying a smirk or laugh in response, he allowed himself to feel connected, instead of using a sarcastic quip to keep his distance, while still appearing friendly and making people laugh.

Cat, the nickname he continued to use with her, consumed Moss's thoughts. He missed her, even knowing she was close by.

Dr. Cameron had decreed Cat should remain at the ranch. She chose to continue living with the Thompsons, which suited Moss.

Moss had an inner anticipation at the thought of marrying Cat. He alternated between excitement and fear at the very idea of marriage—not the running away kind—but the I'll-be-a-husband-and-father-and-my-life-will-change fear that a man takes seriously, knowing that he'll be protecting, providing for, and seeing to the well-being of his loved ones for the rest of his life.

The few lucky days of wedding weather ended as the sunshine

vanished behind clouds and rain, and when the temperature got cold enough—and it often did—snow flurries. The ranch hands had to stay close to the cattle herd as the cows began dropping their calves. The work was long, hard, cold, and exhausting. He barely saw Cat, unless she got up early in the morning for breakfast or the cowboys were close enough to the house to stop in for dinner. Otherwise, they ate the food Mrs. Toffels had packed and sent along with them.

Moss saw Cat for a few minutes at supper if she dropped by the kitchen to sit in the rocker by the stove and hear the cowboys' tales of the day. After a while, more and more of the men relaxed and began contributing to the conversation. Sometimes in the evenings, if the men hadn't gotten in late or he wasn't too tired, Moss washed up, changed, and visited in the parlor with her, surrounded by the Thompson family.

As much as he craved to be alone with the woman he hoped to marry, Moss also enjoyed spending time with her and the Thompson family. He liked seeing the boss's interactions with his children. Moss had never given much thought to being a parent, and he didn't have a good example from his own Pa. But if he became a father to Bobbie, he wanted to be one like Wyatt. So with fresh eyes, Moss studied the boss as he assisted the children with their homework, showed them how to do tasks on the ranch or work with the animals, encouraged them to share, taught them history, and imparted life lessons.

More and more, the Thompsons drew Cat into their family. Moss watched her become a favorite of the children. She exhibited patience with them, joined in their teasing, and helped Daniel and Christine with their homework. If the children finished their homework early, she seemed to relish playing games such as checkers and spillikins. Or, everyone would take turns reading a book aloud. This month's tale was *Robinson Crusoe*, selected by Daniel.

On rare Sundays, if the weather allowed, he stayed at the ranch with her while the rest of the family and some of the cowboys attended church. They took walks or sat in the parlor and talked. If no one was in the house, he rubbed her back, and once, he scandalously coaxed her out of her sturdy, worn shoes to rub her stocking feet.

All the time, during this quiet courtship, Moss waited for Cat to tell him she'd become his wife. He didn't need much. One simple word would do. *Yes.*

As the days ticked off until the birth of the baby neared, Moss's optimism about marrying Catriona O'Donnell waned, as she refrained from discussing marriage. But he kept his promise and remained silent, even though the thought of not having her for a wife and Bobbie for his child made his heart ache.

Without a definite answer from the lady, all Moss could do was prepare for a wedding, as if Cat's answer was yes. He took Wyatt into his confidence, just in case he had to take time away from work for a wedding ceremony. Bridget and James helped by undertaking the errand of buying fabric for a wedding dress. Bridget refused to make the dress, however, saying Catri was a better seamstress and would prefer to make her own.

Moss also sent a note with James to pass along to Reverend Norton. He didn't reveal Catri's true circumstances, just wrote that he'd asked her to marry him and had left her to decide when the ceremony would take place.

Now, all I can do is wait.

Catriona, too, waited, although she knew time was running short. She waited for Flea's birth, and she waited for Moss to declare his love for her. Until he did, she had no intention of marrying the man. Although willing to take a chance on him, she'd learned from her mistakes and refused to trust her life and that of her baby's to a man who wasn't clear and upfront about his feelings.

So she visited with Bridget and Sally, played with the Falabellas, helped Mrs. Toffels cook and clean, and sewed baby clothes out of flannel scraps given her by Samantha. She cherished her time with Moss, whether they were talking up a storm or being together in companionable silence. He hadn't kissed her again, even though they found many occasions to touch. She'd take his proffered arm when they strolled, and when making courteous gestures, such as helping her up the stairs, his hands would linger on her body. Best of all was when he'd rub her back. And the scandalous foot rub.... *Oh, my!*

Moss seemed to care for her, but he frustrated her to no end by not saying so. His eyes lit up at the sight of her, and his smile—the special one reserved only for her—carried Catri through the day.

Bridget had showed her the beautiful lilac fabric Moss bought for her potential wedding dress. Even though Catri longed to begin creating her special dress, feeling superstitious, she refused to even touch the material until she knew she'd actually wear it. But she couldn't stop imagining how the dress would look. In the bottom of her travel satchel, she carried several dress patterns that she'd drawn on butcher paper and then cut out. The styles were mostly unusable in her pregnant state. Even the sleeves wouldn't work. With the new dress, she wanted fashionable puffed sleeves.

So she allowed herself to design patterns, at least for the neck and sleeves, and pondered the best way to convert a dress made for a heavily pregnant woman to one she could wear after the baby's birth, all the while looking as stylish as possible.

Dreaming about her dress, forming the tucks and ruffles in her mind, gradually gave way to daydreaming of her baby. For the first time, Flea started to take form as a child. Maybe because Moss's proposal allowed Catri to see the baby in the context of a *family*, instead of the unwanted, illegitimate child of a foolish, fallen woman.

The dreams helped her cope with a perpetually sore back and

swollen feet, a girth that expanded until she felt bigger than any of the pregnant cows in the pasture, the uncertainty about her future, and the fear of childbirth—all of which combined to make her irritable. She had to take care lest she release her peevish mood on those around her, biting her tongue a dozen times a day.

A few weeks before Flea was due, Catri woke up with back pain, a usual occurrence, for she'd been having what her mother had called *practice contractions* for a while now. In some discomfort, she got ready, and then hurried downstairs.

I missed seeing Moss. Drat. Obedient to Dr. Cameron's orders, she often slept in, losing out on the opportunity to see Moss when he and the other cowboys came into the kitchen to eat breakfast.

After breakfast, Catri helped Mrs. Toffels wash and dry the dishes, pots, pans, and silverware. While the housekeeper started gathering the ingredients to bake pies, Catri put away the clean dishes, taking time to sort through the silverware drawer and stacking the utensils into their proper places.

Once finished, Catri straightened and pressed her knuckles into the small of her back, rubbing at the pain she'd awakened with.

"Having those practice contractions again?" the housekeeper asked with a raised eyebrow.

Catri grimaced. "Yes. I should distract myself by baking something. That's what my mother always told women to do. By the time the cake or bread is finished, the pains will be over."

"That's true, dearie, and you'll only have to do this a few more weeks or so."

"*If* this baby comes on time." As the daughter of a midwife, Catri knew about childbirth, even if Alana was the one who'd followed in their mother's footsteps. "First babies often are late."

"I'm baking pies, so why don't you do a cake? How about the whiskey cakes your sisters had for the wedding? They told me Irish tradition says to save one cake to eat at the christening of the first baby."

"What a lovely idea." Catri clasped her hands together. "Oh, I should have started months ago." *Or at least when Moss asked me to marry him.* "The cake is better the longer it ages."

"Well, I'm sure we'll enjoy the treat on the christening day, even if the cake's only aged a few weeks, instead of months."

The housekeeper took pie pans from the cabinet. "Quite a lot goes into that cake, as I recall, but I have everything on hand. Good thing I had you stone the seeds out of an extra batch of raisins on Monday."

"Only to keep me sitting."

"Right you are, dearie." Mrs. Toffels beamed and nodded. "And we had a nice chat while you did so. If you wouldn't be so stubborn about working too hard, then I wouldn't have to resort to such methods." She pointed with a pie tin. Now, while you get started on your cake, I have pies to bake. What do you think about blueberry?"

"Every dessert ye make tastes wonderful. I can't choose."

"The blueberry pie is tasty, if I say so myself." Mrs. Toffels gestured toward the cellar door. "Are you able to bring me three jars of stewed blueberries?"

"Certainly." Catri carried a basket to the cellar to find the stewed blueberries, as well as the raisins and the other supplies she needed. Then, upstairs again, she rummaged in the pantry. Once she'd assembled everything on the kitchen table, she poured water into a small pan, added the raisins, and set the mixture on the stove to boil. Soon, Catri was engrossed in her preparations and tried to ignore the practice contractions as they came and went, even if sometimes she had to stop, brace a hand on the table, and breathe through one.

Think of Moss. The pain won't hurt so much.

Suddenly, Catri realized how childish she'd been, waiting for him to magically get the message that she needed to hear him say *I love you.* Moss did care greatly for her, or he would never have given up his travel plans to propose. *All I have to do is ask him for the words.*

I'll talk to him as soon as the cake is done, Catri decided and felt a shiver of anticipation.

Finally, she removed the round cake from the oven and inhaled the spicy-sweet scent. She admired the lumpy brown surface studded with raisins.

Mrs. Toffels left the rabbit stew simmering on the stove to join her in peering at Catri's creation. "That looks fine. Good thing your uncle left us a bottle of his potato whiskey. You'll have plenty to soak your cake over the next weeks."

After the cake cooled, Catri flipped it onto the cheesecloth, gathered the edges, and bunched them on top. She lifted the cake to nestle the bottom into the round tin that Mrs. Toffels used in the fall for the Christmas fruitcake. Folding back the cheesecloth, she slowly soaked the top of the cake with whiskey.

As Catri stood staring with pride at the finished confection, a pang of pain squeezed across her back and wrapped around her front. *The cake is baked, so the practice contractions should have eased.*

Another of her mother's sayings came to mind: *If, by the time ye've finished baking and the contractions haven't stopped, then they aren't practice. They're real.*

Catri fought a feeling of panic. *I'm in labor!*

Chapter Fourteen

Moss beat the other cowboys back to the barn by a good fifteen minutes and hurried to unsaddle and groom sweating Traveler. He was determined to speak with Catriona while he still might have some privacy before the other cowboys rode in and descended on the kitchen to eat. After several days of thinking, he'd figured out a way to talk to her about marriage without "pressing" her and breaking his promise.

Outside the barn, he saw Bridget heading for the ranch house. He lengthened his strides to catch up.

Bridget carried a bulky package wrapped in brown paper and tied with a string, which she hefted in his direction. "Catriona's dress material. I'm showing her the fabric again in hopes of enticing her to actually make the dress. If that stubborn mule doesn't start soon, she'll run out of time and have to be married in Mrs. Toffels's black dress."

I'd wed Cat even if she wore rags. "Seems we're on the same errand. Do you think it's a better strategy for you to go first, or for me?"

She slanted him a sly smile. "Maybe we can gang up on her."

He chuckled. "Your sister doesn't strike me as someone who bows to pressure. I think she'd be more inclined to dig in her heels."

"Like I said, Catri's a stubborn mule." Bridget laughed. "Ye know her well.

Warmth spread through Moss's chest. "You couldn't give me a better compliment."

"If ye were a different kind of man, I wouldn't be pushin' her to marry ye."

He touched his hat to her. "I'm glad you're on my side."

In accord, they trotted up the steps and entered the kitchen to the smell of something sweet baking.

At the same time, Wyatt and Samantha entered the kitchen from the other direction.

"We followed an enticing smell," Samantha said gaily, "hoping for handouts."

Bridget walked over to the table and peered into a black tin. "Catri, how wonderful! Ye made an Irish wedding cake." She whirled. "Do ye have news for us?"

Cat stared back at them, a panicked look frozen on her face. "It's two weeks early." She grabbed the back of a chair, wrenching down on a cramp. "Alana's not here yet."

A spike of fear went through Moss. "The baby's coming? Now?"

Bridget rushed over to Cat's side, flung the package on the table, and took her sister's arm.

"But, I'm not ready." Cat glanced at the five of them, her brow wrinkling.

"Babies come in their own time," Samantha soothed, stepping toward Cat.

"I'm the daughter of a midwife," Cat snapped. "I know about labor." Her eyes widened, and her hands flew to cover her mouth. Inhaling, she lowered her arms. "I'm so sorry! I must have sounded like such a *shrew.*"

Samantha's eyes were full of understanding. "I imagine you'll be saying much worse before too long. Shall we establish that, until the baby is born, you have license to be *shrewish*—" she said the word with a smile "—loud, and scream at the top of your lungs, even?"

"Curse," Bridget added. "Remember some of the stories Mama told us?"

"At least, I don't have a husband to curse at." Cat straightened, seeming to gain her composure. But then her expression crumpled. She held out a hand to Moss, her expression tragic. "I'd decided to tell ye today that I accept yer proposal."

Relief propelled him forward, and he took her hand. "For a woman who's about to give birth, you're sure handing out a lot of unnecessary apologies," he teased.

Her expression didn't lighten. "I was a fool to wait. I should have married ye weeks ago."

"All that matters is that you want to do so now."

"But it's too late," she wailed, shaking her head.

"Shush, shush, sweetheart. Don't upset yourself so." Moss sent Bridget a silent message to release her hold on her sister. "We're now officially betrothed. He gently pulled her toward his side, sliding an arm around her back. "Reverend Norton is only a few hours away."

Cat looked up at him, sudden hope in her eyes. "Will ye ride for Reverend Norton, then?"

He stiffened. "I'm not leaving you."

"Wyatt will send someone for Reverend Norton and for the doctor, too," Samantha told Cat. "But in case he doesn't arrive—" her gaze moved to the housekeeper "—Mrs. Toffels is more than capable of delivering your baby."

"So am I," Bridget said in a resolute tone. "Growing up, Catri and I were present at many a birthing, often in one-room crofts. So we saw and heard everything, as well as fetched and carried for our mother."

Wyatt's jaw tightened, and a shadow lurked in his gray eyes. "I'll send young Deuce. He's the only one around." He moved toward the door. "Let's pray that both men are home and not out on calls at far-away households."

Moss groaned at the idea.

Samantha frowned at her husband. "Now, let's not borrow trouble. We'll pray that both men will be here soon."

His expression grim, Wyatt placed a hand on the doorknob. "I'll also have Deuce send a telegram to my lawyer in Crenshaw. Mr. Keniston will arrange for someone to ride out to the Gallagher place with the news. We've luck with the train schedule. Provided Patrick and Alana pack quickly and don't delay, they should be able to catch today's train. If you'd waited a day, Catriona, it wouldn't have been possible."

Hearing the boss lay out the plan eased some of Moss's tension, until Cat made a noise of pain and placed a hand on her stomach. His innards tightened in response.

"Breathe, Catriona Siobhan," Bridget ordered. "Remember Mama always said breathing through the contraction was important."

Hand on her stomach, Catri panted until the contraction eased. After catching her breath, she said, "Just knowing that Alana might, no, *will* be here—for my sister will move heaven and earth to deliver my baby—relieves my mind tremendously."

Wyatt nodded, but his expression didn't lighten. "I'll also have Deuce arrange with the livery for the surrey and a horse to be waiting when the train arrives. Then Patrick and Alana can drive here straightaway."

Samantha smiled at her husband in evident approval. "A sensible plan, my dear."

Wyatt lifted his hands in a helpless motion. "That's the best I can do." He gave Catri a direct look. "I remember how long Christine's birth took. I think it's reasonably possible for Alana to get here in time to deliver your baby."

What no one mentioned but everyone knew was that Alicia Thompson, Christine's mother, had died in childbirth.

Several hours later, Moss, who'd been pacing the parlor, heard the sounds of hoofbeats and wheels. He raced to the window to see Reverend Norton's shabby surrey pull into the side yard.

No sign of the doctor.

Moss pivoted and strode out of the room, down the entry hall, through the kitchen, which seemed empty without Mrs. Toffels—and threw open the door. He hurried outside and over to where the minister had halted the surrey. "Glad to see you!" he called.

By the time Moss reached the vehicle, Reverend Norton had dismounted. He handed the reins to Buck, who emerged from the barn to take charge of the horse.

Buck nodded at Moss, his expression concerned, although he didn't speak. The two men had repaired their friendship, and Buck's silent support mattered a great deal.

Reverend Norton looked at Moss his gray brows lowered. "Dr. Cameron was called out this morning to another confinement. "I cannot predict when or even if he'll make it here." He laid a hand on Moss's shoulder. "We must trust that God will bring Catriona and the baby safely through this."

All Moss could do was dip his chin.

"Shall we get you two married?" The minister lowered his arm.

"First, some things you should know about Catriona's background...." Moss sketched in the details Reverend Norton needed, all the time watching the minister's face for any sign of condemnation. *Not sure what I'll do if he disapproves. I can hardly punch a man of God, especially if I subsequently want him to marry us.* When he finished, Moss held his breath, waiting.

Reverend Norton's expression remained grave. "I can see why Catriona made the choices she did." A sudden smile lightened his austere face. "It's good this marriage removes the necessity for her to live a lie, and I'm glad the child is to be born in wedlock."

Unexpected emotion clogged his throat. Moss exhaled and tilted his head toward the kitchen door of the house. "Shall we?"

They walked inside, their boots echoing on the wooden floors.

"I will just wash up and join you upstairs," Reverend Norton said. "Catriona's in the guest room, I assume?"

While the minister used the bathroom, Moss washed his hands and face at the kitchen sink. He looked down at his work clothes, smelling faintly of horse, and wished he'd changed to his Sunday best for this wedding. Then he realized, in Cat's state, him dressing up would be ridiculous. *Outshining the bride isn't a good idea.*

A few minutes later, Moss knocked on the bedroom door, the minister beside him.

Bridget opened the door. When she saw the minister, her worried expression changed to gladness. "Reverend Norton, I'm so glad ye could make it." She stepped aside so they could enter.

The two men moved to where Cat sat in Mrs. Toffels's rocking chair, which Moss had earlier brought up, along with two chairs from the dining room, so the four women would have seating.

Mrs. Toffels dabbed a towel over Cat's face, and Sally sat on the other side, holding her hand.

Samantha rose and came over to greet the minister.

Moss walked passed her to crouch in front of Cat.

His bride wore a blue dressing robe. Her hair was in a long red braid. Tendrils curled around her face, which looked drawn, but her lips turned up at the sight of him.

"My dear Cat, are you ready to be married?" Moss asked.

Cat plucked at her robe. "My impromptu wedding gown from Samantha. Borrowed and blue." Her gaze met Moss's, and she held up a handkerchief. "From Bridget for luck, which is my something new." She twisted off her ring and gave it to Moss. "Something old from my grandmother."

His jaw dropped. Sheepishly, he took the ring from her. "I thought I'd prepared for everything."

"I'd prefer my grandmother's *claddagh*, anyway. So I'm ready. More than ready." She reached toward him.

Moss took her hand and brought it to his lips, pressing a kiss on the back. "Thank you for trusting me. I promise you won't regret your choice."

"I'll hold ye to that," Cat teased, and then looked at the minister. "Better hurry along."

Moss rose to his feet; Bridget, Sally, and Samantha gathered close to them.

"Under the circumstances," Reverend Norton said, "I think, we will dispense with the ritual and go right to shortened vows. But first, we'll begin with a prayer."

They bowed their heads, and Reverend Norton asked for a blessing on the marriage and a safe delivery for mother and child.

Moss had never prayed so fervently in his life.

When the minister finished, they all looked up.

"Do you…" Reverend Norton paused, looking at Moss. "I'm sorry. I don't know your given name."

Moss flashed a grin at Cat. "Robert. Robert Gordon, though it's been many a year since I've been called that."

She rolled her eyes and squeezed his hand. "Oh, ye!"

His grin widened. "Growing up, I was Rabbie Gordie."

"Rabbie Gordie." She smiled. "I like that."

Reverend Norton looked at Moss. "Do you, Robert Gordon Callahan, take this woman to be your lawfully wedded wife?"

"I do," Moss said, without taking his gaze from her.

Cat breathed more deeply. She kept her gaze on him while her free hand massaged her belly.

"And, do you, Catriona Siobhan O'Donnell, take this man to be your husband?

She squeezed Moss's hand hard. "*I…do!*" she grunted, rocking forward and closing her eyes.

"Then I now pronounce you husband and wife." Reverend Norton smiled at Moss. "Mr. and Mrs. Robert Gordon Callahan."

"I'm kissing the bride," Moss announced. "As soon as the contraction ends."

They watched her breathe until the spasm eased.

Finally, Cat relaxed, rocking back. She opened her eyes and beamed at him. "I'm all right. Just working hard."

"You are indeed." Moss pried his hand from hers, held up the *claddagh,* and slipped the ring on her finger. "Guess I was supposed to do this a minute ago, but you were too busy," he teased.

Letting out a sigh, Cat closed her fingers on the ring and clasped her hand to her bosom. Clearly the *claddagh* was precious.

Leaning over, Moss cupped her cheeks and looked deeply into her eyes before brushing her lips with his. "I look forward to seeing you with Bobbie in your arms. Don't keep me waiting long."

Bridget made a shooing motion. "Away with ye, now, Moss. Leave Catri to go about her business."

Chapter Fifteen

The following hours were the longest of Moss's life. He alternated between pacing the parlor and sitting in a wing chair, staring into space, and formulating prayers for Cat and the babe's safety. He tried to avoid looking at the portrait of Alicia Thompson hanging over the fireplace, an evocative reminder that women died in childbirth.

For a while, Reverend Norton kept Moss company in support, talking quietly of a man's responsibilities in marriage, reading the Bible, or closing his eyes in prayer. Then he had to leave in time to be home before dark.

The parlor was far enough from the birthing room that Moss couldn't hear any cries…or cussing. He rather thought his Cat was the cussing type. From time to time, Bridget hurried in for a minute with the latest update, which to his mind consisted of a lot of nothing. *Her strength is fine, Moss, not to worry.* And later, *She's closer but not to worry.*

At one point, Mrs. Toffels pressed a sandwich in his hand and left a mug of tea on the table next to him. He ate mechanically, not even aware of doing so, before rising to pace again.

With each turn of the room, a nebulous feeling grew stronger until solidifying into an emotion he could identify. *I love her!* The realization slipped into an empty place in his heart like a key fitting into a lock, clicking open a whole new future—*if Cat survives*; *if Bobbie lives and thrives; if she loves me.*

Do I hold the key to the lock of her heart?

Moss collapsed into a wing chair, pondering the question.

A haggard-looking Wyatt walked into the parlor and sprawled in the wing chair opposite Moss. "Amazing the chores you can find to do outside when trying to avoid entering your own home."

"Scrubbed out the horse trough, eh?"

"Just about." Wyatt rubbed his forehead with the palm of his hand before lowering his arm. "I've faced my own death a few times in my life, but *nothing* is worse than waiting for your wife to deliver."

Moss had been married only a few hours. Caught up in the consuming fear for Cat and the babe, he hadn't even begun thinking of her as his *wife. I'm a husband,* he marveled.

"At first, I was naïve about Alicia's confinement," Wyatt told Moss. "I knew plenty about birthing calves and foals, but nothing about babies. Dr. Cameron and Mrs. Toffels were with my wife. Like a fool, I was already outside celebrating with the men. Since the doctor had established his practice in Sweetwater Springs, the death rate for mothers and babies had gone down considerably. I thought dying in childbirth was something *other* women did—poor women, older women, ones worn out from too much childbearing…."

Moss had been telling himself the same thing. He nodded.

"Not ones who were young and pretty and vivacious like my Alicia." Wyatt looked up at the portrait over the fireplace for a long moment. "We were—if you can believe it of me—giddy in love, the future shiny with all the possibilities of our life together." Wyatt shook his head and rubbed his jaw. "We never had the years to rub off some of that polish."

Moss didn't want to hear Wyatt's story. Didn't even want to dwell on the possibility of Catriona dying. But Wyatt needed to talk, and when a man—especially one as reserved as his boss—needed to share something troubling, then a friend's responsibility was to listen.

Huh, the boss and I might just be turning into friends.

"Samantha won't hear of me taking down that portrait," Wyatt went on. "Strangely enough, she feels connected to Alicia and wants Christine to know her mother's memory is respected."

Moss had wondered a time or two why the portrait was still in place. He'd always figured the boss had been the one to put his foot down. "You're a lucky man, Boss. Samantha is one of the most assured ladies I've ever met, and in my travels, I've met a lot of women. She has no reason to doubt your love for her or feel threatened by a portrait."

"Samantha wants a baby," Wyatt said in a weary voice. "I don't want her to take the risk. I couldn't bear to lose…." He broke off, inhaling a shuddering breath. "We have plenty of children and could always adopt more. The world is full of children in need of a loving family."

"No man wants his wife to take the risk of childbirth, but we have no choice. That's how babies are born." Moss shrugged. "Heck, a woman could be walking across the yard as safe as could be. Then she trips, and breaks her neck or a tree branch falls on her head. Accidents like that happen."

"I know," Wyatt said, his tone heavy.

"I think the timing of our death, well, that's up to God. Got to trust in that, else you'll wind up tighter than a spring—fearing death rather than living life."

"I agree."

Moss raised his chin in the direction of the portrait. "If Alicia were able to talk to you for a few minutes, maybe she'd say her sacrifice for the sake of her daughter was worth everything."

"And if I lose *both* Samantha and our baby?"

Helpless, Moss shook his head. "I ain't the minister, here," he drawled. "Despite coming close to sounding like one, I don't have the answers." He thought back to the pain of his father's abandonment—the impact on his life. "Losing your wife and baby would change *everything*," he conceded. "At times, the pain would probably bring you to your knees."

Wyatt propped his elbow on the arm of the wing chair and rested his chin in his hand. "I might not be able to get back up."

"You've survived loss before, and you have five children who'll need you for many years." Moss leaned forward, his elbows on his knees, and stared across at his boss. "What's far more likely, given that it's not her first child, is that Samantha and your baby will be *just fine*. You'll have another arrow in your quiver—" he liked his Biblical reference "—and your life will be enriched."

"You do have a way of putting things, Moss."

They fell silent. Darkness slowly descended in shades of gray to midnight blue to black. Neither man moved to light the lamp or start a fire.

Finally, Wyatt stirred, the soles of his boots scraping the rug.

Moss heard the sound of a match striking, accompanied by the smell of sulfur and hiss as a flame sprang to life.

Wyatt lit the lamp. As the warm glow pushed back the darkness, his gaze met Moss's. "Guess you and Catriona will have to make a trip back from Crenshaw to stand as godparents."

Moss laughed. "We'd be honored." He waited a beat before jabbing a finger at Alicia's portrait. "After your baby is born and has grown to look like a real person, you should have a family portrait painted and hang it above the mantel. Alicia's can go on another wall in here someplace." He looked around, and then pointed to the corner. "I heard you bought the piano for her, so hang the picture over there."

For the first time, Wyatt smiled and nodded. "Might just have to do that."

Moss slid down in the chair, extended his legs, and tilted back his head, once again thinking of Catriona's travail. Closing his eyes he murmured, "Everything I said earlier is cowpucky when it's *your* wife having the baby."

Chapter Sixteen

When her confinement was over, Catri sat on the four-poster bed in the guest room, the green-and-pink quilt covering her legs. She held her son in her arms, still in shock that Flea, who was supposed to be a *she*, was a *he*!

All the women except for Alana had left—Bridget to bring the good news to the waiting men, and Mrs. Toffels, Samantha, and Sally heading to the kitchen to put together a middle-of-the-night hot meal for everyone. But first, the women had surprised the new mother by bringing out baby gifts, lovingly made in secret.

Catri had already examined every inch of her son, marveling over his delicate fingers and toes. When Alana had taken him to be wiped off and dressed, she returned the baby clad in the little flannel gown Catri had sewn, over one of the flannel diapers made by Alana and Bridget, covered by the tiny soaker pants knitted by Sally. Booties crocheted by Mrs. Toffels kept the baby's feet warm, and a small green, pink, and blue quilt, pieced together by Samantha, was wrapped around him. The green fabric matched the patches on the quilt of Catri's bed.

During the birth, lamps taken from other areas of the house had lit the room like sunshine. But now only two—one on the table, and one on the chest of drawers—spread a soft glow in the darkness, enough to see by, but not too harsh for an infant's eyes.

Her son had a black tuft of hair, and the shape of his features told her exactly who'd sired him. *Bartley*.

I was never pregnant with Godfrey's child. I didn't have to run away with another man after all. For a moment, regret wrapped around her. Then Catri realized that she wouldn't wish away those months with the peddler. She'd finally experienced the adventure she'd craved. Bartley had made an interesting traveling companion, and she'd seen a great deal of her country before leaving forever.

In the process, Catri had also learned that what she wanted wasn't out *there*, wherever *there* was. Her sense of peace, of belonging—lay at home, with *people* not places—at first with the twins. Then her O'Donnell relatives and her brothers-in-law joined their circle. She smiled at her baby. *The most important additions to the family were added in the last day.*

Alana, who'd been straightening up the room, came over to sit on the bed. She took Catri's hand, peeked at the baby, and tears welled in her eyes. "He's so beautiful. I think he's going to have the O'Donnell eyes."

Catri hoped so.

"Only a few months ago, we were naught but girls in Ireland." Alana released Catri's hand to touch her shamrock pendent. "We could never have imagined such magic would happen to us."

"Magic, indeed."

"And hopefully much more to come." Alana donned her healer expression. "Now, tell me. How are ye feeling?" She felt Catri's forehead.

"Exhausted. Exhilarated. Philosophical."

"Philosophical?" Alana asked, lifting an eyebrow in askance.

Catri tried to put her musings into words. "If I hadn't been heavy with child and felt weak, I probably wouldn't have fainted into Moss's arms. Without our encounter at the train station, I wouldn't have ended up married to him."

"Ye probably wouldn't have met him at all," Alana pointed out. Then she gave a soft smile. "Life is funny that way. Just like with ye and Moss, if Patrick hadn't been attacked by robbers who tried to steal his horse, he wouldn't have stayed at Uncle Rory's, giving us time to fall in love."

"Lots of good comes out of bad."

Alana nodded. "To keep changing history…. If ye hadn't run off with Bartley, ye would have immigrated to America with us. Once here in Sweetwater Springs, ye'd have gone with me to our aunt and uncle's, for two of us living in Sally and Harry's home…." Wrinkling her brow, she shook her head. "Too much for those newlyweds."

"On the day of yer wedding…." Catri thought through what might have been. "Moss would still have left the ranch in the morning. He'd have gotten on the train and rode south to Texas. He probably would have continued being a rolling stone for the rest of his life." She imagined Moss growing old and lonely—a whole life spent drifting from place to place without forming connections. *Speaking of connections….* She frowned down at the baby and sensed something was missing—a lack inside of her.

Alana leaned forward. "What is it? Are ye in pain?"

Catri met her sister's gaze. "Shouldn't I be feeling…more?"

"More what?"

"I don't know…intensity? Attachment? Love?"

Her sister lifted her eyebrow. "What *do* ye feel about yer baby?"

"Caring." She pursed her lips, thinking. "Curiosity."

Alana sat back. Her lips turned up. "That's a good start."

"I'm numb," Catri admitted, too ashamed to meet her sister's eyes.

Alana reached out to cup the baby's head. "Ye didn't want him, Catri. Ye didn't say so, but I could tell." She touched Catri's leg.

Catri lifted her gaze to Alana's.

"Be patient with yerself. Ye've just given birth, an exhausting ordeal, to be sure. Ye'll feel better after some rest."

"What if my feelings don't change? If I'm not capable of…."

Catri's chest tightened, and she couldn't even form her concerns.

"This baby has two aunts who already adore him," Alana said in a no-nonsense tone. "He has two uncles and a new father, who I'm sure can't wait to meet him. And that's just those of us who will be living in Crenshaw. Then there's our family here and the people of this ranch who care about ye and the babe. He won't lack for love."

"That's true." The tightness in her chest eased.

"Falling in love with yer child is not unlike falling in love with a man. Sometimes it's instant, and sometimes the connection develops gradually. I promise, the deeper love will come."

"When did ye get so wise, little sister?"

Alana just smiled and shook her head. "Have ye decided on a name?" she asked.

"Yes." Catri gave her a mischievous smile. "But I'm telling Moss, first."

"I can wait. But not for long." Alana held out her arms for the baby. "Let me show off my nephew to the men. I'll bring him back soon."

Catri kissed the baby's head, inhaling his sweet scent, and allowed her sister to take him. Then she snuggled back on the pillows, trying to find a comfortable position for her aching body, and drifted into sleep.

Something pulled Catri awake. Drowsy, she opened her eyes to see Moss sitting in the rocking chair that he'd pulled right next to the bed.

Wearing a tender expression, he gazed down at the baby in his arms.

Her chest expanded with such warmth, she could have floated off the bed. But she didn't speak or move, wanting only to look her fill at the precious tableau.

"I'm your pa," Moss said softly, his voice trembling. He traced the baby's cheek with one finger. "Fancy that."

A lightning bolt of love struck Catri—for Moss, for her son, burning away her numbness and filling her heart with light. *Thank you, Heavenly Father and Blessed Mother Mary.* "We'll call him Bobbie."

Startled, Moss looked up and grinned.

"Robert after *his* new father—" she tilted her head toward Moss, enjoying the moment "—and Seamus, after mine."

"Robert Seamus Callahan. Quite a mouthful for a little mite."

"He'll grow into it." Catri reached out and placed a finger in the baby's palm.

His miniature fingers curled around hers.

She relished Bobbie's healthy grip. *This is what maternal love feels like!*

"He's a strong one," Moss said proudly.

"I never thought I could love him," Catri confessed. "I just wanted him out of me. Even when Alana put him to my breast, I was numb. Afraid I'd never feel what a mother should toward her baby. My sister tried to reassure me, but not until I saw ye holding my son—"

"*Our* son," Moss gently corrected.

"Our son," Catri repeated with a smile. "A *miracle* happened when I saw ye hold the babe with the most moonstruck expression on yer face!" Tears welled in her eyes, and one dripped down her cheek. "Ye gave that to me." She shook her head. "To think that I hated my babe. That I didn't want him born. I'm so wicked." She wiggled her finger from her son's grasp.

"Hush, love. Never think that again." Moss rocked the baby. "Our Bobbie is here and healthy. You're safe and healthy. He has a fine start in life, which is a mother's job, and you did it admirably. *Now* comes the time when he'll need your love and mine for the rest of our days."

"Am I really yer love?" she asked. Her voice quavered.

His gaze remained steady on hers. "My love and my life." Moss stood. "Scoot over, my darling Cat."

She slid sideways to make space on the bed.

He leaned over to give her Bobbie, careful not to jostle the sleeping baby, and settled himself beside her, his long legs on top of the quilt. Propping himself against the pillows, he put his arm around her shoulders. "I can't believe you doubted me."

"I doubted ye at first, but ye soon proved yerself to me." She wrinkled her nose at him. "But ye didn't tell me ye loved me. When ye proposed, all ye mentioned was the baby being legitimate. Otherwise, I would have thrown myself into yer arms with a resounding *yes*."

"You've a fool for a husband, Cat." With a rueful expression, Moss shook his head. "The thing is…this love business and coming to terms with my father's abandonment turned me…." He grinned. "Tea*pot* over spout. But I knew for sure I loved you, when terror struck me as I waited for the babe's birth, not knowing if you'd live or die, but realizing how bleak my life would be without you in it."

Her smile bloomed.

"You are my joy and my delight. You have my heart."

"Ye've the Irish way with words, boyo." Catri peeped at him from under her lashes. "But I like it, sure 'n I do."

Moss chuckled and glanced down at the baby. "I'm afraid you have to share space in my heart with this little fella."

"That's acceptable," Catri said primly, but she was sure her eyes danced. "Fair, too, for ye and Bobbie share my heart."

Smiling, he cupped her cheek. "You're glowing."

"Ever since seeing the happiness of Sally and my sisters, I've wanted to glow." In spite of herself, her eyes grew heavy, and she yawned.

He pulled her close. "Rest now, love."

Cat settled the baby more securely and snuggled her cheek against her husband's chest. *Husband. How wonderful to think of Moss as my husband!*

He pressed a kiss to the top of her head. "There's one more thing you should know."

Eyebrows lifting, she looked up at him.

"Catriona Siobhan O'Donnell Callahan—" Moss touched a finger to the tip of her nose before thumping his knuckles on his chest "—this rolling stone has come to rest."

COMING SOON!

Here are the upcoming titles in the Montana Sky series:

Singing Montana Sky

Release Date: August 22, 2017

Beautiful, wealthy, and sophisticated, opera star Sophia Maxwell is living the life of her dreams. As the Songbird of Chicago, she's lauded for her pure, rich voice and has a constant circle of admirers vying for her jaded attention. Then she loses her voice during a performance. Her doctor warns her to rest her larynx, or she'll never sing again. Devastated, Sophia retreats to the frontier town of Sweetwater Springs to stay with her sister. She's determined to recover and once again take the stage by storm.

An injury to logger Kael Kelley forces him to return to his parents' home outside of Sweetwater Springs until he can heal enough to return to the logging camp he manages. He's impatient to recover and concerned about his men, who've been left to work under the incompetent overseer who was responsible for his accident.

When Sophia and Kael meet, they have an immediate attraction. The handsome logger is as different from Sophia's sophisticated suitors as can be. She decides a summer flirtation is the perfect way to enliven her boring convalescence. Then the unthinkable happens, and the Songbird of Chicago falls in love.

Bright Montana Sky

Release Date: March 1, 2018

1896

Jilted seamstress Constance Taylor travels to Sweetwater Springs to live with her estranged father, the livery stable owner. She plans to open a dressmaking shop and bring sophisticated clothing styles to the uncouth frontier town.

Angus Cameron is a young doctor, who's bitter and discouraged from his work with upper class Londoners and the wretched poor in the East End slums. He arrives in Sweetwater Springs to share the medical practice of his brother, the town doctor.

Although Constance and Angus don't want to live in Sweetwater Springs, both are determined to change the town in ways they think are important. They clash over her fashionable creations, which Angus knows are unhealthy, and Constance refuses to change. They deny their attraction to each other until Constance falls ill from the arsenic used in her favorite purple and green fabrics, and Angus must fight to save the life of the woman he's come to love.

Dear Reader,

Thank you for reading *A Rolling Stone*, book three of The Irish Sisters Trilogy, although there really are four stories, beginning with Sally O'Donnell in *Irish Luck*, a short story in *Montana Sky Christmas.* You'll also see more of the O'Donnell family—Rory, Henrietta, and the children in *Healing Montana Sky*.

In Bridget and Alana's wedding, I took the liberty of slightly modifying and modernizing the ritual. I took Reverend Norton's words directly from *Common Prayer* (published 1892.) But I switched the timing of when Rory gave the twins to their grooms, which actually came later in the traditional ceremony. Also, I'm sure in 1895—a much more proper time—a kiss wasn't included in the ceremony. In fact, the modern Catholic ritual and some Protestant denominations still don't officially have a kiss in the ritual, but priests and ministers may include the kiss. Since the kiss has become such a special part of a wedding ceremony, it seems strange and not as romantic to exclude, the "You may now kiss the bride."

The next book I'm writing in the Montana Sky Series is *Singing Montana Sky*, book two in The Maxwell Sisters Trilogy, available for preorder on Amazon and releasing on August 22nd. Book One in the Trilogy is *Painted Montana Sky*. In *Singing Montana Sky*, opera star Sophia Maxwell loses her voice and returns to Sweetwater Springs to recuperate at the Dunn Ranch and spend time with her sister and baby niece. The beautiful woman, who's used to having everything she wants, now struggles to find whom she is when she can't talk or sing. Kael Kelly (whom we briefly met in *Mystic Montana Sky*) is undergoing his own recuperation for a broken arm.

I'm not forgetting that I've promised K.C Granger's story in *Montana Sky Justice.* That's going to be a much bigger book, and I want a few things to first happen in Sweetwater Springs before the sheriff falls in love.

Can't get enough of Sweetwater Springs and Morgan's Crossing? While you're waiting for the release of *Singing Montana Sky*, check out the Montana Sky Kindle World books written by various authors. There are currently thirty-six Montana Sky Kindle World books, with more to come. Some authors are even writing mini-series within the Montana Sky series. For more information on these books see the Kindle World tab on my website: http://debraholland.com/kindle-worlds.html

If you haven't already, please join my newsletter list to learn when new books are released and other news I might have.

All the best,
Debra Holland

Montana Sky Series

in Chronological Order:

1892

Beneath Montana's Sky

1886

Mail-Order Brides of the West: Trudy
Mail-Order Brides of the West: Lina
Mail-Order Brides of the West: Darcy
Mail-Order Brides of the West: Prudence
Mail-Order Brides of the West: Bertha

1890s

Grace: Bride of Montana
Wild Montana Sky
Starry Montana Sky
Stormy Montana Sky
Montana Sky Christmas
A Valentine's Choice
An Irish Blessing
Painted Montana Sky
Glorious Montana Sky
A Rolling Stone
Healing Montana Sky
Sweetwater Springs Scrooge
Sweetwater Springs Christmas
Mystic Montana Sky
Singing Montana Sky
Bright Montana Sky *(March 2018)*
Montana Sky Justice *(August 2018)*

2015

Angel in Paradise

About the Author

DEBRA HOLLAND is the New York Times and USA Today Bestselling author of the award-winning *Montana Sky Series* (sweet, historical Western romance) and *The Gods' Dream Trilogy* (fantasy romance.)

Debra is a three-time Romance Writers of America Golden Heart finalist and one-time winner. In 2013, Amazon selected *Starry Montana Sky* as one of the Top 50 Greatest Love Stories.

When she's not writing, Dr. Debra works as a psychotherapist and corporate crisis/grief counselor. She's the author of *The Essential Guide to Grief and Grieving*, a book about helping people cope with all kinds of loss, *and Cultivating an Attitude about Gratitude, a Ten Minute Ebook*. She's also a contributing author to *The Naked Truth About Self-Publishing*.

To learn more and join her newsletter list go to her website:
http://debraholland.com

Made in the USA
Middletown, DE
31 March 2021

36584384R00241